D0174731

SCENT OF
MURDER

SCENT OF MURDER

MURDER

JAMES O. BORN

A TOM DOHERTY ASSOCIATES BOOK
NEW YORK

SCENT OF MURDER

Copyright © 2015 by James O. Born

A Forge Book
Published by Tom Doherty Associates, LLC
175 Fifth Avenue
New York, NY 10010

www.tor-forge.com

Forge® is a registered trademark of Tom Doherty Associates, LLC.

The Library of Congress Cataloging-in-Publication Data is available upon request.

ISBN 978-0-7653-7847-7 (hardcover)
ISBN 978-1-4668-6162-6 (e-book)

Forge books may be purchased for educational, business, or promotional use. For information on bulk purchases, please contact the Macmillan Corporate and Premium Sales Department at 1-800-221-7945, extension 5442, or write to specialmarkets@macmillan.com.

First Edition: April 2015

Printed in the United States of America

10 9 8 7 6 5 4 3 2 1

For my parents, John and Jane Born.
I didn't know it at the time,
but they did everything right.

ACKNOWLEDGMENTS

Barbara Gould, the perfect reader and woman.

My thanks to the many dog handlers who shared their stories and insights on the wonderful world of police service dogs: Johnny Rivers, from the Palm Beach County Sheriff's Office; Robert Haight, from the Palm Beach County Sheriff's Office; Ray Ruby, from the Palm Beach County Sheriff's Office; Rich O'Connor, from the Palm Beach County School Board Police and a former K-9 officer with the Boynton Beach Police Department; Tim Fischer, from the New York State Police (retired).

SCENT OF
MURDER

Very few cops, including Tim Hallett, ran away from a chance at seeing some excitement. Maybe after a few more years on the job he'd slow down, but he hadn't become a sheriff's deputy to let others have all the fun. He looked up for any sign of the helicopter as he maneuvered his Chevy Tahoe down a narrow, pockmarked, shell-rock road wedged between a Florida Water Management District canal and a sugarcane field near Belle Glade.

The Tahoe bounced violently, tossing his partner, Rocky, a Belgian Malinois police service dog, across the passenger seat. His biggest fear right now was catching a pothole wrong and careening into the canal. In his time on patrol, he'd pulled five bodies out of submerged cars from the crisscrossing canal system of southern Florida. He didn't want some rookie deputy telling the story of how he pulled a K-9 cop and his dog out of the murky water.

Hallett grabbed a quick glimpse of his partner and said, "Sorry about that, Rocky."

As usual, Rocky didn't answer unless he had something important to express.

They were pushing the edge of safety to reach the other deputies who'd been called to the remote sugarcane field after a fisherman reported a possible abduction. To Hallett, the terrain looked much more like a third world country than Florida. The entire area around Lake Okeechobee was dotted with small towns and vast farms. The poor people were very poor, and the rich people didn't give two shits about them.

As the big SUV bumped along the canal's edge, Hallett said, "This is the kind of stuff we signed on for, isn't it, Rock?" He gritted his teeth against another hard bounce and added, "If everyone gets their shit together, maybe we can clear this up quickly." He didn't mind his coworker's silence. Rocky was the best partner, human or nonhuman, he'd worked with in his eight years at the Palm Beach County Sheriff's Office. It was unlike any other relationship he'd ever had with a colleague, or with anyone else. He looked across the space between them, then reached over with his right hand and ruffled Rocky's brown hair.

He cleared a line of pine trees, which acted as a windbreak for the sugarcane, and saw the other patrol cars parked along the edge of the canal with uniformed deputies getting their gear together. As he slowed the SUV, Hallett leaned across the console and pressed his forehead against Rocky's, in his normal ritual to psych both of them up for whatever assignment awaited them. Then he planted a kiss almost between Rocky's eyes.

Hallett said, "Time to get to work." He opened the door and slid onto the rough road. Rocky climbed across the console, let out a short bark, and landed on all four feet with the grace of a much smaller dog. Rocky looked like the classic Belgian Malinois, slightly smaller than a German Shepherd but the same shape, with a thick tan coat and dark muzzle. The sheriff's policy dictated Rocky ride in the secure rear seat caged area, which had a hatch that opened to the passenger compartment, but whenever they had to drive for a long distance Hallett preferred to have his partner sitting next to him. Rocky enjoyed the freedom.

It only took a few seconds to open the tailgate of the Tahoe and pour some water into Rocky's favorite dish, the one with Garfield on the bottom of the bowl, as if mocking the dog. Rocky's sheer exuberance for life put him in a class of his own. He never walked when he could run. There was no such thing as easing them into a situation; the muscular Malinois had to jump in with all four feet, so to speak. Bred in Malines, Belgium, in the mid-nineteenth century, the Malinois was one of four Shepherd breeds from the area the American Kennel Club recognized in the 1950s. The only issue for the dog here in Florida was the heat. Hallett took his responsibilities to keep Rocky groomed and cool very seriously. The rear of his SUV was littered with Gatorade and water bottles he and Rocky had emptied during their long shifts. He'd brush out his partner for an hour after this job was done. It was tough keeping an eighty-five-pound dog cool in Florida.

As Rocky lapped at the water, Hallett got his gear in order, checking his tactical vest to make sure his flashlight, Gerber folding knife, and radio were all in place. He knew that whatever the situation, the K-9 units would be at the very front of the effort. That's why he had taken this assignment over three years ago.

He was happy to see Sergeant Helen Greene already directing the other deputies. It took him a second to recognize the detective sergeant. He'd heard she'd lost weight, but the woman in the slacks and white shirt organizing things hardly resembled the woman the other detectives had nicknamed "Mount St. Helen." She turned toward him and gave him a quick smile and wink. St. Helen might not be mountainous anymore, but she really was a saint. She'd helped him when his career as a detective turned south, reminding the sheriff of the benefits of Hallett's rash acts, and she was known for protecting others as well. After the brief, silent greeting, the sergeant was back to work pushing other deputies to get ready.

Hallett hooked a sixteen-foot leash, or lead, on Rocky's harness and trotted toward the group of deputies. He kept chatting lightly to the dog, making everything they did a game. Every once in a while he would throw in Josh's name and smile at the dog's reaction. Hallett's son, Josh, commanded the dog's complete attention when they were all together.

Rocky was bounding forward, anxious to start their game and making some of the regular patrol deputies nervous.

The other two K-9 units from his special squad were on their way out from headquarters, but depending on how hard they pushed their own vehicles it could be another ten minutes before they reached the scene. There were three things a cop never hesitated to move on quickly: a missing child, a death notification, or a call for help from another cop. Hallett doubted Sergeant Greene would wait for the other K-9s if the information indicated there was really a kid at risk. Most times these calls were flawed and the witness had only seen a family argument or misinterpreted the entire situation, but no one wanted to risk a child's safety, even on a bogus tip. No one wanted a family to hear about the death of a loved one from the media, and no cop hesitated to help another in trouble. The scariest radio call was 10-24, which meant send help but was usually associated with an officer down. Hallett knew if he was ever in the shit and called for help, every available cop would be on the way instantly.

If this call was legitimate, this was exactly the kind of activity Hallett needed to help him feel like he'd made the right choices in life. Lately they'd been hard for him to justify. He didn't worry about any of that as Rocky strained at his lead and pulled Hallett toward the gathering deputies.

■　■　■

He took a moment to catch his breath after slogging through the drainage ditch between the two cane fields, each over six feet high. Somehow, the fields reminded him of growing up in Indiana. Sugarcane was like scratchy cornstalks with snakes and alligators. He was lucky it hadn't been harvested yet or he might really be in trouble. As he scrambled up the other side of the drainage ditch he could almost hear his father yelling, "Move your fat ass, Junior. You're never going to drop any of that weight if you don't start getting some physical activity." Twenty-one years later, everyone in Indiana still called him "Junior." He hated that goddamn name.

The other name his father continued to call him was "the dickless wonder." The sour old bastard called everyone by some derisive nickname, but "dickless wonder" implied Junior couldn't take a chance or make a ballsy move. That wasn't true. He was proving it at this very moment. Somehow, his siblings had escaped the old man's wrath and attention. On some level, it comforted Junior to know he was the only one his father screamed at and berated. At least he was interested in Junior's life. However, it also made him wonder how much the old man had affected him.

The old man had caused a lot of trouble since relocating to the Sunshine State, but he sure could pick some stocks. If things kept going like they were, Junior might be able to live off investments before he turned fifty.

So far, the day had not turned out like he had expected. He had such high hopes for it. In fact, he'd dreamed about it for weeks. Maybe not details like this cane field or cops chasing him, but more his encounter with the pretty blond girl named Katie. He had followed her to the Wellington Mall and waited. He knew where she would be. It was a lucky break to catch her in the parking lot so quickly. She had surprised him by being so quiet and compliant until she was out of the car. She'd been scared by the blindfold and being stuffed onto the floorboard of the beatup Toyota Tercel he'd stolen from the parking lot of the Palm Beach Outlets Mall. But as soon as her feet felt solid ground, she'd managed to slip his grasp and then guessed the right direction, scurrying through the cane like a rabbit, and he would've still been chasing her if not for the canal. But now he was pretty certain the old fisherman had seen enough to call the cops. The old man had pretended to be focusing on his efforts to catch something on his three cane poles wedged between rocks on the edge of the canal, but Junior was sure he knew something was up. These isolated fields rarely saw any excitement, and the commotion would have caught the man's attention.

Thank God the Tercel was parked on another access road fairly close. He'd already spent too much effort screwing around with this girl. He usually enjoyed his time with these young women, but today had been very unsatisfying. He needed to invent some new kind of blindfold, maybe use a burlap sack over their heads, but he enjoyed looking at their pretty faces even if they did have a rag and duct tape around their eyes. This girl had cheekbones like Christie Brinkley and thick, full lips. He'd seen her plenty of times without any obstructions on her face and knew so much about her that it hurt to be fleeing the scene without accomplishing everything he set out to.

Junior was lucky to have heard the old fisherman's truck drive off down the access road to State Road 80. He had heard other vehicles coming back and had to assume they were police cars, but he never panicked. He prided himself on never panicking. No matter what.

Now, if he could make it to the beat-up Toyota, then back into West Palm Beach within forty-five minutes, everything would be cool.

The pistol stuffed in his pants felt awkward when he tried to run, but he was never built for running anyway. Too much jiggled.

Junior thought he heard a dog bark at the far side of the cane field and was glad he had crossed through a couple of drainage ditches in case they tried to track him. Dogs scared the holy crap out of him, and the idea they were chasing him like an animal was disturbing on a number of levels.

■   ■   ■

The western section of Palm Beach County was separated from the eastern section by a stretch of wilderness known as the Twenty Mile Bend. Tim Hallett could think of few places in America where twenty miles made so much difference. On the coast sat Palm Beach with its mansions and world-famous beach, but out here, a forty-minute drive away, it looked more like the Mississippi Delta. Wide plains of crops, hot, stagnant air, and alligators were the dominant features. When the cane fields were burned for harvesting, the smoke hung in the air like a noxious fog for days.

Now, as he stood in a wide semicircle with four other deputies, the air in the cane field was thick with humidity and sun-warm, but not unbearable. It was still a little early for the bugs to start eating them alive, but he knew there were plenty of them concealed out there.

Sergeant Helen Greene said, "We have a report of a man chasing a young girl at the edge of the field. An elderly cane fishermen thought it was a white man and a white girl, but he didn't get a good look. This happened almost an hour ago because he didn't have a cell phone and had to drive into town." Her dark skin had a sheen of perspiration, and her light Glades accent made her seem natural in the setting.

The sergeant continued. "Looks like there was a scuffle in the cane field up ahead. We're gonna send Tim and Rocky into that field and use the other two K-9s to check along the canal and the far cane fields." Her dark eyes scanned the group of six deputies. Then she said, "If this info is right we've got a tough job ahead of us."

Hallett took a moment to assess the situation like the detective he once was. He noticed the older black man sitting in the front seat of the sergeant's car. The old man had done a great job going to get help, and now the sheriff's office—or SO, as most people in the agency called it—had to live up to his expectations.

Just as he was about to start the search, his partners, Darren Mori and Claire Perkins, bumped down the shell-rock road in Chevy Tahoes similar to Hallett's. The task force they were on was funded by the federal government, which had not only provided money to train the dogs in different disciplines but bought the deputies high-end cars, weapons, and other gear that generally made the average deputy jealous as hell. Cops love equipment, and the three K-9 officers had more than they could ever use.

Although he was impatient to get started, Hallett knew it was better to have all three dogs on scene and ready to go at the same time. It didn't take long for Darren to get Brutus on his lead and, of course, Claire hopped out with Smarty ready to go on a sixteen-foot lead.

Hallett was the team leader. It was an odd, almost honorary rank within the sheriff's office, and his authority was implied rather than specified. He did receive a small bump in pay, but he was not considered a sergeant and had no administrative duties. Instead, he made decisions on tactics and how to deploy resources during a callout. He also worked with Ruben Vasquez, the canine trainer who'd been assigned to the unit when they got the grant. The guy was a former army dog handler and smart as a private school math teacher, but Hallett recognized he didn't have much experience in police work. It took a cop to know what was needed on the street in certain situations. It didn't always require a dog willing to bite anyone in sight—although sometimes it did.

Being a team leader might have been a promotion, but it meant nothing if his partners didn't accept him as the leader. Like a lot of things in police work, his authority was implied rather than specified. It was an easier path than dealing with liability and promotional exams. Luckily, both Darren and Claire appreciated his experience, and he had proven his ability to make decisions. Hallett had also proven that he wasn't afraid to work long hours and do whatever it took to get the job done.

At five foot eight, Darren was constantly trying to prove his worth even though he was widely respected in the agency. Darren always had to be the first in a fight, the best possible shot, and the most eager to work. But his exotic good looks and athletic build, and the fact that he was the only Asian in town, made the twenty-six-year-old Japanese American popular among the women in Belle Glade. As Brutus pulled him along on the lead, he smiled at Darren's annoyance about being issued a Golden Retriever instead of a traditionally more frightening Belgian

Malinois or German Shepherd like Claire and Hallett worked with. It turned out Brutus was just about the smartest dog any of them had ever seen and had been trained in several disciplines, including article searches, bomb searches, and cadaver searches. If he had to, Brutus could be aggressive, but generally the snarls and barks coming from a Golden Retriever failed to instill the terror that Rocky could spread in an unruly crowd. Brutus wasn't trained to apprehend suspects, or track them, but he could find a body or bomb with incredible skill. The way the unit was organized and trained, everyone chipped in when the others were working. Brutus could follow a scent, or at least look like he was.

Claire's dog, Smarty, looked like he could pull her off her feet. A couple of inches shorter than Darren, with blond hair usually tied in a ponytail, she could pass for a pissed-off cheerleader. A number of shitheads had learned too late she was not the deputy to make stupid comments to. And despite his name, Smarty had a vicious streak that worried Hallett.

He gave his partners a quick rundown of what the sergeant had said. As usual, Claire just nodded and knew exactly what to do, while Darren had questions.

"Are we looking for a live girl or a dead girl?"

"We don't know."

"Any indication the suspect is armed?"

"No, but what do you say we just assume he is."

Darren was about to ask another question when the sergeant shouted, "Let's get the dogs moving. Now."

Hallett waited a moment while Rocky sniffed the ground where the soil had been disturbed and the old man said he thought he'd seen a scuffle. As was his unique custom, Rocky froze for one second as he picked up the scent. Just that momentary pause in the action thrilled Hallett because he knew they were about to do the job only they were trained for. Then the dog pulled him directly into the cane field, and Hallett lost sight of him just a few feet ahead. The heat brought out just enough perspiration to make his skin tacky, so tiny bits of the scratchy sugarcane stalks stuck to his bare forearms.

He knew Darren would be taking Brutus along the canal to the south and Claire would take Smarty into the next cane field. The other uniformed deputies fanned out behind each dog team, cutting lines into the fields. If one of the sheriff's office helicopters had been available, the pilot would've seen a design like an ant farm as the search teams spread out, but the sergeant had said the nearest helicopter was at least forty-five minutes out due to a search for survivors of an airboat crash near the Arthur Marshall Wildlife Refuge at the entrance to the Everglades.

Now he had a moment to think about what he and Rocky might discover. Rocky was definitely onto something, which meant the old man was right about the scuffle. Dread seeped into his consciousness as he pictured finding a girl dead in the middle of the cane field. He had to block it out and focus on this task. His right hand reached back and touched the handle of his .40 caliber Glock on his gun belt. His lightweight combat boots protected his ankles from the rough base of the sugarcane stalks. The late September Florida heat was amplified by his ballistic vest and the effort it took to move through the sugarcane as his heart rate picked up from the physical activity and excitement of the chase.

Hallett was monitoring the radio, and he could hear detectives arriving on the scene and calling out. He'd been one of those detectives. It was a good assignment for the two and a half years he was in the D-bureau, but there was something about working with Rocky that brought him more satisfaction. He'd found missing kids with his new partner, tracked down a dozen robbery suspects, and was even occasionally asked to speak at schools. It made his job with the sheriff's office more fulfilling. Even if his mom and ex-girlfriend completely disagreed with his career choice.

Rocky pulled him through a break in the cane and paused as he sniffed in each direction carefully for a few seconds. They had managed to lose the deputies behind them, and suddenly Hallett realized how alone they were. Rocky tugged him toward a drainage ditch with a few feet of skanky water at the bottom.

A Florida snapping turtle the size of a hubcap was sunning himself on the edge of the ditch. Rocky paid no attention to him at first, focusing on his task instead, but the turtle twisted his head and opened his mouth. These turtles, which filled the canals and lakes of Palm Beach

County, were one of the more underrated risks to dogs. Maybe they weren't as fast as an alligator, but they were just as aggressive and rarely backed down from a curious pet. Finally Rocky growled at the turtle, regarding it as a threat until it twisted and flopped into the water and disappeared under the murky film of the surface.

Now Rocky pulled him along the edge of the drainage ditch, and Hallett sensed they were getting closer. He used his left hand to hold Rocky's lead and instinctively pulled his pistol. Hallett looked over his shoulder, but there was no one even close for backup. Picturing an injured girl who needed his help, he knew he couldn't wait for the other deputies and started to trot as Rocky pulled harder and harder in the same direction.

Rocky froze again and emitted a low growl. From experience, Hallett knew something was about to happen. He crouched slightly and held his pistol up until Rocky pulled him into the next field of sugarcane, then through another drainage ditch. Hallett tried to jump over the shallow water, but his boots sank in the mud on the far side. It only took Rocky a moment to find the scent again, and he was off.

That sixth sense every good cop possessed told Hallett they were about to find something, but he had no idea what.

■   ■   ■

Rocky tried not to tug and pull Tim's hand, because this was his favorite game in this place with the tall grass that he liked more than anything. The only way this could be better was if Tim just let him run free to find the man who had someone else with him. The *bad* man who had someone else with him. Those were the only people he and Tim ever chased.

Rocky felt that Tim held him back too much sometimes. Rocky knew the difference between good people and bad people, and he knew how to handle the bad people that Tim chased. All he had to do was bite them. Hard. They were bad people. He could sense just how bad some people were. It was so simple to him. There were good people and bad people. He knew he should bite the bad people, but Tim rarely let him follow his heart. Tim always pulled back on the lead or ordered him not to bite people.

It didn't matter if Tim was wrong. Rocky still loved Tim. And someone had to watch out for him. Especially when he didn't know how to deal with bad people.

Rocky stuck his nose to the ground again. There were two clear scents mixed together. One of them was fear, and the other was something he had never really smelled before. It was almost like a predator going after prey. It was the oddest odor he had ever sniffed, and it was making his brain tingle. He knew this was what Tim wanted him to find. And waiting while Tim and the other people communicated only made him want to chase whatever left the smell more.

Once in a while Tim would let him run free in this tall grass and he would chase rabbits or other swift creatures because it seemed natural to him. He liked running in front of Tim because it felt right to take the scent and not worry what was ahead in the tall grass. He could find anything.

Rocky didn't really care what he was doing as long Tim was with him. He liked seeing his other friends who played with their own people. But nothing really compared to seeing Tim and Josh at the same time. The stimulation was too much, and he played until he just had to lie down. Those were the times when nothing else mattered. Not food, not water, and not sleep. Just Josh and Tim.

In the early morning, when Rocky was still asleep, he remembered being a puppy with his mother and three siblings. It was a special time with nice people that fed him and kids that named him Rocky. It was a different place than here. It was wet, swampy, and warm. It seemed like there were endless days where he would play and play until the day he saw Tim. A lot of people had been nice to him, especially after his mother had been killed. He had been lonely and lost after that evening when his mother tried to protect the other dogs from a predator who had come from the water. But the day Tim came, Rocky knew they were meant to be together. Somehow, when he saw Tim walking across the wide lawn, Rocky understood he had to protect him.

Tim and Josh made losing his mom a little easier.

Sometimes Rocky wished he understood more of how people communicated. Their grunts and growls held no clue, just certain sounds like his name and the names of others around him. Then there were the words Tim used in his games. Sometimes he wanted Rocky to find the bags with funny smells, sometimes he wanted him to run after people. Sometimes Rocky was supposed to bite people if they didn't lie on the ground. And a few times, Rocky had to protect Tim. Usually Rocky sensed the danger long before Tim did. And if Tim would let him, Rocky could handle it before Tim was ever at risk.

But this game, where he would follow the scent while Tim hung on to him, this was one of the most fun games. Sometimes it didn't seem like Tim had as much fun on these games. This was one of those times. Rocky tried to control how fast he ran, but excitement pushed him hard and Tim struggled to keep up. It had to be hard with only two legs.

Suddenly, Rocky could tell a difference in the scent trail. Something had happened. At first the two scents were not together. They were close and crossed each other, but they were no longer tied to each other. It was confusing and made him stop for a moment. When he glanced back at Tim, he saw his friend holding the thing that made loud noises. It sounded like thunder and used to scare him, but they played so many games with the noise all around him that it no longer was frightening. At least not when Tim did it.

In the distance, he could hear the distinct bark of his other friends. One was on each side of him. He knew their people friends would be with them, too, all playing the same game, and all hoping to get their treat when they were done.

People did things that confused him all the time. They gave off a smell of fear, but still played games. Sometimes, they would shout at Tim, but he wouldn't react and just stayed calm. Rocky didn't smell Tim's fear very often. But he could smell the fear of other people when Tim talked to them. It seemed like there were only a few people who ever made sense to him. Tim and little Josh were two of them.

Now Rocky had a scent and followed it down to a low, wet area. He followed so closely that he barely noticed the turtle that rolled off a log and plopped into the water. He tried to remember where this place was because he had to come back and explore that turtle more closely.

He sometimes was afraid of swampy areas. They reminded him of where he was born. He would think of his mother and what happened to her in a low, wet place just like this.

Then he heard Tim making the game sound. It wasn't clear, like some of the sounds Rocky had learned, it was just an idea that Tim wanted him to find what they were looking for. Rocky moved along the wet ground.

Something was close.

Claire Perkins rarely needed to communicate verbally with Smarty. They had a connection unlike any other dog handler and canine. The brawny German Shepherd could easily have yanked her unmercifully across the rough ground. Smarty, at 110 pounds, only weighed five less than Claire, but he understood her limits just as she understood his. The connection was immediate, and it developed through training and their home life.

Two years ago, Smarty was raw, or, as the dog trainers would say, "green." He was also high-energy, and when he was about thirteen months old, Smarty had wrecked Claire's townhouse. Furniture was chewed, couch cushions shredded. It looked like a crime scene. The dog raised hell until Claire was forced to get tough. It was a learning experience for both of them. Claire pulled the old "alpha dog" maneuver by flipping Smarty onto his back, then going face-to-face with him to explain who was boss. It hadn't taken long for Smarty to calm down and show some respect. It was a lot like raising a kid. Not like how Claire's father had raised her, but more like how she intended to raise her own children once she started having them.

There was almost nothing she enjoyed more than playing with Smarty at home. He was the real constant in her life right now, and she was happy to have someone so fun-loving and reliable. Still, she needed to find a human counterpart. Maybe someone who understood the stress of police work and would tolerate another male in her life. Even if the male was American Kennel Club certified.

Once they got home, Claire would shower Smarty with all the affection he wanted, but in this man's world of law enforcement, she didn't think it was professional to be rubbing his head and planting kisses on him no matter how much she loved the dog. Tim Hallett was another story. He could get away with it because of his tall, muscular frame and rugged good looks. He was always hugging Rocky and talking to him like they were best buds. It just seemed natural to him. Then again, Tim was clueless on certain issues. He had no idea how the faded scar above his left eyebrow set off his blue eyes and probably attracted more attention from women than his uniform.

Even Darren Mori could show affection to Brutus because the dog was a Golden Retriever and everyone thought he was cute. She knew it burned Darren up that he got stuck with a cute Retriever while she had a badass-looking attack dog.

Claire had heard Brutus bark a couple of times in the distance as she and Smarty pushed through the sugarcane, with two large detectives struggling to keep up. The Golden Retriever had a tendency to shout out for joy at being involved in a job like this. Technically, Brutus was a cadaver and explosives dog, but he could follow a track, and their unit, the Canine Assist Team, had to be adaptable. The federal trainer, Ruben Vasquez, didn't want them to decline any assignment.

She focused on Smarty, who was moving at a decent pace but hadn't seemed to pick up any particular track. From what the sergeant had said, Claire knew the most important issue was finding the girl. The suspect was secondary.

Smarty suddenly picked up the scent of something and turned, waiting for Claire to make the turn with him instead of jerking her along. She thought they were probably about to come out of the cane and be facing another drainage ditch. It was easy to forget how vast and confusing these fields could be, especially the ones that bordered pine patches.

This was exactly why she had signed on to be a dog handler. If she didn't have Smarty, too many other deputies would say something like "Leave the cute chick to watch the cars." She didn't have to put up with that shit in K-9.

Claire loved working in this specialized unit. They had all benefited from Tim Hallett's example. The veteran cop, who had been on patrol as well as a respected detective, had taught her as much about life as he had about dogs. She wondered how Tim was faring as two large deputies tried to keep up with her and Smarty. Tim had said, "Never let the male cops know you care what they think of you or how you're doing your job. Being snotty is better than being sorry." Her favorite hobby was making men who underestimated her feel like assholes.

■   ■   ■

Junior tried to control his breathing as he realized he was disoriented and not sure exactly where his car was parked. Everywhere he looked was sugarcane. He'd run to a row of pine trees where he thought he'd left the car, then realize he'd gotten turned around while chasing the girl.

He heard a dog bark again in the distance. A few minutes earlier, he had heard the unmistakable sound of a voice over a radio. There were definitely cops in the area. He pulled the 9 mm Beretta hidden in his waistband. Experience had taught him it never hurt to have insurance when dealing with volatile young women like the ones he was interested in. But he'd never fired at a human being. He held the pistol up in his shaking hand and pointed it at the closest row of sugarcane, imagining what he would do if the cop burst out right in front of him. Satisfied he'd be able to pull the trigger, Junior yanked out a rag he kept in his pocket to wipe down the cars he stole, blotted the sweat out of his eyes, and worked up enough energy to start trotting toward the next line of trees, away from the sounds of his pursuers.

As he started to jog away, his side hurting from a cramp, Junior wondered if they had found the girl yet. His only hope was to get out of the area. Fast.

■   ■   ■

Tim Hallett read Rocky's subtle moves and pauses. This same sort of behavior had befuddled him before Ruben Vasquez had taught the team the art of dog handling. The wily army vet had turned the process into a Zen-like exercise. Now Hallett felt he could communicate with his dog better than he ever communicated with his ex-girlfriend. Four-year-old Josh had picked up the talent without ever attending class.

Hallett knew Rocky was very close to a discovery. The muscular Malinois would pause, then shuttle forward, nose to the ground, then up in the air, searching for the exact track. This was definitely something. Hallett glanced over his shoulder, hoping there were other deputies close by, but he and Rocky were still alone. They scrambled through the thick cane field, and Rocky started to strain on the lead. Hallett pulled him closer, in case what was ahead was a suspect with a weapon. He still had his pistol in his hand.

Rocky burst out of the sugarcane into an open space. Hallett felt the slack in the lead as the dog came to an abrupt stop. A second later, Hallett fought through the last few stalks of sugarcane and froze next to Rocky.

This was not what he had expected to find. Rocky, sensing the same delicate circumstance, immediately sat in place. The overheated dog started to pant loudly.

Hallett holstered his pistol.

Curled on the ground in front of him, quietly sobbing, was a teenage girl with long blond hair. Twigs and torn stalks of sugarcane were stuck on her shirt and in her hair. She tugged her knees tight into her chest and let her eyes move from Rocky up to Hallett.

He said in a soft voice, "It's all right. You're safe now." He couldn't keep from scanning the open area in the rows between the sugarcane stalks for any threat. He kneeled down, careful not to come too close and upset her more. "Which way did the man go?"

All the girl could do was shake her head and sob more intensely.

Hallett started to feel the familiar anger course through his body at the thought of someone abusing a sweet young girl like this. He didn't think he was radiating his emotions until Rocky nuzzled up next to him in an obvious attempt to calm him down.

No matter what Rocky thought, Hallett knew somebody was going to pay for this shit.

■　　■　　■

Rocky turned toward the scent he smelled most clearly. It was fear. More than the scent, he could hear something ahead of him in the tall grass. It wasn't a threat, and it didn't sound dangerous to Tim. He pulled his friend in that direction and worked his way through the tall grass, but he slowed slightly.

As soon as his head poked through the grass into the open area, he saw a person sitting on the ground and making a sad noise. He had heard it before and knew that it didn't represent a danger.

Rocky felt Tim pause behind him and glanced over his shoulder at his friend, who still had the loud thing in his hand. Then Tim made some soft noises directed at the person on the ground. That's when Rocky knew for sure the person was no threat.

He eased forward, smelling the ground and trying not to upset the person sitting down. He realized it was a female and she had rolled herself into a ball. He placed his nose next to her and pushed, hoping she would rub his head or scratch under his mouth the way he liked. She didn't respond, and Tim stepped forward and told Rocky to back away.

Rocky knew to just sit quietly, but he stayed alert, wondering if the person who made the other scent would come this way. He knew that was a bad person. And that was his special game.

He loved to catch bad people with Tim.

■   ■   ■

Junior was panting and sweating from the combination of fear and exertion. At last he saw the goddamn car parked up ahead. He'd be able to drive out on the rear access road and with any luck avoid having to explain himself to the cops. He had a feeling he'd be able to talk his way past them anyway, but it was better to avoid them altogether.

His legs felt wobbly, and he knew this wasn't over. He'd never had something like this go so bad. He dreaded the evening, when he could think about what happened and obsess over how to fix it.

As he approached the vehicle, he wiped his face again with his rag. It was a good thing he had the torn-up towel, because a handkerchief wouldn't have been enough to soak up his sweat.

Then he heard another bark. This one was close. Closer than he thought they'd ever make it. Just before he reached the car he slipped in the muddy soil and landed hard on his butt.

"Shit," was all he said as he struggled to lift his girth and make it to the car. The damn dog barked again.

He started the car by crossing the exposed wires and resisted the urge to stomp the gas. He wanted to ease out of the area.

As he pulled away, his eye caught something on the ground. A dog barked again. He looked down at his white rag on the rough dirt near the road and calculated that it was more important to leave the area than to pick it up. They couldn't link him to the rag. They couldn't link him to anything.

He was invincible.

■　　■　　■

Rocky felt they were close to their prey. Whatever had made this odd scent had been by here, and now it had changed and added a tinge of fear to the scent. Tim urged him on, and Rocky knew it was important to find what had made this smell.

A rabbit ran off to his side, but he didn't even look up. He smelled something dead, but quickly saw it was a bird that was lying directly in front of him. It had nothing to do with the scent they were following. The scent almost hurt his nose and made him want to whimper and put his paw on it. It was the oddest thing he had ever followed, and now he had to know what it was.

He paused and listened ahead of him to see if he could pick up the sounds of whatever was fleeing. But there was a lot of noise around. The sound of other people behind him. The barks of the other dogs. Birds that made noise in the trees and the loud birds that floated on water. He tried to block them all out and focus the way he knew Tim wanted him to.

It was hopeless. The only thing he could do now was follow the scent. The scent that had changed to a nasty combination of odors that were completely unnatural.

Rocky had decided this was a *very* bad person.

Tim Hallett sat on the tailgate of the Tahoe with Darren Mori while Rocky and Brutus rested in the shade of the truck. They had been unable to find whoever had abducted the girl, and it was eating at Hallett. The dogs were spent. A search like this would wear anyone out. After the girl had been taken to safety, they tried to pick up the track of the suspect but had no luck. Now the girl was back "East" at the Palm Beach County Sheriff's Office headquarters. The residents out here in the communities around Lake Okeechobee referred to the urban areas along the coast as "East," usually with a hint of disdain and distrust in their voices.

Hallett casually looked over to make sure Rocky was okay and was pleased to see him breathing normally, not panting, which was a sign of overheating. He had lapped up plenty of water and eaten a few snacks. Now Rocky sat in his "Sphinx pose," his front paws lined up and his head held high. Hallett could stare at the dog for hours when he took certain postures. It was another way the dog communicated nonverbally. This pose signified satisfaction and calm. Rocky looked regal sitting in the shade. He turned his head to look up at Hallett, and his left eyelid closed. It was a wink. Hallett could never convince other dog handlers that his dog winked at him after a tough assignment, but he had not imagined it. The Belgian Malinois winked at him to let know everything was cool.

Hallett often studied other dogs to see if they displayed the same behavior. Sometimes he worried that if he saw another dog wink he would end up in the uncomfortable position of explaining how dogs winked at him alone. He knew it would earn him an odd nickname, so he was just as happy Rocky was the only dog who chose to communicate that way.

Darren's Brutus, with his thick hair, had a harder time keeping cool but had managed to sprawl across the shaded road and seemed perfectly content. "Why did Claire have to go in with the detectives?" Darren asked.

"The girl formed a quick connection with her. She was comfortable talking with Claire, and no one wanted to screw that up when they needed so much information from her."

"Too bad she didn't get a look at the guy. But it sounds like the same suspect grabbed a couple of girls in the past few years."

Hallett nodded, committing the description to memory. Tubby middle-aged white male with thinning hair. None of the girls had seen much other than a black pistol. He had come up behind them and forced them to wear blindfolds. It was always a different car. The creep had performed oral sex on the first two girls in addition to fondling them; the detectives in sex crimes said it was common for the same sex act to be performed each time. Both crimes were committed in wooded areas, and no one knew about it until the girls returned home. One of them was so ashamed she hadn't even told her mother for over a week, a very common situation with young girls who'd been molested. It was a similar circumstance that had caused Tim Hallett to punch a suspect named Arnold Ludner until he revealed he'd left a terrified eleven-year-old girl in the wooded area of a park off Forest Hill Boulevard. The stunt had gotten Hallett booted out of the D-bureau, but the sheriff was a stand-up guy and refused to screw someone who had saved a little girl. Helen Greene had been outspoken in her support and had influenced the sheriff. One of Hallett's options was to join the K-9 unit, and he had never looked back.

Darren said, "I don't know about you, but I'm dog-tired." He laughed at his own joke. It was a good thing he was close with Brutus, because no one else liked the puns.

Hallett sat up straight as he heard a call over the radio asking for a K-9 unit half a mile south of where they were now.

Darren said, "I recognize that voice. It's John Fusco, isn't it?"

Hallett just nodded.

"Didn't that jerk get you kicked out of the D-bureau?"

Hallett shrugged and said, "No, *I* got me kicked out of the D-bureau."

■   ■   ■

Claire Perkins waited in the undersized interview room with low ceilings as Smarty sat very properly next to her on the linoleum floor. The girl they'd found in the cane field, Katie Ziegler, refused to allow Claire or Smarty out of her presence. Although Smarty was terrifying to most people, Katie had seen past the facade and was on her knees in front of the beefy Shepherd, calmly patting his head and running her fingers through his thick coat. Smarty would occasionally nudge the girl to let her know it was a two-way street and he appreciated her, too. Katie had only spoken to Claire since she'd been found. That frustrated the detectives, but they went along with it.

Katie never saw the man who kidnapped her. She had intended to apply for a job at Ruby Tuesday's and was in the parking lot of the massive Wellington Mall when she heard a man's voice and felt his pistol against her head. The next thing she knew he had put a blindfold over her and wrapped tape around it to keep it in place. She didn't know how long they drove but thought that it was less than half an hour, and as soon as she felt firm ground under her feet she ran as hard as she could, pulling at the blindfold as she did. The first thing she saw was the sugarcane and thought it offered her sanctuary. The man ran after her and called her by name but was only able to grab her arm once, just as she came out the other side of the cane field near a canal.

The detectives on the case were scrambling to figure out how the suspect knew her name. Katie was certain she hadn't told him.

No matter what angle Claire took, she got the same information over and over again. She felt sorry for this girl, but at the same time, she realized being asked to sit with Katie and question her was a tremendous opportunity for her career. She knew there were detectives on the other side of the mirrored panel watching everything she said and did.

Claire said, "Your mom should be here any time."

Katie just nodded.

"Does your dad live around here?" She hadn't heard the girl or anyone else mention her father.

Katie shook her head, then, in a quiet voice, said, "He's in jail."

"I didn't know that. Why's he in jail?" She knew it was a question she didn't have to ask, and it might keep the girl from talking more, but curiosity got the better of her. She thought back to some of the lessons Tim Hallett had taught her. One of the more important ones was "Never deny your own curiosity. That's what makes a good cop."

Katie said, "He was on probation for possession with intent to sell cocaine and he violated. Now he's doing six years at South Bay Correctional. I get to see him every other weekend."

Instantly Claire's mind started racing, and she wondered if Katie's abduction had something to do with her father's involvement in the cocaine business. Then she remembered the two other girls and how closely the incident matched. Kidnapped, blindfolded, molested—there were too many similarities. This wasn't a crime of profit. They had something much worse than an enforcer for a cocaine distributor; they had a serial sex offender targeting teenage girls.

And he seemed pretty smart, judging by the way there were no leads to work with yet.

■ ■ ■

Hallett brought the Tahoe to a stop about fifty feet from the crime scene tape set up on a road that ran east along a row of pine trees. Darren parked right next to him, and they hooked the six-foot leads on the dogs. He could see Detective John Fusco directing a couple of crime scene techs and another detective. Fusco stood tall. It was a rare moment when the detective removed his expensive suit coat and worked only in a shirt and tie. As Hallett and Darren walked over, Hallett knew exactly what Fusco was going to say.

Fusco turned toward them, smiled, and called out in a loud voice, "Look, the kittens are here. Oh, sorry, the CAT."

Cops being cops, they had naturally come up with the nickname CAT for the Canine Assist Team. Not very original, but not objectionable, either, until a dickhead like Fusco got hold of it. Cops loved nicknames and acronyms. In a profession that could get you killed, they risked everything, but most of them knew the value of a good laugh and blowing off steam.

Since he was prepared for Fusco's greeting, Hallett just nodded and said, "How's it going, Fusco?"

"Not bad, how about you, Farmer Tim?"

Hallett shrugged but didn't acknowledge his personal nickname. He'd earned it by living in a trailer behind a Christian school in Belle Glade and having a growing menagerie housed next to him. It had started with a teacher building a small pen for an injured raccoon, but somehow Hallett was now in charge of the original raccoon, two possums, a chicken, a boa constrictor, a goat, and, incredibly, an alpaca someone had left abandoned on State Road 80.

John Fusco was a detective in the crimes/persons unit. That title covered anything that happened to a victim physically short of death, where homicide investigated. It was a catchall phrase and everyone used it to distinguish between them and the less prestigious crimes/property unit, which dealt mainly with burglary and thefts. Fusco was the highest profile and most effective detective in crimes/persons even if no one wanted to admit it and give the puffed-up prima dona any more reason to swagger.

Fusco said, "Don't you guys live out here in this shithole?"

Hallett mumbled, "In town."

"I thought this *was* Belle Glade."

Darren was the one who said, "What do you got, Fusco?"

The tall detective looked down at Darren in a show of power and said, "What's the hurry? Got a date?"

"We're tired and the dogs are worn out. Could you, for once, get to the point?"

Fusco purposely kept quiet for a moment. Hallett knew it was to show he wasn't bowing to pressure from anyone in a uniform. Then he said, "The crime scene techs are photographing the area, and we found a rag that could've come from the suspect. Can either of you geniuses make your dogs sniff it and see if it's related to the track they had earlier?"

Darren said, "What do you think the dogs are going to do, Fusco? Smell it, then turn around and tell us it belongs to the same guy?"

"I don't know what kind of voodoo you guys do. But I've seen Hallett's dog do some pretty amazing things besides just grabbing someone by the balls and throwing him down." He twisted to look in every direction. "It's getting late. We gotta get this show on the road and clear out of here. This is the last damn place I wanna be caught late in the afternoon. The gators would love a big chunk of Italian sausage like me." He cackled at his comment, then gave them a hand motion that said to speed things up.

Hallett mumbled, "Give me a second." He scanned the scene and noticed the pretty young crime scene tech standing by with a plastic bag to process the white rag that was on the ground near her. As he stepped closer, Hallett heard Fusco say, "Sorry there's no one to beat up in this case. I know that tends to make things easier for you. We're following the book on this one."

Hallett felt his face flush. He saw the embarrassment on the face of the pretty evidence tech, so he worked hard to keep his mouth shut. He wanted to explain to the young woman that he didn't beat people up arbitrarily, but he was tired of telling the story. He let Rocky get closer to the rag, then leaned down and said, "*Ruiken*, Rocky, *ruiken*." It was the Dutch command for "smell it." He'd worry about what they could learn from it after Rocky got a whiff. That's when he got a surprise.

Rocky leaned down, sniffed the rag, then stepped back and moved his front left paw against the rough ground as he made an odd sound in his throat, like a lawn mower. Hallett looked over at Darren, who just shrugged. It was the first time he'd ever seen his partner do something so unusual in relation to a scent.

One more mystery to ask Ruben Vasquez about.

■　　■　　■

Junior worked hard to make his "dates" with the young women undetectable to the police. The rag was an anomaly, but they couldn't say it was actually connected to the incident, and he didn't think they could link it to him. Even if they got a DNA sample from it, he wasn't in any databases. He left the beat-up Toyota Tercel in the same spot where he had found it off Palm Beach Lakes Boulevard and was careful to wipe down the interior so even if the owner had reported it stolen, it would be excused as a lapse of memory.

He'd spaced out the first two girls over two years, and as a result, there hadn't been much news coverage. The second girl, Lily, only rated a short story in *The Palm Beach Post* over a week after his intimate encounter with her. That sort of coverage and the current lack of effort by the police led him to believe that he had chosen the right girls. Looks were important, but so were the family history, their age, their actions, and their connections. Junior had the system figured out and knew he'd never be caught.

Sometimes it was just his disciplined practice of observing the girls from a distance that was enjoyable. He loved the anticipation of what was going to happen, but the idea that he could watch them so closely, and no one ever knew, started the chain of events that made him feel so special. Using the computer to learn their family history also made him feel sort of like God. He wondered what guys like him did before computers. The old stereotype of the creepy stranger in a van with free candy was a little low-tech, but probably still effective in the right circumstances today.

Ultimately, it was his close and intimate interaction with the girls that satisfied his complex desires. He recognized they were like a drug to him. Each experience felt more intense. Each girl had to have a slightly different attribute to make the encounter as satisfying as the one before. But this was his form of relaxation. He didn't smoke, drink, or use drugs. He felt like everyone was entitled to one vice. God knew he had earned it by putting up with his father. Even now that he was an adult, the old man tended to bully him. Junior had caught himself doing things he hoped his dad would be proud of. No matter what he did, his father would rant and bluster. But this activity was his own private secret. He was in charge. It was a feeling he rarely got to enjoy.

Junior never tried to justify what he did with the girls. He just liked doing it and thought, maybe, at some later point in life the girls might appreciate what he did for them. He wasn't crazy. A nut wouldn't think it through as well as he did. He left no evidence and chose the right girls. He was untouchable.

Now he thought about Katie Ziegler with her soft, wavy blond hair and full lips. He'd followed her and researched her. She was no angel. He didn't feel like he was doing anything she hadn't done before. Junior hadn't counted on her being so sly, sitting calmly until she had the opportunity to run. The incident had put him far too close to being caught. But it also proved to him that planning things out carefully always paid off in the end. He considered using Katie again. That would drive the cops crazy. Then he realized the difficulty of the task and the risk he'd have to take to try again. It wasn't something he could accurately predict.

He needed to release this tension as soon as possible. Not only had it been a while, but his needs seemed to be growing at an exponential rate. He wondered how long he'd be able to contain them.

Junior felt the first stirrings of the urge that compelled him to act. It was unavoidable. Usually it took longer to develop, but this date had not been like any other.

He knew he wouldn't be able to sit still during the night.

Tim Hallett and Darren Mori stood on the edge of the field where, a few hours before, Rocky had made the odd alert on the rag. It was a pretty big leap of faith to just assume the rag was associated with the kidnapper, but this was the kind of shit a good K-9 officer followed up on.

It had cooled off like most evenings in the fall. This wasn't the kind of place that tourists visiting Florida saw. And reality TV shows couldn't convey the mud, mosquitoes, menacing sounds of various predators, and the stark beauty of rural Florida. Hallett recalled a high school creative writing teacher asking him to imagine an evening just like this one. In his youth and ignorance all Hallett called it was "nice." Now, after living in Belle Glade for a couple of years, he found remote places like this invigorating and calming at the same time. It was awesome in a quiet way. It was the most contradictory place Hallett had ever seen. These miles wedged between Florida's coasts were a mystery that no one ever really understood.

With the wide canal at the edge of the field and the pine trees running up to the water, this was a spot he'd bring Rocky and Josh to go kayaking one day soon.

Crickets in the pine trees chirped, and frogs along the banks of the canal sang their annoying love songs, while the occasional gator croaked a low bass to all the amphibian musical instruments he would eat later.

The two K-9 officers had cleaned up since the search for Katie Ziegler earlier that afternoon. Now they were just in jeans and T-shirts as Brutus and Rocky explored the woods, chasing rabbits and playing together. It was a way to unwind before Hallett asked Rocky to get down to business.

This time of the evening, as the sun set and a hazy twilight enveloped them like a fog, was the dogs' favorite time to run. Especially Brutus. The Golden Retriever never seemed to run out of energy.

Darren said, "You wanna get this started?"

"Let's wait for Claire."

"I'm getting hungry. Why should we wait?"

"Because we're a team and Claire might have an insight after talking with the victim all afternoon. It wouldn't hurt to have a little extra info and look for something specific."

Darren just nodded as he turned back to the sketchpad lying on the hood of Hallett's unmarked white Tahoe.

"Don't pout, she'll be here in a few minutes." He turned to look at the designs and logos for a new Canine Assist Team T-shirt Darren had been drawing for days. Aside from being smarter than just about anyone Hallett had ever met, Darren had some real artistic ability.

Claire pulled her Tahoe off the shell-rock road and parked next to Hallett's. After she got out of the vehicle with Smarty on a six-foot lead, she saw the other two dogs bound out of the woods, so she kneeled down to release Smarty to trot over to his friends.

As she approached her partners she said, "Let me guess, you're still working on a new logo."

Darren smiled and held up his sketchbook. "I like *You can run but you can't hide* or *Release the hounds.*"

Brutus ran up to Claire, wagging his tail wildly. When she squatted down to pet him she said, "How about *Cute dogs finish first.*"

Hallett and Claire started to laugh. Brutus reinforced the slogan by jumping up and licking Claire.

Darren said, "Et tu, Brutus, et tu?"

Hallett restrained a smile at the rare moment when Darren let slip how well read he really was.

Now Darren changed the subject and said, "What are we doing out here in severely fading light? We could be having a burger and a beer at Cooters."

Hallett said, "The dogs are rested and fed, and I thought we could just check the area again. Now we have an idea of where to start looking. Fusco rushed us along this afternoon." He turned to Claire and said, "Did the victim give you any ideas of what to look for?"

Claire said, "The victim has a name. It's Katie. All she really remembers is that the guy was heavy and he had a black pistol. She's not even sure where she ran from him. She thought it might be a smaller car just by the way the interior felt, but she never got a good look at it."

Darren said, "So we're doing all this based on a rag?"

"Why not? We got nothing else."

Darren shrugged, and they all got the dogs ready to search the area. To the dogs it was just another game, and this time their human partners were joining in. Each of the dogs was secured on a six-foot lead and started spiraling out in a concentric circle.

Hallett was still learning all of Rocky's capabilities. Any decent K-9 officer knew there was always something to learn, about the dog and about himself. Hallett was careful not to focus his SureFire flashlight in front of Rocky. That might inadvertently lead Rocky in its direction. Hallett felt a burning desire to find something they could use, but he didn't want his desires to override good police work. He hoped he was doing all this for the right reason, which was to stop this asshole and make Katie Ziegler feel safe. Not just to show up Fusco.

But that would definitely be a perk.

■   ■   ■

Junior's efforts to satisfy his desires by searching the Internet for his next target had proven futile. He could no longer sit in front of the computer. He could no longer concentrate. All he thought about was Katie Ziegler and how he'd handled the whole incident. Not just letting the girl run on him, but how close he had come to being discovered and losing the rag out in the field. Normally he kept a rag or two with him in case the girls needed to be gagged or he started to sweat. He realized there was nothing to worry about; it just bothered him that he had made any mistakes at all.

Ultimately, that's what drove him to leave the house in his father's car. There was something inside him that made him avoid using his own vehicle for anything related to this part of his life. Besides, the old man didn't need it. It was just taking up space in his driveway.

He lived a compartmentalized existence. Sometimes this compartment and work overlapped. It was just a bonus. But he recognized he could never let anyone, not even his brother, know about this part of his life. The secret desires and drives. Occasionally, he even felt revulsion when he saw news stories on sex offenders in court. The further he stepped back from his actions, the more unnerving they became.

These were simply private moments he shared with these girls. Under the best circumstances they would be too ashamed to share these moments with anyone else. Or at least, as in the past, by the time they shared them, it was too late. Maybe that's what had made him overconfident and sloppy.

If he really wanted to do all he could to cover his tracks, then the idea of the rag he'd lost in the woods and the fact that Katie Ziegler had gotten away from him compelled him to take action. The urge was just too strong. It pushed him out the door into the twilight. His father's well-maintained Oldsmobile hadn't been driven in a while but cranked right up.

Junior's brain hurt as he considered his options and tried to decide what would satisfy this nagging drive.

Anything was better than just sitting still.

■　　■　　■

Hallett took the time to study each dog on almost every assignment. He learned something from watching the dogs work as well as watching how the dog handlers worked. These three dogs were as different as the deputies who worked with them. In a way, the K-9 and human on each team had similar personalities. Hallett didn't think it could be a coincidence.

Brutus had two speeds, play and all-out romp. Just like a lot of other Golden Retrievers, he didn't have a mean bone in his body and needed to be in almost constant motion. Darren Mori had that same active gene.

Smarty, like his handler, was serious. If any dog could be called serious. He also tended to keep to himself. He and Rocky had a special friendship. Sort of a dog romance. They respected each other, but the Shepherd was clearly the badass, bigger brother.

Rocky had a freewheeling side, but, like many other Belgian Malinois, once he set his mind to a task he never backed down. It struck Hallett that he'd been described in much the same way. One of his early evaluations at the sheriff's office said, "Has potential, if he just learns to let things go occasionally."

It was a curse. Once he got stuck on something, everything else fell to the side. He tried to get past it—God, he had tried—but the right case, the interesting assignment, just consumed him. And it cost him. Cost him more than he could ever calculate.

The first thing that always popped into his head when he started to think about things like this was his relationship with Crystal. He'd had something special with her, and there was no one but himself to blame for why he now lived alone in the trailer behind the Christian school in Belle Glade.

Maybe his family wouldn't be so weird if he was around more. His mom, brother, and sister all went weeks without seeing him, but he was at least trying to do better with them. Even if his brother drove both him and Rocky to distraction. Rocky couldn't be in the same room with his stoner brother without alerting on him every ten minutes.

Now, in the field, each of the dogs had staked out his own area in his own style. Brutus kind of looked around, making a game out of sniffing even if he wasn't sure what to seek.

Smarty walked the perimeter like a guard at a prison making sure everyone was safe and occasionally checking for a scent.

Rocky was just determined. He'd detected a scent earlier, and something told Hallett the dog knew what he was looking for. Rocky showed no interest in a rabbit he flushed from a bush, or a dead bird lying across his path. He had his nose just off the ground and seemed to sense the urgency Hallett felt.

■   ■   ■

The sedan bounced and rumbled over the uneven, unpaved shell-rock road, giving Junior a headache.

"God damn, it can get dark out here," he muttered. There were no streetlights on either side of the road. There wasn't even a streetlight in sight. Just the sinking rays of sunlight behind some clouds far to the west. The early evening seemed even darker with a thick clump of scrub pines and underbrush on the right side of the road.

His annoyance and irritability were trumped by his urge. Or possibly caused by it. He lost all common sense when these moods came on him. He'd learned a long time ago not to fight them anymore. But this was the first time he had gone with the feeling so decisively. Maybe he was evolving.

Junior realized he'd been lucky with the first two girls before today. They had gone smoothly. Maybe they had made him overconfident. He missed that feeling of competence. He needed it in at least one compartment of his life.

It didn't matter. Whatever the weird origin of his urge, he was doing something about it now. Junior slowed and shut off the headlights. He could barely see the white shell-rock road in front of him.

5

Hallett paused, still keeping the beam of his flashlight pointed in front of Rocky. It was always a concern that a police service dog would read or be influenced by subtle, inadvertent clues from the handler. In training, Ruben Vasquez went to great lengths to keep the handler in the dark as to where practice drug bundles were hidden so the dog had to find them on his own. Now Hallett wondered if he was violating that dog handler commandment by shining his light in front of Rocky, in effect leading him where Hallett thought might be the best place to look.

Rocky hesitated, and Hallett waited patiently, not wanting to rush him.

Darren and Brutus walked over, but Hallett raised his hand to give Rocky a moment more. Then the dog leaned down, put his paw over his nose, and made the same funky lawn mower sound.

Darren asked, "What is it?"

"Not sure. But you heard that abnormal alert, too. Just like this afternoon."

"It didn't sound like any alert I ever heard or saw before."

Hallett stepped back and spread his beam over the soft, muddy ground just off the packed white shell-rock road between the fields and the pine windbreaks. He was missing something.

Claire and Smarty walked over, but they stopped well outside the perimeter of where Rocky was alerting. She didn't want to contaminate their potential crime scene. She called out, "Any idea what we're looking for?"

Hallett shook his head. "I don't see anything in the area. Not even a branch or leaf."

Claire said, "Maybe it's not something we can see on top of the ground."

Hallett said, "Rocky would start digging if it was buried."

"That's not what I'm talking about. Maybe it's just a strong scent." Claire carefully walked around to Hallett. She surveyed the scene like a movie director, changing position and squatting low to look along the plane of the ground. Finally, she said, "I see three things of interest. It looks like a tire tread right here"—she placed the beam of her flashlight on a patch of ground—"a shoe print here, and the ground has been disturbed over here."

Now that she pointed them out to him, Hallett noticed all three disturbances in the soft ground. He pulled out his phone and snapped a few photographs. "You think we should call crime scene? Fusco was in charge earlier, but I didn't see them take any notice of these imprints."

Claire let out an exasperated sigh. "We're supposed to be trained and adaptable. We don't need crime scene just to take a few photographs and make a plaster cast of a shoe that may or may not involve the case."

Now Darren said, "You can make plaster casts?"

Claire just shook her head and walked over to her Tahoe. A few minutes later she came back carrying a plastic box with the material needed to make a cast of the imprint.

As she mixed and poured the plaster, Claire said, "There's not enough of the other two imprints to make a cast. But I would guess the tire is small enough that it went to an import. The other imprint might be someone's butt where they slipped and fell."

Darren had to say, "That's a pretty big butt."

Claire snapped a few photos as the plaster dried.

All three of them froze at an unusual sound on the quiet night air.

Darren said, "You hear that?"

It was a vehicle.

■   ■   ■

Junior took his foot off the gas and allowed the Olds to coast as he edged it toward a small stand of pine trees. There was someone on the edge of the road up ahead. He couldn't make out any details, but he could see the shadow, and it threw off his plan.

He'd thought he'd be able to creep in unseen and do what he had to do. He *had* to creep in unseen for the plan to work. As his eyes adjusted to the light he could make out that the figure was a man.

Junior patted the Beretta in his belt. Was he ready to get drastic? The urge told him it might be time to take a few risks.

■ ■ ■

Hallett did a quick assessment of his team. None of them wore a uniform, but each of them had a pistol concealed under a loose shirt. He was considering all the factors for the worst-case scenario. Every good cop thought in those terms.

Claire stepped toward him and said, "Who the hell would be in this place at this time?"

It was now completely dark, and the absence of any city's ambient light made it feel like they were in a cave. The closest building was miles away. All three shut off their flashlights immediately.

Hallett felt responsible for his partner's safety. He always did. Even as a kid, he looked after his brother, no matter how infuriating he was. The only fights he had been in were defending his brother's odd behavior. Now his instinct was to send his friends to safety, but he had to understand that they were trained professional police officers and equal to any of the challenges that they ran up against. There was no telling who was in this vehicle, and he definitely needed the help.

Darren said, "A fisherman?"

Claire said what everyone was thinking. "The kidnapper? What are the chances?"

Hallett calculated the odds. It would be weird, but possible. Crazy things happened on this damn job every day. He tensed as all three of them backed to the edge of the woods and watched the vehicle as it slowed, then turned toward the canal at the far end of the field.

Now Hallett could clearly tell the vehicle was a pickup truck. It looked like a four-door Ram Charger. The truck drove along the edge of the far stand of pines to the bank of the canal. Although it was an isolated spot just to fish, that seemed like the easiest explanation.

The front passenger door and the rear doors opened simultaneously as three men stumbled out. All three were loud and drunk. One man wobbled like a broken toy, and Hallett figured they were just drunk rednecks. The driver, a kid, about seventeen, stepped out of the driver's door.

Hallett's hope that this was the kidnapper evaporated.

Darren whispered, "Why the hell would you drive all the way out here to fish?"

Claire added, "I thought they might be dopers, but I haven't heard any planes, and there are no airstrips in the area."

Then they heard two small dogs yapping. That caught the attention of Rocky, Smarty, and Brutus.

Hallett immediately realized what these assholes were up to. By the light of the open door, he could see two poodles on homemade rope leashes sitting in the rear seat. Hallett thought, *Son of a bitch. I'll make them sorry.* He was all about justice no matter how it was handed out or who dealt it. He turned to his partners and whispered, "Gator poachers."

Claire muttered, "Assholes."

■　　■　　■

Now that his eyes had adjusted to the dark and there was light coming from the double-wide trailer's living room window, Junior clearly saw the thickset man leaning on the mailbox with a Confederate flag painted on it. He was smoking a cigarette. And he hadn't noticed Junior.

The trailer was on a permanent cement pad forty feet off the road and marked the beginning of the park that held twenty double-wides. Junior could see from the light that the front yard was sprinkled with old, cracked kids' toys, and a satellite TV dish dangled from the side of the trailer.

He wondered where Katie Ziegler lived inside the trailer. She had a younger brother, but he was pretty sure the place would have three bedrooms.

Junior took a moment to fantasize about what she would be wearing at this moment. He'd like it to be young, preppy, and not too slutty.

This sparse, shitty trailer park was only on the left side of the road. The right side of the road was scrub brush and canals. It'd been Katie's address for the last four years. Two years before Pops went up the river.

So this guy smoking by the mailbox was a squatter. He must've moved in on the mom while Dad did his six-year stint for possession with intent.

Junior considered this for a moment. Was there a way to slip past this guy, grab Katie right from her room, and do what he needed to do to calm the thunder in his head? He liked to think bold even if he rarely acted boldly.

Could tonight be the night?

How would he be able to remain anonymous?

What if there were no witnesses?

A smile crept over his face.

■　　■　　■

Hallett stepped forward with Rocky close by his side as he called out, "Hey, fellas, what's going on?"

The man closest to him was startled and immediately stepped toward the bed of the big truck. Any poacher would have a shotgun or rifle in there.

Hallett used his best official police voice to shout, "Don't reach into that bed." He knew that even though he wasn't in uniform, these creeps had to figure they were cops. Then Hallett added, "You two on the other side of the truck, come around to this side and keep your hands where I can see them."

The other two solemnly stomped around the truck while the heaviest of the three, the one already facing Hallett, said, "We ain't breaking no laws. People fish back here all the time." The man's belly made the plaid shirt drape off his stomach like an awning. His crew cut was uneven around his ears, and the soiled baseball cap was a size too small and sat on the top of his head like a clown hat.

"Let me have a look at your fishing poles."

That brought the man up short. Then he said, "You got any ID? You could be rent-a-cops or some kinda community aide, like that fella in Central Florida that shot that kid. I like to know who I'm talking with." He had a heavy southern accent, and Hallett didn't recognize him. This was no Belle Glade crew.

Hallett considered the request and what he'd like to do to these jackasses, then decided he'd rather not be identified for the moment. It was obvious Claire and Darren agreed, as they joined him with their dogs at their sides but no badges came out.

The three men approached them, with the young driver, obviously terrified, standing by the open door to the pickup. The fat guy, who'd been doing the talking and appeared to be a hired guide, looked at Darren and laughed. "Look, it's an actual Seminole. And he's got a cute little puppy with him."

Hallett knew the crack about Brutus would bother Darren more than the racial slur. Brutus didn't help the fact by wagging his tail furiously and straining to reach the man so he could jump and lick.

To his right, Hallett heard Smarty unleash a sinister growl. He was glad the dog was on his side.

Claire said, "Those your hunting dogs?" The two dogs were clearly visible now on the edge of the seat. They were ungroomed poodles and continued to jump around and yap.

Sometimes gator poachers staked out dogs like these on the side of a canal to attract the large alligators they'd come to shoot. They usually didn't care what happened to the dogs. As far as Hallett was concerned, there wasn't a prison sentence long enough for behavior like that.

Claire said, "Where did you get the dogs?"

The fat guy said, "Where'd you get the Seminole?"

Claire had a hard edge to her voice as she said, "You think this is a game?"

"I think this is some kind of shakedown and we don't have to put up with it." Now the big man had some confidence. "Look at the cute puppy with the Indian. I think I'm gonna give that puppy some love." He stepped forward and started to bend over.

Now all Darren said was, "Don't do it, redneck."

The fat man straightened like a man ready for a bar room brawl.

Hallett stepped forward. "Hang on, Tubby, before you say something that'll get you punched."

"Do you know who you're talkin' to, boy?"

"Ralphie May's father? No, wait a second, Orson Welles's son?"

"What? What the hell are you talkin' about? Are you crazy?"

"I gave you references that should cover two generations. You didn't get either of them? You see, they're both famous fat guys. Maybe I should've stuck with Louie Anderson."

"You don't talk like no cop I ever met. You must be crazy."

Now Hallett got in the man's face. "I'm not crazy, I'm pissed. I'm pissed that assholes like you abuse little dogs for a few thrills."

"And some good money. We ain't bothering no one. Leave us alone."

Hallett glanced down at Rocky as the dog looked to his right at Smarty. Rocky winked. Hallett was certain he saw it this time. Rocky was letting his partner in on what they were going to do. At almost the exact same time both dogs leaped up, straining at their leads, snapping at the fat man, pushing him backward. Hallett decided to see what would happen. He let go of the lead. Claire did the same.

He could see the herding instincts at work in both the dogs. They never came too close to the man, simply barked and herded him back to his friends and then pinned them all against the side of the truck.

All three of them had lost their bravado, and the fat man started whimpering, "Okay, okay, you win. Call them off."

■　　■　　■

Junior had driven his car past the trailer and parked on the other side, down the dusty road. Whoever had been by the mailbox walked back into the trailer, and now Junior was trying to psych himself up. It made him think of his father yelling at him to *act like a man*. He hated to think how much his father had done to mold him into the man that he was today.

He had the Beretta slipped out of his belt line and sitting on his lap. The sleek black weapon made him feel like God. He'd almost used it once, back in Indiana. After one of his first attempts at a date. He was very young and it was clumsy. The girl's older brother came out, not realizing how serious he had been about taking the girl. The brother, a big farm boy, had used a buck knife to threaten him. The idea of putting a bullet between Farm Boy's eyes appealed to Junior. But then he thought about the consequences and somehow rational thought kicked in.

Now he calculated the consequences of doing the same thing. Only this time he wouldn't be caught.

He felt an incredible thrill rush through him at the idea. He considered the practical aspects, like the noise from the pistol and the attention it would draw from the other trailers, but the two trailers closest to Katie Ziegler's house were dark with no vehicles in the driveway. People that lived here were used to gunfire, and a few shots wouldn't draw any attention.

Junior would have to take Katie to a secluded area because he couldn't waste time here after he had caused a commotion. The more he thought about it, the more he realized he might be capable of pulling it off.

Hallett suppressed a smile as he noticed the bloom of a urine stain on the fat man's pants; the guy could no longer hold his bladder in the face of a snarling Belgian Malinois. They had herded the men to one end of the pickup and, sure enough, found a rifle in the bed of the truck, along with ropes and heavy knives and a meat cleaver, all used in dressing a dead alligator.

Hallett turned his attention to the two men who'd paid the fat guide to bring them gator hunting. The older man, about fifty and lean, with a smoker's voice, said with a thick Brooklyn accent, "Give us a good reason to keep hassling us or leave us alone. We paid to have some fun and we're going to have some fun."

Hallett knew these types. Moved down from New York and thought they understood how to work the system and intimidate people. They were a minority and a stereotype, but they were all the same. Hallett thought about dogs being used as bait and something snapped. He kicked the rear door so hard it crinkled around his foot. There was no turning back now. He'd ruined any chance he had of making a criminal case. But it had certainly gotten these morons' attention.

He said in a very low voice, "I don't think you guys want to say too much right now. Our friends down here don't like it when people abuse animals." All three men looked at the dogs.

Hallett pressed his knee against Rocky's shoulder—their secret cue for the dog to growl—then rubbed the knee down slightly so that Rocky snapped at the men, making them scatter a few feet. This dog was 100 percent pure ham. He loved to play-act.

Claire was talking to the teenage driver at the front of the truck, and

Hallett heard him admit to what they were doing. His father was the fishing guide from the town of Moore Haven on the north side of Lake Okeechobee and had promised that these jerk-offs could catch an alligator.

Claire said, "Who did they steal the dogs from?"

The young man said, "He didn't steal them, he bought them. There's an old lady in Clewiston who sells them for a hundred dollars apiece."

That really pissed Hallett off. Now he had the immediate problem of teaching these asswipes a lesson.

Hallett said, "We have two ways we can deal with the situation."

The guide knew he was in over his head. All he said was, "Yes, sir, what are our options?"

"Dump all your poaching equipment in the canal, including the rifle. Give me your word you'll never do anything like this again and be out of our sight by the time I count thirty."

The New Yorker said, "Or else what happens?"

"I let my hairy friend loose and see if three against one is a fair fight. Chances are only one of you will lose your testicles and the other two will just have severe lacerations that require stitches."

The second customer, the one who hadn't said anything, immediately grabbed the rifle by the barrel, along with two gaffs, and tossed them hard toward the middle of the canal.

The guide said, "Hey, wait a minute." But then he looked at Rocky and didn't say a word. He scooped up some coiled rope and a long chain with a nasty-looking meat hook on the end and tossed them.

Then the men just stared at Hallett until he said, "One. Two."

All three men scrambled to get back in the truck.

Claire had calmed down the young driver, who casually stepped toward the open driver's door.

Hallett said, "Leave the poodles."

"Say what?" said the guide.

This time he had his own growl in his voice. "I said, leave the goddamn poodles here."

The fishing guide said, "I paid a hundred bucks apiece for them."

Hallett dug in his pocket and pulled out his meager wad of cash and threw it in the car. "There's forty-three bucks. I think you're getting a bargain." To emphasize the point, Rocky gave him another snarl.

The guide tossed the small poodles out of the truck onto the damp ground. They started running around in circles with the rope leashes trailing behind them, yapping at the bigger dogs.

Hallett felt a sincere wave of satisfaction as he watched the taillights of the truck disappear down the shell-rock road.

Claire said, "We let them off easy."

Hallett smiled. "Joke's on them. I only had thirty-three bucks in my pocket."

■   ■   ■

Junior had just about convinced himself to leave the safety of his father's Oldsmobile and take action when, in the calm night air, he felt a vibration and heard a low rumble. At first he thought it was thunder, but the sky was clear. Then, at the far end of the road in the direction of the highway, he caught a glimpse of a headlight.

Maybe it was just a neighbor coming home. With any luck they lived at the far end of the park. Then Junior noticed a second and third light. *What the hell?* It didn't take long for him to realize the lights belonged to at least five motorcycles, and the motorcycles had to be Harleys, judging by the noise they were throwing off.

He almost could have predicted they would pull into the driveway of Katie Ziegler's trailer. Junior could clearly see the burly men dismount from their motorcycles. They all had on vests, but he couldn't see which club they belonged to. Then the light came on and all he saw was the word OUTLAWS. Essentially the most feared motorcycle gang in the country.

Common sense finally overwhelmed his urge. Junior headed home with enough guilt and shame built up in him to do something really nasty, really soon.

Hallett carefully set the cardboard box he had the two little poodles in on the backseat. As he closed up the tailgate to his Tahoe, Darren stretched and said, "Gotta get home, too. I'm having breakfast with my parents and have to come up with a lie about my future. They'll demand to see my transcript from this semester if I appear too irresponsible. Living up to a stereotype is tough."

Hallett laughed and patted his buddy on the shoulder, saying, "You really care about police work. That should be enough for them."

"I've tried to explain it's about duty and answering the call, whatever the call may be." He leaned down and scratched Brutus's back. "Brutus and I are ready as long as the call involves a tennis ball or Frisbee."

That earned another laugh. Hallett said, "Rocky and I need to check on the animals."

Hallett watched as Rocky and Brutus silently sniffed around each other, then stood almost nose-to-nose. It looked like a good-bye from Hallett's perspective.

Darren said, "I'll trade you my trailer behind the Baptist school for your trailer behind the nondenominational school." He kept his face emotionless, as if they were playing poker, and Hallett couldn't tell if he was joking.

Hallett smiled. "What difference does it make? They're both free and pay utilities. All we have to do is keep an eye on the place at night."

"The Baptists are tough. They don't want me drinking or bringing women by the trailer. Your people don't even check on you and let you keep that zoo right there."

"It's not exactly a zoo. It's just a few animals, and one of the teachers uses them with the kids."

"A few animals! You got a goddamn boa constrictor. Not to mention the llama and how many cats?"

Hallett looked down at Rocky, who was anxious to leave, his farewell to Brutus complete. "It's not a llama, it's an alpaca. The exact count on the cats is in dispute. And, for your information, the school is not crazy about the cats. Now there's so many of them running around, the school administrators worry it might be a health hazard."

Darren said, "You still got a better deal than I have with the Baptists."

Finally, Hallett said, "I've got the morning to spend with Josh, so I better get some sleep." He patted his friend on the shoulder, turned, and followed Rocky out to the Tahoe. That was one of the reasons he was anxious to leave; he could sense Rocky wanting to head home for the night.

■　　■　　■

Rocky could hardly contain himself, he was so excited about the new additions to the family. All he wanted to do was play with the odd-looking little dogs. They reminded him of when he was little and had so many other puppies to play with on the wide, open fields. Except now *he* would have to be the mother to these dogs. They were small, and funny-looking, but they had interesting scents. They also yapped a lot, but he understood they were just scared and this was a new place to them. He couldn't wait till they saw the animals in the cages. No dog could be used to all those different kinds of animals.

Earlier in the evening, Rocky had sensed how angry Tim had been with the men who had the little dogs. He was about to boil over he was so mad. It made Rocky want to bite those men, but Tim wouldn't let him. Now Tim was back to his usual self. Fun, light, friendly. And Rocky liked the way he chuckled every time he looked down at the new little dogs.

Every night he and Tim always explored the property. First Rocky would run along the fence line as Tim jiggled the gates to make sure they wouldn't open. Rocky knew to make sure there were no predators on the property, but he sometimes got distracted by the cats or rabbits that wandered past the fence. After they were done with that, he would walk with Tim through the area that held all the strange animals. He knew a few of the names of the animals from hearing Tim or Josh say them over and over again. The white fluffy things with long ears were rabbits. The things that walked around freely and never seemed to be in a good mood of any kind were cats. Turtles had hard shells, and some of them tried to bite him. After that, Rocky just knew if animals were big or small, dangerous or not. The most interesting animal to him was white with a long neck and the sour smell. It was not ever friendly, but it was still his responsibility to keep it safe.

As they walked back toward the house, Rocky saw a chance to play a game that always seemed to make Tim happy. Tim called it "tag." It was a simple game where he nipped at Tim and then Tim tried to catch him. It got his heart racing, and he liked seeing Tim happy. It took a while for Rocky to understand that Tim showed his happiness by baring his teeth. He was learning new things about his man every day, and that was fine with Rocky. All he wanted to do was make Tim happy.

■   ■   ■

The Belle Glade Christian School where Hallett lived in a trailer had twenty acres of open fields, buildings, and long perimeter. He lived rent-free in exchange for keeping an eye on the sprawling complex. Every time they arrived on the school grounds, Hallett and Rocky conducted the customary survey of the area before heading to the double-wide. He never found anything wrong, but it was the least he could do considering they provided him with a place to live and paid his utilities.

Tonight, Hallett and Rocky stopped at the trailer before moving to the rest of the property. Hallett fumbled with the box he'd retrieved from the backseat of his Tahoe. Rocky had carefully walked along beside him and was anxious as Hallett set the box on the ground. Rocky poked his head over the edge of the cardboard that contained the two poodles.

The little dogs were not nearly as active and loud as they were earlier. Hallett thought it was a little ironic that they were more afraid of him and Rocky than they were of the morons who were going to use them for gator bait, but he preferred them in this docile state.

He looked at Rocky and said, "Do we really need more animals around here? I'm not sure how to take care of these two." He was so used to chatting with Rocky that sometimes he imagined the dog answered him. At least he rationalized that he was picking up on the dog's cues more effectively. He didn't want to think he was going crazy from living alone too long.

Hallett made a bed for the small dogs in the carport, behind a low fence he had built to house animals on a temporary basis before they got adopted or, more commonly, moved into his little zoo.

A Florida Highway Patrol trooper had lived in the trailer before him and was transferred to North Florida just as Crystal had booted Hallett from the house they shared in Royal Palm Beach. He knew it'd never work with her, but he tried hard to do what was right once Josh was born four years ago. He still liked the idea of marriage and settling down to have more kids, but Crystal wasn't built for it. At least not on a cop's salary.

She was a great mother and mostly a good person, but she didn't much care to have a uniformed deputy sheriff living with her. She needed a high-end lawyer or doctor who kept regular hours.

He knew that was an easy excuse. In fact, when he and Crystal had first moved in together, he thought he'd found true peace. He couldn't spend enough time with her. She was fun and they were in love. But a lot had happened from their first six months to the last six months of cohabitation.

Neither family had ever accepted the arrangement, and it had nothing to do with the fact that Crystal's family was African American and his was not. Crystal's family thought being a policeman was not the type of job that could support their daughter, and Hallett's mother resented the attitude that no one in Crystal's family tried to hide. Her father was a prominent pediatrician and community leader who'd hoped his daughter would go on to medical school. Instead her looks had gotten her some modeling jobs while she was still a junior at the University of Florida, and it sidetracked her education. It had nothing to do with Hallett, but her father always seemed to blame him somehow.

Adding to the stress of the relationship was how their jobs had changed. Crystal lost a high-paying hostess job at a swanky Palm Beach

restaurant, and he went from being a regular day-shift detective to working all kinds of shifts in uniform with a K-9 partner.

Rocky presented another challenge, but Hallett still had to take responsibility. He drank more, took his frustration out on Crystal, and mis-
judged what their little verbal sparring matches were doing to her.

Now it was just easier to make jokes about her and dismiss the whole
relationship. In truth, though, he still missed her and what they once
had. He was just too proud to ever admit it to anyone.

Hallett leaned down to pick up a plastic cup that had blown onto
the grounds and he felt a pinch on the seat of his pants. He knew what
that meant. Hallett stood up quickly and spun to face Rocky.

The dog was crouched with his hindquarters high in the air. It was
his favorite game. Tag. It always started with Hallett bending over and
Rocky giving him a friendly nip on the butt. Then he would challenge
Hallett by crouching and moving in the opposite direction. It was a fast,
choppy game that never failed to make Hallett laugh. It was like playing
with another son.

Sometimes the games lasted an hour and sometimes only a few
seconds. Hallett never refused, because he knew it was Rocky's way of
forging a bond by doing something they both enjoyed.

After the game of tag, Rocky trotted along beside him gave a quick
look at the school grounds across the open field and then walked back
toward the trailer. His approach caused a stir of excitement in the animal pens next door. He was amazed that all the different critters, separated by chain-link fence, seemed to live in relative harmony. There was
no doubt Rocky was the monarch of this little animal kingdom. He could
stick his nose into any pen and no animal would snap at him or make a
threatening sound.

After he built the pen for Randall the raccoon, the school had been
amazingly tolerant when Josh wanted a cat and a bunny. Then came Wally
the wood stork, with a broken wing. Once Josh's face lit up at the sight
of the odd-looking bird, Hallett knew he was a permanent addition to
the growing menagerie. Then a teacher at the school, Leah Martin, had
asked if Hallett could house a boa constrictor. The beautiful teacher was
about his age with a nine-year-old son, and her smile made it difficult
to refuse any request. Over the following months he'd added the alpaca

he'd found on the side of the highway. Josh had immediately named him Albert, and Hallett had quickly learned alpacas were not terribly pleasant, although he had grown to admire the undying defiance of this distant cousin to a camel. There was something about his cadre of animal friends that made him feel at home even though the trailer on the edge of the woods behind the giant Christian school was as far from his middle-class upbringing as anything he could imagine.

Hallett liked to keep a regular sleeping schedule no matter what shift he worked. The special unit worked a variety of shifts but rarely mid-nights, when not enough happened to justify three hypertrained dogs. He wanted to always be available for the days when he could see Josh. Having the boy every other weekend was just not enough. He'd worked it out with Crystal to take Josh a couple of days a week, then drop him off at her mother's house in the afternoon when he went on shift. Some-times the schedule wore him down, but it was well worth it to see that perfect smile and those twinkling brown eyes. He also had to share the boy with his own mother, whose only goal in life was to populate the state with her grandchildren.

Another reason he'd always tried to maintain regular sleeping hours was for his health. Too many cops experienced problems later in life from screwed-up working hours—one reason why retired cops live an aver-age of nine years less than the general public. Civilians always thought of bullets or knives as being the biggest threat in a policeman's life. Once again, TV had skewed people's view of the profession. The fact was that more cops were injured by years of carrying heavy-duty belts than by bullets. He didn't know a single patrol deputy over forty without serious back problems. That was one of the few reasons he missed working in the detective bureau.

At ten o'clock, he sat on the edge of his bed. "What do you want to watch?" he asked Rocky.

The dog trotted up with a DVD in his mouth. A line of slobber ran down the case.

Hallett pulled it free and groaned. "C'mon, Rocky. Really? *Marley and Me* again? Can't we try something else for a change?"

The dog sat motionless, staring at Hallett.

"Owen Wilson is a whiner who doesn't deserve Jennifer Aniston."

Rocky wagged his tail.

"The book is great. The guy who wrote it lived right here in Palm Beach County."

Rocky bowed down and let out a slight whimper.

That did it. Hallett sighed and popped the DVD into the player, then settled back onto the bed to be bored into sleep by the sappy movie he had watched more than fifty times. The first few were great. Up till the time he knew the dialogue by heart, he still enjoyed the film. But now it was like a bad dream and he couldn't wake up.

After a few minutes, he sensed Rocky stir on the rug next to the bed. The dog rarely moved during his favorite movie. A moment later, he caught just a flash of a headlight as a vehicle came onto to the school grounds. He automatically looked across the room at the locked metal box that contained his .40 caliber Glock model 22 duty pistol.

■　■　■

Junior sat in the La-Z-Boy his father had given him years ago. The blue fabric that covered the chair was stained and had a dingy odor, but he had never felt more comfortable. That's what he needed to get through this night. Comfort. He couldn't believe how badly things had gone and how unlucky he had been. Of course he should've remembered Katie Ziegler's father was connected to a motorcycle gang. He had been their drug dealer.

They had effectively cut off that avenue of respite from his urge. He had to do something and do it soon.

He might not have finished what he had started with Katie Ziegler, but it wasn't a total loss. His interaction with the girls was only one of his needs. He had plucked Katie from a list of potential candidates, learned everything there was to know about her, including her schedule, then grabbed her at will. If that wasn't God-like behavior, he didn't know what was.

No one would be able to pin anything on him. He had watched the ten o'clock news, but there had been no mention of the incident near Belle Glade. In a way it was good that the public wasn't aware of his activities. But it hurt him as well. No one thought it was worthwhile enough to put on TV. That didn't seem particularly God-like.

Now he scanned page after page on the computer to find someone that fit the profile. Someone had to satisfy his urge.

He considered his father and wondered how he could possibly be sane. It didn't matter. He had to keep going.

Junior settled on three young women, all about the same age, any one of which would be suitable. This was the safest part, and it kept his interest, but it lacked the thrill of actual contact.

That would come.

■　　■　　■

Tim Hallett was out of his bed and Rocky at the door silently listening and sniffing the air. Hallett had not opened the lockbox containing his gun yet, but he'd put the combination into the small lock and was standing right next to it. The box ensured Josh could never get to the gun accidentally.

Anxiety got the best of him. He opened the box, pulling out his pistol and sliding it out of the holster. He slipped a T-shirt over his head and walked to the front door in just his sleeping shorts, T-shirt, and bare feet. Rocky hadn't made any sound, which was typical. The dog was the equivalent of a ninja. He loved to sneak up on people.

Hallett opened the door and peered through the crack. Whoever it was had parked directly in front of the trailer and wasn't trying to hide the fact that they were here. He and Rocky had managed to make several enemies since they had been on the CAT. They had broken up a drug-smuggling ring that used State Road 80 and U.S. Highway 27 as a corridor to transport hundreds of kilos of cocaine. Hallett had arrested three of the drivers, and Rocky had inadvertently bitten off the finger of one of them.

The local gangs were also pissed off, because just the sight of Rocky had cut into their drug sales and cast doubt on their courage. Few thugs could stand up in the face of a badass police dog. But Hallett doubted any of those morons would be brazen enough to pull up in front of his trailer and park.

He stuffed the pistol in his shorts and pulled his T-shirt over it but kept a tight hold on Rocky's collar. Then he saw the newly revised form of Helen Greene step out of the car and flash her brilliant smile at him.

Hallett smiled back as he stepped down the three stairs from his trailer. Rocky followed him step for step. The newly arrived poodles stirred from their padded bed and started to bark in short, shrill spurts.

Sergeant Greene said, "Those two are new. Where did you get them?"

Hallett hesitated, not wanting to tell a boss at the sheriff's office he had essentially stolen them, no matter how good his reasons. "I just picked them up. I'm looking for a home for them. You interested?"

She held up her hand. "Not since you talked me into taking the gecko for my son. I ended up buying dead crickets and feeding him."

Hallett grinned and waited to hear why the sergeant had come by his house after ten o'clock.

After a moment, Sergeant Greene said, "I'm sorry I didn't get a chance to chat with you this afternoon. You and Rocky did a fabulous job finding the girl." She held out her hand for Rocky to sniff, then, after his approval in the form of not biting her, she reached down and rubbed the clean, brushed fur on his head.

Hallett nodded and watched his partner display his warmth by letting the sergeant pet him. "It's hard to put a value on a happy ending. I was just lying in bed thinking what a good day it had been."

"Ain't that the truth? Saving a girl like that can lift the spirits of the entire detective bureau. But I'm afraid we're gonna be back to reality tomorrow."

He sensed the edge in her tone and said, "What's wrong?"

"This guy is almost certainly the same guy who grabbed two other girls over the past few years. And we might have a list of suspects."

"Anyone special?"

She nodded.

"Is that what brings you out here to the wilderness this time of night?"

She was now leaning on the handrail to the stairs, letting Rocky smell her left hand. "Nothing ever gets by you. I really liked that in the D-bureau. I was so disappointed when you shipped out, but maybe it was the best for everyone involved."

"So that's why you're all the way out here?"

"That, and I'm meeting someone."

Sergeant Greene dug a photo out of a file and held it up so he could just see from the light coming through the open door. Hallett took the photo and stepped inside to get a better look. The round, splotchy face and thin comb-over made his stomach turn. He cut his eyes up to the sergeant and didn't say a word.

"That's right. One of the suspects is Arnold Ludner. I thought I should tell you before you found out somewhere else."

"So the girl I found when I was a detective . . ."

"Would have been an early victim. If he's our man. He had a different style. There's no direct link. Our theory is he changed in his short time in jail. The timeline all fuses together."

"But he's on your list for a reason."

"Him and about forty others. He's known to do this kind of shit, and no girl was reported missing while he was in jail after you caught him."

"He should have been in a lot longer."

"And you shouldn't have been transferred, but things are what they are."

"Any chance I'm gonna be able to help in this?"

"For obvious reasons we can't let it look like you're after revenge. But we could use Rocky to match scents from the rag we found in the field. We've still got a few things to check out. I just want you to get this straight in your head before we ask you for any help."

"I'll have everything straight by the time I see him."

The sergeant nailed him with her legendary terrifying look. "Tim, I'm not fooling around. If you screw this one up, getting transferred will be the least of your worries. You may be the first cop in history whose dog is in charge of his daily assignments."

Hallett looked down at Rocky, who appeared to like the idea.

8

As soon as Tim Hallett pulled up in front of his former residence in the suburban town of Royal Palm Beach, his ex-girlfriend, Crystal Gibbs, appeared in the doorway of the modest, one-story home.

In the sunlight, wearing a form-fitting dress, she looked like a work of art, and he felt much less responsible for any of Josh's good looks. Having a child had not affected her lithe figure, and she always held herself very straight. He knew she was going to spend the morning with her grandmother at a nursing home near Lake Worth. Usually Crystal would take time to visit just about every other resident before she left for the day. Hallett knew this because he took Rocky there, too. The elderly people loved it. Josh was a big hit as well.

Neither of them ever acknowledged something nice like that. It was too much fun to be snarky to each other.

He left his personal Dodge Dakota King Cab running with Rocky comfortably sitting in the backseat. Knowing how the dog reacted to a potential threat, he didn't want to risk bringing him anywhere near Crystal.

Before Hallett had reached the front door, Crystal said, "I need four hundred and thirty dollars."

"In cash?" He hoped his voice hadn't cracked like a kid going through puberty.

"As long as I get it by Friday, I don't care."

Hallett didn't even ask what it was for. Despite the unceremonious way Crystal had dumped him, she was an excellent mother and didn't milk him for money she didn't need. He just nodded and took a moment to gawk at the statuesque black woman who, even at eight in the morning, brought her best game. Her dark complexion was flawless and her brown eyes clear. On the rare occasion she used her smile, it was stunning.

"Is Josh ready?"

"He's been bouncing off the walls waiting for you." She didn't ask him inside as she turned her back and returned a moment later with Josh's Spider-Man backpack filled with snacks and a change of clothes. "Have him back at my mom's by eleven thirty."

"What if I leave him at my mom's for a few hours?"

"No."

"Why not?"

"She's a racist."

"That's not fair. She doesn't hate all black people. Just you. In all honesty, don't you think she has the right?"

Crystal betrayed no emotion when she looked at him and said, "As an African American I don't trust the police, especially you."

"That mean yes?"

A slight smile crept across her pouty mouth as she just nodded, never willing to admit defeat.

Josh came darting through the house like a guided missile and flew into his father's arms. His light brown hair was only a shade darker than his creamy complexion. He wrapped his tiny arms around Hallett's neck and squeezed, and suddenly nothing else mattered.

The boy kissed his mother good-bye and waved to a neighbor as he walked to the truck hand-in-hand with Hallett. Before he had even opened the door, Rocky was frantic in the rear seat, wagging his tail in anticipation of seeing Josh. The dog loved the boy as much as Hallett did.

Josh climbed into the car seat but first reached around and gave Rocky a hug.

The dog whimpered with excitement as he licked the boy and leaned his head on the boy's chest.

Although this was exactly what Hallett lived for, his mind started to wander. He noticed a chubby man about five foot ten, walking a small dog on a leash, and the only thing he could think of was Arnold Ludner.

■   ■   ■

Hallett had smiled so hard during the morning, his face hurt. He, Josh, and Rocky had spent the morning at a series of parks in downtown West Palm Beach along the Intracoastal Waterway. Josh loved to run through the fountain at the end of the touristy Clematis Street. Rocky would follow him, collecting more and more water in his thick coat, soon becoming his own water toy as spray shot out in all directions from his tail. After a thorough drenching, the three of them moved to a wide-open green space where Rocky showed his prowess at snatching Frisbees out of the air and Josh showed his ability to throw Frisbees like any other four-year-old—poorly and without even getting them into the air sometimes.

This was one of the few times he had ever been distracted while with his son. He didn't want to be the stereotype of the cop who was always on duty, who ignored his family and then retired to a lonely life. But he couldn't get Arnold Ludner or his sons out of his head. The sons had been so protective of their father they refused to believe any of the charges against him. Two of the sons had each been arrested on drug and gun charges in the past and held a healthy dislike for cops. When Hallett admitted how he got Ludner to tell him where the girl was, the youngest son, who was an attorney, had a deal in place instantly to make it all go away with simple probation and time served. Those were the lowest days of Hallett's career.

Right now Rocky, Hallett, and Josh sat next to a stand of coconut palm trees as traffic drove by on Flagler Drive. Days like these kept Hallett going. The boy didn't expect anything except his time, which was convenient since he didn't have much money. He wished he'd had this kind of relationship with his father, but his dad had worked a conventional job and liked to have a few beers after work, so that Hallett and his brother and sister only saw the old man a few minutes a day. He hadn't spoken to his father in four years, since the former tax accountant had run off with one of his clients, a forty-year-old massage therapist named Mitzi. Hallett had nothing against Mitzi, but just the mention of her name put his mother into a serious funk. His dad knew Josh existed but had made no effort to meet his grandson, or either of Hallett's sister's children.

His brother Bobby, the baby of the family at twenty-five, had no children. Thank God. Bobby still lived at home with their mother and had neglected to grow up. He'd been a professional student and now commuted two days a week to South Miami to take classes at Florida International University toward his Master of Fine Arts. Whatever the hell that was. He'd earned a degree in English literature from Florida Atlantic University and tried moving out on his own but found that he liked living with his mother. Secretly, Hallett envied his irresponsible brother and was glad his mom had some company. Even if it was a perpetually stoned, would-be writer.

Josh asked, "Do you have this much fun at work with Rocky?"

"Sometimes."

"With Rocky around you never get lonely, do you?"

If the boy only knew. But all Hallett said was, "Rocky is a good friend to have around." Too bad there was more to life than friendship.

■　　■　　■

Junior was shocked how quickly he found a new girl that was suitable to "date." Perhaps it wasn't quite as shocking as he thought, because he'd considered this girl once before.

He had an excellent idea of what the cops were doing on the Katie Zeigler case and felt he had time to act again. The question was if he could find this new girl, Tina Tictin, in the right situation. He was able to locate one photo of her by using his false Facebook identity. She looked tall and a little awkward but had a very dark, pretty face. The photo could be a couple of years old, and girls that age tended to move past the awkward stage awfully fast.

She met all of his requirements. She was eighteen years old, athletic-looking, and he could find her near her house in a crappy neighborhood west of Military Trail. Junior was willing to bet Mom was at work and Tina was an only child. It didn't look like Tina had a job, so she'd be bored and alone at home.

But not for much longer.

9

Tim Hallett took a few moments to gather himself in front of the detective bureau entrance on the second floor of the main building of the Palm Beach County Sheriff's Office. The bureau had seen some great work and brilliant detectives over the years. No one considered Hallett one of them, he was sure. He felt a little foolish, making sure he appeared neat and prepared before he walked through the door for the first time in more than three years. Rocky gave him an odd stare as he spent one more moment running his fingers through his hair and pulling his uniform shirt tight. He didn't want anyone in the D-bureau to think he was trying to come back. He wasn't. But the last time he walked out these doors he felt like a failure. At the time he was.

It really was Rocky who turned things around. He still remembered the trip to the breeder's ranch. The sheriff's office was getting away from buying dogs from Europe in an effort to save money. Instead, Hallett had been sent to pick up a Belgian Malinois at the pastoral compound in Louisiana with about forty young dogs in various stages of training and maturity. The place was no puppy mill; the dogs were given wide, fenced-in areas to run and play.

Hallett knew which dog was Rocky before anyone pointed him out. There was something about his eyes and the way he looked at Hallett that made it clear they were supposed to be together.

The older man who ran the place had two of his teenage daughters with him, and they made a fuss over Rocky. They were obviously sorry to see him go.

The man, who looked like a stick figure and had an odd Cajun accent that Hallett was not used to, said, "They got 'tached to the dog after his mama got kilt by a gator who come up the canal onto the property. The Malinois mama kept the gator from getting up into the pens. Probably saved a lot of dogs and me a lot a money." He gave a rheumy laugh as he nudged Hallett with his elbow.

Hallett stepped closer to the young dog and went to one knee, and Rocky immediately loped over and put his head in Hallett's hands. As Hallett rubbed his head, the dog let out a slight whimper. They'd been together ever since.

Hallett might have rescued a lonely dog who had lost his mother, but Rocky had done much more for Hallett, and by extension Josh, too. Now Hallett considered them all just one odd, goofy family. And he wouldn't want it any other way.

It bothered Hallett that being in the detective bureau seemed to affect how he was feeling. He had everything he could want. This was just childish.

Hallett reminded himself of the work he'd done since he left, of his bonding with Rocky and the life he had made for himself. Finally, he'd psyched himself up enough to step into the detective bureau he had left so long ago. He opened the door, and Rocky slipped through in front of him, commanding everyone's attention. Before he could even say hello to the secretary, Hallett heard John Fusco's loud voice saying in his Long Island accent, "I can't believe they let you work with us again."

Great.

■　　■　　■

Darren Mori looked around the Palm Beach International Airport and shook his head. He was a little annoyed he couldn't be at the detective bureau with Claire and Tim Hallett, learning about their new assignment. Especially considering all the crank calls that were made to places like the airport saying they had planted a bomb. They were always hoaxes. Always. But no responsible public servant could just ignore them. These were the types of assignments they needed to complete to make the federal grant program look good. He knew their administrator and trainer, Ruben Vasquez, would like to have them out on ten calls a day like this, detailing how one deputy with a trained dog, like Brutus, could save a fortune on manpower and other specialized units.

At the other end of the terminal, Darren saw the exact example Ruben often used: the bomb squad. In Iraq, or maybe even Israel, these highly trained and truly dedicated specialists earned their pay every day and paid for themselves a thousand times over. But in places like Palm Beach County, Florida, the unit was wildly expensive compared to other specialties and hardly ever dealt with an actual explosive device. They waddled in their fancy padded suits and had equipment that looked like it was from the next century, but it was a rare day they dismantled something capable of exploding. The bomb squad had destroyed more forgotten backpacks than all the middle-schoolers in the county combined.

One old-timer said that when he was on the road, back in the late seventies, he used to pay homeless guys to shake suspicious packages and nothing bad ever happened. That conversation did two things. It made Darren wonder why a guy had been working since the seventies and made him appreciate the bomb squad a little more. If it was so easy, why didn't everyone apply?

Now, as Darren made one last pass through the terminal with Brutus on a six-foot lead, he tried to think of something witty to throw toward the bomb squad guys, who were sitting quietly at the end of the terminal.

In fact, Darren really didn't know the nature of the threat or why they were using a dog instead of closing down the terminal. He suspected that the prankster had not sounded authentic and there was a reason someone believed it was a hoax.

As he passed the row of rental car counters, one young female clerk in particular made it a point to smile, then lean over the counter to get a look at Brutus. She was in her early twenties, a few years younger than Darren, and she was Asian. That was something he didn't see much in this part of the country. He wanted to play this cool, so he just nodded hello as he continued on his path to meet with the bomb squad commander.

Although usually he liked to hear how impressed other units were with Brutus and would listen to praise all day long, he was already thinking of how he could hurry this along. The muscle-bound sergeant gave him a quick wave. Darren had worked with the sergeant on the road in the past and considered him a pretty good guy. As he approached the four bomb squad members, preparing himself to deflect the imminent praise, the sergeant's phone rang.

Before Darren could even reach the group, the sergeant was hustling to get his men moving. As they passed, he said, "Thanks, Darren, we gotta run." They were out the door in a matter of seconds.

He glanced around the terminal. Several passengers turned to watch the bomb squad but quickly lost interest in a uniformed deputy with a Golden Retriever on a leash. He tried to act casual as he turned and slowly walked past the rental car counters again.

The girl behind the Hertz counter knew he was going to stop there. There was no way he could hide it, but he didn't want to risk not talking to her. As Darren approached the counter the young woman said, "Everything safe now?"

She had delicate features and shoulder-length jet-black hair. He tried to be suave instead of his usual self and said, "I would never let anything happen to someone as pretty as you."

She didn't seem offended by the clumsy comment. "I like your dog."

Darren braced for the inevitable *he's cute.* Instead, she said, "I don't see many Japanese in uniform."

Darren said, "Wow, I'm so used to hearing 'Asian' that hearing 'Japanese' sounds odd."

The girl giggled and said, "I know exactly what you mean. People work so hard not to be racist that they end up being a little racist by lumping all people of Eastern decent together."

He wasn't confident enough to say she was Japanese. But she saved him by saying, "My name is Kim."

"Is that short for Kimiko?"

"No. For Kimberly. Kimberly Cooper."

Somehow he managed to stammer, "I'm Darren Mori. It's very nice to meet you."

She stepped out from behind the counter, and Brutus immediately wagged his tail as he slid up next to her. She went down on one knee and rubbed his head but looked up at Darren and said, "My dad was a marine and met my mom on Okinawa. I hope you're not this obviously clueless all the time?" She gave him a dazzling smile to let him know she was just playing.

It wouldn't have mattered if she'd stood up and slapped him across the face. Darren believed he had just fallen in love.

■ ■ ■

Hallett waited with Rocky at the front of the detective bureau while the sergeant finished up some business in her office. He had purposely avoided John Fusco after his initial encounter and hoped the loudmouthed New Yorker would stay at his desk. A couple of detectives said hello as they walked past, but none of his close friends were on duty right now.

Hallett recognized he had nothing to be down about. Being a detective seemed important once, but now he had a different perspective. His personal life had straightened out once Crystal and he split up. He focused on Josh much more and didn't feel the stress of a day-to-day relationship. And he had learned there was a lot more to police work than just arrests. He had to get some distance from the competitive detective bureau to recall how he felt about cops when he was growing up. As a kid, he worshiped cops. Things were different today. It was a true public-relations battle for the hearts and minds of the general public. TV shows like *Cops* had helped people understand what the challenges facing a road patrolman were like. Investigations were still a mystery.

Any cop who cared about the profession cared about how the public perceived police officers. It was important to overcome the stereotypes of the bullying, doughnut-eating flatfoot. Times had changed and so had police officers, but the public's view was stuck somewhere in the mid-1970s.

Firemen had it easy. When they showed up, everyone was happy to see them. With a police officer, usually only half the crowd was happy to see you. Only people losing a fight, or the victims of a drunk driver, were thrilled to see someone in uniform. If someone was winning a fight or was a poor driver, the last thing they wanted to see was a cop.

One of the things that lured Hallett into his chosen career was reruns of TV shows like *Hill Street Blues* and *Miami Vice*. Now he recognized the shows were a product of excellent writing and not necessarily any research at all. In fact, as best Hallett could tell, Sonny Crockett, the hero of *Miami Vice*, could shoot people one moment and be ready to fish the next. The sign of a true psychopath.

Real life for a cop was much different. It was different from TV, different from public perception, and different from any other profession in the United States. A modern cop had to be able to adapt and think on his or her feet, generally had some college education, had to be familiar with the law, and had to be able to deal with other professionals like lawyers, as well as be tough enough to withstand a physical assault if it came to that.

He was knocked out of his thoughts when a young woman, about twenty-five, with long, dark hair tied neatly behind her, wearing green fatigue pants and a gray shirt that identified her as a crime scene technician, smiled and said, "Hi." She had intelligent brown eyes and a very pretty face. It took Hallett a moment to figure out where he knew her from. She was the technician at the scene when Rocky found the missing girl.

The pretty evidence technician said, "I'm Lori, Lori Tate," and stuck out her hand.

Hallett shook her hand as he tried to gather his wits and mumbled, "I'm Tim Hallett."

Lori gave a quick laugh. "Everyone knows you and Rocky. You guys did a great job yesterday." She looked at Rocky and asked Hallett, "Is it okay if I pet him?"

This girl was sharp. Most of the uniformed cops didn't have enough sense not to harass a trained dog without permission. More than one patrolman had been nipped on the hand by a moody canine. Rocky was good about attention from other people, but that didn't mean he always liked it. It was one of the areas Ruben had been helping Hallett understand. Rocky displayed subtle indicators of what he enjoyed and what he didn't. Sometimes it was the angle of his head or the movement of his tail. The longer Hallett spent with Rocky the more he understood.

In turn, Rocky had learned from Hallett's different postures. If he stood with his right leg back and his hand resting on the butt of his gun, Rocky was ready to pounce on anyone in a heartbeat. If he stood with his arms folded or leaning against the wall, Rocky would take that opportunity to sit and rest for a moment.

Now Hallett looked at the beautiful girl in front of him, then down at Rocky and noticed the dog's head bowed slightly as he anticipated a gentle rub. Hallett smiled and said, "I don't think you'll get any argument from Rocky."

Lori kneeled down directly in front of Rocky and ruffled the hair between his ears. It was obvious the burly Belgian Malinois had been instantly tamed by this evidence technician. After a minute of rubbing Rocky, Lori stood and said, "What're you two doing here?"

"Our whole unit is going to help out in the investigation of whoever grabbed that girl."

"It's good to be making use of your investigative experience."

Hallett felt his face flush as he realized the girl knew about his career in the detective bureau.

He kept calm and said, "I think they're more interested in Rocky's skills than mine."

"With a case like this I think any help we can get is important. I'm looking forward to working with you." She cast a quick, sharp glance toward Fusco working at his desk, and Hallett realized they shared the same feelings toward the brash detective.

■　　■　　■

Junior peered through a set of hunting binoculars that belonged to his father. It was one of the few things of value he had gotten from the old bully before he packed him away in his new home. The afternoon sun cast odd shadows over her body. The girl was stretched out in the front yard of an old Florida shithole of a house on a cheap plastic lounge chair. She had on a green sundress and had clearly grown out of the awkward stage.

His head was spinning at the speed of his own actions. But now it felt right. Thank God he had the freedom at his job to come and go. No one ever asked questions. Everyone was overwhelmed.

Junior wasn't about to risk driving past the house, even if he was driving an F-150 pickup truck he had taken from the outskirts of a Home Depot parking lot. His hope was that the truck belonged to a manager who wouldn't walk outside until after the store closed. He'd easily have the truck back in time, even though he wouldn't be able to hide the effects of hot-wiring it. Junior was willing to bet the car owner would write it off as a failed burglary attempt and probably not even report it to the police. One of the benefits of his chosen profession was learning things like how to hot-wire a car. It was amazing what people were willing to show others to prove how smart they were.

He hadn't thought he'd get started in earnest so quickly, but he saw the opportunity. The time might come when those things changed and he'd be forced to either move on or act radically. But for now he liked the idea of getting back into the groove of things immediately.

Tina Tictin wasn't the same kind of eighteen as Katie Ziegler. He knew she had flunked out of beautician school and had been in trouble with some boys in the neighborhood when she was younger. She hadn't even pretended to look for a job or find a class to take today. He'd seen her around the house as early as noon.

He watched as she stood from the lounger and stretched her long, lithe body, lifting the sundress high on her hips. She pulled the tie from her curly black hair and shook her head, which gave her a wild look. He wondered if she expected people to be watching from the other houses and she was just showing off.

She walked inside, and he considered calling it a day. He set down the binoculars and checked his watch. If he'd had a clear opportunity he would've acted, but Junior wasn't about to risk discovery.

He froze as he saw her come back out of the house, now wearing a pair of sandals with three inch heels. She walked with purpose up the street toward the convenience store where he was parked in the corner of the parking lot.

His chance might have come.

10

Ten minutes after arriving, Hallett sat in the sergeant's office across the room from a restless John Fusco, who obviously felt it was a waste of time bringing Hallett up to speed on the case. Rocky was sitting next to him while Fusco made sure the sergeant realized he had made no mistakes on this investigation, and he absently rubbed Rocky's head. Rocky had the same effect as a tranquilizer on Hallett in situations like this. He had to keep the dog close and continue to rub his head in order to keep his cool. It was a crutch, but one Hallett never wanted to give up.

The sergeant said, "We believe the incident yesterday is connected with two earlier abductions that happened over the course of two years. I think you've read the briefing. The fact that it was different police departments working each case didn't help anything."

Hallett controlled a shudder when he thought about what the creep did to the girls.

Fusco said, "Katie Ziegler sealed it in my mind. We're dealing with one suspect. That makes this a serial case. Not only will everyone in the sheriff's office be looking to me for results, the media will be all over it."

Hallett said, "Where does CAT come in?"

The sergeant said, "We'll use you in several different areas. But mainly, like I said last night, we have a list of potential suspects, our usual suspects, convicted child predators living in the county and matching the vague description Katie Ziegler gave. Although I told the captain you and the CAT would be available for other emergencies, I hope we have full use of you for at least a week or two. We want to try to wrap this up as quickly as possible."

Hallett couldn't resist looking across at the sharply dressed detective and saying, "We'll be happy to bail out Detective Fusco. This is exactly what our unit was made for. It doesn't matter what kind of mistakes he's made in the case already, we'll help grab this guy, especially if it's Arnold Ludner." He noticed the sergeant didn't say anything and was trying to hide a smile. She probably realized this arrogant ass needed to be put in his place.

Fusco nearly jumped to his feet, saying, "I wasn't even working the case for the first two abductions. And Ludner wasn't even considered a suspect as far as I can tell. The girls that have been kidnapped by this guy were older than the ones Ludner liked. The first girl was seventeen"—he looked at some notes—"the second girl was twenty, and Katie Ziegler is eighteen."

Rocky reacted to the outburst by standing and flexing his back. It had the desired effect on the detective, who immediately regained his composure.

Hallett said, "What about forensics? There really wasn't any DNA found?" Now he was just trying to rile the detective.

"This ain't *CSI: Miami.* We did a rape kit on all three girls, but there wasn't anything obviously worthwhile. The first girl, two years ago, admitted to consensual sex with two other men before she was grabbed. Plus he never penetrated any of the girls vaginally. As far as we can tell he prefers oral sex and leaves no semen at the scene. The second girl waited eight days before she even reported it. And Katie got away before the asshole could do anything." He waited a moment and threw in a halfhearted "Thank God."

Hallett knew that a guy like Fusco only cared about clearing the case. He really wasn't happy that the girl hadn't been raped, because a rape would've provided him with some decent DNA to enter into the database run by the Florida Department of Law Enforcement. Detectives like Fusco saw victims as potential evidence and not much else.

Fusco said, "I think the guy was even smart enough to pick up the blindfold that Katie had ripped off. All we have is the one rag that may, or may not, be from our suspect. And your dog sniffed it. Maybe he can match us up with Ludner when it's time."

Hallett said, "You think the plaster cast of the shoe is anything worthwhile?"

Fusco just snorted.

Sergeant Greene said, "We'll look at it. One of the techs pointed out that it's a hiking boot with a waffle bottom, missing one of the rubber squares in the heel. It might come in handy."

Fusco mumbled, "Bullshit."

Sergeant Greene looked at Hallett and said in her usual even tone, "I got your unit assigned to us for assistance. I'm going to go by your guidance as far as the dogs are concerned. I know they can do a lot, but you know the capabilities better than anyone."

Hallett wanted to play it cool but blurted out, "Will I be able to check out Ludner?"

The sergeant hesitated, then slowly nodded and said, "You can, but no direct contact yet. The TAC guys haven't even seen him around his house. Fusco's going to talk to his probation officer tomorrow and see if we can get a better fix on him. I'll send Claire Perkins with him so your whole unit will be involved from here on out."

Hallett felt a flicker of excitement at the prospect of facing the biggest creep he had ever met in his years of police work.

■　■　■

An hour later, in the detective bureau squad bay, Hallett wanted to be certain Claire knew what her assignment would entail. When the sergeant said she would work closely with Fusco, Hallett felt his stomach turn. It took him an hour to realize that Fusco probably wasn't a bad guy to work with. He just didn't want to do it.

Hallett was happy the sergeant was perceptive enough not to stick Darren Mori with the bullying detective. Darren appeared to be reserved, but Hallett knew he had a temper. Almost no one in the sheriff's office knew he had the skills to back up that temper. No matter how funny it would've been to see Fusco find out what one of his smart comments might cost him, Hallett didn't want his partner to get in trouble.

Now, looking professional in a sharp uniform, Claire Perkins stood her ground and offered a firm handshake and listened to what Fusco had to say.

Fusco, wearing an expensive Joseph Abboud suit, looked from Claire to Smarty. Claire strategically had the dog sit right next to her and stare at Fusco. Hallett could see how the dog would intimidate anyone.

Fusco stammered, "I guess you're coming with me to talk to the probation officer in the morning."

Claire just nodded and said, "I'll be ready anytime you want."

"Meet me here about eight thirty and we can drive over in my car."

Claire shook her head and said, "I won't leave Smarty alone in the Tahoe. And you wouldn't care to be a passenger with him in the back. We better take separate cars."

Hallett wanted to smile but suppressed the urge.

Fusco, to his credit, kept his calm and plowed ahead. He showed Claire and Hallett a forensic artist's rendering of the suspect from Katie Ziegler's vague description. Fusco said, "This is the same creep that grabbed the other two girls. I can feel it."

Then Claire asked the right question. "Do you think the guy is on our suspect list?"

The way Fusco hesitated told Hallett everything he needed to know. All Fusco said was, "It's possible."

Hallett had to admit he was impressed at the detective's openness. Some men were thrown off by Claire's appearance. Even with a big dog and wearing fatigues, she was pretty. But now Fusco had to realize she was smart, too.

Fusco said, "I'm not convinced it's one of these guys. The asshole could be anyone, but we gotta tell the sheriff we're doing something. The media has gotta be satisfied, too. I can think of worse leads we've run out on."

■　　■　　■

Junior could tell by the way Tina shoved the door of the convenience store open when she came out that she was pissed off about something. Then she spoke to a man in his midthirties before he walked into the store. When the man shook his head and walked past her, Junior realized she was trying to get someone to buy her a beer. She asked a woman a minute later. The woman not only refused, she scolded Tina.

He felt like this might be his chance. But he didn't want her to see his face. His one saving grace was that no one had a good, detailed description of him and none of his victims could identify him. He wondered if he could work out some sort of trade with Tina. Then he realized it wouldn't be the same. He needed the power. He wanted to smell her fear. To know how superior he was. He had to introduce her to a whole new world. It wouldn't be anything at all like what she was used to. He also realized she couldn't see his face. Unless . . .

The idea bubbled in his head briefly, then took on a life of its own. He'd never really considered it except as a last resort. She could see his face if she was unable to talk to the police later.

Tina turned and looked in his direction, then began to walk tentatively toward the truck at the edge of the parking lot.

His heart started to beat faster and he felt a tingling in his chest. He pretended not to notice her and acted like he was concentrating on his cell phone. Somehow he managed to look startled when she rapped on the passenger window.

She had a pleasant smile as the window whirred down. He noticed several crooked teeth and blamed her father for not working a steady job to pay for braces. Tina said, "Can you help me out?"

"Whatcha need?"

"I left my ID at home, and that jerk inside won't sell me beer."

Junior forced himself to wait a moment before answering so he wouldn't sound too anxious. He grunted, "Sure," as he pulled the handle on the driver's door. As he stepped out onto the littered asphalt parking lot he said, "Wait in the truck. It's a lot cooler in there."

She hesitated, looked through the window to make sure he was out of the truck, then pulled the door open and slipped into the passenger seat.

That's when he pulled his Beretta from under his shirt and hit the automatic lock button on the open driver's door.

Tina gasped but didn't move.

In a very calm voice Junior said, "I'm not going to hurt you." His mind raced as he stepped back into the truck, pulling the door shut behind him. This was going to be a wondrous afternoon. Then he would see if he could take things to the next level.

He pulled out onto Military Trail, then turned west at the next light. There were always wide-open empty areas to the west.

11

The girl was terrified, and that excited Junior. If what he was doing was a drug, then he'd just mainlined heroin. He didn't know how long he could last, and he hadn't even parked the truck. Since his first sexual encounter with his ninth-grade music teacher, Miss Trooluck, Junior had loved the feel of performing oral sex. It seemed so dirty at the time. Worse than intercourse. Her moans had frightened him at first; then he developed a fascination with it. A fascination that had grown since that day. Some people might call it an obsession, but Junior didn't care. It was one of the few things he looked forward to in his dreary life.

He turned off onto two unkempt farm tracks with heavy brush on each side of a canal. Except for the occasional fisherman, no one would ever have a reason to come out here. He was glad he'd borrowed the big F-150 pickup as it clattered down the road. He could hear tools rattling in the toolbox in the bed behind the cab.

Tina had hardly said a word during the trip. He'd asked her a few questions and couldn't ignore the electricity he felt when she looked him in the eye. This was something he'd missed with the previous girls. They'd always worn blindfolds and sort of flailed around aimlessly. Now he could see the emotion in her face and knew that he'd tapped into a fear she had never considered. He'd surprise her. Eventually she'd like his attention. He realized she had no idea what he intended to do, and if Junior thought about it, neither did he. That was part of the thrill.

He found a number of trails that led away from the canal through brush and sporadic crops. Cornstalks grew up through Brazilian peppers mixed in with Australian pine trees, all of the nonnative plant species that people bitched about.

Junior had the Beretta tucked in his belt, but he had a number of other options still available to him, even if Tina Tictin did not.

■   ■   ■

Darren Mori listened while Tim Hallett briefed him and Ruben Vasquez on their duties with the detective bureau. After the adventure at the airport, Darren had gone on a cadaver call with Brutus and missed the meeting. Turned out there was no cadaver. Just a pissed-off drunk who had wandered away from the Salvation Army and someone reported him as dead in a field. It was just one of many incidents that made him smile now but horrified him at the time. All dog handlers experienced stuff like that.

Police service dogs had a long history that could be traced back to over three hundred years ago in Europe. In the United States, Boston and New York had working dogs by the end of the nineteenth century when Florida was a mysterious swamp no one wanted to visit. Both the First and the Second World Wars taught military trainers the value of using dogs for different tasks, but it wasn't until as late as the 1960s that a Miami police trainer named Jay Rapp instituted the training protocols that were the basis for modern K-9 units.

None of the CAT members would've guessed the amount of training that went into preparing a dog for work on the street before they joined the unit. The initial courses for patrol and drug-sniffing dogs were nine to twelve weeks each. The courses covered everything, including legal issues. The academies were long because once a K-9 unit hit the street they were pretty much on their own. But unlike most squads in police agencies, the K-9 units trained together on a regular basis, often as much as once a week.

Although Ruben wasn't a sworn law enforcement officer, he administrated the grant that funded their unit and was a consultant for training the other K-9 units. After Hallett had finished, Ruben gave them one of his rare smiles. "That's good you're doing something different. The only way this program will work is if you move from assignment to assignment and make a reputation for yourselves."

Somehow Ruben's voice always seemed to captivate the dogs. He insisted that no matter what the discussion or issue, dog handlers should always have their dogs with them. At this moment both Brutus and Rocky stared at Ruben as if they were apostles listening to Jesus.

Darren and Hallett had often discussed how old they thought Ruben might be. Neither of them had enough balls to ask him. A scar that ran along the right side of his face made it difficult to judge his age. He also had a slight limp, which he told them was from an IED in Iraq. The blast had ended Vasquez's military career. Even with all that information, the best estimate they could make was that his age was somewhere between thirty-two and forty-five. Darren also openly envied Ruben's thick, dark hair. Even cut short, it showed no thinning or gray. That was a sore spot for Darren. He cut his hair short so he could use different products to hide his ever-growing bald spot. His new favorite baldness cure was a spray that filled in the round patch at the crown of his head. Unfortunately, Darren's height made it easy for anyone over six feet to look down on his scalp.

Ruben said, "The dogs will be invaluable on a case like this." He looked at Darren and said, "Just remember, Brutus is not trained to run after someone and apprehend them. He's a seeker. He'll find cadavers, explosives, and even the track of a fugitive, but don't use him in ways he wasn't meant to be used." Ruben was always in teaching mode, even during an administrative meeting like this.

Ruben turned to Hallett and said, "Do you got your head on straight? There'll be a lot happening, and this will be new for Rocky."

"I'm not worried about Rocky. He'll have less to concentrate on than me."

"Really? That's what you think? You don't believe that if your olfactory sense was a million times better than it is now and you were able to change your outer ear to focus on a particular sound, you wouldn't have enough to concentrate on?" Ruben paused and wiped his face with a handkerchief. "I know you guys are good cops. And you're good dog handlers, too. But sometimes you, Tim, overlook the obvious things Rocky is trying to tell you. I can't teach you every specific mannerism or sound. I can only show you how to open your mind to understand what he's saying."

Darren learned a lot when other people were getting scolded. He noticed Hallett shift his eyes up like a kid talking to a teacher in elementary school.

Hallett finally said, "He did do something yesterday I've never seen him do before."

"What's that?"

"When he sniffed a rag that was possibly used by a suspect, he made a sound I'd never heard. A cross between a growl and a yelp that made him sound like a lawn mower starting."

Vasquez nodded his head and steepled his fingers under his chin as he contemplated this information.

Hallett said, "What does it mean?"

Vasquez leaned down and looked Hallett in the eye. "You're asking me what it means?"

Hallett nodded.

"Who do you think I am, Dr. Doolittle? Do you think I can talk to the animals? He's *your* dog. Get your head out of your ass and start paying attention to him."

Hallett didn't mind the trainer talking to him like that. Most cops were used to it. Besides, if a guy like Ruben, wounded in Iraq, couldn't be a tough guy, no one could. He decided to get his head out of his ass and figure out what Rocky's alert meant.

■   ■   ■

Junior felt very satisfied with his selection of locations. He had barreled onto a dirt road west of U.S. 441, and there didn't appear to be anyone around. Thank God he'd worn his single pair of decent ankle-high boots. There was nothing in the field or on the bank of the canal that would penetrate them. He hadn't rushed, and instead enjoyed the subtly changing light around him as the sun slowly set. The girl, on the other hand, had become more and more frightened despite his efforts to calm her down. And her fear had only excited him more.

He'd left his clothes on and enjoyed the feeling of power as he tried to open a world of excitement to the young Tina Tictin. She had shaken and quivered, and he honestly didn't know if it was from fear or sexual excitement. Now she sat in the passenger seat of the stolen F-150 with her legs tucked under her and her sundress still clinging to her body. The whole experience was intoxicating. The fact that she didn't have a blindfold and her dark brown eyes focused on him with such intensity made him almost lament that he'd never looked into the eyes of one of the girls before this. That left him with another dilemma: She could easily identify him. From the mole on his upper forehead to his ears, which stuck out just a tad too far. But the solution had stuck in his head the moment Katie Ziegler had run from him. He almost shot her in the back as she ran, but he had held out hope he could use her.

Junior had no idea how killing this girl would affect him both physically and psychologically. He thought about the gun tucked in his waistband, but there were two issues: the mess and the evidence. He didn't want to leave a lead round for the police to recover, and he wasn't interested in digging it out of her body, either. He'd seen a big fishing knife, a tree saw, and a couple of shovels in the toolbox in the bed of the truck. A knife was messy, though, and he wasn't sure it was something that He would be able to appreciate.

She looked up at him with those big brown eyes. They were moist, but she'd stopped crying. He noticed a tattoo peeking out from the top of the sundress near her right shoulder and blamed her parents for not being strict enough. This girl needed some guidance. Maybe not the kind of guidance he had given her today, but she needed something in her life.

She started to sob quietly and pulled her knees up in front of her body. She had a hitch in her throat and couldn't breathe enough to maintain her crying and it gave Junior the perfect idea.

He felt an electric charge surge through him as the idea formed and solidified. This would solve all of his problems, but it was also the most exciting thing he'd ever considered.

Junior said, "It's probably time to drive you back to your house."

Tina looked at him and released her legs, sitting up straight in the seat. She said, "Really?"

Her voice now had a little-girl quality that thrilled him. He'd also managed to distract her enough to make his move. Slowly at first, without any threatening movement, he turned toward her and extended one hand. Then, with a conscious effort, he swung his left hand around as he slid his right hand off the back of the seat and set them firmly around her graceful neck.

It took longer than he expected for Tina to quit squirming under his grip. As soon as he was certain she was dead, he realized that now the real work would start. He couldn't risk her being found. There was just a hint of daylight left outside, but he had a pretty good plan already formulated in his head.

This had been totally worth it.

Tim Hallett didn't want to be one of those children that avoided their parents, but sometimes his mom made it hard. She clearly didn't like his career choices and thought K-9 duty was beneath the D-bureau. The public rarely understood anything about police work, and his mom in particular based all of her assumptions on what she watched on TV.

He had set up the lunch to see if his mom would adopt the two poodles he had liberated from the gator poachers. Josh had already fallen in love with the little dogs and named them Sponge and Bob. Hallett laughed every time Josh yelled, "C'mon, Sponge, Bob."

Now he tuned out his mom's monologue on the dangers of not eating enough fiber. His mind drifted as he wondered about the investigation into Katie Ziegler's abduction. Once Sergeant Greene had told him that Ludner was a suspect, it all made perfect sense to him. These were exactly the kind of girls a pervert like Ludner would seek out.

In the case that Hallett had against Ludner, when he was in the detective bureau, it had not been so clear. The case also pointed out how a predator like Ludner evolved, always wanting more stimulation. Two young girls had been molested a couple of months apart in an area west of the town of Lake Worth. They had both been from immigrant families, and Hallett had a hard time gaining full cooperation from the parents. That wasn't unusual. There was often a well-deserved distrust of the police among people from some of the Caribbean islands and Central American countries.

The first girl had been picked up and released an hour later. She was dazed and provided very little useful information. The second girl said her attacker was a heavy white man. She clung to her mother and also sparked something in Hallett. He couldn't let this happen again. He became obsessed and lost track of time and shifts.

Finally he caught a break and focused on Arnold Ludner.

Ludner, a money manager, led a somewhat normal life with a wife at home and three grown sons. Two sons were mixed up in the ubiquitous Florida drug trade, and the other was a successful attorney. The detectives made jokes about how the lawyer had been kept busy by just his own family.

Hallett had put together a number of clues that pointed directly at Ludner. The first attack provided little informations, and the investigation went nowhere. After the second attack, Hallett learned Ludner had been given a speeding ticket a block away from the spot where the second girl had been molested. The ticket was two days before the crime but it pointed to a suspect who carefully followed victims prior to abducting them. These were not impulsive acts. Someone had also caught two digits of his license plate and a description of his car speeding away from where he had grabbed the eleven-year-old. Hallett had searched the state motor vehicle records to come up with a list of forty possible suspects who had similar cars and the same two digits of the license plate. Then he cross-referenced that and found the speeding ticket from the area where the second girl had been taken. That's when Hallett developed tunnel vision and focused all of his energy on Arnold Ludner.

When a third girl disappeared, he didn't hesitate to pick up Ludner. From the moment he had the man in cuffs, he had no doubt this was a predator.

At the time, the concern was for the missing girl. She was twelve years old and had been gone six hours when Hallett arrested Ludner. He had no time to waste and immediately started pressuring Ludner, who refused to talk. All Hallett could think about was Josh and how he would feel if someone took his boy from him. He lost it and threatened Ludner. It had no effect until, without conscious thought, Hallett punched him in the face. Not a gentle tap or slap to get his attention, but a full-on punch that knocked the smirking child molester off his feet and across the hood of Hallett's car and onto the asphalt parking lot outside the sheriff's office headquarters.

Hallett hated to admit it, but he was prepared to go much further when Ludner told him exactly where the girl was. Deputies found the girl cowering in woods very close to her house, too terrified to move or seek help. There was no telling what would've happened to her if someone hadn't found her.

Hallett often thought about that day, but if he were to be honest with anyone who asked, he had no regrets whatsoever.

■   ■   ■

At the moment, Hallett was sharing a basket of muffins with his mother as they sat in front of a bagel place on Clematis Street, watching Josh play in a fountain while Rocky stood like a statue, keeping watch over the giggling four-year-old boy. Even a silent Belgian Malinois was enough to scare the occasional pedestrian to the other side of the street.

Hallett's mother, Jane, said, "It's creepy how he stands there so still and lets Josh jump all over him."

"My buddy Darren says he's like the good Terminator sent to protect Josh at all costs."

"I think Darren is an idiot. When are you going to move back into the city where you're around a better class of people?"

"Belle Glade has some advantages."

"Like what, you're always the smartest person in the room?"

"C'mon, Mom, that's not fair and you know it. The only difference between Belle Glade and West Palm Beach is the average income."

"And average IQ."

"I'm starting to set down roots out there. I've got a nice place to live that's free and a new hobby of raising every possible breed of animal."

His mother flashed her blue eyes the way she had since he was a child; it was a way to get his attention. It worked on his brother, too, but it always scared his sister away. Jane Hallett said, "I just wish I got to see Josh more. I don't get to see any of my grandchildren as much as I'd like." It was one of the few arguments she could make that was valid. He'd been over it with her many times.

His mother said, "I think one of the reasons you don't want to move back is that you don't want me meeting your girlfriends. Trust me, after Crystal, I won't ever object to another girlfriend."

Hallett let out a laugh. "It really has more to do with me not wanting to meet your boyfriends." He'd met several already. Hallett recognized that his mother, at fifty-three but telling people she was forty-five, was still very attractive, with blue eyes and short brown hair. She worked out most days and watched what she ate. But he couldn't bring himself to think of his mother as anything other than the only woman who loved him no matter what.

Jane blushed slightly and said, "A woman has needs."

"Which her son doesn't want to hear about. Ever."

"Good thing your brother doesn't feel that way."

"Why, otherwise he might have to move out on his own? Good God, what a tragedy that a twenty-five-year-old college graduate might consider paying his own bills."

His mother said, "Don't pick on Bobby. He's going to do great things."

"Like use up the world supply of marijuana?"

"Let's change the subject."

"Sounds great, what would you like to talk about?"

She said, "Any chance you could be a detective again?"

He rolled his eyes. "I'd rather talk about Bobby."

She just kept that stare on him. "Any chance?"

"Not any time soon. Besides, I still have a lot to learn about being a good dog handler. The sheriff's office doesn't want the baggage of some of my past actions weighing down investigations."

His mother just nodded as if he'd been the victim of a conspiracy. He'd admitted to her that the allegations against him were true, but she never wanted to believe her son could do anything wrong.

A man walking a Chihuahua on a pink rhinestone-studded leash let the dog sneak up and sniff Rocky. Even though Rocky didn't move or acknowledge the tiny, annoying Chihuahua, Hallett called out, *"Eenvoudig."*

His mother said, "What's that mean?"

"'Easy.' Just keeps him calm in case he was thinking about having a snack."

"Why do you speak German to him?"

"It's Dutch. And it doesn't matter what language I teach him the commands in as long as most mopes on the street don't understand. Plus, when they hear the guttural commands it tends to scare people."

"Does he know any English?"

Hallett let a smile slip across his lips.

"What's so funny?"

"I did teach him the word 'sit' means to bark and act aggressively. It tends to freak out the people that walk up and think they can control him. It's also good for a laugh."

"Does he understand anything in English that's not a sick joke?"

"He must, because he loves to watch *Marley and Me* and listens when I read Josh *Clifford the Big Red Dog.* It's the damnedest thing I've ever seen."

His mother said, "Are you working on anything interesting now?"

"Yesterday my entire squad was assigned to help on a kidnapping investigation."

"Are the dogs a big help in something like that?"

Hallett thought about it for a minute and said, "I've got a feeling they're the only chance we have at all."

■　■　■

Claire was running a little late, but she made sure she had time to put on makeup, even though she rarely used it while in uniform. So rarely that she stared in the mirror and said out loud, "Really?" Then she checked her hair. "Come on, give me a break." She was a little embarrassed because usually she spent more time fussing over Smarty, making sure his coat was brushed out and clean, than she did with her own appearance.

Right now, her partner and closest friend in the world sat in his favorite odd place, between the toilet and tub. He barely had room to move but she thought it might have something to do with the comfort of the cool tub touching his backside and the toilet coming across his chest. Smarty stared up at her like a beauty school student trying to pick up pointers.

Claire stopped what she was doing and looked the dog right in the eyes. His brown eyes locked on hers. It was a weird connection, like he could read her mind. Claire said, "I know, rumor is that he's a jerk. He loves himself too much. Most of all, Tim Hallett doesn't like him. But I have to represent the unit well. Ruben is always telling us we have to promote the unit and do a lot to keep the federal funding."

Now Claire kneeled down and rubbed his head. "So you're okay with a little sprucing up, aren't you?" As she stood and turned toward the mirror, she added, "At least I didn't bother to shave my legs. I just want to look as nice as John Fusco usually does." A smile spread over her face.

■   ■   ■

Forty-five minutes later she was pulling her Tahoe, with Smarty secured in the rear compartment, behind John Fusco's Ford Crown Victoria into the parking lot of an old Target store that had been converted to a giant church. It was just before nine in the morning, and the vast parking lot was empty. It struck her as odd that the probation officer they needed to talk to chose this parking lot for their meeting, but Claire was just as happy she didn't have to walk through the shitty probation office and leave Smarty in the car. God knows he couldn't interact with the felons that weren't even tough enough to get sent to prison.

Cops and probation officers always had a tenuous relationship. Cops viewed probation officers as nothing more than social workers who obstructed their investigations. Probation officers thought cops were mindless enforcement machines. But Claire realized John Fusco recognized the value of a decent probation officer. They had jurisdiction cops didn't. If a suspect was on probation, his probation officer could enter his house and, in most circumstances, search.

Claire contained a smile as she watched Fusco step out of his black unmarked Crown Victoria and stretch his legs. His Brooks Brothers suit shifted slightly on his body, showing off a broad chest in a white shirt.

Claire said, "Looks like your wife spent a few extra minutes dressing you today."

"She rarely looked at me when I left the house back when we were married, and in the three years we've been divorced she hasn't commented on my clothes once."

"I'm sorry, I didn't realize you were divorced." In fact, she had heard a rumor that she'd just confirmed. "Do you have any kids?"

A broad smile passed over his face and he said, "Two little girls. Caitlin and Lauren."

She liked the way he automatically reached for photographs of the five- and seven-year-old girls.

A Ford Taurus with a crappy tailpipe rumbled off Southern Boulevard into the parking lot and stopped a few spaces away from the Crown Vic. As soon as the guy stepped out of the Ford, Claire knew it had to be the probation officer. He was dumpy, about forty-five, with a cheap polyester tie clipped onto a short-sleeved white shirt and white running shoes. Classy. The only thing unusual about the porcine man was an Indiana Pacers baseball cap. Claire saw a lot of Jets, Giants, Yankees, and Mets paraphernalia down here in the Sixth Borough, but she rarely saw anything from the Midwest unless the odd Chicago Bears fan rolled through town.

The probation officer gave the deputies a sour look and said, "You Fusco?"

Fusco nodded and stepped forward, extending his hand.

The probation officer said, "I'm Bill Slaton, pleased to meet you." He leaned against Fusco's Crown Vic, leaving a greasy handprint on one side. "What's with the uniformed deputy?"

"Deputy Perkins and her team are assisting in the investigation. Why?" Claire liked how Fusco had immediately explained her professional role.

"I don't mean to be rude, but you guys don't usually call us unless you need us to do something. Generally you treat us like a Muslim in a bulky jacket at the airport."

Fusco looked the man in the eye, then fumbled with his words. "We, er, I'm working on a serial kidnapper. We've developed a list of suspects from the FDLE roster of sexual predators. I was told you supervise more than half the predators on probation."

Slaton nodded his head. "Same old story. Instead of trying something innovative, just go to the list of regulars."

"They do cause most of the problems."

That comment made Claire recall that 2 percent of all convicted felons accounted for 90 percent of serious crimes, but she wasn't going to throw that stat out now.

Slaton said, "Is it so hard to investigate?"

"That's what I'm doing." His voice edged up to match the pudgy probation officer's tone.

Slaton said, "By making me do your job?"

At this point Claire wanted to introduce the probation officer to Smarty.

Fusco didn't take the bait. Instead, he said, "I was hoping to work *with* you to get current addresses and any insights you might have on some of the men on our list."

Slaton sighed and said, "You don't think the state gives me enough to do? I have a caseload of over 150 probationers and parolees. All I can do is identify the worst five percent and try and focus on them. It'll take me hours to go through a list with you."

"It could be a huge help and maybe lead to this guy's arrest."

"Or it could be a huge waste of time and lead to me getting further behind on my daily casework."

Now Claire was getting frustrated. This guy was supposed to be part of the team. Is this what detectives had to put up with? Who could argue with an effort to capture someone who kidnaps teenage girls?

Finally, Fusco said, "Here's the list. Let's take a few minutes and go through it right now." He left no room for the probation officer to weasel out of his responsibilities.

Claire held one end of the fifty inch printout containing a list of the sexual predators they were interested in. She and Fusco spread it across the warm hood of Fusco's Crown Vic. After looking through the list, Fusco and the probation officer narrowed it to about three dozen suspects. Arnold Ludner was one of them. She knew to look for the name. He was tied to Tim Hallett too closely to ignore it.

The probation officer said, "Ludner definitely could be a suspect in something like this. He's off probation but has the sexual predator tag for life. He never gave me any trouble, but he's hard to get a fix on. He lives west of Military Trail and south of Tenth Avenue west of Lake Worth. Eight or nine guys on this list live in the same neighborhood."

Fusco said, "Can you tell me anything else about Ludner?"

"Two of his sons did time on a drug rap and aggravated assault charge. The youngest son is a lawyer and accompanied his dad to every meeting at our office. He's big into the intimidation bullshit and is constantly threatening to sue someone. He claims his father was railroaded and abused."

Fusco nodded and said, "It was one of our guys who made him tell us where the girl was."

Claire was surprised how proud he sounded talking about Hallett's action a few years ago.

"I heard all about it. I can't believe the sheriff didn't fire a guy like that."

Claire watched the probation officer scan the list again, and all she could think was, *Thank God I don't have a job like his.*

■   ■   ■

Junior felt a wave of relief as he watched the noon news on the tiny TV he kept in his office and heard no mention of a missing teenage girl. He wasn't even certain Tina Tictin's mom would have reported her missing by now. He understood how families like that worked. First, it was minor neglect. Then, once they were annoying teenagers, it was easy to totally ignore them. That's why he wasn't surprised to hear the airwaves quiet about her disappearance.

After his busy morning with meetings and reports, he was glad to take his mind off his job for a few moments during lunch. His bosses thought they knew him, and it was all he could do to keep from smiling about everything he kept concealed. They were idiots, just like everyone else.

The other thing he focused on was how well he'd hidden Tina's body. With a shovel from the truck, it hadn't been hard to dig along the bank of the canal, then dump the cooling body into the hole. Even as she thumped into the muddy grave, water rushed in, pushing dirt and sediment over her. By the time he was finished shoveling the watery dirt he had dug out back into the grave, Tina's body was completely covered with water.

A couple of lucky moves by water management officials could raise the water level in all the canals. Something like that would put her body out of reach for anyone who might be looking for her until the dry season. It wouldn't surprise him if she was never found. And if she was, the water and mud would have scraped her body clean of any incriminating DNA or microscopic evidence.

He chuckled out loud at his brilliance as he opened the page on his Internet Explorer and looked at the information he had gathered on his next potential date. His encounter with Tina Tictin had taken it up a notch, and he realized he could probably never go back to the boring old blindfold again. Maybe he had time to act once more before the police scrutiny became too strong.

It was fun being the smartest person in the state.

Tim Hallett and Rocky searched for the address in an older neighborhood known as Westgate. He had one uniformed patrol deputy following him in a cruiser. John Fusco and Sergeant Greene had come up with a list of convicted sexual predators that they wanted found and talked to. Based on Hallett's background in the detective bureau, they didn't feel it was necessary to waste a detective with him. Hallett felt like it was a make-work detail, but if it was a lead they could clear up that steered them toward a quick capture of the kidnapper, he didn't mind one bit. This could be the lead that broke open the case. It was at least plausible. Any of these suspects could be potential child predators. He knew it wasn't the time to cop an attitude about assignments.

Darren Mori and Brutus had been sent to a neighborhood west of Military Trail in Lake Worth. One of the names on his list was Arnold Ludner. Hallett wished he was the one looking for Ludner, but he understood the sergeant's decision. Rocky showed no particular interest in Arnold Ludner.

Claire Perkins and Smarty were near the same neighborhood as Darren. In some cases, where the offender was still on supervision from the Department of Corrections, a probation officer would assist. Theoretically, the investigators would be able to eliminate each of these suspects quickly because they had to account for their whereabouts at all times.

Hallett was concerned Claire was being sucked in by Fusco's supercool act. The thought of a smart young woman like Claire wasting her time with a jerk like Fusco turned his stomach. He viewed Claire like a little sister and would act like a protective brother if Fusco stepped out of line.

Hallett slowed the big Chevy Tahoe as Rocky sat in his rear compartment, checking out the sights. One advantage to leaving Rocky in the back was the "bail-out button" attached to Hallett's tactical vest. If Hallett was out of the car talking to someone and got into an unexpected scuffle, all he had to do was press the button on the transmitter and the door to Rocky's rear compartment in the Tahoe automatically opened, allowing Rocky to enter the brawl. He'd never had to use it because he brought Rocky with him almost every time he left the car.

The houses in the neighborhood were a little run-down. The area used to be called the "redneck ghetto," but in the last decade and a half, the demographics had switched to largely Caribbean islanders. The old, unincorporated neighborhood held enough of a mix to be known as one of the more dangerous areas in the county. No one seemed to get along with anyone else, and there was constant conflict between the various ethnic groups and the rednecks who clung to the belief that they still controlled the streets.

There was a strong correlation between social economic standing and registered sexual offenders. The Florida Department of Law Enforcement kept a detailed list of offenders that could be viewed as a map on a computer. Hallett had noticed the congregation of red dots on the map of Palm Beach County. Each concentration corresponded to trailer parks, low-rent apartments, and housing developments. That wasn't to say there weren't plenty of sexual offenders spread out in the rest of the county. Even the town of Palm Beach had several. But they tended to be higher profile. A neighborhood like this had a disproportionate population of sexual offenders.

One of the statistics classes that Hallett had taken at Palm Beach Atlantic University had taught him to look at all the factors in any analysis and consider the reasons behind statistical statement. He understood that one of the reasons for this grouping of sexual offenders was that they couldn't afford attorneys that might get the charges dropped, or at least reduced.

Hallett had read in the newspaper about a guy in Palm Beach who'd been caught with two underage girls. His argument was that it was a consensual act. Sometimes it was difficult for the public to grasp that there was no such thing as consensual sex with a minor. Since the jerk was wildly wealthy, he had a team of lawyers drag out the proceedings and attack the police chief needlessly. The chief of Palm Beach was widely respected and handled the situation with class, but some of the cops in the county wanted to lynch the pervert who had started it all. In the end, he was convicted of some lesser charge and ultimately designated a sexual offender. Hallett doubted anyone in this lower-income neighborhood would get the same treatment. For them it was arrest, arraignment, public defender, plea, sentencing, jail, and then spend the rest of your life tagged as a sexual offender. He thought the system to designate sex offenders was sound, but he hated the inequality between the rich and the poor. The system needed tweaking. Unfortunately, removing attorneys from the system wouldn't be one of the tweaks.

Hallett had fought back against any injustice since he was a kid. He hated the idea that some kids didn't have enough to eat before school; he hated it that some parents showed no interest in their kids. At least on law enforcement matters he and Rocky could stand up to injustice. No one seemed to realize that it was an injustice when residents were too scared to walk down the street or store owners went bankrupt after too many robberies.

Hallett found the address listed on the sheet John Fusco had given him. It was a single-family, one-story house with duct tape over one of the windows in the front and six dead bolts on the front door. As he and Rocky stepped out of the Tahoe, the skittish deputy walked over from his cruiser.

The guy was wiry, in his early twenties, probably about the same age as Hallett when he started with the sheriff's office. He wore leather gloves. Hallett didn't like the practice, even if it was safer. He felt it gave the wrong impression to the general public.

The deputy stayed several paces away from Rocky. Smart move. Before they could start heading toward the front door, two young boys peeked from around a scraggly hedge. Hallett smiled at them and squatted down next to Rocky, encouraging the boys to step closer.

They were both about six years old and slowly stepped away from the bushes and edged closer to Rocky. Their eyes were wide with excitement.

One boy said, "Can we touch it?"

"Rocky is a 'he,' not an 'it.' Would you like to be called 'it'?"

The boys both shook their heads vigorously.

Hallett smiled and said, "Go ahead, boys, you can pet him. He won't hurt you."

The other deputy said, "You sure we have time for this?"

Hallett didn't take his eyes off the boys and spoke without turning his head. "We always have time for good boys."

Both the boys smiled when they heard Hallett talk about them. And it put him in an instant good mood.

Finally, Hallett sent the boys on their way and led Rocky up the uneven front path to the door with six locks on it. Rocky seemed to have a bounce in his step after the encounter with the boys. No one could calculate how valuable a little investment of time like that could be.

The other deputy stepped to the side of the front door in a good tactical move, but he seemed far too eager to get into a scrap. Hallett knew it was actually a lack of confidence and a need to prove himself.

Rocky was the biggest reason for Hallett's confidence in most situations. Everything they'd been through together made their bond strong. There were few situations Hallett worried about when he had Rocky ready to jump in.

They waited after he knocked on the door twice and heard a long succession of locks turning. As the door opened a crack Hallett noticed Rocky cower down slightly and take a step back. He couldn't imagine what would cause this reaction in his fearless dog until the door opened all the way.

As he looked up, all Hallett could say was, "Holy shit."

■   ■   ■

Rocky didn't know this area at all. It was an interesting mix of odd scents and crumbling sidewalks. There were scraggly trees and no animals in sight except one scrawny cat darting across the road. That was the only thing that grabbed Rocky's attention. The absence of life spooked him. The bright sun was directly overhead and cast very short shadows.

As soon as he was out of the vehicle and on a lead, Rocky discovered a whole new set of smells. Other dogs had been here. A lot of dogs. He strained to sniff the base of the tree as Tim shifted to meet another man. This man was dressed the same way a lot of people Tim talked to were. He had the loud thing on his hip, and Rocky could tell immediately Tim was a little annoyed at him. Rocky decided he would make Tim happy and have a little fun at the same time. He turned toward the man, stepped next to Tim, and emitted a low growl. That made the man jump back. Rocky had to resist the urge to wag his tail. Tim and the man communicated while Rocky explored as far as his lead allowed. Then he noticed two young people creep forward. Their eyes were wide, and after a moment, when Tim spoke to them, their fear changed to wonder. Tim had him sit and let the young people come up close and pat his head. Rocky liked the attention. After a few moments of this, Rocky followed Tim toward a house.

As he approached the door, Rocky sensed something was not right. When Tim called into the house, Rocky heard steps. Something heavy. He saw a shadow and sensed the fear in both Tim and the other man. Then he felt the fear wash over him as he saw the man inside the house.

Rocky heard Tim say something, but he didn't know what the words meant.

He had to be strong for Tim.

■   ■   ■

Claire Perkins had enjoyed working with John Fusco earlier in the day. It was one of her first efforts in investigations. The fat probation officer had been abrasive, but she liked how Fusco had handled him. He had been calm but didn't let the probation officer try to bully him. They really did need his help.

But that was this morning, and at this moment, shortly after lunch, Claire didn't want the tall, muscular road patrol deputy to ride in the Tahoe with her and Smarty. Secretly, she had been hoping John Fusco might decide to accompany her on the assignment, even though this made more sense. Fusco was busy with the overall case. The deputy who had been assigned caught the hint that he wouldn't be riding in her Tahoe. They had six names on their list to locate. Given her lack of experience in sex crimes and looking for fugitives, she assumed these were six of the less likely suspects in the kidnappings.

The first thing the other deputy had said when he met her was, "You're a cute little thing." In reply, Claire hummed a note that caused Smarty to bark and snap at the startled deputy. The moron still didn't catch on.

After they'd gone through the list of suspects and talked to John Fusco about them, the road patrolman asked her if she had a boyfriend.

Claire said, "Maybe, why?"

He looked surprised at her answer. "I'm not used to answers like that from women."

"What kind of answers are you used to?"

The tall deputy, who was a member of the SWAT team, and known as a serious player at all the local singles clubs, said, "It, I don't know, seems like a weird response to my question."

Claire looked the deputy up and down and said, "I have a question for you."

"What's that?"

Claire took a moment to assess his sense of humor and said, "A train leaves Chicago traveling west at fifty miles an hour . . ."

"What the hell are you talking about?" The deputy looked kind of like Smarty when he cocked his head to one side.

Claire patted him on the shoulder and said, "Don't worry, at least you're pretty." She was afraid her sarcasm had been lost on the dim-witted muscle-head. At least she felt good about herself.

Now they were driving to the second address on their list, after having questioned one suspect who could prove he was at his job as a law clerk at a local firm. Tim Hallett had told her and Darren to stay alert because the interviews were important and sent a message the CAT could tackle any assignment.

Claire checked her rearview mirror to make sure the uniformed deputy was still behind her, then called back to Smarty in his rear seat compartment and said, "If you get a chance to nip this idiot who's following us, I won't be upset." Smarty just looked at her through the cage, and she knew he understood. She parked in front of a duplex with a wide field behind it. Old, dried-out plastic lawn furniture was strewn across the front yard, mixed in with the weeds and exposed dirt. A quick scan of the neighborhood confirmed no one else moving around.

Smarty followed her out of the Tahoe as she attached a six-foot lead. The other deputy paused to make sure his fitted uniform shirt had no wrinkles and reached down to feel the handle of his pistol in his tactical holster. Then he strutted toward her until he remembered Smarty and froze in his tracks at the edge of the Tahoe.

Claire said, "You want to go around the back wall and I'll knock on the front door?"

"It's not like this guy's a fugitive. We're just gonna talk to him."

"You never know what a convicted felon is gonna do."

"That's why it's important he sees someone like me at the front door."

Claire decided to treat this dope with maternal neglect and started to walk toward the front door with Smarty at her side. At least the dog kept the deputy a few paces behind her. As she stepped into the messy courtyard between the two front doors, she could see someone standing in the living room.

She knocked on the front door and heard a rustling inside and then a crash. She looked through the front window to see the rear door wide open and a figure running into the open field. Claire didn't hesitate to force the front door open. This looked wrong, and she wanted to know what was going on.

From behind her the deputy said, "I thought the guy that lived here was in his forties. The guy who just ran out the door couldn't have been more than twenty."

Claire looked around the shabby two-room duplex, then ducked her head into the open bedroom door. A chunky middle-aged man lay naked on the dirty carpet with blood coming from his head and nose. He turned gray eyes up to her but didn't say anything. Claire kneeled next to the injured man. "Are you seriously hurt?"

The man gasped, "I don't think so."

"What happened?"

"He called me a faggot, then just started to beat me. He took my money out of the dresser." The man pointed at a shabby wooden dresser with the top drawer open.

Claire stood quickly, stepped into the main room, and said to the deputy, "Take your cruiser over to the next block on the other side of the field and don't get out until you hear me on the radio."

She looked out across the field to see the young man running fast and about halfway across the open area. She yelled, "Stop. Police. I'm going to release my dog." It was more of a formality. Called "broadcasting intent," it was a chance for a runner to save himself some pain. Something she would be able to tell her supervisor she did later on. It got no reaction from the runner.

She kneeled down and unhooked the lead from Smarty and hummed a high a note, then said, *"Hol ihn."* Which meant "go get him" in German. The dog sprang up and was in a full gallop in a split second.

■   ■   ■

Tim Hallett couldn't help but swallow as he stared up at a black man who was at least nine inches taller and two hundred pounds heavier.

The giant said, "What do you want?" His deep voice reverberated in Hallett's eardrums.

Rocky was uneasy but now stepped up to support his partner. Hallett never wanted to take bravery and loyalty like this for granted, but Rocky displayed it so often that he expected it more often than not.

Hallett looked down at his paperwork again and said in a shaky voice, "I'm looking for Roger Randall. You don't fit the description we had on him."

The big man said, "Mr. Randall is resting. I'm his nurse."

Hallett felt such a wave of relief, he thought he might need to use the restroom. But from behind him, the wiry deputy with leather gloves said, "Nurse? You look more like a professional wrestler."

Hallett wanted to turn around and tell the kid to shut up, but the big nurse said, "Used to be. Way too tough on your body."

As he was standing there, Hallett saw a middle-aged man in a bathrobe walk into the living room. "Who's here, Tyrus?" he asked.

Hallett stepped past the big nurse and said, "Sheriff's office, Mr. Randall. We're just doing our regular check."

The man in a bathrobe stepped back and flopped onto the couch. "I wish I had enough energy to get into trouble again. As you can see, I'm so ill, Medicaid has to supply me a nurse full-time. You can check all you want."

As soon as Hallett saw the man, he realized he'd been sent on a wild goose chase. His next stop was going to be at the detective bureau, where he and John Fusco would have a few words.

Hallett paused at the entrance to the detective bureau, where he saw John Fusco sitting alone at his desk, concentrating on reports and other information spread in front of him. Sitting on the floor next to him were two stacks of information sheets on sexual predators from the annual sweeps conducted by the sheriff's office.

As Fusco read a report, a low growl from Rocky broke his concentration. The detective lifted his eyes from the neatly typed page to see the dog less than a foot away, baring its teeth. Hallett inched back, Rocky's signal to drop the mob enforcer act. The dog quieted and sat down, but his eyes never left the shaky detective.

Fusco worked hard to keep his cool but couldn't hide his Adam's apple bobbing as he swallowed hard.

Hallett made it clear he was not happy as he pulled the dog back a few inches and said, "Did you think that was funny?"

"What are you talking about, Farmer Tim?"

"Sending me to check on the registered sex offender who's been too sick to leave his house for the last six months."

"It wasn't meant to be funny."

"What was it meant to be?"

"Look, Tim, if you want to talk about this, make your pooch back off and let's sit down and talk about it."

Hallett didn't react right away. Then, slowly, he took a step back and grunted, *"Kalmeren,"* to Rocky. The dog sat right where he was and seemed to immediately lose all interest in Fusco. Then Hallett calmly shoved some papers off the chair next to the desk, sat down, leaned toward Fusco, and said, "I'm listening."

"It wasn't my idea. I'm not sure I'd even have you working on this case."

"Whose idea was it?"

"The sergeant thought it was best to keep you away from Ludner, but there were so many suspects out in his vicinity that we gave you the sex offenders farthest away."

Hallett looked around the office and said, "Where's Sergeant Greene now?"

"I dunno. She's busy. But it's not really her fault. She's only doing what she thinks is right."

"That doesn't change the fact that I really want to do something useful on this case."

Fusco said, "One of the biggest questions I have about the Katie Ziegler incident is how the suspect knew her name. I could use your opinion on a few things like that."

Hallett paused, considering the detective's request. Was it a bullshit way to placate him? Finally, he said, "My first idea is that Katie imagined he called her by name. A situation that stressful can do funky things to witnesses' perceptions."

"I know, and her mother is no help. She distrusts the police and said her husband was in jail on trumped-up drug charges. You know how bikers can be."

Hallett nodded. Everyone who had a brother or cousin in jail believed it was some kind of a setup or crazy police conspiracy. If that was true, who the hell was committing all the crime? It drove Hallett nuts that people were never willing to accept responsibility for their actions or the actions of their relatives.

Fusco said, "The first victims of this creep seem much more interested in forgetting the incident than trying to recall any details that might help."

"Can you blame them?"

"I can't even have a sketch made because none of the girls actually saw their attacker. That makes the guy extremely lucky, extremely smart, or extremely prepared."

"I hope the guy was just lucky, because eventually luck runs out. If he's smart and prepared, this could be a long case."

Fusco said, "He's smarter than the average predator, who's usually driven by urges. They act without thinking and take advantage of situations, not planned encounters. But this guy seems to choose victims carefully and space them out. I've wondered if the guy had purposely planned to take the girls from different police jurisdictions, knowing it would be more difficult to coordinate an investigation."

Hallett shook his head. "That would be good planning."

He had been through the juvenile sexual offender classes required by policy, but it seemed like just a bunch of terms and labels to him. At the basic level this guy was a predator that needed to be put down like a rogue alligator or a lion in Africa that developed a taste for human flesh. Hallett didn't need some class developed by administrators to motivate him to stop a child molester. Every time he looked at his son he knew he had to get a monster like this off the streets as quickly as possible.

As he considered Fusco's sincerity, the alert tone went off on Hallett's radio. It was Claire Perkins calling for him to switch channels. Hallett acknowledged and was on the next band in an instant.

She said, "We have a runner at a house in Lake Worth, and Smarty is running down a suspect now."

Hallett was out of the seat and headed to the door without another word.

■   ■   ■

Claire stood at the back door after broadcasting the chase over the radio and telling Tim Hallett what was going on. She watched Smarty rocket toward the fleeing man, then checked over her shoulder once more to make sure the victim she'd found on the ground was okay. She started to trot after the graceful German Shepherd as he zeroed in on his prey. At the far edge of the wide field, she saw the deputy pull his cruiser into position. He wasn't quite as stupid as Claire thought, because he stayed in the car. People believed the dogs could distinguish between uniforms and suspects not wearing uniforms, but once they were in a chase, any moving human could be a target. The more experienced patrolmen knew it all too well.

The fleeing man looked over his shoulder more frequently as Smarty got closer. Once Smarty was directly behind him, he made an extra bound, launched into the air, and grabbed the man by his inner thigh and twisted his whole body, throwing the man onto the ground like a wrestler performing a body slam.

Claire could hear the hard thud of the man when he struck the ground.

Just like he had been trained, Smarty left his jaws on the man's leg, not causing any additional harm but holding him in place.

As Claire approached, the other deputy came from his cruiser with his gun drawn. Smarty released the man and sat in the open field. The man was moaning, and when he turned, a geyser of blood shot up through the hole in his jeans. The stream of fluid was taller than Claire. She'd seen it before, but not with Smarty involved. It was a severed femoral artery—a risk for anyone fleeing from a trained police dog.

She was about to get on a radio and call for fire rescue when the other deputy stared at the diminishing geyser of blood and casually remarked, "You don't see that every day."

She was glad she could entertain the troops once in a while.

■   ■   ■

Darren Mori was pissed off he'd missed Claire's chase and Smarty's bite. He'd been ordered to keep checking the sexual offenders on his list. He was less than two miles away but realized there wasn't much he could do after the guy had already been captured.

He knew this was important and was excited to be working something different. He loved the variety of assignments he got on CAT.

Now he was meeting up with the patrolman assigned to help. He knew the tall, lanky Puerto Rican from his days on the road.

The deputy parked next to Darren's Tahoe and stepped out of his cruiser to meet his friend. He looked down at Brutus on a six-foot lead and said, "Cute dog, Kato."

Darren didn't mind his old nickname nearly as much as he disliked Brutus being called "cute." Brutus was a professional, working police service dog. Just because he didn't look like a killer, everyone thought he was a cuddly play toy.

Darren just wanted to prove he and Brutus could do something big, especially on this case. Maybe it was because he had some kind of inferiority complex. He was, after all, a short Asian man stuck with a Golden Retriever. He'd already bucked the system and renamed the dog. It was a long-held superstition among dog handlers that it was bad luck to change a dog's name. The superstition was always backed up when a dog with a changed name was injured in the line of duty. In reality, it couldn't be used as proof because so many dogs got hurt.

The dogs coming from Europe always had tough names like Horst or Blitz or, if the European trainer knew some English, Zeus, Smarty, or even the occasional Killer. That would've been cool, a dog named Killer. But he got a domestic dog that some redneck had named Bingo. Just like the kid's song. So Darren had pleaded with the sergeant at the time and was finally allowed to rename the dog as long as the name started with the letter *B*.

Now Darren faced the much taller deputy and wished Brutus would bark or snap at him just so he could see the smug bastard jump back. Instead, Brutus wagged his tail ferociously and allowed the deputy to scratch his back while he slobbered all over the ground.

Darren refocused the deputy on the business at hand. "We gotta talk to a few guys in this neighborhood, starting with one named Arnold Ludner." He knew this was the guy Hallett had punched and had gotten kicked out of the D-bureau because of it. There was no real need for Brutus or any other dog in this situation, but it wouldn't hurt to let him have a sniff.

So Darren drove his Tahoe two blocks west of Military Trail and turned another two blocks north with his tall buddy following him in his cruiser. He found the address and was impressed with how well the large ranch-style house was maintained. There was a series of vacant lots behind the whole block of houses.

The tall deputy could not have looked less interested in the assignment as Darren led the way to the front door and knocked firmly. After a few moments, an older woman answered the door with a look of concern.

Darren said, "I'm looking for Arnold Ludner."

"Is something wrong?" asked the woman.

"I just need to talk to him for a few minutes, ma'am." He saw her eyes flick to the other deputy, then down to Brutus.

She said, "Just a minute, please." Then she shut the door before Darren could say anything.

As Darren was about to knock on the door again she opened it, holding a cordless phone in her hand. She said to the person on the other end of the call, "Yes, they are both in uniform." Then she stuck out her hand and said, "Here."

Darren took the phone tentatively and simply said, "Yes?"

Immediately, a professional voice said, "I am Joe Ludner. Arnold is my father, and I am his attorney of record. As his attorney, I'm telling you I don't want you to talk to him without me present."

"He's a registered sex offender. I can talk to him anytime I want."

"Actually, you can check his residence anytime you want. But the law does not compel him to speak to you. As his son and attorney, I will certify that he lives at the residence you're at right now. And I will say one more time that I do not want you to speak to him without me present." The line went dead.

Darren gave the phone back to the woman, who looked apologetic. He needed to tell someone about this as soon as possible.

■　　■　　■

Later in the afternoon, Tim Hallett was told to check registered sexual predators in the neighborhood west of Military Trail and take over for Claire Perkins, who'd been pulled off the shift to complete the stack of paperwork related to Smarty's bite incident. It was a clean bite, and she was justified in using the dog. All she had to do was articulate the circumstances and say she had probable cause to believe the fleeing suspect had committed a felony. As it turned out, the registered sex offender she checked had hired the young man to help him around the duplex. The young man had decided to rob him and figured a sexual predator wouldn't report the crime. He was probably correct. Too bad for him, Claire had been sharp enough to look into the duplex as she approached. It was also too bad for him he couldn't run just a tiny bit faster. Now he was in the hospital ward of the county jail recovering from thirty-two stitches in his leg and lucky he didn't bleed out from the injury.

Hallett had made a routine check and cleared another suspect from the list. Now he sat in his unmarked Chevy Tahoe with both the windows down and the air on so Rocky wouldn't get too hot but they both could get some fresh air.

He had the Tahoe parked at the end of the block behind a convenience store that faced Military Trail, making a few notes and trying to decide how to make Rocky comfortable while he had dinner with the squad at a restaurant that wouldn't allow the dogs inside. It was a tradition after an incident like Claire's that they get together with Ruben Vasquez and discuss the progress of the squad and how they were all reacting to the dog bite. It was Ruben's idea, but Hallett realized it fostered closer camaraderie as well as provided him with a chance to teach them things they might not be open to hearing during the course of training.

Ruben was an odd guy who was obviously driven by goals. It wasn't a military thing. It was the way Ruben was raised, or maybe something in his DNA. He was going to make the unit a success, and nothing was going to stop him. He had said as much in training.

As Hallett wrote his notes, a woman about forty years old approached the Tahoe tentatively.

The woman said, "Excuse me, do you think you could help me?"

He turned to the woman and said, "If I can't, I can find someone who will." That elicited a nervous smile from the woman, who looked more closely to see Hallett's uniform and make sure she was talking to a sheriff's deputy. The unmarked vehicle confused a lot of people.

"It's my daughter. I haven't heard from her since yesterday."

"How old is she?"

"Eighteen." There was a hitch in her voice.

Hallett relaxed slightly because at least he wasn't looking at a missing toddler. He'd learned over his career that most teenagers who disappeared had actually run away and would come back after a relatively short time. But the sheriff's office had implemented a very efficient and specific protocol for any missing person who was considered "at risk." He knew he was going to have to call one of the people from missing persons to come out and talk to this lady but decided to get a little information first.

Hallett stepped out of the truck but kept his small notebook and pen in his hand. He looked at the attractive woman and said, "What's your daughter's name?"

The woman said, "Tina. Tina Tictin."

15

Tim Hallett nursed his beer as he sat at an outdoor patio table of a restaurant not far from the sheriff's office's headquarters. It was known as a deputies' hangout, and he'd never spent any time here until Darren Mori suggested it as a convenient place to meet after work. Hallett had found he liked the relaxed atmosphere, and by sitting on the patio, he could look directly into his Tahoe to make sure Rocky was comfortable. Darren didn't say anything, but based on his glances to his own vehicle he felt the same way. Claire had to do something at the detective bureau. Hallett understood that shouldn't bother him, but he knew Fusco and worried about Claire. He didn't know why he worried about a woman capable of crushing most men and also had a dog more ferocious than a lion at her disposal. But he still worried. It was in his nature.

The sergeant and another detective had joined them. The first thing Sergeant Greene said was, "Nothing about the case for fifteen minutes." It was a standard request when things got tense in the office.

Sharing a beer after one of the dogs had bitten someone was a ritual observed by many canine units. A K-9 bite was a big deal. It was something dogs trained for every week but rarely had to put into action. They weren't celebrating the fact that the dog committed violence; they were celebrating the fact that under pressure, and when it counted, the dog performed the way he was trained. They had the same ritual when a dog successfully tracked someone. That made Claire's absence that much more glaring.

Every dog handler was proud of his dog that chased someone down. No one wanted to admit it, but they enjoyed the thrill.

Everyone had cleaned up at the headquarters and wore casual clothes. Ruben Vasquez had come from his house and was wearing shorts. It was the most relaxed Hallett had ever seen the dog trainer. He noticed a spiderweb of white scars running down the dog trainer's muscular leg. Just another mystery he'd never have the courage to ask Ruben about.

The bar had changed its image over the years from a dark, smoky pickup place to its current incarnation of a restaurant/lounge that wasn't family oriented. Management had encouraged it to become a hangout specifically for employees of the sheriff's office. With almost three thousand of them just down the street, it was a decent base of customers to start with. Add to that the women who wanted to hook up with a cop, and all the friends and family of the employees, and the business ran almost totally on law enforcement.

Darren had been bragging about his wild single life, most of which Hallett knew to be a sham. Then Darren looked across the table and raised his beer to Hallett and said, "What are you doing tonight, Tim? You and Rocky watching *Marley and Me* again?" Everyone laughed.

Hallett said, "I think we're changing it up tonight. We might try something else."

Darren said, "Let me guess, *Old Yeller*. Or is that too sad for Rocky?"

Once again, Hallett laughed, then looked across the table to Ruben Vasquez, who didn't see the humor in Darren's comment.

Tim said, "What's wrong, Ruben?"

Ruben ran his hand across his right eye. Finally, he said, "Nothing's wrong. But that's a movie that has affected me since I was a kid. Think how you'd react if you had to shoot your own dog. It's like Disney made a movie to terrify kids." He picked up the napkin and blew his nose.

Sergeant Greene reached across and patted Ruben on the back. That's when Hallett realized it wasn't a joke or an act. The guy was broken up by the movie *Old Yeller*.

Darren turned to the sergeant and said, "Anything new on the girl reported missing to Tim?"

"That's why I was in the office so late. We've got someone working on it, but it turns out the girl has run away a couple of times, plus, legally, she's an adult. Her mom thinks she skipped beauty school yesterday. The only troubling thing is that a convenience store worker thought he saw her get in a brown pickup truck, he thinks it was a Ford, after she tried to buy beer. He said it looked like she got in the truck voluntarily, but he wasn't paying that close attention. We should know more tomorrow."

Hallett thought back to the pretty woman who had approached him earlier in the afternoon. He could feel her pain but also an undercurrent of doubt. Clearly the woman wasn't sure whether her daughter had run away or something more sinister had happened.

The next hour was relaxing as they ate an assortment of appetizers and had a few more beers. Hallett checked on Rocky one time and let the dog stretch his legs, then use the grass on the swale along the edge of the parking lot as a restroom. He could tell his dog was tired, and he knew he'd be headed back to the trailer in Belle Glade before too long.

Not long after he got back to the table, Sergeant Greene stood up and said, "I'm gonna get a good night's rest before what promises to be a shitty day." She stood quickly and gave everyone a wave before she walked from the outdoor patio a few steps to her black Crown Victoria. That started the flood, and everyone but Hallett made their exit.

As he reached down to take one more bite of a chicken wing, he heard someone call his name. He turned and saw Lori Tate with a group of her friends standing near the outside bar.

She didn't hesitate to walk over to him, saying, "I can't believe they all left you alone so quickly."

He smiled and shrugged.

Lori touched his arm and said, "You don't have to rush off, too, do you?"

Hallett couldn't keep the broad smile from spreading across his face.

■　　■　　■

Claire Perkins didn't mind missing the get-together that was somewhat in her honor. Well, technically it would be in Smarty's honor. She enjoyed hanging out with the other members of the Canine Assist Team and could've used a bite to eat and a few minutes to relax. But she got to see those guys all the time, and this was one of the few times she had been asked to get involved in an actual investigation. John Fusco, the lead detective on the case, needed help going through some old police reports to see if there were any links to the current investigation. It wasn't something the unit was supposed to do specifically, but since the sergeant wasn't paying overtime out of her budget she had no problem with it. Claire knew better than to say anything to Ruben Vasquez. He was specific about how the money from the federal grant should be spent. He wanted the dogs working for the money, not the dog handlers.

Worrying about politics and being covert was not something she was familiar with. Claire's mom had not been thrilled about her decision to go into police work. Her mom thought Claire's interest in biology would eventually lead her into the sciences or possibly medical school. But Claire had gotten bored while attending Florida Atlantic University and was intrigued at a job fair where a female detective from the Palm Beach Sheriff's Office told her about the career she had. It was so different from the way she was raised. Aside from disappointing her mom, Claire had no regrets about joining the sheriff's office. She'd learned a lot about people, and if she hadn't become a deputy she never would've met Smarty.

Now, dressed in casual clothes, with Smarty sleeping comfortably in the corner, Claire pored through reports, occasionally chatting with Fusco. She felt like a guilty mother dragging Smarty into the D-bureau and making him wait for her rather than sleep on his favorite rug or on the bed. He never let on that he minded, and she appreciated his attentive glances in between short naps.

Fusco said, "I like the idea of making a lawyer meet us at the sheriff's office after eight o'clock. It makes us a little OT but also seems to annoy the attorney."

Claire said, "He won't come up here, will he?"

"Oh, hell no. We'll go down and talk to him in the lobby."

"You want me to go with you?" This was not what she had been assigned to do. She wasn't complaining, it was just surprising.

"Absolutely. You can never meet with an attorney by yourself. They'll twist your words and say all kinds of shit in court if it helps their client. The typical defense attorney cares more about winning the case than anything else. It's their livelihood. That's why there are so many jokes about them." Fusco stretched in his chair and said, "You know how you can tell when the defense attorney is lying?"

Claire shook her head.

"Their lips are moving."

Claire gave him a smile at that one. Then the phone rang and the secretary said there was someone in the lobby for Fusco.

■　　■　　■

Claire didn't like waking Smarty, but she didn't want to leave him unattended in the detective bureau either. Fusco liked the idea of the fearsome-looking Shepherd coming with them, and it made her feel like at least she was utilizing Smarty in accordance with the federal grant.

As they walked down the stairwell, Fusco said, "This time of night there's no one around, and I don't like bringing lawyers into the detective bureau. It's also a way to show slight regard for the attorney and his family."

As soon as they stepped through the downstairs stairwell door, Claire saw an average-looking man about thirty, dressed in a suit with a loosened tie. The man appeared tired and more than a little frustrated. She did like that his eyes flicked down to Smarty at her side, but he didn't make a comment. She knew this was Arnold Ludner's son Joe. She had been trying to figure out the family dynamic that sent two brothers into the drug business and one to an extra three years of college.

The first thing Fusco said was, "I thought your father was coming with you."

The lawyer hesitated slightly, perhaps giving Fusco an insight into what was happening. "I thought it was best if I talk to you before I brought my dad in."

"Why is that?"

"Because of some of the tactics your detectives have used in the past. It traumatized him."

"As badly as he traumatized the little girl he left in the woods?"

"I don't know if it's appropriate to get into that right now."

"You're the one who brought it up, counselor. I didn't call you to exchange pleasantries. I said I needed to talk to your father, and I was giving you the courtesy of calling you about it first."

"I would hardly call the right to counsel a courtesy, or are you not familiar with the Constitution?"

"Are you familiar with the concept of a registered sexual offender?"

"Apparently more familiar than you. My father is no longer on probation. All he has to do is advise you of his residence, and you are allowed to check to make sure he lives at the residence. You don't have a right to search his house, and you certainly don't have a right to order him to talk to you like he was some kind of lifelong indentured servant."

Claire felt Smarty ease forward as he sensed the growing tension in the conversation. Fusco's voice had raised enough to catch the attention of two young women waiting in the lobby near the front door.

Then Fusco gave the attorney his own smirk and said, "I guess I'll just be going past your dad's house until I can verify that he's there."

The attorney started to say something. Fusco interrupted him.

"I believe this meeting is over, counselor." He turned and shoved the door that went into the stairwell. Claire paused a moment, looking at the speechless attorney, who was now completely focused on Smarty. She let out one of her low-pitched musical notes, and Smarty knew to give him a good snarl with a complete showing of his front teeth.

As Claire and Smarty turned to follow Fusco upstairs, she felt like she had contributed something to the encounter.

16

Hallett liked how Lori had casually taken the seat next to him and let him order her a beer. She was in a pretty print sundress and looked like she was at a resort in the Caribbean the way she leaned back in the chair and sipped her Corona. He still kept thinking about poor Claire having to spend time with John Fusco.

Lori said, "You guys meet like this often?"

"Sometimes, but we always meet after a . . ."

A smile spread over her pretty face as she said, "After a what?"

Hallett hesitated.

Just her inquiring look pushed him to answer. He sighed and said, "After one of the dogs bites someone." A moment later he added, "Sorry, that's a little morbid, isn't it?"

"I've worked here for years in a couple of different units, and they all have their little wacky rituals. The SWAT guys celebrate after they're able to use flash-bangs. Some of the patrol units have a drink after a new guy has his first fight. Even the computer guys celebrate when they crack the password on a seized computer. And the narcotics guys, forget about it. They celebrate every arrest and drug seizure. They're out almost every night."

Every police agency Hallett was familiar with had at least a few legendary narcotics agents. They modeled themselves after an earlier generation of hard-working/hard-drinking zealots. There were even some hotels that refused to host the annual convention for the Narcotics Officers Association. The story of them dumping a grand piano into a fountain at a Hilton in Orlando was enough to scare any hotel manager.

Hallett said, "When do crime scene techs celebrate?"

"When one of us gets a better job."

They both laughed at that.

Lori said, "Seriously, we all try to better ourselves. I have an application in with the FBI and the new Department of Homeland Security evidence unit."

"Why do they need evidence? I thought they did mostly immigration and customs stuff."

"Still need forensics. And they pay well." Then Lori sat up in her chair, leaning in close to Hallett, and said, "You want to go somewhere else for a drink? Maybe get away from every single person we work with?"

Hallett wanted to, but he looked over his shoulder at his Tahoe holding Rocky and thought about the day he had planned with Josh. Then he said, "I wish I could, but I have an early day tomorrow."

"How long is your shift?"

"I'm not working tomorrow; I'm picking up my son first thing in the morning."

He couldn't tell from her expression if she was surprised, disappointed, or intrigued. But she certainly had caught his interest.

∎　∎　∎

Although Kim Cooper occupied his mind more often than he would admit, Darren Mori didn't want her to think he was a stalker. Since he had met her two days ago, he had tried to find reasons to go by the airport. He had not seen her at the counter again and was beginning to think he'd have to ask someone at the Hertz desk about her.

But tonight, wearing the casual clothes he had worn to the bar and leaving Brutus comfortably in the back of his issued Tahoe, Darren saw Kim behind the counter talking to a man in a suit who looked quite agitated.

Now he worried that she would be too occupied to speak to him, and he didn't want to seem needy by waiting. He even worried for a moment that she wouldn't recognize him out of uniform. But as he approached, Kim looked over and smiled at him, then said to the business traveler, "If I give you a Lincoln Town Car instead of a midsize, will that make you happy?"

The man looked shocked and said, "Yeah, sure. What do I have to do?"

Kim slapped a set of keys on the counter, told the man the location of the car, and said, "You have to pick up the car in the next three minutes."

"What do I have to sign?"

Kim showed her frustration and said, "Nothing, you're all set. Just bring it back in three days."

The man virtually sprinted from the counter, leaving Kim with a broad smile as she said, "This is a very nice surprise, Deputy Mori. I was hoping I might run into you again."

Darren tried to contain his glee at her pleasant greeting. He jumped right to it and said, "When do you get off?"

Kim casually said, "Usually about ten minutes after I start."

Darren was shocked and knew that he was blushing.

Kim gave him a playful smile and said, "You're cute. I finish work in about fifteen minutes. And I would love to go anywhere for a quick bite to eat."

Suddenly Darren didn't care that he had missed Smarty's bite. He'd rather have a bite with Kim. This was turning into a pretty good day.

■   ■   ■

Junior gained more confidence with every newscast that went by without mentioning Tina Tictin. He checked the *Palm Beach Post* Web site, too. Nothing yet. Now he was getting annoyed at her mother. Had the woman not even reported her daughter missing yet? Maybe he had done Tina a favor.

He also checked the detailed *Palm Beach Post* crime blotter and found no mention of a truck burglary at the Home Depot lot. It was starting to look like he was a genius. Even if they did find a way to track down Tina's body, there was absolutely no evidence to connect it to him. And he knew the cops had suspects in the other kidnappings already.

Junior couldn't believe how much time his obsession now took up. He had never acted on his urges to teach young women the pleasure of oral sex until a few years ago. At least with this new fetish. It was almost like his previous life, the one before now, hadn't existed except to point him in this direction. Even his earlier memories were hazy. This had focused him.

The prostitutes he had paid for never wanted him to do it or seemed to think they were too good to show appreciation. He had a hard time finding ones with the right look for it to be exciting. Then he got the idea to do it forcibly. It was just a joke at first. Then he started to fantasize about it. The satisfaction he'd felt from these fantasies was unlike anything he'd ever experienced. That lasted more than a year, until he started to envision specific girls. At first it was just girls he'd see at the mall or on the street. Then he found himself frequenting the places young women tended to congregate.

Then he noticed a neighbor's daughter. Her name was Melanie, and he was under the impression she was only nineteen. That taught him a lot about his own interests. It was then he knew he was stuck on the idea of a young woman he could dominate. Not just when they were alone but without her knowing it. He didn't care about the age of consent. He loved that elegant phrase that no longer applied in most states. To him it was someone unsuspecting. It represented innocence. It represented the drug he needed to make himself feel important.

It was just chance that the first girl he picked was eighteen. She looked younger. But once he identified her, he stalked her quietly, using both the computer and his ability to blend in. He was all stealth and had learned a few tricks along the way. He realized no one had ever noticed him in his whole life, and now he was using that to his advantage. His father's voice nagging him to do something with his life would fade. Maybe for only a few minutes, but it got out of his head.

It had taken more than a month of constant surveillance for Junior to build up the courage to act. He had taken her as she walked home from a bus stop. It was so much easier than he thought it would be. He just waited in the right spot and stayed behind her. He kept her looking forward and used the simplest of blindfolds: a Carnival Cruise Lines sleep mask with a strip of duct tape to hold it in place. He had learned to make more effective blindfolds, but that one worked for his first try.

He had never thought about hurting the girl physically. He had the Beretta with him and let her know, but it was purely to intimidate. He took her to a nearby wooded area he had scoped out, kept her there for more than an hour and a half, then left the girl, naked, not three miles from her house. He left her without clothes because he thought it would keep her from just running away as soon as he left. From reading the news accounts he wasn't sure how long she had stayed, but it was clear the local cops had no idea who had done it.

After that, his fantasy life improved so dramatically he didn't think he'd ever have to risk grabbing another girl. But after many months the urge started to come over him again, and he realized it was pushing him to kidnap another girl. The risk never entered his mind.

Along the way he discovered his own pattern, his cover, so to speak, by accident. But it was working. Now he had taken it all the way and felt the ultimate thrill. He had felt the power of life and death and had seen the look in Tina Tictin's eyes as his hands slowly cut off any chance she would have of growing old. And he had found in in one day. Astounding.

He wanted to capitalize on his good luck. He could still act, there was time. And if he did it right, he wouldn't draw any attention to himself once again. But this time it was different. He had satisfied his needs with Tina and didn't need to be rushed. He wanted to enjoy the chase as much its results.

He'd been sitting in front of his computer and considering the incredible number of possibilities. It took some time to do the background and figure out ages and relationships, but computers were a wonderful thing and made his job that much easier.

He found a candidate. An excellent candidate. He opened a browser and navigated to Facebook. The name wouldn't have many matches. He typed in slowly "Swirsky Florida." With the touch of a button he had a perfect photo of Michelle Swirsky posing with three friends at one of the local beaches. He smiled when he looked at her pretty face and saw that she was a cute, athletic-looking nineteen-year-old.

This was going to be sweet. He felt a chill and a tweak to his vision that always meant something wild was going to happen.

Tim Hallett liked Sergeant Greene, but she'd made it perfectly clear that the detectives were driving the investigation and CAT was in support, no matter what someone's prior experience may have been. Hallett couldn't blame her. She had to show confidence in her own people. Sergeant Greene had an excellent reputation, and she was known for being tough. She had no problem explaining expectations clearly to other cops. It was one of the things about the profession that Hallett appreciated. Like anywhere else, there could be politics in a police agency, but on a one-to-one basis, most supervisors were pretty straight shooters.

That didn't make his current circumstances any less frustrating. It had been ten days, he wanted to get out there and stop this kidnapper. The sergeant didn't want him interfering with an ongoing investigation. He had practiced developing patience over the last two years while he worked training Rocky as well as raising Josh. He wasn't sure which was a more daunting challenge, but both jobs had taught Hallett that patience was truly a virtue.

Hallett was hoping to demonstrate his newfound patience by not pestering John Fusco or Sergeant Greene about following up on Arnold Ludner. It had been more than a week since Fusco had told him he'd get his chance. Hallett could taste it. He'd made a couple of surreptitious passes by the former financial manager's house, but had yet to see the man himself. Hallett had managed to see the wife twice and even one of the adult sons, but never Arnold Ludner.

Hallett realized the delay probably had something to do with Fusco hoping to build a case. He understood that. The time he'd spent in the detective bureau had taught him the importance of exhausting every piece of evidence before confronting a suspect. He noticed patrol deputies didn't usually have that patience. They liked to start things and wrap them up all in one shift if possible. The idea of leaving something hanging was unthinkable to a road patrol deputy. Hallett realized his time would come.

As he and Rocky waited in the detective bureau for a new stack of leads, a shadow crossed over him and he looked up to see Sergeant Helen Greene.

The sergeant took a moment to gather her thoughts. "I know what you must be going through with this whole Ludner situation. In reality, you shouldn't be involved in the case in any way. But people tend to cut heroes slack."

Hallett just stared at her. No one in any position of power had ever referred to him as a hero, at least in respect to his dealings with Arnold Ludner.

The sergeant continued. "That's right, a lot of people admire what you did. But that doesn't change the fact that you have to stick to the script. Fusco is the lead. He gets the chance to review all information. If you have any questions, you go to him."

"He's a pompous ass."

"An ass that gets results. If you took a few minutes to sit back you'd see he's a good teacher, too. He could impart a lot of good habits to your two young partners."

"So I'm just along for the ride?"

"No, you're here to do a job." Sergeant Greene gave him an intense stare. She spoke a little louder. "A job I know you can do. You may have gone off on some crazy tangents once in a while when you were in the D-bureau and tried to make some wild-assed theories work, but you were a good detective. Rocky could come up with less emotional insights into the kidnapper. If it weren't for your crazy theories, you might be considered one of the legends to come through the D-bureau."

"What crazy theories are you talking about?"

She smiled. "The county commissioner who was supposedly running a loan shark operation."

Hallett tried to keep from smiling himself. "He was."

"It's called a bank."

"He's still a crook. Taking advantage of the poor people in the Glades."

She laughed. "Sometimes I think you'd make a better superhero than cop. You want to help the oppressed when our job is to serve and protect. Everyone."

"That's—" He caught himself before he said any more. "I think I get it, Sarge."

"Oh, I doubt that. But you will. You will present information and theories to Fusco. You and Rocky will do the jobs assigned you. And you will not give me a reason to jerk your ass off this case or to doubt your judgment. We're friends, but I have responsibilities. I can't cut you any more slack." She leveled a good scary glare at him and said, "Now, do you got it?"

He gave her a weak smile as he nodded and raised his hands in surrender. "I got it. I'll follow the rules this time."

∎   ∎   ∎

Claire liked how John Fusco tried to teach her some investigative tricks while they worked. He'd point out things written in reports and how they might relate to a prosecution later. She also realized that Fusco had gone to Sergeant Greene directly and asked for Claire to help. She was still assigned as a K-9, and that took precedence over anything else, but when she was not out on a lead with Smarty, she'd work in the office for Fusco, and he always had something for her to do. A lot passed between them during the hours on the job.

She could tell Fusco was frustrated because the case had stalled. Everyone in the detective bureau knew it, and now, apparently, the command staff knew it as well, because he had been assigned an unrelated aggravated assault. Fusco didn't want the case to be put on a back burner until the kidnapper struck again and ruined some other girl's life. Claire was getting insight into the detective and realized how much of his life revolved around his two young daughters. She was waiting for the right time to explain to Tim Hallett that he might've been wrong about John Fusco.

Sure, Fusco was a little odd and definitely flashy, but when you got down to it, he was a decent guy.

Claire was amazed at everything that went on in the D-bureau. The missing persons detectives were working on a dozen missing teenagers. Fusco was constantly checking with them to make sure none of the missing girls could be a victim of the kidnapper. He was already looking at every chunky, middle-aged man suspiciously. Hell, that description matched half the men employed by the sheriff's office.

Fusco said, "The real challenge of this job is to stop guys like this. Most mopes that commit aggravated assaults and robberies are crack heads or morons too lazy to work." He paused and then added, "Sometimes I feel sorry for the downtrodden men and women we arrest because they just got nothing going for them. It's the rare case like this that makes me feel like I'm earning my salary and the hefty pension all the politicians are bitching about now."

Claire didn't mind his grandstanding. He somehow was able to make it very personal as he leaned in and said, "Like most cops, I feel a certain responsibility to the victims of violent crime. Not only do we owe it to Katie Ziegler to find this creep, but we definitely owe it to the next girl that might not be as lucky as her."

Sergeant Greene had done a great job of organizing the effort to question the registered sexual offenders in the area. There were still a few to talk to, and that asshole Arnold Ludner had yet to turn up. The son knew all the angles and had forced the sheriff's office administrators to back off the efforts to interview him. Something his son had spouted had convinced them he wasn't a viable suspect right now.

Fusco had told her the worst thing that could happen to a cop was to let the frustration of the everyday job get to him or her. It manifested itself in a dozen ways, from indigestion to a constant state of irritability. Claire had already seen it destroy careers as well as family lives.

Fusco had told her one way he avoided the frustration was to recall some of his good cases over the years. Like the two different times he had found missing kids while on patrol. His first year in the D-bureau he arrested a group of robbers who'd shot a gay bar patron in Lake Worth, then bragged about it. That led to one of the early uses of hate crime charges in addition to the assault charge. He even locked up a builder who'd bilked a million bucks from low-income families. But it was the open cases that absolutely haunted him. Like the asshole who assaulted a navy recruit at home on leave; the kid was paralyzed. Or the shithead who left a young mother in a coma after pouring poison into a tub of mayonnaise at a local sub shop. There was never any reason or suspect identified. He visited the woman at the long-term care facility once a year.

As Claire and Fusco studied more reports, one of the younger property crimes detectives walked up to him and cleared his throat.

Fusco looked up at him and said, "Whatchu got?"

The young man held out a traffic ticket with a photograph of a pickup truck. "You might be interested in this."

Fusco looked closer and said, "Why would I be interested in a red-light camera ticket?"

"This came to me in a roundabout way. The guy who owns the truck works in the garden department at Home Depot. He was at work the day this photograph was taken. I even saw his timesheet that showed him on the job from one P.M. to nine thirty P.M. and says he remembers finding some wires hanging loose under his steering wheel and thinks someone might have hotwired his truck that day."

"That seems like a lot of work to get out of a traffic ticket." Fusco took a moment to check out the earnest young man's face and said, "I don't see what it has to do with me."

The young detective said, "I saw a flyer for a missing teenager. One of the information lines said the girl might have been seen getting into a brown Ford F-150. If you look at the camera date and time stamp, it's the same day the girl disappeared. I heard you were working on the kidnapping case and thought this might be related." The young man started to step away. "I didn't mean to bother you."

Fusco reached up and snatched the photograph of the pickup truck.

Claire immediately realized the implications of the photograph. The intersection at Lake Worth Road and U.S. 441 was not too far from where the girl was last seen. Then it clicked in her head how each girl that had been taken by the kidnapper had ridden in a different car. Maybe this wasn't such a long shot after all.

Fusco looked at the handsome young detective and said, "You did good. I'll talk to the sergeant about having you assigned to the case." Then he looked at Claire with a grin on his face. Not like he was happy, but the sort of expression a predator might have once he picked up the scent of prey. The look almost reminded her of Smarty before he was about to pounce on someone.

Fusco said, "Maybe we can keep this young detective from the type of frustration we've been talking about?"

18

I t was a short training session, late in the afternoon, when it felt like the temperature and humidity had sucked the life out of Tim Hallett as he tried to grip his pistol, which was loaded with simunition. The training bullet was simply a piece of colored soap, which fired through his actual duty weapon with a special barrel at a low velocity. It might sting a little bit, but it wouldn't injure anyone participating in the training. Other people in the training scenario were using blanks, which didn't fire a projectile but were very loud, like real bullets. The idea was to get the dogs used to noise and distractions.

Tim Hallett dreaded a lot of the training all cops are forced to go through to keep their certification. Profiling, crimes against the elderly, and human diversity could be used as sleep-inducing agents if packaged right. Frankly, Hallett thought he should get a pass on the human diversity topic simply for the fact that he had lived with a black woman and had a biracial son. But that wasn't how training worked. Not that he didn't think crimes against the elderly were important, just like avoiding profiling, but he hoped most cops had enough common sense to not need the classes, which were usually nothing but jargon he would never have to use.

Training with Rocky was another story. Anything to do with K-9 training was interesting to Hallett.

Both Claire and Darren had been called off on other duties, but Hallett had used the training session as a chance to take a break and get perspective.

Ruben Vasquez had walked him through two or three different scenarios where the dogs would find fugitives who turned out to be armed.

So far, Hallett and a couple of dog handlers from the main K-9 unit had been effective drawing a weapon and firing into the heavily padded suits worn by the training aides. The suits weren't designed to lessen the impact of the simunition—that wasn't even necessary; the pad was to take a bite from the dogs.

In this scenario, Hallett and Rocky were supposed to be tracking a fleeing armed robber. They moved quickly through a series of obstacles into the wide, wooded area behind the training field. Ruben hustled along right behind them, watching everything they did.

Rocky was on the track, and after about two minutes they surprised the training suspect, who was hiding between two buildings in his thickly padded suit with a steel mesh mask over his face. Hallett saw he had a blue plastic gun in his right hand just as Rocky sprang onto the man's chest, gripping the pad on his upper arm.

Rocky seemed to know this was a game, too, but held on tight as Hallett drew his pistol and said, "Police, don't move," as he had been trained to say every time he drew his pistol from its holster. Then he shouted, "Drop the gun." He watched, but the training suspect still held the pistol in his hand. Hallett realized he was supposed to shoot in this scenario, but he didn't want to risk hitting Rocky, even with the soap bullet.

Behind him Ruben shouted, "Shoot. Shoot now."

Hallett still hesitated. Then Rocky lost his grip and slipped off the man's chest and Hallett fired twice, striking the man dead center of his chest. The double tap was so clean that both pieces of simulation touched each other in a pink splotch on the padded suit.

Ruben shouted, "Break. Clear." He stepped forward and got right next to Hallett, leaning his face into Hallett's like a drill sergeant in the army. "What the hell was that?"

Hallett took a step back to regain his personal space as he holstered his pistol. "What was what?"

"That suspect had a pistol. Why didn't you shoot immediately?"

Hallett hesitated, then said, "I was worried about hitting Rocky."

Ruben sighed in frustration. "Look, I know you love your dog. I love him, too. But don't lose sight of the fact that he is a tool to protect you and the citizens of Florida. You don't risk getting shot just to avoid shooting Rocky. Is that understood?"

Hallett just stared at the dog trainer.

This time Ruben raised his voice and said, "Is that understood?"

Hallett nodded his head.

"What exactly do you understand?"

Hallett mumbled, "A police service dog is a tool for the officer." It was a line from one of their training manuals. "Is that good enough for you?"

"It is if you really believe it."

■   ■   ■

Junior ate a sandwich while he waited outside the Palm Beach Community College, or whatever it was called now. Most of the community colleges had been converted to state colleges and offered bachelor's degrees. He couldn't figure out bureaucracy. The campus was too big to watch every building, but he knew her last class and had made an educated guess. It made him feel like God knowing what this girl would do before she did it.

Junior had used some of the skills he'd developed over the years to find the perfect surveillance point and spotted Michelle Swirsky almost immediately as she walked out of the Health Science Building with her bright red backpack.

He already realized she'd be much more of a challenge than the other girls. She actually went to school when she was supposed to, and it appeared that her mother kept a very close eye on her. Maybe her home life wasn't as bad as it looked on paper. His research made him think the family was a train wreck. He'd have to reassess after he watched her a few times. His concern was that if he spent the time watching her, he'd become fixated and not be able to move on to a more reasonable and safe target. That's what had happened every time in the past. Besides, he had a time frame. He didn't know how long he could keep flying under the radar, but if he acted quickly, Michelle couldn't be connected to him. And no matter how he looked at Michelle, he knew he couldn't go back to just letting the girls go without seeing him.

He'd finally seen a flyer for Tina Tictin. It was on the bulletin board of the county courthouse, and it was clear that no one thought she'd been abducted. He noted the line at the bottom of the flyer that said, *Last seen possibly in a late model brown Ford F-150 pickup truck.* He didn't own a pickup truck, so once again no one would ever connect the two of them.

Michelle hopped into a new blue Honda CRV driven by a nice-looking woman with flowing brown hair. Junior recognized her as Mrs. Swirsky, although her photograph didn't do her justice. He followed the blue Honda, which drove away from the school and out Sixth Avenue South in Lake Worth. It was easy to stay five cars back and still keep the Honda in sight. He was starting to understand how cops were able to follow people without being noticed. After a couple more turns, the Honda pulled into the parking lot of a Publix grocery store. He was shocked to see the cute Michelle pop out of the car wearing a Publix uniform shirt. Her mother had driven her to work. She kept a schedule.

Perfect.

19

Tim Hallett watched John Fusco and Claire Perkins as they walked toward him. The two looked more and more like partners, and he felt a pang of jealousy. But the surprise at seeing John Fusco at the K-9 training facility off Forest Hill Boulevard was nothing compared to the shock Hallett felt when he learned the detective came specifically to ask for help. He grudgingly admitted that Fusco had swallowed a lot of pride and come up with a creative theory about the missing teen Hallett had made the initial report on.

They had waited until Sergeant Greene and Darren Mori joined them at the training facility. Ten minutes later, they stood in the classroom with a gigantic map of central Palm Beach County spread out on the floor. Hallett could see that it was a South Florida Water Management District map and showed more detail than anything he had ever seen before.

Hallett didn't comment about Claire wearing plainclothes instead of her CAT shirt and fatigues. She didn't say a word as Fusco explained the situation.

Fusco said, "The F-150 was photographed running the red light at U.S. 441 here." He jabbed at the map with his index finger pointing to Lake Worth Road and U.S. Highway 441. "That was about ten minutes after the clerk saw Tina get into a similar-looking truck here." He moved the same finger across the map to a store on Military Trail just north of Lake Worth Road.

Fusco looked up but stayed on his knees so he could point at different spots on the map. "The garden shop manager at Home Depot didn't leave the store all afternoon and found evidence of a break-in that evening, but never reported it. The kidnapper in this case has used a different vehicle each time he grabbed a girl. I now think he might borrow them. It makes perfect sense if he knows how to hot-wire a vehicle. It also means he's very smart."

Hallett had caught on and appreciated the detective's leap of faith. This was the kind of thinking that solved complex cases, but it was becoming less and less common as people expected scientific means to be used to gain convictions. Goddamn *CSI*. Hallett said, "So the kidnapper, using a stolen truck, grabbed Tina and headed west, past U.S. 441 on Lake Worth Road."

Fusco said, "That's the theory. We're taking the truck into evidence and processing it just in case."

Hallett smiled and said, "Not bad, who helped you? Is Claire getting you to open your mind to new things?"

All Fusco said was, "Funny."

Darren Mori spoke up. "But where was he headed? He could cut through Wellington, end up on Southern Boulevard, and be out in Belle Glade in forty minutes."

"That is a definite possibility. But it is also possible, if not more likely, that he was looking for an open area like this." He brought his finger down hard on a wide area of undeveloped land. "This old farmland was bought up but hasn't been developed yet because of the real estate crash. There's no reason for anyone to be out that way. It's isolated and fits in with where he took the girls before."

Claire Perkins said, "So what's the plan?"

"We use cadaver dogs to search as much of the fields as possible. We have Mori and his dog, plus three other certified K-9 units from other local police departments. If we need more, we can call FEMA and they'll have some registered in the area that they can recommend. For now, it's just a search. Who knows, we may get lucky."

Hallett recognized that lucky breaks were responsible for about half of the big cases solved by any police agency. TV shows never wanted to take that into account. Of course, even he realized that often the luck was a result of extremely hard detective work. But in this case, having a red-light camera take a photograph of the truck no one reported stolen was nothing but pure, freakish luck.

■ ■ ■

Out in the field, Tim Hallett kept his mouth shut. This was not Rocky's area of expertise. If they were looking for drugs like cocaine or marijuana or some type of explosive chemical like TNT or ammonium nitrate, Rocky would be all over it. Cadavers were an entirely different specialty, and Brutus showed unbelievable ability in the area. He found everything from a single human tooth to a few strands of hair during training, and Ruben Vasquez had commented that he had never seen any dog with as strong a drive as Brutus.

Now Sergeant Greene stepped over to the group of three deputies, holding their dogs as they talked about the plan to search the area. The sergeant said in a low voice, "It's been more than a week since the girl disappeared. Obviously if she's still here we're looking for a body."

They all nodded.

After the sergeant had walked away, Hallett turned to his partners and said, "We conduct the search as a unit. Brutus may be the one sniffing, but there's nothing to say we all can't help. This is a long shot, but it's exactly the sort of thing we were designed to handle." He looked over at Darren and clapped him on the shoulder. "Keep it light and fun for Brutus, and he'll keep going and going. We've got a few hours of daylight left, and the other dogs are gonna conk out long before the sun sets." He looked at several dog handlers who were not assigned to the CAT unit. They milled around their vehicles, not organizing like a team. Each was used to working individually.

Hallett had known the area when it was farmland, before the town of Wellington was developed. Now sprawling minimansions and horse farms had laid waste to the area that was once a wildlife sanctuary. He knew it was tough on the farmers to resist the big payouts on land that wasn't providing them much profit, but he hated to see the county jammed with so many northern transplants in hastily constructed houses.

John Fusco was walking from his black Crown Vic toward the K-9 officers. Hallett was surprised to see him wearing something much less formal than his usual suit and tie. He had on a pair of black tactical pants and a white shirt with a badge embroidered on it and the words DETECTIVE FUSCO under the badge.

Hallett caught the smile Fusco threw Claire as he approached.

Fusco said, "I thought we could start by covering the perimeter of the fields, then work our way in as we have to. We'll do as much as we can today and pick it up again tomorrow."

Hallett listened, but his mind started to drift as he realized Tina Tictin didn't live too far from Arnold Ludner's house. He knew something was keeping the sheriff's office from going after Ludner. It was probably some restraining order the shithead son had filed with the court. He wished there was a way to get to the former financial adviser.

Then an idea popped into his head. No one had looked at the other two sons. The two that had been involved in the drug trade for many years. They could be the key to finding and questioning Arnold Ludner.

And sniffing out narcotics *was* part of Rocky's area of expertise.

■　■　■

Darren Mori and Brutus had only found one other body in almost two years of working together. And that one barely counted. It was an elderly woman who had fallen in her bathroom and died. Darren happened to be on patrol that day and got the "suspicious activity" called in by a neighbor. The neighbor was concerned because she hadn't seen the old woman in three days and she wouldn't answer the door or her phone. As soon as they had stepped onto the porch by the front door, Brutus started acting funny, almost as if alerting to narcotics. He paced back and forth in front of the door and scratched at it. Usually Brutus would sit down by the area where he'd smelled a cadaver or body part. He wanted to get to that area. With the neighbor standing right behind him, Darren decided that was enough to enter the house forcibly. After knocking several times, he broke a small frame of glass with the back of his flashlight, then reached in and opened the door.

Brutus dragged him through the house directly to the decomposing woman on the floor of the tiny bathroom attached to her bedroom. Two cats hissed at Brutus from the far side of the body. The big gray tabbies looked like they were keeping watch. Darren realized it was more likely they were hungry and preparing to start gnawing on their former master.

It wasn't exactly a mystery or even anything to brag about, but at least he could claim that he and Brutus weren't virgins when it came to finding cadavers.

This was an entirely different circumstance. Darren was nervous, but he couldn't let anyone know, especially Brutus. He had to stay calm and upbeat to keep the playful Golden Retriever from getting bored or worn-out. Not only was the rest of the squad counting on him, there were detectives, other K-9 units, and uniformed deputies milling around the scene as well. Darren knew most of them and didn't want anyone to have any ammunition for jokes about him later. He didn't mind the names like Kato. He no longer explained himself to the rednecks who couldn't tell the difference between a fictional Chinese character and someone whose grandparents emigrated from Japan. In one sense, it was politically correct to call all people from the Far East "Asian," but in another sense, it lumped everyone together. Europeans and Americans no longer made an effort to distinguish between people from China, Korea, or Japan—even though the culture and language of Japan were as different from China's as from America's.

Darren realized he was building this search up in his mind to mean more than it really did. Whether Brutus found a body or not, it wouldn't really affect racial stereotypes across two continents. But it would mean something to him. He took a deep breath and looked out over the area they expected Brutus to search. The field was substantial. He could see where someone had tried to grow different crops and apparently just abandoned them after selling the land. One area held corn; another looked like it was growing wild tomatoes that used to be in some kind of order. There were the usual scrub-brush windbreaks between the fields and the seemingly never-ending maze of canals. The canal system in South Florida was complex and allowed the South Florida Water Management District to prepare for an oncoming hurricane by dumping water before it arrived. It was also a means by which to manage the gigantic Lake Okeechobee. Here it was just another impediment that Brutus would have to overcome while he searched for a dead teenage girl.

■　■　■

Junior couldn't believe he'd given in to his urge to enter the Publix where Michelle Swirsky was working. Usually he'd fantasize about things like this, but he rarely took the extra step of actually risking contact with the girl before he was ready to consummate their relationship.

Like most Publix supermarkets, this one was a bustling, crowded montage of noises and people. It reflected South Florida with accents of every flavor and no two faces the same color. As soon as he stepped in the door he risked being caught on camera. He panicked for a moment and wasn't sure what to do. He didn't want to appear too nervous or do anything to attract the attention of anyone who might review the footage from the security cameras later. He stepped on into the store and down the pasta aisle, pretending to inspect a bottle of Ragu spaghetti sauce. Once he was safely in the middle of the aisle he looked up to see if he could notice any video cameras. There were none obvious, but there were several large domes with blacked-out glass bulging from the ceiling at strategic locations. He knew those were cameras that could be moved in any direction. Staying close to the shelf, he inched toward the end of the aisle, glancing each direction until he could see the cash registers.

His heart skipped a beat when he saw her bagging groceries on register five. Michelle had a bright smile as she chatted with the elderly man while he paid for his groceries. He watched her push the full cart as the man followed her slowly, using a cane in his left hand. Her long dark hair was tied in a ponytail and bounced when she walked. She didn't seem to be anything at all like the girls he had dealt with in the past.

That didn't really matter as her image burned onto his brain and he knew that she would be his next choice. He didn't have much time to waste and wondered if it would be too much to grab her this evening.

He loved when his mind had so much to occupy it.

20

Tim Hallett stayed at the dirt-road entrance to the field with Rocky next to him. There wasn't a lot for Rocky or Smarty to do during the cadaver search, but Hallett realized he could learn a lot by watching how things were organized. He'd seen the training that Ruben put Darren and Brutus through. Using just a few strands of hair or a tooth or a bone fragment obtained from the medical examiner's office, Brutus had been taught to search out the decaying material and human scent. At first, Darren had tried to make it a rigid exercise for the dog, but it was Ruben who knew Brutus's true nature and turned it into a game with rewards and incentives. They had all been shocked how much progress Brutus had made from his first day trying to locate a pair of human teeth in a small area. After the intricate training Ruben put him through, now just a few strands of hair could attract the dog's attention.

But this was different. This was real. And it wasn't a guarantee. A crime scene team had set up a loose grid marked by wooden stakes in the ground, in case the search went on for more than just today. Darren would take Brutus through each section until the dog tired; then when he searched again he wouldn't search the same area twice. There were also crime scene photographers and a lieutenant who looked nervous. He knew the tall, skinny lieutenant of the detective bureau didn't have the balls to call out this many people on a hunch. This was all Sergeant Greene's doing. That was one of the things he respected about Helen Greene: She called out a tremendous amount of manpower and resources to follow up on what some would call a far-fetched lead, but she never flinched in making these decisions.

Rocky panted as his eyes followed Brutus's progress. Hallett ran his fingers through Rocky's coat and tried to move him completely into the shade. Out of habit, he picked burrs out of Rocky's fur. It calmed him to watch this with his partner. His friend.

Hallett wanted to be out here supporting his other good friend, Darren, but his mind was now stuck on the idea of going after Ludner's sons as a way to get to the man. The sergeant still hadn't assigned him leads like that, and she would shoot down his idea if he suggested it. He'd have to do it quietly. That's why he had called one of the crime intelligence analysts and asked her to come up with some addresses and phone numbers for Arnold Ludner's sons. She kept him on the phone chatting for a few moments. He was trying to place her face and match it to the pleasant voice. Just as he was about to give her a clever comment, he looked up and saw Lori Tate standing next to him. He thanked the crime analyst and hung up.

He smiled and said, "Hey, Lori." For some reason he felt guilty flirting on the phone with the analyst.

She returned the smile with her white, straight teeth. "Looks like you guys have been busy."

"Now it's all up to Darren and Brutus."

"How late do you think you'll be out here?"

He caught the hint that she was looking ahead to the evening. "I have no idea. If we find something, my guess is you'll be out a lot later than us."

"You're probably right," she said as she leaned over and gave him a quick kiss on the cheek. "That's for luck." She trotted over to the group of investigators and crime scene technicians on the other side of the field.

■   ■   ■

This place really reminded Rocky of home. It was wide open and filled with all kinds of animals. Rocky could smell a dozen different scent tracks that crossed in every direction. He didn't notice any water close by, so he wasn't scared. But the place did remind him of the low, wet lands where he was born.

Rocky sat and sniffed the air. Just that morning, as he was starting to wake up, he remembered that day when his mom fought the animal in the water. He had seen more of them and heard Tim say over and over the word "gator." Rocky was sure Tim didn't understand that now just the word "gator" startled him. He remembered the gator trying to come up from the water into the puppy pens and the way his mother raced down to the water to stop it. He had never heard barks like that, and the gator simply made low grunts. Its long tail whipped the water, and it snapped its wide mouth filled with teeth toward his mother.

His mother slowly gave ground and looked over her shoulder to see if anyone had heard the commotion. Lights were coming on outside the house, and help would be there soon, but the gator moved so swiftly his mother never had a chance. Rocky could still hear his mother's yelp of pain as the gator's jaws closed on her neck and pulled her into the dark water that led up to the edge of the pens. There were fences there designed to keep the dogs from going in the water, but it looked like the gator could come right through them if it wanted.

The fight between his mother and the gator had caused every dog on the property to yelp and bark as the man from the house raced down to the puppy pens. But he was too late.

Now Rocky let Tim's hand on his head comfort him, and he focused on the sights and sounds around him. There were a lot of people here. His friend Brutus seemed to be at the center of the attention. Brutus was fun to play with, and he could find anything and win any game his man set up for him.

Rocky started to pant to throw off the heat of the day. He moved back slightly into the shade of the vehicle and was happy when Tim sat down on the ground next to him and looped his arm around Rocky's shoulder, pulling him close.

This may have been Brutus's game, but Rocky couldn't have been happier.

■　　■　　■

Right off the bat Darren Mori realized this was nothing like their training environment. As word spread about the search for the missing girl, more sheriff's personnel got involved. That's the way things always seemed to unfold. Especially in the afternoon on a weekday, when shifts were slow and deputies were always interested in seeing something unusual. Cops were just like anyone else; they wanted to be around when things happened. But with cops there was no one to come up and say, "Show's over folks, move along." Now Darren had the added stress of not being able to find anything in front of twenty witnesses.

At least Brutus didn't seem affected by the commotion. There were a couple of sergeants, the missing persons detectives, Fusco, and a homicide guy, as well as several crime scene technicians who had laid out some markers to help keep track of where Brutus had searched.

Finally, Fusco looked over at him and nodded, twirling his fingers in the air to indicate it was time to get this show on the road.

Darren had a sixteen-foot lead on Brutus and leaned down and said, "Seek, boy, seek." He wished he had the cool Dutch or German commands the patrol dogs used, but since he didn't have to worry about some thug on the street running away and being chased down by Brutus, he kept the commands simple. At one point he thought about using Japanese, even though he didn't speak any himself. It was more of a nod to his heritage and his family. But he didn't want to extend any of the stereotypes some of the detectives held about Asians.

Brutus surprised Darren by darting off into a clump of old corn and what looked like sugarcane. The long lead got caught in the stalks, but Darren was able to quickly catch up with the enthusiastic dog. By the time he cut through the old crops, Brutus was sitting down next to a mound of dirt. It was a classic alert behavior that he'd been taught. The cadaver dogs were trained to sit quietly because no one wanted to risk the dog digging down to the body and disturbing evidence.

None of the crowd could see Darren from this position, and he wasn't sure what to do. He didn't want to disturb potential evidence, but he didn't want to seem subservient to that pompous Fusco. He walked over slowly, patted Brutus on the head, and said, "Good boy." Then he looked at the mound of dirt, squatted down, and used the edge of the flashlight from his belt to scrape some of the dirt to one side.

He saw a tiny bone and brushed away more dirt and realized it was a dead possum. That was another thing that never happened in training. There were rarely other dead animal parts in the confined area where Ruben Vasquez hid different artifacts. These were the kinds of things he needed to bring up with Ruben, who was very progressive in his training techniques.

Darren walked around the clump of corn and encouraged Brutus to start searching along the road leading to the field. He kept his voice light and playful, saying over and over, "Seek, boy, seek." Brutus would start in different directions, full of energy.

After more than an hour and a half, with several water and food breaks in between, Darren noticed Brutus starting to slow down. But he had not nearly reached his limit. Darren was beginning to understand some of the things that Ruben did in training to teach him more about reading his partner.

The sun was about to set, and he was surprised how cool the breeze from the east felt against his face. As he moved along the edge of the road near the canal, he sensed a slight hesitation from Brutus. Then the dog continued in the same direction he'd been walking. Brutus paused again. He walked back to the spot where he hesitated and acted somewhat agitated. He kept leaning over the edge of the road that dropped down into the canal.

Darren looked over his shoulder and noticed John Fusco easing his way from the group of detectives. When he got about fifteen yards away he stopped and said, "What do you think, Kato? It's getting kind of dark out. Is Brutus showing any interest in anything?"

Darren didn't mean to ignore Fusco, but he liked the idea of it anyway as he focused on Brutus and his odd behavior.

Fusco edged closer, careful not to upset the dog.

Finally, Darren said, "You see that uneven ledge just under the water?"

Fusco leaned over to look at the ledge three feet below the road. "How could the dog know there was something under the water?"

"Brutus is onto something right here. It's up to you, but I think it's worth checking out."

Fusco said, "Be my guest."

Darren thought about it for a minute, then handed the lead to Fusco. Brutus was still sitting right at the edge of the road but looking down at the ledge. Darren slipped off the side of the road into a few inches of water. The main part of the canal was three feet to the side, where it dropped off precipitously into the standard black water of Florida waterways.

Darren used a stick to poke into the mud a little and immediately felt it bump against something hard. At the same time, Brutus let out a quick bark. Darren didn't hesitate to pull out his flashlight and pop it on. He squatted and used his hand to dig in the mud. Normally, if they had a stronger lead, they would call a crime scene technician to process the area, but this was still classified as a long shot.

It was a long shot until he pulled out a human hand and forearm in an advanced state of decay. He immediately dropped the hand and looked over his shoulder at Fusco, who in turn shouted over his shoulder for help.

Even in the heat of the moment, Darren remembered to look up and say, "Good dog, Brutus. Good dog."

Brutus answered with a vicious wagging of his tail.

■　■　■

Tim Hallett felt pride in Brutus's accomplishment. It was clearly the sort of thing Ruben Vasquez was trying to instill in the squad. An *all for one and one for all* type of attitude. Police agencies had a built-in competitiveness, and Hallett supposed he was as competitive as the next guy. It was always fun to say you had the most arrests or caught a dangerous criminal. But this was an entirely different feeling. He imagined it was the way he'd feel if his brother ever achieved anything.

Now, in the dark, the attention had shifted from the cute Golden Retriever to the grim business of recovering a body someone had managed to bury under the water. Hallett was only able to catch a quick glimpse of the crime scene but saw that the killer had taken advantage of a ledge and probably buried the girl when the water in the canal was a little lower.

Hallett sat on a towel he'd laid out on the ground with Rocky next him. He had his arm around the dog, absently rubbing his shoulder and chest while he watched the crime scene people set up a bank of floodlights powered by a generator in the rear of one of their vans. Lori Tate was one of the busy crime scene technicians conferring with the detectives about how best to retrieve the body and all the evidence in the grave. Hallett couldn't deny she was pretty and he was drawn to her. The fact that he'd watched her every move tonight made that obvious.

Rocky laid his head on Hallett's shoulder, exposing a spot on his neck he liked rubbed. It was cooler since the sun had gone down, and the Belgian Malinois breathed quietly and seemed content.

The real reason Hallett was sitting there was to hear the conversation between an agitated John Fusco and the perennially calm Helen Greene. As was her custom, the sergeant let the detective rant and rave for a full minute before she said anything. Hallett wanted to point out that the dead girl, assuming it was Tina Tictin, lived less than a mile from Arnold Ludner's residence, but Fusco beat him to it.

Even though they were a good distance from the crime scene, Fusco's loud voice carried over the field on the night air, and he didn't care one bit.

Fusco said, "Why can't we grill that asshole Ludner? He's a decent suspect and lives near the victim."

Sergeant Greene held up one hand, saying, "First off, we haven't identified the person in the grave. Secondly, we've been talking to his attorney, who won't allow it. He's gone so far as to get a court order."

"Why would he have to do that?"

Hallett caught Helen Greene glance in his direction. It could be argued that if Ludner was involved, this was Hallett's fault. On the other hand, if he hadn't acted the way he had two years ago, another girl could be dead in the field.

Fusco said, "There's got to be another way."

"There is. Build a case against him."

Then Fusco looked over at the homicide detectives scurrying around the crime scene and said, "On top of everything else we're gonna lose the case to them. They'll freeze us out of everything they do."

"John, you need to calm down and dial it back a few notches. We all work together. Sergeant McAfee and I will decide what's going to happen."

Hallett knew Fusco didn't like the idea that homicide was considered the top of the food chain. It was a specialty like anything else. If Fusco really wanted to work homicide, he could put in for it. Right now, it was just a personal, minor turf war with the surly detective.

Hallett saw the tall homicide sergeant stand from a crouch near the edge of the canal and casually stroll over to Sergeant Greene, casting a sideways glance at Fusco. The sergeant had an excellent reputation around the sheriff's office and didn't put up with the petty politics that Fusco was ranting about now. He didn't even look at the detective but focused on Sergeant Greene instead.

McAfee said, "Here's the scoop, Helen. We'll hold what we've got and leave a deputy here overnight to maintain the crime scene. In the morning we're going to use the good daylight to do this thing right. We called the Water Management District, who's gonna send someone out to seal off this canal and drop the water level about three feet by morning. That should make everything easier. Then we'll use a backhoe and come at this thing from the land side."

Sergeant Greene gave him a smile and nod and said, "Thanks, Rick. I appreciate you keeping us in the loop." She looked over at Fusco as if to emphasize the point that he was going out of his way to be informative and helpful.

Of course Fusco didn't acknowledge it.

As McAfee turned, he looked over at Darren and Brutus standing at the back of their Tahoe and called out, "You did a hell of a job."

Hallett knew the comment was as much to annoy Fusco as it was to compliment Darren. He caught the sergeant looking over his shoulder to make sure the jab struck him.

■　　■　　■

Darren and Brutus had to take a moment by themselves away from the crush of people interested in excavating the body they had found. To Brutus it was just a game, and he had been rewarded with his favorite chew toy, a doll made out of rope. Darren thought the doll was a little creepy, but for some reason Brutus loved it. He never damaged the doll, just held it in his mouth without pressure.

They both sat on the ground next to Darren's Chevy Tahoe. The first thing he had done was make sure Brutus had enough to drink and got a snack. Now he was just spending a few mindless minutes, taking the burrs and twigs out of Brutus's coat.

He heard someone say, "You two doing okay?" When he looked up he was surprised to see Sergeant Greene approaching by herself. She plopped down next to them and groaned like an elderly woman who had been on her feet too long.

Darren didn't say anything as he continued to concentrate on Brutus. The dog, on the other hand, turned so he could stick his snout right in the sergeant's face as he wagged his tail incessantly. The rope doll dropped to the towel.

The sergeant said, "I don't think you realize what a big deal this is." She waited, but Darren didn't say anything. "You made the whole sheriff's office look good, and the detective bureau in particular."

Darren gave her a weak smile. He was too exhausted to do much else.

"What I'm trying to say is that I owe you and Brutus. If you ever need anything, anything at all, just give me a call and I'll take care of it, no questions asked. I never forget when someone helps me out like this."

Darren was touched. It really meant something for a good cop to make a commitment like that. And it did open his eyes to the fact that he and Brutus had done something important today. It might've been because she was a really good sergeant or it might have just been chance, but Sergeant Greene had lifted his spirits with that short chat.

21

Tim Hallett spent some time trying to sort out his emotions. He was willing to bet it was the same reaction everyone else on the squad had. Brutus might have shined and possibly performed the greatest feat of any cadaver dog, but no one felt like celebrating. And no one was happy about leaving the body in the water overnight. He understood the homicide detectives' decision, and it made sense. Have a deputy maintain the crime scene overnight while the Florida Water Management District cuts off water to the canal and lowers the water level, and preserve more evidence when you excavate the body. It was pretty basic police work, but it was the kind of thing that ate at Hallett.

People often turned to police work as a profession because they had an innate sense of justice. Leaving a dead girl in a watery grave was the ultimate injustice, and it pissed Hallett off as he drove, with Rocky sitting halfway in his compartment but leaning his head and paws out onto the console of the Chevy Tahoe. Even Rocky seemed subdued. Hallett was tired, but without any interest in going home to bed. It was still relatively early. The one urge Hallett had was to visit his son, Josh. It was probably because he had been thinking about the woman that approached him last week about her missing daughter and the fact that they had probably just found her body. It made him thank God for the healthy, happy little boy that loved him more than anything in the world. At least that's what Josh told him when his mother wasn't around.

He thought about calling Crystal first but realized she might think it was too late and say no. He didn't want to explain the day to her. They bantered maliciously, but she wouldn't deny him access to Josh and would help if she knew the turmoil he was going through. He just didn't have it in him to talk about the events. Instead, he kept driving north on U.S. 441 knowing he was going to turn on Southern Boulevard and into the village of Royal Palm Beach. He was stopped at the light at Forest Hill when a panhandler standing on the median walked across the two empty turn lanes and rapped on the window of Hallett's unmarked county car.

The grizzled man, about fifty, lost his smile the instant he saw Hallett's uniform. Then his cloudy eyes caught sight of Rocky giving him a silent, warning stare. The man stepped away from the Tahoe and almost into the path of a Kia in the turn lane.

Hallett reached out quickly and grabbed the man by the arm, pulling him closer to his SUV. He said, "Whoa there. If you're gonna cross traffic lanes you probably need to sober up."

The man was scared now and said, "I'm sorry, officer. I was just looking for a few bucks to eat."

Hallett looked at the man's scarred face and thought of Ruben Vasquez's combat scars. "Were you in the service?"

The man nodded and mumbled, "Army."

Hallett glanced at the clock in his dash, but the time didn't really matter. He popped the locks on the car and said, "Jump in and I'll take you wherever you want to eat."

The man looked at him suspiciously and said, "This ain't some kind of trick, is it?"

"Not unless getting some food in you is a trick."

"What about the pooch?"

"He's got enough food in him right now that he shouldn't be a problem. But don't do anything stupid. He snacks on guys like you."

The homeless man caught the humor and hustled around to jump in the passenger side of the car.

Rocky whimpered slightly and backed into his compartment completely. Hallett caught a whiff of the man a moment later and wondered how the dog's sensitive olfactory system hadn't shut down completely. He tried not to wince when he said, "What do you feel like?"

"I feel like a loser, but I'd like to eat a thick, rare hamburger."

Hallett smiled and made an illegal left to pull into the parking lot of a Ruby Tuesday's. He got no argument from Rocky when he told him to stay in the car and had to endure a couple of annoyed stares from the hostess and the waitress as she led them to their table.

The man said his name was Harold and his drinking and meth problems had kept him from working a steady job.

Watching him gobble down a hamburger, Hallett quietly waved the waitress over and ordered a second one for the man to take with him.

Harold said, "I was afraid you were going to arrest me."

"Why would I arrest you?"

Harold shrugged and said, "I probably got all kinds of prescription pills on me. I figured your dog would alert."

Hallett smiled and said, "First of all, don't admit to any crimes in front of me. It's the polite thing to do. Secondly, drug dogs don't alert on prescription pills because they aren't probable cause. You could have a prescription for them."

"What about meth?"

Hallett sighed and said, "Harold, are you telling me you have meth on you right now?"

He hesitated and his eyes darted to his pockets. When he looked back at Hallett he said, "No, I'm just trying to figure it out for future reference."

Hallett started to laugh and said, "My specific dog is not trained on meth. The chemicals are dangerous. Besides, I'm pretty sure your personal odor shield would keep any dog from coming close enough to alert on you."

"That's been my plan all along."

That line alone was worth the price of a couple of hamburgers.

■   ■   ■

Claire had a hard time getting a grip on her emotions as she sat in a booth at a Denny's with Smarty under the table and his head resting on the bench between her and John Fusco. One of the reasons she ate in this particular Denny's was that they let Smarty hide under the table without any comment. It was almost like the German Shepherd was acting as a chaperone, because he clearly was able to scare John Fusco to the other side of the booth.

She had picked at her eggs and ham, occasionally slipping a piece of

ham to Smarty. She didn't just hand him a piece but placed it on his
nose to reinforce his patience until she hummed the combination of notes
that told him it was okay to move his head and catch the falling ham in
his open mouth.

It was all just a ploy to keep her mind off the body she had just seen
half-buried on the side of the canal as the professionals at the Palm Beach
County Sheriff's Office worked efficiently and quietly to gather any evidence possible. She had seen plenty of bodies, but having lived with a
poster of Tina Tictin around the office she felt like she knew the girl.
There was still no guarantee that the body they found was actually Tina
Tictin, but it was everyone's best guess based on the time she disappeared
and the level of decomposition.

Claire decided she just wasn't hardened enough yet. Maybe that would
come in time. She noticed Fusco was quiet, too.

She said, "Do you ever get used to stuff like that?"

"I hope not." He took another sip of water as he stared straight ahead.
"This is why I work so hard in crimes/persons. If we keep homicide out
of it altogether, everyone wins."

"Do you want homicide to stay out of it because of your career or it's
what's right?"

Fusco shrugged and said, "Both."

Claire appreciated this complex man and his honest answers. She
could learn a lot from him.

■　　■　　■

Having a quick dinner with the homeless guy had thrown Tim Hallett
off his schedule, but he knocked on the front door of his ex-girlfriend's
house just the same. He had planned to rationally explain to her why he
just needed to see Josh for a few minutes, even if he was asleep, then
he'd be on his way. He didn't know what he could trade for this favor
but hoped that Crystal wouldn't be pissed at the late hour and that she'd
honor his request.

He was surprised to see her in a beautiful long dress when she jerked
the door open. As he was about to apologize for intruding, she cut him
off.

"Tim, what are you doing here?"

"I, um."

She reached out and grabbed him by the arm, pulling him into the house. "It doesn't matter. The restaurant wants me to work an exclusive party for some Hollywood execs, and my babysitter just canceled. Can you take Josh?"

His only question was, "When do I have to give him back?"

"Tomorrow afternoon."

A smile spread across his face as his emotions from earlier in the evening evaporated in an instant. "You got a deal."

Crystal pulled him into her for a hug and then kissed him on the lips. Something she hadn't done since he'd moved out.

He felt like he'd been given a shot of adrenaline. Her hands gently moved to cradle his face and her tongue slipped into his mouth. Her full lips locked tighter on his.

She pulled away suddenly. "I'm sorry."

"Don't be."

Crystal looked down to hide a smile. "I still worry about you."

"And I worry about you."

"You know what I mean. Going out on patrol is a different kind of danger. It causes a different kind of worry. When you were a detective, I could rationalize that you weren't in harm's way every day, but seeing you leave in uniform felt like someone was punching me in the stomach. And I had no one to talk to about it. No one can understand what it's like. My sisters would act like they got it, but worrying about their stockbroker husbands was not in the same league as what I felt every morning you left the house."

He just stared at her. Finally, he said, "I had no idea."

Crystal swallowed hard, then turned, ignoring him, and shouted, "Josh, get your stuff together. Your dad is going to take you."

■   ■   ■

Hallett couldn't resist taking the boy by to see his mother even if it was late. She had been thrilled by the phone call, and when Josh walked in wearing his Spider-Man pajamas, she held back tears as she grabbed the young man like a wrestler ready to throw someone to the ground.

The only thing Hallett had not considered was his younger brother,

Bobby, who was apparently so worn out from his hard day of not working that he couldn't get off the couch and motioned for Josh to come to him for a hug.

Rocky hopped up on the couch and sat right next to Bobby.

Bobby said, "Why does this stupid dog always do that right next to me?"

Hallett rolled his eyes and said, "Because he's alerting on the marijuana odor, you moron."

Bobby eased off the couch and backed away from Rocky, then hustled into his room at the rear of the house. Hallett's mother ignored the whole exchange, as she had since Bobby started smoking pot at about sixteen. He had always been a slacker, and now, with the addition of THC to his system, he was lazy even for a slacker. Hallett wondered if they had a word for that.

She insisted on making a small meal for him and Josh, even though his hamburger with the homeless man had filled him up. He sat back and listened while his mother asked Josh all kinds of questions about what he'd been doing and what he would like to do tonight.

She looked at Hallett and said, "I'm going to have to pull rank as your mother and insist you spend the night here."

Hallett considered his obligations and said, "I need to feed the animals out at my trailer."

His mother said, "I know you have a cute teacher out there who will do it for you."

His head was spinning from the roller-coaster day. Crystal's show of affection and confession had surprised him. Finding the body had drained him. How could a cop not take something like that home at night? He didn't think he could ever work homicide. Hallett smiled and acceded to his mother's wish as Bobby sheepishly came back into the room in different clothes and sat on the couch with Josh between him and Rocky.

Hallett needed a night like this with his family because tomorrow he was going to start bothering someone else's.

■   ■   ■

It'd been a long day, but Rocky had grabbed several good naps. He wasn't sure exactly what had happened, but Tim had been very sad after they left the field where Brutus was playing. Another man had gotten into the vehicle with them and he smelled bad. There were other smells that sometimes Rocky would associate with a game, but mostly his scent made Rocky's eyes burn and he was happy to sit back in his cage behind Tim. He was even happier when Tim and the man left the vehicle for a while and he could just sleep.

Then Tim had picked up Josh, and Rocky couldn't believe how happy he was. Usually they picked up Josh when the sun was still in the sky. This was different. And now they were at the house with the other people that Tim seemed to love.

It was a confusing house for Rocky. The other man in the house who Tim called Bobby always smelled like the game he played with Tim. The one that if he sat down next to the smell, Tim gave him a cracker. Although when he sat down next to Bobby, it just seemed to make Tim mad.

It didn't really matter because he had Josh with him that night. Rocky missed checking the fences and the animals at their home, but he would trade it for the few moments with Josh and Tim together.

The problem was that Rocky couldn't keep his eyes open. It had been such a long day and he had done so much that it was time to sleep. He curled up on the floor while Josh lay next to him and rubbed his ears. He wanted to stay awake and gaze at the boy, but he was so relaxed and so happy, all he could do was put his head down and close his eyes.

He knew he could never understand why Tim got angry or sad with other people. All that mattered was that Tim was happy with Rocky and Josh was there, too. He fell asleep happier than he had ever been.

■　　■　　■

Claire was nervous. Not like on the job when she faced down a gangbanger. These nerves were legit and well founded, but not as much fun. Or maybe they were. She said she needed to get Smarty home, but John Fusco had taken it as an invitation. Claire was too intrigued to say no. But now, as Smarty marked his territory near her front door, she realized she wasn't up to much other than talking. She didn't think she could fall asleep even if she went to bed. Every time she closed her eyes she pictured Tina Tictin left in the canal.

At the moment Fusco stood by his car, on his phone. She could hear him saying, "Yes, sir, I'll handle it first thing."

Claire felt a thrill of the unknown as he closed the phone and turned toward her. She said, "Problems?"

"Always."

As the tall, well-built detective approached her she felt her resolve melt. Then Smarty growled. Out of instinct she scanned the area and then realized he was growling at Fusco.

The detective had frozen in place, cutting only his eyes up to Claire in an effort to see what the next move should be.

Was Smarty thinking for the both of them now?

■   ■   ■

Claire looked into John Fusco's dark eyes. With his perfectly combed hair and receding hairline, expensive shirt, and silk tie, he was exactly the kind of guy her biological father would've hated. He was ambitious, intelligent, industrious, and, from her father's point of view, completely corporate.

She appreciated the fact that he never tried to move her off the comfortable couch, and he had listened with a great deal of interest to her babble about her childhood and early days at the sheriff's office. He'd reached over to play with her hair once, but Smarty's intense gaze and guttural sounds had put a stop to any of his moves.

Claire said, "I'm sorry, I just wanted to talk. I guess Smarty had the same idea."

"He's better than a dad with a shotgun."

"It doesn't mean that I'm not interested in you."

Now Fusco took a minute to gather his thoughts and said, "It might be better this way as long as you're working on the squad. There is a policy about fraternization within squads, even though I doubt anyone follows it."

Claire smiled. "That's a much more mature attitude than most men would have."

"Is that a shot at my age?"

She let out a giggle that sounded more like a teenager's than she had intended. "How old are you?"

"Thirty-five."

She let a sly smile slide across her face and said, "Yeah, I guess it is a shot at your age." Seeing the look on his face, she had to kiss him.

22

Tim Hallett enjoyed the casual morning at his mom's house. It was almost like he was a kid again, sleeping in the same house as his brother, in his old room with Josh on the other single bed and Rocky sprawled on the carpet between them. He had awakened to the smell of his mother's famous pancakes and bacon.

After breakfast, while he worked on his mother's shutters, Josh and Rocky played in the front yard. Bobby joined them after a while and fulfilled the stereotype of the stoner who could throw a Frisbee five hundred different ways. At least he'd cleaned up enough that Rocky wasn't alerting on his every move, and his spectacular Frisbee skills were a challenge for Rocky.

Hallett had changed into his spare uniform he kept in the Tahoe, then managed to drop off Josh a few minutes early to Crystal, who gave no hint about her feelings toward the kiss the night before. Women were one of the puzzles he would never figure out. But he enjoyed trying. He was glad his mother got to spend the evening with Josh and even happy that his brother got to see the boy for a while.

He realized this quick respite was the quiet before the storm. Everyone involved in the kidnapping case knew they now had to find this creep before he struck again. Any hope that he had gotten bored and moved on was gone. Tina Tictin fit the profile of the victims perfectly. Theoretically, there were no specific suspects, and the effort to go down the list of usual suspects continued, but for Hallett there was only one target: Arnold Ludner.

Now Hallett was parked down the street from the odd residence of Arnold Ludner's sons. It was more of a compound, with a lot of land between it and any neighbors, and two separate houses on the lot, both two-bedroom, two-bath, with one house in front and one sitting way back on the two-acre lot. The county tax records showed one person owned both houses. His address was listed as the rear house. The common assumption was that the boys were renting the house in the front.

Rocky fidgeted in his rear compartment in case Hallett needed to hit his emergency button and open the rear door. He had no real plan, but he knew that both of the sons had extensive criminal histories. Between them, they'd been arrested sixteen times for everything from a marijuana possession to aggravated assault. One of the narcotics agents in the office had told him they were smart enough to fly under the radar, and they were tough. They cut off the ring finger of a pot distributor who owed them money. The laid-back marijuana dealers weren't used to that kind of violence. One of them had told a deputy, "If I wanted to get my ass kicked, I'd sell crack."

Hallett had a criminal intelligence analyst looking for a contact number for the owner of the houses, but so far it had proven difficult. His general idea was to find a way to hook up the two brothers on dope charges and use that as a way to loosen Arnold Ludner. No father, no matter how depraved he was, wanted to see his kids in trouble. At the very least, the third son, the attorney, might agree to let his father be interviewed so that Fusco could eliminate him as a suspect and focus his interest on other people.

Rocky sat in the back patiently as Hallett scanned the large piece of land with two houses through a set of Tasco binoculars. In the last hour he'd seen both of the Ludners as they came from the house to the Toyota Highlander parked next to it. One of the brothers was lanky, over six feet tall with long hair. The other was short and beefier. Even though there was only a year and a half's difference in their ages, the chubby one looked much older, with thinning hair. Hallett had to check twice to make sure he wasn't looking at Arnold Ludner Senior.

The taller brother carried something from the house and opened the rear door to the SUV. Hallett couldn't see clearly but it looked like he placed something in the back seat of the vehicle. Then both men got into the gold Highlander, and it slowly backed down the driveway.

Hallett said out loud, "It's show time."

.   .   .

Claire Perkins had been helping interview girlfriends and schoolmates of Tina Tictin. It was not an assignment that required her K-9 handling abilities or gave Smarty the chance to do something spectacular, but it was different from her normal days of patrol. John Fusco had recognized her ability to talk with Katie Ziegler and thought she might have a better chance of gaining information from one of these younger girls. The handsome detective had been an advocate for her to the sergeant and higher-ups. She hoped it was because of her ability and not due to their burgeoning personal relationship. She put the idea out of her mind as she interviewed girl after girl, desperate to find a shred of information that might tie the case together. So far no one had any idea who could have kidnapped and murdered Tina Tictin.

She knew the crime scene people were still out by the canal where Brutus had found the body, which they had somehow already identified. Claire was just glad she wasn't sitting out there doing nothing.

A break in the interviews gave her a chance to sit and think about the evening she spent with John Fusco. It was nothing serious, yet it had pointed out how lonely she had been. Did she really want to be one of the cops who had nothing but work in her life? She'd have to consider this more closely when she had more time, or when work wasn't dominating her life.

Claire didn't like leaving Smarty in the Tahoe. He was her partner, but she didn't want to scare the girls at this technical school not far from Tina's house. Smarty appeared relieved to rest quietly in the air-conditioned vehicle. Claire ignored her "no public affection" policy and leaned in to kiss Smarty on the head and pat him. He gave her a rare wag of his tail, sighing as if ready to sleep.

Claire and a young burglary detective who had been assigned with her had just finished the final interview and decided they had learned nothing new about Tina Tictin. She seemed to be a pleasant girl with an extreme wild streak.

Her cell phone rang, and she pulled it from the pouch on her tactical vest.

Tim Hallett didn't wait for her to speak. He just said, "Are you busy?"

"I just finished some interviews."

"I'm going to try a vehicle stop over near Fruity Acres. Can you give me a hand?"

"I'm on my way."

Tim Hallett added, "Let's use the cell phones and keep it off the radio."

Claire wasn't sure she liked the sound of that.

■   ■   ■

Darren Mori kept to his policy of shutting up and listening whenever he got a chance. Sergeant Greene had asked him if he minded sitting in on a meeting with John Fusco. It had nothing to do with his abilities as a dog handler. They just wanted another body in the meeting. He was smart enough to recognize it was a way to use manpower from another unit that was paid for from a federal grant. But he didn't mind the change of pace, and Brutus enjoyed the cool room and comfortable rug. He had curled up under the conference room table and had his head draped across Darren's boot. Every once in a while Darren could catch the sound of him breathing deeply as he snoozed.

Darren understood there were some politics going into the investigation. He'd caught on that homicide considered this part of their case, but Fusco wasn't going to give up that easy.

Fusco said, "I've been careful to cover myself in reports by mentioning Ludner's name here and there, but I never gave it the star billing. I don't want someone stealing our thunder." He looked like one of Darren's professors lecturing the class. "These sorts of games between the different squads go on all the time. You don't get to be a detective without being at least a little devious. No one wants to have a case scooped out from under them. The media never catches on to these kinds of maneuvers, and in some police agencies, neither does command staff. We're lucky at the sheriff's office. Everyone on our command staff has worked investigations at one point in their career. They understand. If not, and if they looked into something like this and decided we were holding up a potential homicide case, I'd find myself pushing a green and white cruiser in western Boca Raton, writing tickets to residents for putting the trash out too early."

Fusco had told Darren that by hosting the two probation officers in the sheriff's office's main conference room, he would have a home-field advantage. Fusco told Darren he was not finding his second encounter with probation officer Bill Slaton any more enjoyable than his first. In fact, it looked like being summoned into the sheriff's office had pissed off the portly probation officer.

Darren quickly realized it was the other probation officer who provided a key to John Fusco's investigation. The younger man was tall and dorky-looking and supervised one of Arnold Ludner's sons, who was still on probation for aggravated assault. Technically, Bill Slaton had nothing to do with this, but he had come along with the younger officer anyway.

The younger officer looked from Darren to Fusco and said, "He lives in a house in Fruity Acres with his brother. He's got about a year left on his sentence and hasn't really caused any problems."

Fusco asked, "How often do you go by the house?"

"I saw him out there about six months ago."

"Have you checked on him since then?"

"He came by the office once or twice."

"Are you telling me he's on probation and you see him about as often as I see my dentist?"

Now Slaton cut in and said, "You got no idea what our caseloads are like and what we're expected to do. You'd be better off if you worried about doing your job instead of worrying about *us* doing your job."

"What's that supposed to mean?"

"I told you that Arnold Ludner could be a good suspect in your kidnapping case. Now that you're finally getting serious about him, you're using us to harass his sons."

"All I'm trying to do is use all the resources available to solve a major crime. You think you could drop the attitude and jump on board?"

The younger probation officer said, "What do you need us to do?"

"You're allowed to search his house, aren't you?"

"Under certain circumstances. Why?" He was nervous and glanced over at his older co-worker for guidance. "I need a reason."

"Like PC?"

"No, probable cause isn't the issue. By policy we need a reason to search a probationer's house. I'd also need another probation officer with me and a police officer to stand by in case there's trouble."

Fusco raised his voice so much he ended up nearly shouting, "Screw policy. I got a dead girl on my hands and a killer who likes to kidnap young women."

Bill Slaton kept calm and said, "We can help you, but we should wait a little while."

"Wait for what?"

"Neither of the brothers are suspects, right?"

Fusco shook his head. "Our suspect is older than either of them."

Slaton said, "Shouldn't we wait to see if Arnold Ludner will talk?"

"Thanks to his prick of a son, we haven't been able to talk to him. Christ, we haven't even seen him in a week. The boys are just a way to get to the father. Give us a chance to speak to them. In reality, we have no specific strong suspect."

Slaton seemed to take this all in and shook his head, saying, "Yeah, we'll help. Maybe I can even talk to Ludner for you. I developed a decent rapport with him while he was on probation."

It was these sorts of arguments that Darren still didn't understand completely. He always thought that probation officers should be on the side of the police. This probation officer didn't seem to care for the police at all. Or maybe it was just Fusco. Darren could understand that.

When Hallett was on patrol he was known for making vehicle stops—not just to write tickets or meet pretty women, but to find a reason to investigate a suspicious car and make a felony arrest. It was his skill in building cases after a vehicle stop that got him promoted to the detective bureau so quickly.

Once he was in the K-9 unit, he quickly learned that Rocky gave him one more valuable tool to develop probable cause. The dog could smell a seed of marijuana from ten feet away. No matter how many times Hallett's brother had showered, Rocky still sat down next to him in alert mode every time he walked in the room. Once he saw the Ludner boys' Toyota Highlander break a traffic law he could start to build probable cause by using Rocky and his own experience to articulate why he thought they were committing a crime. He already figured, based on their record, it would be some kind of drug possession.

The older neighborhood they lived in, west of the city of West Palm Beach, was called Fruity Acres. Each lot was a minimum of one acre, and some much larger. At one time most of the lots had citrus trees on them, which had resulted in the name of the area. The neighborhood had a true old-Florida feel to it, with rough roads, pine trees, and plenty of rednecks.

He stayed well behind the Highlander until Claire rolled into the area. The two men had stopped at a run-down auto parts store on Southern Boulevard, then turned back into their own neighborhood. Hallett finally saw them roll through a stop sign and waited while Claire got a block ahead of them. He flipped on the Tahoe's extensive police light system and was surprised to see them pull over quickly.

Before he even got out of the car with Rocky, Claire pulled around the corner and parked directly in front of the stopped Toyota SUV. Hallett waited twenty seconds before he started to get out of the Tahoe. The short wait tended to make people nervous as their imaginations worked overtime. He hadn't called the stop out on the radio. He knew there were no current warrants on either of the men, so the less anyone knew about him getting involved with Ludner's family, the better.

Hallett opened the rear door and hooked a six-foot lead on Rocky. He assessed the Toyota as he and Rocky slowly approached. It looked like it had driven the Baja 500, with dings and paint scratches but no major damage.

The window was rolling down as Hallett and Rocky came to a stop. Hallett was surprised the dog hadn't alerted yet. He let Rocky sniff from the rear hatchback all the way to the door. Still nothing.

Behind the wheel was the younger man, Neil Ludner, who snapped, "Why'd you stop me?" His time in prison had honed his shitty attitude.

Hallett stayed calm and professional. "You didn't come to a complete stop at the sign back there." Hallett took the time to check out the two men in the interior of the SUV carefully. The other brother sat perfectly motionless with both of his hands on his lap. They'd been through this drill before and knew what drew attention from the police.

The driver said, "You're shitting me. It's a four-way stop. There's never any traffic back here."

"It's still the law to stop at stop signs. It doesn't say anything about whether a car is coming or not." He knew he had to play this by the book. "License and registration, please."

While Hallett engaged the driver, Claire brought Smarty out along the rear and other side of the vehicle. He caught the slight shake of her head, indicating Smarty had been no more successful than Rocky in detecting any drugs.

Hallett leaned back down and said, "Would you guys mind stepping out of the vehicle, please?"

The driver said, "Do you have a reason for us to get out?"

Hallett calmly said, "For our safety and yours, sir."

That was a hard reason to argue with, so both men got out of the car, steered clear of the two dogs on either side, and walked to the rear of the Highlander. Then the leaner brother, who had been driving, said, "What's this really all about?"

Hallett assessed the man, who was about thirty-three years old, and said, "Just waiting for the info on your license and registration and trying to figure out why you're in such a hurry."

Neil seemed to catch on then. He looked directly at Hallett and said in a loud, clear voice, "Am I under arrest or am I free to go?"

Some shithead jailhouse lawyer had come up with that phrase years ago, and regular lawyers, who sometimes weren't even as good as the jailhouse attorneys, started to tell their clients to use it whenever they were stopped by the police. They somehow believed it was a magical phrase that would force the police to either make an arrest or let their client go free.

Hallett said, "You'll be free to go in just a minute, sir." He couldn't believe how much he was enjoying this. Rocky moved back and forth across the car and passed the two men, knowing exactly what Hallett expected him to uncover. There was still no alert behavior from Rocky, but he would occasionally omit a low growl and stare at the two men with his ears back. The dog was as big a ham as Charlton Heston. This kind of acting could win him an Academy Award.

Hallett looked over at the other, heavyset brother and said, "What's your name, sir?"

This one was much cooler than his agitated sibling and panned his dark eyes over to Hallett, saying, "Arnold Ludner."

Hallett realized this man looked just like his father. Even chronologically, he looked older than he was. But unlike his father, up close this one had a hardened, street look to him. He had moved a lot of dope and collected a lot of money over the years.

He looked back at Neil Ludner and said, "Where do you live? Is the address on your license good?"

"Of course it's good. It's a crime to not change your license information if you move." He nodded his head down the street and said, "We live at the end and to the right. Why?"

Hallett had to think fast but managed, "You said you knew there was never any traffic at this four-way sign. I'm trying to figure out if I should cut you a break."

Neil mumbled, "Maybe I'll cut you a break sometime in the future, then."

"What's that supposed to mean?"

Now Neil Ludner knew he had caught his vague threat. He obviously liked the idea that the cops could be afraid of him. All he said was, "You don't want to know."

Hallett didn't want this moron thinking he'd gotten into his head. So he made a veiled threat of his own. Leaning in closer to the man, Hallett let Rocky step up and issue a deep, guttural growl. Then Hallett said, "I bet you don't want to show me now, do you, tough guy?"

This time it was the other brother, Arnold Ludner, who said, "Are we under arrest or are we free to go?"

Hallett wanted no official record of the stop, so he stepped back and said, "Have a safe day." He ached to call the mean-looking, heavier brother "Junior," but that would tip off that he knew their father.

■　　■　　■

Junior was tired from a long day with a lot of hassles, but somehow just thinking about Michelle Swirsky energized him. Now he found himself sitting outside the community college in the late afternoon again waiting for her mother's Honda to roll to the curb and Michelle to bounce out from the Health Science Building. As he had predicted, he'd become fixated on only one possible target and recognized his window for action was closing quickly. He was hoping this would give him enough to dream about for months or possibly years to come. She certainly seemed to be the total package. Pretty, athletic, innocent, and only nineteen years old. He wasn't sure he could find another target this perfect even if he wanted to.

He saw the blue Honda pull to the curb at almost the same time as it had the day before. Once again, Michelle scurried out from the building, waving to her mother as she approached, then hopped in the backseat of the nondescript car. He assumed it was to change into her Publix uniform. But as he followed, the car turned onto Military Trail in the opposite direction of Publix.

Junior liked using his surveillance skills. His simple car blended into almost any neighborhood. He knew the two women had no idea he was directly behind them. He followed the blue Honda as it pulled into a strip mall on the east side of the busy highway and realized it was very close to her house.

As he tried to figure out what they were doing here, Michelle popped out the rear door, this time wearing a karate gi tied with a brown belt. What an impressive girl. She really was full of surprises.

Junior felt an erection while he fantasized about teaching her all the tricks he'd learned while she wore the gi top. This girl was so different, she might move him in an entirely new direction.

He decided to wait during her class. It was so close to her house she might even walk home alone. Junior debated trying to grab a car from one of the nearby lots just to be prepared.

24

Tim Hallett sat with his partners at a picnic bench in Okeeheelee Park, wolfing down a sub for dinner and watching the last of the day's joggers finish up their workouts, while the dogs alternated between lounging and roughhousing in the grass. It was good to leave them untethered for a while every day so they got used to being around each other. When they first met, Brutus was subjected to several snarls and angry snaps by the more powerful Belgian Malinois and German Shepherd, but he had earned their respect by not backing down. Hallett wondered if Rocky thought of Brutus as "cute," too. God knows every human seemed to love Golden Retrievers. After so many training days where they all worked together, the dogs had formed a close bond just like their handlers.

Hallett finished his sub first. He wanted to get back on the road to run down leads, but didn't want to rush the other two. Claire was sending a text to someone between bites.

Darren looked across the table and said, "What's wrong, Tim? Still trying to find a home for Sponge and Bob? I thought Josh was opposed to their adoption."

"We're still negotiating. I have to admit they grow on you." Hallett hadn't realized he'd been brooding.

"Then what's bothering you?"

"The goddamn Ludners. I know those assholes were holding. That compound just screams *grow house*, and I saw them put something in the Highlander. Why didn't the dogs alert?" Rocky walked over and sat next to Hallett away from the other dogs.

Claire set down her phone and said, "We'll get him. We just have to approach it from another angle. At least we got a decent look at the two of them."

"But they saw us, too. And they saw the dogs. That could jeopardize something we might do in the future. They're not stupid. They know they have to be careful." Hallett noticed Rocky sitting gingerly, almost the way he did in alert mode. "The two Ludner boys are like my stoner brother Rocky alerts on constantly."

All three of the deputies laughed. They'd heard Hallett's stories about his brother.

Hallett noticed Rocky stand and walk in a circle, then sit down again like he was alerting. He dismissed it as some sort of game the dog was playing.

Hallett said, "Even an old homeless guy I met knew enough to be concerned about Rocky. He sort of admitted he was . . ." Hallett just stared at Rocky, unable to continue speaking.

Claire said, "Tim, what's wrong?"

"That's it."

"What's it?"

Hallett stared off into space while he pieced it all together, or, more correctly, after Rocky had pieced it all together. Hallett said, "The homeless guy was holding meth. None of our dogs are trained to pick up on meth. But Rocky can smell pot from a block away."

Claire snapped her fingers and said, "You're a genius."

Darren looked between his partners and said, "I'm not following you guys."

Hallett said, "The Ludners are making meth, not growing pot. That's why Rocky didn't alert."

Darren said, "You need to thank your brother for the training tip."

Hallett was excited to investigate his theory and was just about to say they should head out when his phone rang, and he was surprised to hear Lori Tate say, "Any chance you're free tonight?"

Claire saw his face and figured out who was calling. She said, "We need some down time. The dogs need rest. We can go after the Ludners tomorrow."

Hallett smiled. That was a good partner.

■   ■   ■

Junior watched Michelle Swirsky step out of the dojo, now wearing shorts and a T-shirt with her gi bundled and tied tightly with her brown belt under one arm. She had on a pair of running shoes and started to jog away from the school, holding the rolled-up gi like a football. Wow, even after karate this girl wasn't satisfied with her fitness. Junior was bowled over.

Junior started the car but stayed in his parking spot and watched her run out onto Military Trail and turn right. She came back past him on the sidewalk, and he realized she was running home. It was only about a mile away. Quickly he checked the pistol in his belt. He even had a plan already if he needed it. He couldn't believe he was acting so rashly.

Could he do it? The idea itself was thrilling to the point of compulsion. He saw this kind of behavior every day at work and thought he was above it, but as he considered Michelle and the things he'd do with her, he couldn't stop himself.

Junior backed his car out, pulled out of the lot, and crossed two lanes of traffic on Military Trail so he could get ahead of Michelle. She was running along the sidewalk, and he kept his eyes open for the likely street she'd turn on. All of the blocks in her neighborhood crisscrossed, so he picked the next one, thinking she'd want to get off the main road as quickly as possible.

His heart pounded. He could see the pattern of blood vessels in his eyes with each beat, it was so powerful. His weight had caused him several problems, including high blood pressure, and for the first time he was worried the excitement might kill him. But what a way to go.

He pulled into the side lot of an auto parts store and killed the engine and lights. He could just see her on the sidewalk. If she didn't turn here he could always pull down another block or two, but he felt confident she'd make the turn. His plan was simple. Get out of the car, get next to her, and show her the gun when she came within arm's reach. He'd worry about everything else once she was in the passenger seat.

This made sense. She'd overcome so much in her background that she was too impressive a target to pass up. He felt like a cat stalking a bird as she jogged closer and closer. It would only be a minute or so. He swallowed even though his mouth was dry.

He realized this was the only thing he lived for now.

■   ■   ■

Tim Hallett sat across from Lori Tate at a casual seafood sports bar in Lake Worth. Like most other minor towns in South Florida, the small city Lake Worth had worked hard to upgrade its downtown and create an atmosphere that would attract tourists and locals with cash to spend. The problem was that most of the city was a shithole. Hallett had his Glock under his shirt and could see the Chevy Tahoe with Rocky in his compartment only a few feet away, parked directly in front of the restaurant.

Hallett said, "I'm sorry I didn't dress better. These are the extra clothes I keep in the work truck. It's too long a ride out to Belle Glade to change."

Lori giggled and placed her hand over his on the table. She looked out the window at the Tahoe and said, "You look great, but is Rocky okay?"

Hallett smiled and said, "I have a portable DVD playing *Marley and Me.* He's content." He often used the excuse of Rocky needing to eat or rest as a way of getting out of social commitments, but at this moment he was glad he'd gone through with the date. It had been a long time.

"This is nice," he said. "The crime scene must've worn you out today."

Lori said, "It took an hour to shower off the dirt and mud. It's probably the first time I ever got sunburned at work."

"I saw one of the homicide guys is working with Fusco on the kidnapping case."

"Danny Weil?"

"Yeah, that's him. Young guy, tall, good-looking."

Lori said, "Sounds like something *he* would tell you." They shared a laugh over that. Then Lori said, "He cut out early to see if he could get a jump on things."

"Like what things?"

"He never tells us. He tends to rely on his good looks and personality to get things done."

Hallett shrugged and said, "If it works for him."

"It works on some girls, but not me." She winked at him.

In addition to being pretty, this girl had a decent sense of humor. Hallett found himself starting to relax and really enjoying himself.

He said, "I'm hoping the sergeant lets me do more on the case."

"Has she been keeping you from it?"

"She's limited my involvement with the suspects. On a big case like this there's always a lot to do, but I don't think the sergeant believes the dogs will come up with the information that would break this case."

"I'd say Darren Mori and his Golden Retriever brought in quite a bit of information when they found the body at the canal."

Hallett nodded, conceding that point. "I'm not sure she believes Rocky and I will break the case. Rocky is trained to find explosives and narcotics and apprehend suspects. Part of the grant money we got requires the dogs be trained in multiple disciplines. It's sort of an experiment and is really innovative."

Lori leveled a stare at him and said, "If you had to do it all over again, would you change what happened with Arnold Ludner the first time you arrested him?"

Although he often thought about this, no one had ever directly asked him that question. He looked into Lori's pretty eyes and beautiful face as he thought about his answer—and he couldn't resist thinking about Crystal and her kiss at the same time. Finally, he said, "No, I wouldn't change how I dealt with Arnold Ludner. No matter what, I know that little girl is alive today at least in part because of what I did. There's sometimes a big difference between doing things by the book and doing things that are right. Anyone who ever looked at that little girl's face never criticized my actions."

Lori let a big smile break across her face. "Do you keep in touch with the girl and her family?"

Now it was Hallett's turn to smile. "Every birthday and Christmas. And I hope it never ends."

■　　■　　■

Junior saw Michelle turn down the street, so he placed his left hand on the door handle, preparing to slip out of the car quickly. He already had the Beretta in his right hand. He had evolved since the first girl he'd surprised more than two and a half years ago. It was a miracle he hadn't been caught in those early attempts. Although he knew everything he needed to about his targets, he had not prepared nearly as well. He didn't understand police investigative techniques, either. Now he had a much better handle on both the victims' mentality and the status of police investigations.

He slipped his hand off the handle and used it to mash the button to roll down his window. She didn't even notice him. No one ever did. It was almost time, and he felt the excitement surge through him. It made him feel young again. She crossed over to the sidewalk on his side of the street, still behind his car, which made his plan more awkward but not nearly impossible.

Just as he was about to pop out of the car, a set of headlights came around the corner and a yellow car slowed. He heard someone yell from the passenger seat as Michelle turned, smiled, and waved.

Now he saw that the car was a newer Mustang. He was helpless and had to sit there like a statue as the Mustang passed his car on one side and Michelle jogged past on the sidewalk. No one in the vehicle or Michelle paid any attention to the lonely man sitting in the parked car. Then the car pulled closer to the sidewalk as the passenger chatted with Michelle.

He had missed his chance and would have to wait. But the urge was so strong it physically hurt him. Now his only focus was to grab her as soon as possible.

allett liked the idea that they all started the shift as a team in the detective bureau. He didn't care if it was late afternoon instead of first thing in the morning. An added bonus was that John Fusco appeared to be frazzled to the point of exhaustion.

It was Sergeant Greene who brought order to the friendly gathering. She said, "The analysts have been working overtime and found out a boatload of information about the house where Arnold Ludner's sons live."

Hallett, along with everyone else, picked up a pen to make notes. The criminal intelligence analysts at the sheriff's office, like most analysts in police departments, were one of the most valuable resources that never got any glory. Using computers and contacts, the analysts gathered information on suspects that no detective could ever uncover, from ancient court cases to links between telephone numbers. A good analyst was as valuable as five detectives.

The sergeant continued, "Both of the houses are owned by a corporation named New Deal Florida Development. The corporate office is the rear house on the property. One of the listed corporate officers is Joe Ludner, Arnold's son. You guys all remember the pain-in-the-ass attorney."

Claire said, "You think the dad is in the rear house?"

Fusco stepped in. "I got the probation officer to agree to a thorough home visit in the morning. The rear house is not listed as a residence, but if we find something, we might be able to push it." Fusco turned to Hallett and said, "Will the Canine Assist Team be able to help us? Can the dogs detect something in the rear house if we're at the front house?"

Hallett felt a stab of panic, wondering if Fusco or the sergeant somehow knew that he had made the vehicle stop and tried to get Rocky to alert on the Ludners' vehicle. After a moment, he said, "We can oblige, but if these idiots are making a chemical-based drug like ecstasy or meth, the dogs won't alert. We don't train them on it. It was a choice Ruben made. Too many extra scents, and he was worried about the harsh chemicals."

Fusco said, "These assholes are pot and coke dealers. Why would you think it might be meth?"

Hallett shrugged and said, "Just a hunch."

Sergeant Greene said, "What if we use some of the federal money that's being poured into your unit for surveillance of the compound tonight? We can get an idea of the activity at the place before Fusco arrives in the morning. Maybe we'll get lucky and see them doing something that will give us probable cause." She looked around the table at the three K-9 officers, who all nodded their heads. No one would miss a chance at something like this.

As the meeting broke up and Fusco scooped folders and photographs into his arms, Darren Mori said, "What's wrong, Fusco? You seem rushed."

The detective ran a shaky hand through his thinning black hair and said, "I got homicide breathing down my neck, and those assholes are waiting to swoop in."

Sergeant Greene said to the three K-9 officers, "Go get 'em."

Hallett smiled at the way she said it. It sounded like she was talking directly to the dogs.

∎　∎　∎

Tim Hallett was sitting on the far edge of the vacant lot behind the compound where the Ludners lived. He'd been scanning the entire lot with a high-powered telescope the marine unit used at inlets to spy on smugglers. Rocky explored the area around them, sometimes pawing at the grass and sniffing out a queasy-making treasure like a dead snake and a half-eaten Twinkie. Hallett had to turn to him and say, "Don't you dare eat that."

Rocky dropped the Twinkie and hung his head as he sat next to Hallett. It was clear the dog wanted to do something active. Hallett knew the feeling well. He felt like he had not accomplished anything in the last few days.

Claire walked over from her Tahoe and said, "See anything at all?"

Hallett didn't remove his right eye from the high-powered telescope. "I think there's an adult male near the rear house. I haven't been able to get a good look at him because of the hedge and a low wall next to the house. He's working on something in the grass." He stepped aside so Claire could slip in and look through the telescope.

After a few moments of focusing on the man in blue jeans she said, "He's gardening, or pruning the bushes right next to the house. It looks like he could get up and go into the house without us seeing his face."

Hallett nodded and said, "That's what I thought, too. If there was just some way we could make him stand up and look behind him, I could at least tell if it was Arnold Ludner or not."

Darren had been using binoculars to scan the front house. He said, "I see the sons by the other house. Do you suppose there's a renter in the back?"

"That's something we should find out before Fusco goes in with the probation officers in the morning."

Claire scratched Rocky's head and said to her partners, "Any ideas on how we could make the man stand and look behind him?"

Rocky barked, hopped to his feet, and trotted around the three deputies.

Darren said, "What's gotten into him?"

Hallett smiled and said, "He just had another brilliant idea. I swear to God Ruben is rubbing off on me. I now understand canine. Even when it has a Belgian accent."

■   ■   ■

Junior had decided tonight was the night he would take action with Michelle Swirsky, no matter what happened. He had to relieve the urge that had built in him relentlessly since the moment he saw her jog down the street, chatting with someone in the slow-moving Mustang. The way he felt at this moment, he was almost sorry he didn't shoot the driver of the Mustang and take Michelle anyway. But that wasn't the way he operated. He liked to think he was too smart for that, but lately his basic instincts had been taking over instead.

He was too late to catch her at school and wondered if she would be at the Publix tonight. The poor girl never seemed to take an evening off. It was time she learned about things other than karate and work. He liked to think he was going to let her go like he had some of the other girls, but something in his head told him the only chance he had to regain this feeling he constantly craved was to go all the way again.

The fantasies he had about Tina Tictin revolved around choking her more than anything else he had done. The power that had surged through him lasted for days and her body proved he mattered in the world. He had the power of life and death. Junior would never forget the moment he saw life flicker out of Tina's eyes.

He knew he would have to do the same thing to Michelle Swirsky.

■   ■   ■

Darren Mori said, "That's the craziest idea I have ever heard. The dogs aren't trained for something like this." He liked thinking outside of the box as much as the next guy, but he never wanted to put one of the dogs at risk needlessly.

Tim Hallett grasped him by the shoulders and almost yelled, "I'm telling you, this is a great idea. We let one of the dogs run past the guy and he'll jump up and look behind him. I'll be able to see his face and tell whether it's Arnold Ludner or not."

Darren knew Hallett wasn't trying to be aggressive, but it was still intimidating to look up at his taller partner. He hadn't seen this much passion in Hallett since they had started in the unit.

Claire said, "It's almost like the dog would be undercover."

"Exactly." Hallett turned so he could make his argument to both his partners at once. "Ruben wants us to think differently, expect more. That's all I'm trying to do. We really do have smart dogs and only use a fraction of their abilities."

Darren glanced quickly at Rocky, then Brutus, and then over to the Chevy Tahoe where Smarty was in his rear secure compartment. "But which dog do we use?"

Claire shrugged and said, "Sorry, but I couldn't promise Smarty wouldn't bite him. Especially if he smells something else, like dope."

Darren said, "Brutus is a seeker. He loves to find stuff, but he wouldn't go in without me. Maybe I could change clothes and wander through, acting lost."

Hallett shook his head and said, "That defeats the purpose of using the dog. I think if Claire went around the block and waited on the other side of the property, Rocky would run directly to her. I know he could do it." Hallett turned and looked at his dog and said, "You can do it, can't you, boy?"

Rocky ran back and forth in a tight square, energized for the game. He looked ready to do anything. Hallett kneeled down and took off the dog's harness, rubbing his hair so it all stood up in a uniform pattern.

Hallett said, "I'm just afraid that if Ludner sees him later, he might recognize Rocky, or if the guy over there is one of the sons, he might remember Rocky from the vehicle stop. He is a memorable dog."

Then Darren Mori had his own brilliant idea. He looked at his partners and said, "Hang on a minute." He hustled to the rear of his Tahoe and rifled through his personal equipment locker. He found what he was looking for and jogged back to his partners with Brutus right next to him the whole time. He held up the can and said, "He doesn't have to be a mostly brown dog. We could give him all kinds of black patches."

Hallett looked at the can and said, "What in the hell is that?"

Claire said, "It's his stupid spray paint for his bald spot."

Darren protested, saying, "Technically it's spray-on hair. And Tim didn't even realize I had a bald spot because of it."

Hallett looked at him and smiled. "I'm sorry, Darren, but I always noticed your bald spot. If you're stuck directly in front of my nose, it's all I see. I just never said anything about the spray paint."

Darren almost screamed, "It's not freaking spray paint, it's a special product for hair. Thank God for Ron Popeil."

Claire said, "Who's that?"

Darren said, "He's the inventor. The guy is a genius. He's invented everything from pocket fishing rods to slow-roasting ovens. But this weird invention of his can make Rocky look any way we want him to." Darren kneeled down next to Rocky and sprayed a hand-sized black mark along his back and side. Then he sprayed half of his head and an ear. He stepped back to admire his work, saying, "Now, no one would recognize him." He glanced over at Hallett in case his partner was about to punch him.

26

Tim Hallett didn't want to admit how nervous he was letting Rocky go, but it was only for a few minutes, and Claire Perkins had driven around to the far side of the property, so, in theory, he would run directly to her and Smarty.

Hallett kneeled down to stroke Rocky's back. He was careful to avoid the black spot Darren had painted on him. Hallett had to admit it made him look entirely different. It probably wasn't necessary, but it'd make for a good story later on. Hallett said in a low voice near Rocky's ear, "Okay boy, just run to Claire and Smarty. Run and bark. Your two favorite things in the whole world."

He scratched his fingers down the dog's spine the way Rocky liked, but just before he was about to let the dog run, Darren Mori said, "Hang on."

Hallett looked over his shoulder at his partner using binoculars.

Darren said, "The Highlander is pulling out."

"Can you see who's in it?"

"One driver. It's the oldest son. Doesn't look like anyone else is inside."

Hallett said, "He's a little bit of a badass."

"But the other one is on probation, right?"

"At this point it doesn't matter who's on probation. I guarantee you John Fusco is walking in there in the morning."

"Amen to that."

Hallett said, "Can I send Rocky now?"

Darren answered with a quick nod of his head.

Hallett released Rocky and called out after him, "Run, boy, run. Run to Claire and Smarty." On the far side of the house, more than a block away, he could just see Claire with Smarty standing in the road so Rocky would know where to run.

Hallett used the thick telescope to focus on the man kneeling by the rear house. Rocky ran so fluidly it looked effortless. He seemed like the fastest dog Hallett had ever seen, though he knew greyhounds ran faster. It had to be an effect of looking through the high-powered telescope. Hallett mumbled, "C'mon, boy, come on."

As Rocky approached the house he slowed slightly, and Hallett could hear him bark at exactly the right time. It was like taking a photograph. The man sprang to his feet and twisted to look behind him at Rocky. Hallett saw his profile, then his full face. At the same time he and Darren said, "That's him."

Ludner screamed something at Rocky, who just kept running.

About half a minute later Claire came over the radio and said, "I've got him, Tim."

Hallett stood, turned, and smiled at Darren Mori, saying, "Now, that really was a special canine assist."

■   ■   ■

Claire Perkins waited on the opposite side of the compound from Tim Hallett. Rocky sat in the rear compartment with Smarty. They enjoyed just hanging out sometimes. It was like buddies who went out for a beer, but in this case they just sat together in the cool compartment on the quilt her mother had made for Smarty. Rocky looked ridiculous with the black hair paint sprayed over his face and on his side, but she couldn't deny it was a hell of a good idea and proved how adaptable their unit could be.

She'd been working closely with Smarty to ease his drive to attack. It was difficult for dog trainers to get past some of the innate abilities and instincts of certain breeds of dogs. German Shepherds had been bred as herding dogs but had a protective streak, as well as an aggressive one. Often people thought training a dog was as simple as giving him a treat when he did something right.

For a police officer of smaller stature, like herself, it was important that she and Smarty trained on the basics of obedience. She worked on the simple commands during the day and practiced in their home when it was just her and Smarty. She wondered who'd picked such an appropriate name as Smarty and realized it could've been one of the dog breeder's children who didn't even realize Smarty wasn't a real American name. The more time she spent with him, the more control she had over the dog's instincts.

She was really enjoying teaching the hand signals and musical notes to Smarty. But despite all that, it was too risky to allow Smarty loose in public without a strong lead attached to his harness.

Claire especially liked assignments out of the ordinary, like this one. K-9 units rarely conducted surveillance. She wanted to be challenged. That was why she had gone into police work. She never expected one of the challenges to be the fact that she was a petite female. But she didn't mind proving herself day in and day out. Sergeant Greene was a great role model. It was just a fluke that Claire now worked on her squad. No one thought of Sergeant Greene as a woman boss. She was just a respected, hard-working boss. That was something Claire could aspire to.

One thing she was learning about surveillance was you had plenty of time to be alone with your thoughts. For no reason at all one of the thoughts that popped into her head was John Fusco. The smug but attractive detective probably had that effect on more than a few women around the sheriff's office. Right now she was glad she had his attention. She knew he'd arrive here on scene in the morning, and she intended to look nice when he did.

That was something most male cops never had to consider.

■   ■   ■

Junior was annoyed he'd been delayed so long that he'd missed Michelle leaving school. It was unavoidable. It would have to be to throw him off schedule. Now he had nothing in his brain but Michelle. The image of her nude body splayed out in front of him made the rest of the world pale by comparison. He had run past her house and seen the blue Honda in the driveway, but that really didn't mean anything. Her mother tended to pick her up and drop her off places instead of bringing her home every day.

Then he got lucky. He had parked in front of the Publix where he'd seen her working and sure enough, after only a few minutes, she followed an elderly woman out of the store, pushing a basket with a ridiculously small payload. Maybe the old lady just wanted company on her walk back out to her Buick Riviera.

Junior surveyed the area. There seemed to be constant foot and vehicle traffic in and out of the parking lot, plus he wasn't certain about security cameras. It would be a tremendous risk, but right now he was wondering if that wasn't his only option. Wait till she was coming back from delivering someone's groceries, pull alongside, point the gun at her, and get on with his life. The biggest flaw in that plan was the fact that he was driving his own car once again.

The other day Michelle had left work around seven thirty. That didn't him give much time to make his move. He felt his stomach growl and decided all of this worrying was giving him an ulcer. As his grandfather back in Indiana used to say, it was time to shit or get off the pot.

27

Hallett took a few minutes off the surveillance to drive Rocky to a car wash down the street and use one of the low-powered hoses and a bottle of baby shampoo to wash the black hair-spray paint off of him. He didn't want to leave it on too long in case the dog had a reaction to it. Rocky enjoyed the short bath. He always did. Sometimes Hallett wondered if the dog got dirty just so he would give him a bath. The dog's favorite activity was a bath with Josh. Sometimes Hallett just put the two of them in the shower with a bottle of baby shampoo and turned them loose.

As Hallett scrubbed away, he felt a cold ball in the pit of his stomach about Arnold Ludner. Had he seen only what he wanted to see? Had he pushed the investigation toward a possible suspect based on his personal feelings? But when it came down to it, this was just a hunch. A gut feeling. And he was basing his entire career on it.

He also wanted to be in on the arrest, or at least have his team on it. The idea that homicide had entered the fray annoyed him. The guys in homicide could be like the FBI sometimes. A lot of information went into them, but not a lot came out. He knew that Lori Tate would keep him updated if she heard anything, but he didn't like to use her that way. He thought he might have feelings for her. She was the first woman he had ever wanted to meet Josh.

This was going to be one long night.

■ ■ ■

Junior saw Michelle step outside the Publix holding her purse, and he knew it was quitting time. Junior had missed his opportunity again. He kept an eye open for her mother's blue Honda. It wasn't quite eight o'clock, and he was surprised how traffic had died in the lot. He figured the retired people in the area didn't like to stay out too much past dark.

As he was gazing at her face through the windshield, he saw a brilliant smile and a wave, expecting the Honda to pull up. To his surprise, the yellow Mustang he'd seen before rolled to a fast stop directly in front of her, and she jumped in quickly.

Junior regained his concentration and focused on the Mustang, catching just a glimpse of the driver. It was a young man with long dark hair and a wide grin. This was a completely new wrinkle. The son of a bitch was trying to steal Junior's thunder. There was no way he could let this happen. He didn't care what he had to do.

■　　■　　■

Darren Mori was bored. He had never been on a long surveillance before, and it blew. Maybe his guidance counselor in high school was right and he had ADD. He didn't like to sit still for long, even with Brutus resting in the front passenger seat of the Tahoe. He was waiting while Tim Hallett bathed Rocky. Darren had already brushed Brutus out, and the dog was curled up and comfortably snoozing.

This sort of duty was not what he'd envisioned when the Canine Assist Team was formed. He wasn't sure what he'd thought they'd be doing, but sitting on the street, watching a house where no one moved, was not his idea of active police work.

He liked to train with Brutus. He especially liked the fact that they had a guy like Ruben Vasquez teaching him all aspects of searching for drugs or cadavers. He knew in his heart how special Brutus was. He was smart, tough, and talented, but Darren wished he had a dog that could bite someone. He never got to be at the front of the search, because they needed the patrol dogs for that. Brutus was a fantastic tracker—it was a natural ability for him that had been easy to develop— but he couldn't apprehend. Darren never got the hot calls of a fleeing robbery suspect because no robber was ever scared of a Golden Retriever.

Looking over at Brutus, though, he knew he had found his partner. Even if they offered him a vicious Pit Bull, he wouldn't trade Brutus now.

They'd been through too much together and had too strong a connection. At least he didn't have to call him Bingo.

Kim was occupying more of his waking thoughts. They had only been on one date, but this girl was special. Darren decided he could fire off a few texts while everything was quiet. He gazed down at his iPhone and wondered if he was in love. He didn't care; he just wanted to talk to this new girl he'd just met. He typed in *hey, what r u doing?*

■　　■　　■

Junior had been shocked to see the Mustang pull into the strip mall at the end of Michelle's street. This wasn't just a simple ride home. These two had plans. She was obviously trying to be sneaky.

Now he was parked down the street from Michelle and her boyfriend. He could see the two individual silhouettes even in the dark and decided he could wait without acting unless the two of them disappeared from view. He couldn't let that snotty bastard steal what was his. He hated the idea of a punk like that having the kind of experience Junior never did as a teenager. His odd sexual history was a blur to him. He couldn't recall ever asking a girl his own age out.

The teacher who had seduced him, Miss Trooluck, was a clear memory, and he had used it as a fantasy for many years. He couldn't recall a cute cheerleader from high school. This kid with Michelle made his blood boil. He reached down and patted the Beretta in his waistband. He could even envision the *Palm Beach Post* headlines the next day. It would only mention one dead at the scene, a male with a bullet hole in his head. But that made him wonder if Michelle would be too traumatized to do anything else.

As Junior watched, the two young people just kept talking, or at least staying on their own side of the car. The whole situation made Junior wonder if she was even allowed to be in the Mustang. There was a chance she might walk home from there. That meant there was a possibility he could make his move tonight.

28

Junior was growing impatient when the passenger door finally opened. He checked his watch. It was just before nine when Michelle Swirsky stepped out of the Mustang and the boy pulled away slowly. She stood in the shadow of the building and waved good-bye as he honked his horn twice and burned rubber onto Military Trail. Now she was alone and had to walk to the end of her street to get home. Finally, his moment had arrived. She would have to walk directly past him.

Junior had pulled in at an angle in the parking lot of the plaza down the street. The most reasonable path she would walk would take her directly past him. He swiveled his head quickly in all directions to ensure there were no witnesses. This was it. There was no escape. He was giddy with excitement, his hand trembling as it touched the butt of his pistol. He savored the feeling and now had his eyes glued on the tall, athletic form of Michelle. As soon as the Mustang was out of sight she crossed the street just as he had expected, then turned to walk toward her house.

He remained motionless in the car, watching her through the rear-view mirror as she slowly strolled closer and closer. Michelle looked like she was daydreaming. His heart pounded in his chest like a piston. Sweat poured off his forehead and soaked his underarms.

When she was at the rear of his car, he jerked the handle and popped out. The surprise was total. He had her by the upper arm before she realized someone was near her. He didn't even bother with his pistol.

That was his mistake.

With no windup, Michelle threw an elbow hard into Junior's side. The blow knocked the wind out of him and forced him back toward the car. Before he could regain his balance she threw a knee, then a front kick directly into his abdomen, dropping him into the open door and onto the front seat.

Michelle grabbed the open door with both hands and slammed it onto his outstretched left ankle. The agony made him grunt like a pig as it shot up his leg and connected with the pain radiating from his cracked ribs. This was not going the way he had planned.

Junior struggled to sit up and see Michelle darting away toward her house. Even if he managed to get the car rolling, she'd be at her front door before he caught her. He reached for his pistol, wondering if he could make the shot. She couldn't have seen his face clearly, but she was the first witness who knew anything about him at all.

He sat straight in the seat, fighting through the pain, and squealed the tires backing out of the spot and speeding away from the area. Every breath was agony, and his left ankle throbbed. He would have to deal with Michelle Swirsky, not only to keep her from being a witness but because he owed her big-time.

■   ■   ■

Darren Mori didn't really want to interact with this crowd. He wanted to listen and learn. John Fusco seemed to sense that and pulled him to the side, saying, "I wore one of my best suits. To use one of your own terms, I wanted to impress upon everyone that I was the alpha dog on this case. Remember that, Kato, you can make a big impression with your clothes. Even a uniform if you wear it right." As he said it, Fusco brushed something off of Darren's K-9 T-shirt. He didn't mind; Fusco seemed like he was sincerely trying to help him.

Then the detective turned and said, "You guys did a great job last night."

Darren realized this was another mind game and Fusco was really saying, *Step aside, now. The real cops are here.*

Right now they were on the street behind the compound where Arnold Ludner and his sons lived. The three K-9 handlers were tired. At the moment, they all stood quietly or slouched against one of their unmarked Chevy Tahoes.

Fusco said, "We should be able to cut you guys loose pretty quick.

As soon as the probation jerk-offs get here, we'll take a quick run through the property and see what we can find."

Tim Hallett said, "You'll find Arnold Ludner. We saw him last night, and he hasn't left the property since."

"I *hope* we find Arnold Ludner, and I *hope* he confesses to all the shit that's gone down the last few weeks. But experience in the detective bureau has taught me that you never know what's going to happen." Fusco turned to look at a Ford Taurus as it pulled to a stop next to their group. "You guys sit tight while we figure out what we're gonna do next." He looked at Darren and said, "Why don't you back me up?"

Darren and Fusco turned to greet the probation officers. They looked like a comedy team walking toward them. The younger one was tall and geeky with wavy hair, and next to him was a man who was mostly round and squat with a Pacers hat covering his thinning hair. His bloodshot eyes and shambling walk screamed "alcoholic." Both men were dressed in similar cheap white dress shirts with short sleeves and clip-on ties and hiking boots.

Fusco leaned in and said, "I can't remember the tall guy's name. The shorter one is Bill Slaton. He's an asshole. Just take any shit he gives us now. We need them." As the probation officers approached, Fusco pointed at their feet and said, "You guys look ready for the Appalachian Trail."

Slaton answered, saying, "We learned to wear heavy shoes during a search when one of our guys stepped on a syringe that popped right through his loafer."

They joined the group. Slaton looked directly at Tim Hallett and said, "Are you the guy that screweded up Ludner's case and allowed him that sweet deal?"

Darren thought it was out of line, but Hallett's scowl shut down the probation officer.

Claire Perkins stared down the testy PO. "He also saved a girl's life."

"But did he cost others?"

Fusco stepped in and said, "Let's get this show on the road."

Slaton's eyes cut over to the dog handlers and then back to Fusco. "We don't need a parade going in there. All we need is one uniformed cop to show his authority and let them know we have some backup."

Fusco said, "I'm coming in, too."

"I don't see what you can add. You got no uniform. You're dressed just like us."

"First of all, I am *not* dressed just like you. This is a damn thirteen-hundred-dollar suit. Secondly, it's my case and I'm going in. It's not open for discussion."

Darren noted Slaton's pissed-off look and dismissive attitude.

Fusco turned to face the entire group. "I need one of you guys to come with us." He looked each one of them in the face. "I want to impress the Ludner brothers right off the bat with a show of authority." He strolled past each K-9 unit like a general inspecting troops. He stopped and winked at Claire. "You look too good to scare anyone." Then he stared down Hallett. "Too much history with the family." Fusco looked at Darren and said, "Kato, you and your dog . . ."

Darren said, "Brutus."

"Whatever. You and Brutus are in the box. We need you to come with us." Fusco looked at Hallett and Claire and said, "You guys cover each side of the compound."

Darren liked the idea of being in the front of the pack where the action happened. It was a new experience.

29

Tim Hallett didn't like standing by. He'd never been one of the guys to hang in the rear of the pack. He disagreed with Sergeant Greene about using CAT because the federal grant paid their salaries. They were a specialized unit, and the dogs' abilities were not being used. But he was an Indian, not a chief. Now he and Claire were strategically parked on each side of the compound in case there was a problem or someone ran. And he was annoyed that John Fusco got to go into the house and do all the close-up work. But his days as a detective were over, and he was slowly coming to grips with it.

Rocky was edgy. He'd been restless in his compartment until Hallett let him out and hooked him to a short lead with a quick release. Did the dog know something? As part of his preparation for taking the assignment in the K-9 unit, Hallett had done a lot of reading on dogs in general and police service dogs in particular. There were hundreds of accounts of dogs sensing things before they happened, and there were a few instances where dog handlers swore the dog was psychic. One handler in Boston said his police service dog flipped out at the precise moment a fire broke out in the officer's home twenty miles away. The dog kept acting oddly until the officer called home, and the phone woke his sleeping wife and children, saving them.

Hallett wanted to believe in these supernatural abilities, but for the moment, it was all he could do to understand the actual, normal abilities Rocky possessed. He rubbed the dog's back, trying to calm him down. What was Rocky trying to convey? Was he psychic? This was one of those questions Hallett wasn't prepared to answer. He wished Reuben was with him to interpret what Rocky was trying to say.

He thought back to the day he found Katie Ziegler curled up in the cane field. How young and terrified she had looked. Now she was safe because they did what they had to. He wanted to help more. Take it a step further and make a whole bunch of young women safe. He had to shake these jitters. Was he just convincing himself Ludner was the right suspect? He'd have to leave that up to John Fusco to decide. Either way, Ludner needed to be interviewed to find out what he had to say.

Rocky let out a nervous bark.

Hallett rubbed the dog's head and said, "I'm with you, buddy. Let's get this show on the road."

■   ■   ■

This was the closest Darren Mori had ever gotten to an actual criminal investigation. He'd had to investigate a few incidents when he was a road patrolman, write reports and interview witnesses to a traffic accident or take a homeowner's report of a burglary, but he really didn't have much experience interviewing hardened criminals.

The two probation officers—funny-looking guys who didn't seem very happy about helping the police—knocked on the door with John Fusco directly behind them. Darren and Brutus were on the walkway to the front door, close enough to hear and see everything that went on. Ruben Vasquez had taught him to listen to Brutus, but he also learned to listen to everyone else around him. He'd probably learned more in the last year just by keeping his mouth shut and his mind focused than he had in his entire life leading up to his assignment on the Canine Assist Team.

The door opened and the younger of the Ludner brothers stood staring at all four men. He was in his early thirties and almost six feet tall. One of the probation officers was at least four inches taller than Neil Ludner, and the other was a couple of inches shorter. But Darren noticed how the drug dealer's attention was focused on Fusco, Brutus, and him, instead of the two probation officers.

After a moment the drug dealer said, "What the hell is this all about?"

The tall probation officer said, "Hi, Neil, we're just doing a check. Mind if we come in and look around?" He made a slight movement to step into the house but was blocked by the drug dealer.

Slaton was much more aggressive. "Step out of the way, we're coming inside."

Darren could see the drug dealer dig his heels into the floor as he said, "Why're the cops here?"

The tall probation officer said, "Per our policy, for safety reasons."

Neil Ludner said, "Let me call my brother."

Slaton pointed past his shoulder and said, "He's sitting on the couch behind you."

"No, my other brother. My attorney." The way he enunciated the word "attorney" made it sound like a threat.

Darren was getting sucked into the staccato bantering and enjoying the show. Brutus sat quietly at his side, showing little interest. If there wasn't something to find, Brutus wasn't engaged in a situation. Smarty would've been barking and snarling as he sensed the aggression and tension growing.

John Fusco pushed his way past the probation officers, saying, "You can call anyone you want, but we're coming in right now." He edged an arm past the drug dealer and shoved him to the side, stepping into the house.

The surly probation officer, Bill Slaton, obviously didn't like being pushed aside. He tried to regain his composure, wiping his boots on the doormat and stepping into the house like an invited guest. Then he turned around and motioned to Darren and said, "Stay right there."

Darren resented being told to stay like a pet, so he ignored the probation officer and eased up next to Fusco. Brutus turned sheepish in the darkened room. Darren didn't like it much either.

Once inside the house, Darren flashed back to his brief stint in narcotics three years ago and instantly recalled why he preferred patrol. These guys were dirt bags. The dark, dank living room had a haze of cigarette smoke and other smells emanating from God knew where. It made his skin crawl. He'd never be able to get this stench out of his uniform or Brutus's coat. He at least knew to stand still for a few moments until his eyes adjusted to the lack of light.

These two shitheads were raised in a middle-class home and their brother was an attorney. What went wrong? How could anyone accept living in conditions like this?

The taller man, Neil, said, "I'm calling my brother."

Fusco said, "So?" He turned toward the hallway at the far end of the living room and started to step that way when the heavier brother, Arnold Junior, bounded off the couch with surprising speed, shouting for Fusco to stop and blocking his way.

Fusco raised his voice to match the shithead's. "Step out of the way and don't do anything stupid. We're just here to look around as part of your brother's probation."

An adult male stepped out from the hallway, but in the dark and haze of smoke, it took a moment for Darren to realize it was Arnold Ludner. The whole reason they were going through this farce was to talk to the father of these two idiots.

The senior Ludner called out, "What's all the racket about?"

The beefy younger Arnold Ludner got in Fusco's face. It looked like Fusco was prepared to let the thuggish drug dealer run his mouth. Most cops are good about letting people blow off steam. They take abuse all day long in uniform, and if they fought everyone who made a smart remark, they'd be nothing but a mass of black eyes and cut knuckles.

Then the drug dealer went too far. He touched Fusco on the chest. It was really more of a poke with his index finger. Once someone touches a cop, all bets are off. When a cop is assaulted, no matter how minor, he or she has to respond with overwhelming force.

Fusco lifted his left hand quickly in a feint, which worked. When Arnold Junior raised his eyes to Fusco's left hand, he drove his right fist hard into the drug dealer's gut.

Darren could smell the man's nasty breath as he exhaled involuntarily in response to the blow. But the guy was tough. He absorbed the shot in the stomach, wrapped his arms around Fusco, and pushed back like a lineman.

Fusco stumbled backward into the probation officers with the drug dealer on top of him. Darren's first instinct was to reach down and grab his pistol on his right hip. That was from the first day of the police academy. Always protect your weapon. For some reason the statistic that 25 percent of all cops killed in line of duty were killed with their own pistol flickered through his mind. Fusco fell on the soft padding of Bill Slaton underneath him, breaking his fall.

Darren moved toward the other brother to block any possible attack.

The drug dealer was still on top of him when Fusco yelled out, "Kato, help."

Darren turned, threw a kick into the heavy drug dealer's ribs, and grabbed his radio quickly, calling out, "I need backup. We've got a fight in the house." He was on the local dedicated CAT channel and knew that only Hallett and Claire would hear his call. They could make the decision if more help was needed from the district.

Darren didn't hesitate to jerk his pepper spray from his tactical vest and give it a quick shake with his left hand. Just as he was ready to let loose with the spray, Fusco yelled, "Not yet, not yet. We're too close to each other."

It was like magic. Brutus barked and all three suspects froze, then looked his way. It wasn't Darren in his uniform, holding pepper spray, that startled them. It was the sight of Brutus. It was obvious none of them realized the biggest threat they had from the Golden Retriever was being beaten in a game of ultimate Frisbee. But it still had the desired effect as the brother and father pulled Arnold Junior off the law enforcement pile and all three spurted through the kitchen and out the back door.

Darren knew exactly what he needed to put out over the radio. "We've got three suspects running out the back door. All three are involved in a felony battery." That was justification to use the dogs if these idiots kept running.

Darren sprinted to the rear door and watched as the three men spread out in the backyard. He knew not to run, in case the dogs were released from each side of the compound. It physically hurt him not to be part of the chase.

30

Tim Hallett heard the transmission about the fleeing suspects just as he saw all the men stumble out of the rear door of the house. He could tell they had experience with K-9s because they were smart enough to split up and run three separate directions. It was obvious to him which one was the father. He seemed to be in more of a relaxed jog than an all-out sprint and slowed to a walk before getting too far from the house.

The toughest of the brothers, Arnold Junior, was running closest to Hallett, who was praying the drug dealer wouldn't stop. Hallett gave the warning just the same. "Stop, police. Stop running or I will release my dog." He waited a few more seconds, then gave the fleeing man a second chance, saying, "You better stop. You're gonna get bitten." Now he was jogging in the direction of the running man and Rocky was straining at his lead. It was *go* time. Hallett had the quick release on the lead and said, *"Krijg hem,"* which meant "get him" in Dutch.

Rocky launched like a missile, sailing through the uncut grass-and-weed mixture that filled most of the wide backyard. He didn't bother to bark and warn the man he was closing on him; he just galloped closer and closer to his prey.

The drug dealer—who was moving much faster than Hallett would've thought such a chubby man would—glanced over his shoulder and, instead of freezing in place the way he should have, tried to turn on the speed. It was futile against the sleek Belgian Malinois.

Hallett anticipated the strike and was afraid Ludner would stop fleeing. Hallett mumbled quietly, "Run, asshole, run." He'd never taken such pleasure in watching his partner run down a bolting suspect. A dozen yards before the edge of the property Rocky launched himself into the air, opened his mouth, and latched on to Ludner's upper arm in one fluid motion.

Rocky twisted his body and brought the big man down with a thud. He never released his grip on the man's arm as Hallett jogged over to them.

Before he even reached the flailing drug dealer, Hallett had a set of handcuffs in his left hand and shouted to the man, "Put your free hand behind your back. Do it now." As he got closer he said to Rocky in a softer voice, "*Loslaten,*" which was Dutch for "let go" or "release." Rocky dropped the man's bloody arm, took a few paces off to the side, and sat quietly like a sentinel while Hallett handcuffed Ludner firmly behind his back, not showing any concern for the man's wound.

Hallett looked up at Rocky and said, "Good boy, Rocky. Good boy."

Ludner moaned and said, "Why did he try to yank my arm off?"

"Because you kept running when you shouldn't have, dumbass."

■   ■   ■

Rocky felt a surge of excitement as he saw three men come out of the house in the distance. He could tell by the way Tim was turned and his body language which man Tim wanted him to chase as part of their game. He was a big, slow man. Good. This was going to be fun. Then Rocky heard Tim say, "*Krijg hem,*" which meant "chase the man and bite him hard." It was one of those phrases Rocky had come to know, and it was the one that made him happiest when they played these games. He knew he had to run the man down and bite him hard so Tim wouldn't be in danger and it might teach the man a lesson.

He felt the release on his lead open and it was like he had no control. Instinct took over, and his paws seemed to barely touch the dew covering the grass as he raced across the open field.

The man looked over his shoulders with wide eyes and sweat pouring off in every direction. Rocky always liked when people looked behind at him. This bad man was scared. Rocky could see it and smell it.

Rocky could've caught up with the man easily, but instead hung back to let him tire himself out more, then paused as he timed his leap. He sprang off the ground and aimed for the man's upper arm. It was easy and fun. Rocky turned in midair and felt the man twist and his feet lift off the ground. He made a funny sound, *"Umph!"* Rocky didn't think it was a real word, but wasn't certain. He could hear the man gasping for air.

Rocky held on to the man's arm the way he had been taught during their other games. Until he heard Tim say, *"Loslaten,"* which meant the game was over and it wasn't fun anymore.

Rocky sat back and kept watch while Tim played his own game with the big man.

■   ■   ■

Claire Perkins enjoyed the excitement of a chase and arrest. The brother that ran toward her was smart enough to freeze the moment he saw Smarty. She took him into custody without having to say a word. Hallett and Rocky had captured the other brother, who was currently getting stitched up at Palms West Hospital. Hallett told her it was mainly superficial, with no arteries or veins severed. The suspect was whining just the same.

The man they were looking to capture in the first place, Arnold Ludner, had run out of gas and sat on a stack of fencing material until someone walked back and took him into custody as well.

It didn't take long for the probation officers to figure out why the three men had run. The rear bathroom of the front house was being used as a small but efficient meth lab. Based on the stack of twenty-dollar bills it appeared to be a profitable operation.

All three of the Ludners were now in custody, and the older, heavyset probation officer was on his way to the emergency room complaining about back pain brought on by having two grown men plop on top of him.

Now Claire stood in front of the house with Darren Mori and Brutus, watching the crime scene technicians and evidence custodians as well as the narcotics agents do their job. Lori Tate smiled and waved as she carried out a small box of cash sealed in clear plastic envelopes.

Lori said, "You guys did a great job."

Claire gave her a smile and was about to say something when Fusco walked past and winked at her. It broke her train of thought. Claire realized that Fusco was about to fight a battle with homicide about who would run the case, but even in this most basic of police investigator activities he had time to acknowledge her. She liked that.

Darren moved closer to the house as Brutus took a sniff of the walkway and stepped into the house. He started circling the area near the front door.

Claire said, "What's gotten into him?" She let Darren focus on his dog, as he looked like he was about to alert. Brutus would walk around in a circle and act like he was going to sit in a classic alert mode, then stand up and sniff the area some more.

Finally, Darren said, "Brutus is giving an abnormal alert from this area. I don't know if it has something to do with the chemicals used in the lab or if it's something that might be related to our case." His eyes cut to Fusco, but he didn't say anything because Fusco was still arguing with Danny Weil.

Lori Tate was walking back with an expensive Nikon camera when Claire said, "Brutus is showing some odd behavior near the front door. I wish I could give you a better idea of what he was interested in. But someone should probably know about it."

Lori looked over her shoulder at the agitated detectives and hesitated. The fight for control had started. She snapped photos of the walkway and entrance as well as the surrounding area.

Darren leaned down and pulled the welcome mat out of the house onto the front walkway. Brutus immediately bounced out of the house and started circling the mat. That's where the odor was coming from.

Lori said, "I don't think it's a good idea for me to get in the middle of homicide and Fusco right now." She shot a glance over to Fusco. "We'll take the floor mat into evidence and let one of the forensic people take a look at it."

Claire liked the practical way this girl thought.

31

Tim Hallett couldn't remember a more perfect Sunday afternoon. Crystal had allowed him to keep Josh a few days. She'd fed him a nice dinner Friday night, and they chatted about their lives. It was more than they had talked since they split up. Her smile came easy. It made him forget about everything that had happened during the week. He hoped there'd be more for him and Rocky to do on the case when he reported back. But when Crystal suggested he spend the night, he told her about dating Lori. Crystal paused and said, "You're too good a guy. No one admits something like that." Then he, and a soundly sleeping Josh, left for their weekend adventure.

They'd spent all day Saturday exploring the edges of Lake Okeechobee in a rented kayak and had watched *Marley and Me* and the beginning of *Old Yeller* on Saturday night. Hallett knew better than to watch the movie to the end. Josh never would've understood why the boy had to shoot his own dog. And he was afraid it would be unsettling to Rocky as well. He had *Beethoven* on the shelf for later today, but Rocky had already shown disdain for the rambunctious St. Bernard. They might revert to *Marley and Me* during quiet time.

But now, as burgers sizzled on the grill and his mother was doing her best imitation of being at the beach, splayed out in a lounge chair next to his brother with Josh and Rocky playing in front of them, Hallett felt like he had turned a corner in his life. Maybe it was the sense of redemption at having finally nailed Arnold Ludner. His life had a rhythm now. Simple tasks added to the feeling. Early this morning, Hallett had systematically taken each of the animals in his menagerie and let them out of their cages. Josh treated it like a solemn duty to exercise each animal as best he could. Albert the alpaca was the only one who proved to be difficult, when he spit on the shirt Hallett had worn to church.

The two new additions, Sponge and Bob, the yappy poodles, had seemed to take on the role of assistant zookeepers with Rocky. They herded the animals that wanted to stray.

Hallett wouldn't have thought herding was an instinct in the poodles' DNA.

Fall had finally started to settle into the communities around Lake Okeechobee, and the property surrounding his trailer behind the city's largest Christian school was a comfortable seventy-four degrees.

He carried a platter of hamburgers over to his mother and brother like a waiter at a ritzy oceanfront resort. He grabbed a burger for himself and plopped into the chair next to his mother.

She said, "It's nice to see you having such a good time. You work so hard, I'm afraid you're missing out on life."

"I like my job, Mom. That's part of life."

"It's not too often I get to read about your work in the newspaper anymore. I cut out both the articles and showed them to all the neighbors."

Hallett had been impressed with Ruben Vasquez's ability to plant a detailed media story about how the Canine Assist Team had helped in solving one of the county's most notorious crimes. He didn't mind admitting that he enjoyed the recognition for the unit, too. There was even an article that referred to their efforts as heroic. It was rare to see a modern newspaper latch on to such a complimentary term in regard to police work. He was still assigned to the detective bureau with the other members of the squad but figured this week would be a cakewalk as he transitioned back to his regular patrol duties.

His brother, Bobby, said, "You and Rocky both looked pretty sharp standing in the background."

Hallett let the dig slide.

His mother said, "Are you sure that awful Arnold Ludner did it? I mean, will you be able to convict him?"

"He's being held on the meth charges now while homicide tries to piece together the case. They probably wouldn't have mentioned his name if they didn't have something already. I know his wife isn't able to give him an alibi for the times that Katie Ziegler was assaulted and Tina Tic-tin disappeared. He supposedly has some kind of job, but he wasn't at work either of those days. His sons swear that he was at the little compound in Fruity Acres all of the time."

Bobby said, "If he's a registered sexual predator, why was he so hard to find?"

"His son, the attorney, says he was afraid of being *tortured* again by the sheriff's office." He had to use air quotes for the word "tortured."

His mother muttered, "Bullshit."

He nodded his head in agreement and said, "I don't think that bully is getting his way this time. He can't do much. Both of his brothers and his father were caught with a decent amount of meth being made in their bathtub, although he already got his two brothers out on bond. We got a favorable judge who's giving us the benefit of the doubt while homicide tries to put the case together. We've got time."

His mother said, "I keep seeing that nice-looking John Fusco on TV."

"Technically, he's still the lead detective on the kidnappings, but homicide has effectively frozen him out of any of their forensic information. I'm glad Rocky and I aren't involved in any of those kinds of politics anymore."

Bobby, looking at his nephew and Rocky, said, "I'm glad Rocky doesn't alert on me all the time anymore." He turned to Hallett. "I really listened to you about the pot."

Hallett sat straight, stunned by this revelation. "You quit smoking pot?"

Bobby shook his head. "No way, man. I showered and put on fresh clothes before we drove out."

Hallett shook his head as he settled back into his chair and watched while Josh stretched out in the lush grass and played some silent game with Rocky, touching his tiny hands to Rocky's paws. The dog looked just as happy as Hallett.

■　　■　　■

Even though there was no game going on with Tim and they weren't chasing bad people, Rocky liked times like this at their house with all the animals. The other people Tim liked were with him, the female and the man who usually smelled like the game Rocky played. But more importantly, Josh was there. Josh liked to play with the two little dogs and Rocky, but if Rocky had to check the fences or investigate a rabbit, he felt comfortable leaving Josh with the two little dogs. They might not be able to protect Tim or Josh, but they could sure make enough noise to attract Rocky's attention if there was a problem.

Tim stood up from the other people and walked over to the animal pens, and Rocky followed him and walked right next to him as he stopped and gave food to each of the animals. The birds and rabbit rarely acknowledged the food, but often the big white thing with a long neck would eat right out of Tim's hand. Although it never seemed happy to be fed and often made hissing sounds at Rocky.

When Tim was done feeding animals, Rocky jogged along the fence line the way he did every night, even though it was the middle of the day. He didn't understand why he felt the need to do it no matter what time he entered the animal pens. He just went with the feeling.

The property was safe and everything was in order, so Rocky walked back over to where Tim and the other people were eating. He walked between the two little dogs—which by now had exhausted themselves and flopped out under some shade—and went directly to Josh. Rocky laid down, too, while Josh played a quiet game with his front paws.

Rocky knew this felt nice.

■   ■   ■

Claire sat in the detective bureau with Tim Hallett, but she was itching to get back out on the road. If they didn't have a specific assignment, she didn't want to waste time sitting around like a mannequin. Unless John Fusco had something he needed her for. Anything. She'd be happy to stick around. They had gone out Saturday night to a nice dinner, but he didn't stay over or invite her to. She was very impressed that he wanted to get up early Sunday to spend time with his two daughters. He made sure every Sunday was devoted to them and almost every Wednesday night as well. He was nothing like the image the other members of CAT had of him.

John Fusco had also explained how careful he had to be working with her. He said he couldn't permit even the appearance of favoritism. When she asked if that was why he had chosen Darren Mori to follow him into the house when they arrested the Ludner brothers, John had nodded his head. She knew there was more to his decision, but she appreciated how he treated her like everyone else at work. She didn't know if there was a future in any kind of relationship with him, but he was smart and funny, and the only negative thing she could say was that he was a little bit in love with himself. Frankly, she understood why.

Hallett said, "Where's Darren?"

"He had a couple of things to do and is going to meet us after lunch."

"Have you seen Sergeant Greene around?"

Claire said, "What're you doing, taking attendance?"

Hallett chuckled and said, "I was gonna see if the sergeant would cut us loose if she had nothing for us to do."

"Amen to that. I'm not sure I like the atmosphere in the detective bureau right now." As if to emphasize her point, John Fusco came banging through the front door, cursing about something. She noticed Hallett smile, seeing the detective so out of sorts. It was an infectious smile.

She knew Tim Hallett couldn't let it pass. He said, "What's wrong, Fusco? Is the sheriff going to restrict the use of hair plugs?"

Fusco scowled at the two K-9 officers. "Homicide isn't saying shit about the Tina Tictin investigation. They're treating me like a goddamn reporter. All they say is bland, general facts without getting into any details."

Claire was happy that Hallett recognized the frustration Fusco was experiencing and didn't pile on. Instead, they headed down to the parking lot to check on the dogs. Almost as soon as they were in the hallway outside the detective bureau, Lori Tate greeted them. Claire noted the warm hug and kiss she gave Hallett, who looked uncomfortable with the public display of affection.

Hallett said, "What are you doing over here?"

"The homicide detectives have us running around like crazy on some of the evidence we took from the Ludner house."

Claire took a second to read Lori's body language. She was completely focused on Tim Hallett, and Claire saw a chance to get some information. She said, "Find anything interesting?"

Lori hesitated.

Claire said, "We'll keep it quiet."

Lori still didn't answer right away. Finally, she said, "The most interesting thing is the doormat that Darren's dog pointed out to us. So to speak. Someone at the lab matched the sand and sediment to the same material recovered with the girl's body the other day."

Hallett let out a whoop and clapped his hands. "That seals it. Arnold Ludner is our man."

Lori said, "Not so fast. I've heard the forensics people and the detectives going back and forth on it. They can't say the sand comes from the gravesite, only that it is from that same canal. It has to do with the levels of phosphates and fertilizer runoff. All it means is that someone in the house had tracked a small amount of sand from that canal, which is more than a mile long."

"It's still decent PC."

Lori nodded. "They're trying to write a probable cause affidavit now. They even mention the cute Golden Retriever who alerted on the mat. He pointed them in the right direction."

Claire said, "They've been busy."

"And there's a question about their authority to take something from the house under a probation search. But I heard the lead detective say one of the suspects gave consent."

Hallett said, "Consent? Really? All three seemed pretty pissed off to me."

Lori just shrugged. "No one tells me anything directly, I just hear it in the squad bay. It's not exactly like the general detective squad, where everyone gets along so well and works together."

Claire thought about crimes/persons and all the squabbling she had heard. She had to let out a short laugh. She wondered how people viewed the Canine Assist Team. They were a unit that really *did* get along well.

32

Hallett and Rocky needed to get away from the headquarters building for a few minutes and grab something to eat. As he pulled his unmarked Chevy Tahoe onto Gun Club Road, directly in front of the sheriff's office, he noticed a gold SUV sitting in the parking lot of the Army Reserve building across the street. It immediately reminded him of the Ludner brothers' car. Was he getting paranoid? He sure did need the training day tomorrow to break up the stress he'd experienced in the last week. The weekend with Josh, and especially the Sunday with his whole family, had gone a long way toward screwing his head on right. Seeing Lori Tate in the office this morning made him think he should've invited her to the cookout yesterday.

Rocky appeared content lounging in his compartment when Hallett pulled into the sub shop near the headquarters building. It was a slightly rougher part of town, and he didn't want to make any of the patrons nervous by walking in with a fearsome-looking dog. It was bad enough wearing the black tactical vest over his black K-9 T-shirt with the image of a snarling dog and PBSO written on the sleeve.

As soon as he locked the doors and turned toward the sub shop, he was confronted by two men. It took a moment for him to realize it was the Ludner brothers.

The chubby one, Arnold Junior, said, "We gotta talk."

Hallett noticed the absence of the third brother, the attorney. That gave him a pretty good idea this conversation was about to turn ugly. He said, "I guess you want me to kick your ass like I did your old man's." He just needed a quick distraction to make his move.

■ ■ ■

Claire stretched her hamstring in the courtyard of the sheriff's office main headquarters. There was just something about the fresh air and sun filtering through the wispy clouds that pushed her out of the gym and into the empty public area. She was glad she'd skipped lunch to grab a workout. Tim Hallett constantly stressed the importance of physical fitness for a good K-9 officer. More than once, while following the progress of foot chases or searches by other K-9 officers on the radio, Claire had heard the phrase "I'm out of dog," which meant the dog could no longer continue to search. Tim said that phrase was the biggest bunch of bullshit he'd ever heard. It was an easy excuse for an out-of-shape officer to use when he could no longer continue. It wasn't that dogs didn't get exhausted and have to rest, it was just that it didn't happen as often as the handler wearing out. With a heavy tactical vest, it was already difficult to keep pace with the dogs for long. Add to that an extra twenty to forty pounds of visceral fat and an out-of-shape K-9 officer could cut the effectiveness of his dog by 80 percent.

She sat down on one of the cement benches, which were vacant during all but the coolest months in Florida. Before she noticed anyone in the area she heard, "Hey, this is a nice surprise." She looked up at John Fusco strolling toward her from the main building. He was dressed like the typical big-shot detective. He loved his suits and being seen as having good taste and professional clothes that matched the homicide detectives, who always felt that they had to dress to rival their serious assignment. The Palm Beach County Sheriff's Office's homicide unit was recognized as possibly the best homicide bureau in the Southeast. They had effectively worked everything from simple drug shootings to decades-old cold case homicides.

Claire said, "I was going to find you soon."

"Why?"

"I heard that the homicide unit is about to prepare an affidavit and charge Arnold Ludner with Tina Tictin's death. They're going to try to charge him while he's still being held without bond for his scuffle with you."

Fusco nodded his head. "No one told me, but it's a smart move. This way they can make a big splash in the media. Credit goes a long way toward getting you resources. Homicide wants to take credit for anything connected to this case, and I don't blame them." He looked at Claire and said, "How'd you find out?"

She wasn't trying to be coy, but Claire said, "I can't reveal my sources." She gave him a disarming shrug and smile.

"You sound like a detective already."

"What's that mean?"

"You're gonna try to get into the D-bureau, right?"

She shook her head emphatically. "No. Not at all."

"Why not?"

"I have Smarty. Together we can do things most cops only dream about."

Fusco shook his head and said, "You don't want to be in patrol your whole career, do you?"

"Don't make it sound like a curse. Besides, I thought that we couldn't see each other if I was in the detective bureau. Is this your way of trying to avoid me?"

"Sorry, I just assumed you wanted to be a detective. I thought every cop did."

"You need to come out of your bubble sometime and look around at the real world. You don't have to be a detective to contribute. I like K-9, especially CAT." Claire could see how uncomfortable Fusco was and that he was trying to extricate himself from the conversation. She decided to help him out by saying, "I gotta finish up in the gym and take Smarty out for a run. I'll talk to you later."

As she turned, she wasn't sure if he was relieved or sad she was leaving.

■   ■   ■

Hallett, facing the two pissed-off drug-dealing siblings, did the one thing that usually gave thugs pause. He smiled. Just a simple, genuine-looking smile. It was an old cop trick. A smile was infinitely more unsettling than a threat. A smile indicated that the cop was not concerned in any way about what was about to happen. It hid an unimaginable potential of possibilities behind a simple facade. And it unnerved anyone who had ever been in a street fight.

The brother closer to him, Arnold Junior, noticed the smile and did a quick scan of the area to see if there was an army of backup, then shuffled away from Hallett half a step, saying, "I didn't put the name with the face the day you stopped us. It wasn't until after we were arrested that my dad mentioned who you were."

Hallett kept his smile as his right hand eased toward the pistol on his hip and his left hand moved up his tactical vest to the emergency release button that opened the door to Rocky's compartment. "How many stitches did it take to close up your arm after Rocky brought you down?"

"The doctor at the jail said it was mostly puncture wounds and didn't need any stitches, but it still hurts like hell."

"Rocky and I won't charge you for the lesson you might use later in life."

"We're not here to thank you. It's no worse than some of the lessons my dad laid on me over the years."

"That's what I figured." Now he was able to casually push the button on the electronic release, and the door right behind the two brothers clicked and swung open, leaving Rocky in the perfect position to jump out and land on the younger brother. Rocky stood there for a moment, emitting a menacing growl. "Looks like you boys brought fists to a dogfight."

Arnold Junior said, "No, wait. We're not here to cause any trouble."

The edge in his voice and look on his face made Hallett call out to Rocky, "*Stoppen. Zitten.*" It was Dutch for "stop, wait." Rocky froze in position then sat obediently, but he kept his eyes tuned to the two subjects in front of him.

The chubby drug dealer stuttered, "You, you've got the wrong idea."

Hallett said, "I think I have the right idea. My idea is to have Rocky here rip you a new asshole." He looked at the other, more terrified brother and said, "You, I might just shoot."

Arnold Junior held up his hands and said, "You got us all wrong. That's not why we're here."

■　　■　　■

Rocky smelled the men before Tim knew they were there. He tried to signal Tim, but he turned around in time. Rocky recognized one of the men as a bad man he had run after and bitten. He scratched at the door, knowing he had to get out of this cage and help his friend Tim. These were bad men.

Tim started to communicate with the other men, and all Rocky could do was pace back and forth in the closed cage and growl, hoping to catch the men's attention and give Tim a chance to act. He needed to protect Tim, but once again Tim was being too easy on the bad men and not letting him do what he was supposed to do. Bite them.

He felt trapped and desperately wanted to be free. Free to bite.

Then he saw Tim bare his teeth the way he did when he was happy, but Rocky could tell he wasn't. Silly Tim. Why wouldn't Tim let him out to bite these bad men? Rocky would never understand humans.

After a short time of more human communication, the door popped open and Rocky was face-to-face with the bad men, and as they turned, he could smell their fear. This was easy.

Then Tim surprised him by saying, *"Stoppen. Zitten,"* which meant the game was over. He didn't understand. These were bad men right in front of him, and Tim didn't want him to bite them. Then he sensed the tension disappearing. He knew he had to stay alert until these men were gone, no matter what Tim said.

•   ■   ■

Hallett let Rocky's presence grab these two morons' attention.

Hallett said, "If you're gonna talk, you better talk fast, because both my dog and I are hungry."

The drug dealer said, "Our dad is innocent." Then he added, "Of this."

"You have got to be kidding me. You really think that bullshit is gonna work on me? You remember my last face-to-face encounter with your father? I think you should talk to your smarter lawyer-brother next time you want to pull a stunt like this."

"He's the one who said that you were actually a decent, honest guy who did what he had to do."

That caught Hallett by surprise.

"My brother said you might actually have enough principles to listen to us. But he couldn't do it officially, and he didn't think you'd want to talk to him anyway."

"You mean after he tried to get me fired from the sheriff's office?"

The drug dealer just nodded his head sheepishly. Then he said, "That doesn't change the fact that my dad has nothing to do with these kidnappings or that girl's death." He paused a moment and looked into Hallet's eyes.

Hallett's gut feeling was this guy was sincere.

"My mom can't swear about my dad's whereabouts because she has mental issues. She's not even sure when he's at the house. We were afraid that Dad was aggravating the situation, so we brought him over to our place. He gets impatient and loud. I already told the detectives that Neil and I can verify he was at our house the two days the girls were attacked, but no one would listen to us."

"Do you think you would seem credible to a cop?"

The drug dealer didn't answer. He just hung his head. "What about my brother Joe? Is he more credible?"

"No, he's less credible than you. He's a goddamn attorney. Most people would rather hang out with a scumbag drug dealer than with an attorney."

Then Arnold Junior said, "My dad has a problem, there's no denying that. That's why we don't hold it against you. You might have saved his life as well as made the neighborhood safer. But it's different now. You can't believe how different he is."

"What are you talking about?"

The drug dealer hesitated, finally saying, "He's taking medicine. Special medicine that helps him with his problem."

"There's no cure for pedophiles."

"This medicine is to chemically castrate him. He knew it was the only way. We've been trying to help him, too."

"Wait. What?"

"He's taking Androcur, a French drug that's used on certain sex offenders. He's doing it on his own."

"So you're telling me that he's taking a drug and between your methmaking shifts you guys are babysitting him. Does that sound about right?"

"We have been advised by our brother not to talk about our business with anyone. But if you can keep that separate, is there any way you could keep an open mind about our father? We'll do anything."

"Go straight?"

"Almost anything. But I'm appealing to you as an ethical police officer and as a human being to consider what we've told you."

Maybe this was the brother who should've been an attorney. He was very convincing.

Hallett didn't see anything he could do in this situation, but it still made him think.

Claire felt bad about the exchange in the courtyard as she sat in the detective bureau with John Fusco, who was obviously desperate to make his kidnapping case before homicide stole all of his thunder and charged Arnold Ludner with the murder of Tina Tictin. Technically, they were supposed to be working together, and command staff wouldn't be happy that Fusco struck out on his own, but the positive media attention would probably keep him from getting in too much trouble.

Fusco had explained to Claire that a true kidnapping case was very rare. An actual abduction for money, like she used to see on the old re-runs of the FBI TV series with Efrem Zimbalist Jr., was extraordinarily unlikely.

This case was nothing but a series of dead ends. The rag they had recovered near Katie Ziegler had resulted in no positive hits in the CODIS DNA database. There was no other viable DNA evidence at this time. The imprint of the shoe would not be useful without something to compare it to. Neither Katie Ziegler nor the two earlier girls could identify the suspect from available photographs or pick Arnold Ludner out of a photographic lineup. The description from all three girls was virtually identical: The way the man surprised them and drove them to a secluded area indicated that it was absolutely the same creep each time. The fact that Arnold Ludner owned no vehicle himself fit the idea that the kidnapper used stolen vehicles.

Fusco said, "I don't like sitting at my desk, trying to work out these problems, but I got virtually no more leads on the kidnapping. The homicide unit is covering all the new leads developed from the recovery of Tina Tictin's body. No one has asked me to come along."

"And you're too proud to beg."

His pout was all the answer she needed.

Sergeant Greene came out of her office and eased down into the chair next to Fusco's desk.

The sergeant said, "Are you two working with homicide?"

"Not really. I want to build the kidnapping case."

Sergeant Greene sighed and said, "You know, John, there's more to this job than winning."

He gave her a wide grin and said, "But if *I* win, *everyone* wins. I may be considered the backup plan now, but we'll see who gets the recognition for Arnold Ludner's arrest."

The sergeant shook her head and said, "The real reason I'm out here is that I'm writing a letter of commendation for the two probation officers who helped us. I need their names and their supervisor, if you have it."

Fusco looked up the younger probation officer's name and gave it to the sergeant. Then he said, "The older, tubby one is Bill Slaton. I want to see his reaction to a letter from us. He's not a particular fan of the agency."

Claire laughed at the depiction of the surly probation officer.

The sergeant said, "He's the one that got hurt, right?"

Fusco nodded his head.

"How's he doing?"

"He said his back and side were sore. He's going to be out at least a more few days. Maybe after he reads the letter of commendation and sees what we had to do to make the arrest, he'll appreciate the police a little more."

■　■　■

Hallett walked into the detective bureau with Rocky close at his side. He saw Claire and Sergeant Greene at John Fusco's desk. He had subtly taught Rocky to give a brief snarl at the sight of John Fusco every time he walked up. He never failed to enjoy the look of fear on the detective's face when the dog walked past, turned his head, showed a few of his teeth, and growled. To Fusco's credit, he had never said a word about it.

Hallett said, "I just had an interesting encounter with Arnold Ludner's sons."

The sergeant said, "Where?"

"At the sub shop a few blocks away. They surprised me and wanted to tell me their father was innocent."

Fusco blurted out, "Oh, please."

The sergeant got more to the point. "Did they threaten you in any way? Is there enough to charge them with a crime?"

Hallett waved off the inquiry and said, "They were very respectful and made no threatening actions or comments. They just wanted to tell me that someone had questioned them about the earlier kidnappings and they could account for their father's whereabouts each time. I guess homicide didn't believe convicted drug dealers."

Fusco said, "That's about the only thing we agree on."

"The sons said their father was on a drug called Androcur that acts as a chemical castration. They said it was part of their father's program to stay out of trouble."

Fusco said, "I guess that explains why there was no semen at any of the scenes and he only performed oral sex on the girls. If you can't get a stiffy, you've got to find other ways to have fun." Fusco looked at Hallett and said, "You're not getting sucked in by this bullshit, are you?"

Hallett held up his hands and said, "I'm not arguing, just informing."

Fusco said, "What if you go back to dog walking and I'll handle the investigation? All we really needed was the cadaver dog anyway. I'm tired of babysitting you guys."

Hallett touched Rocky's rear leg with his knee so the dog would snarl at Fusco again. It made him feel a tiny bit better.

■　　■　　■

Claire jumped at the chance to be involved in another interview of a young girl. This was just the way to start off Tuesday morning.

Remembering how Smarty had served as a focus for Katie Ziegler after she was rescued in the cane field, Claire brought the dog into the detective bureau with her. She didn't want to rush things along but really wanted to meet the gang out at the training facility as soon as possible.

She also was responding to the tone of John Fusco's voice. He had never before used the phrase "I need your help."

Fusco met her as soon as she entered the detective bureau and said, "This girl wants to talk, but I thought you might connect with her better than me. Young girls confuse me."

Claire said, "You sure you're not just confused about young girls? It would explain a lot about your extravagant fashion sense."

Fusco rubbed the sleeve of his expensive suit coat and took it as a compliment, saying, "This *is* extravagant, isn't it."

Claire sighed and said, "Where's the girl now?"

Fusco led her through the squad bay to the rear interview room. As he was about to open the door he said, "She claims she was attacked Thursday night but was afraid to come forward. She and her mother are waiting inside."

Claire said, "What's her name?"

"Michelle Swirsky."

■   ■   ■

Darren Mori sat at the end of the long conference table between Tim Hallett and Claire Perkins. They all appreciated Sergeant Greene including them in a meeting specifically about an investigation. The meeting really had nothing to do with their dogs' special abilities. He would've chuckled at John Fusco's hysterics if it hadn't been such a serious subject.

The sergeant had already given an overview of the interview of a young woman named Michelle Swirsky who had been attacked Thursday night. Darren had never been involved in investigations, but even he could tell that every detail matched the previous attacks. The subject was a chubby, middle-aged man. The location was not far from where Tina Tictin had been snatched. His approach had been a surprise, and the victim fit precisely into the age range the kidnapper had been targeting.

The twist on this encounter was that Michelle was a brown belt in tae kwon do and immediately fought back with everything she'd been taught. Her sensei's name was Rick Morris and he was a retired Coral Springs cop who now worked for the School Board Police. The advantage of having a police officer teach self-defense was that he taught her to fight dirty. She used her elbows and knees the way he had shown her, and when her assailant fell backward into his car, she slammed the door on his legs. This was some special kind of girl.

The sergeant said, "Michelle was with a boy the night it happened and was too afraid to tell her mother anything. It was the news stories about recovering Tina Tictin's body that made her think she might be able to help the investigation." She looked at John Fusco and said, "What's your take on the girl?"

Fusco said, "She's straight up. I know we sometimes take teenagers' accounts of events with a grain of salt, but this girl didn't seem like she was making anything up at all. Her mother sat in on the investigation with us, and I could tell they were both very serious about what happened."

No one stated the obvious. Finally, Hallett said, "So you think this is the same guy as the other attacks?"

Fusco hesitated, and the sergeant didn't answer at all.

Hallett was more forceful this time. "Come on. Even a copycat wouldn't get things this close."

It took a moment for Darren to catch on to the hesitation. Then Hallett spoke his thoughts aloud. "If she was attacked Thursday night, the attacker couldn't have been Arnold Ludner. We had him covered on surveillance. He has the greatest alibi of all time. *The police were watching me every minute of the evening.*"

Now Fusco mumbled, "Bullshit. You been listening to his kids too much."

Darren heard the anger and frustration in Fusco's voice and thought back to what Ruben had been telling them. He was trying to read the other subtle clues from the detective, and they told him Fusco wasn't convinced completely either.

Hallett gripped the end of the table and said, "What good does it do us to arrest the wrong man? That means there's still a killer out there even if this one gets convicted. Does Ludner have any of the injuries this girl inflicted on her attacker?"

Sergeant Greene stood and did the equivalent of stepping between two brawlers. She said, "Hang on, now. Let's see what homicide comes up with. There's a lot of evidence to go through."

That set Fusco off. "Who cares what they find? Homicide is trying to trash *my* case. This doesn't change shit. Either the girl has her times confused or you guys screwed up the surveillance and let him slip past you."

Darren saw Hallett was angry, but instead of saying something insulting he just said, "Could be."

That brought Fusco to his feet screaming, "Could be? It *has* to be." He looked over to Sergeant Greene and said, "Why don't we send this guy back to the dog patrol?"

Darren had learned a whole lot about the politics of investigation in just this one meeting.

■　　■　　■

Junior had seen the news and understood that now was the time to lie low. He could just creep back into the woodwork where no one would notice him. Not that anyone did anyway. If he could control himself and keep from acting, he'd never have to worry about jail time. After all that he had seen, jail was not an option.

The only problem with his plan to lie low and sit quietly at home was Michelle Swirsky. The very thought of her made him ache. The idea that she thought she was better than him kept him awake at night. The idea that she had taught him something was insulting and absurd.

He didn't know if he could ever rest again until he set things straight.

34

Tension bothered Claire. It had since she was a little girl. It reminded her of the arguments her mother and father would have about everything from money to her father's reliance on all types of drugs. Back then, her bunny, Beulah, calmed her down. She'd stroke the white bunny's fur as if it had a sedative in its pelt.

Now she found herself doing the same thing with Smarty in the detective bureau. It might have looked like she was trying to calm down the German Shepherd as they sat in the corner together, but they both knew the truth. Not that Smarty minded. At home he acted more like a puppy, following her from room to room and lying across her lap, craving any attention he could get. But he seemed to understand the rules at work and wasn't used to affection like this in the middle of the day.

Things were tense in the detective bureau since Hallett had brought up the idea that they had arrested the wrong man. She knew it had to be hard for Tim to express his theory when all he wanted in the world was to keep that creep off the streets. She couldn't have admired him more for his position. So far it seemed like she was the only one who felt that way.

Claire Perkins noticed John Fusco sulking at his desk. She had to ask, "What's wrong?" She could tell he didn't want to admit that Arnold Ludner wasn't good for the kidnappings and homicide. He already had the asshole in custody. But none of the girls, including Michelle Swirsky, could pick him out of a photo lineup. He was already in the CODIS DNA database from his previous arrest and didn't match anything found in this case, not from Tina Tictin's body or the rag found near Katie Ziegler.

The only tangible evidence anyone had from the Michelle Swirsky case was a still photo taken from a video surveillance camera on the edge of the building where she was attacked. It showed the partial hood of a sedan. She identified it as the car her attacker was driving. Only a few feet of the hood were visible, and you couldn't see the emblem or manufacturer. Fusco had taken the photo down to the auto theft task force, and they said it looked like an American sedan but couldn't be any more specific.

Claire sat down next to him, not sure what she could say or do to make him feel better. She knew he was simmering about losing all the work he'd put into the case. Just then one of the homicide detectives strolled into the crimes/persons unit and gave Fusco a friendly smile.

The younger detective said, "We got a problem, hombre."

"What's that?"

"Your man Tim Hallett is running his mouth about how we got the wrong guy in jail."

"So what do you want to do about it?"

"We need to find a way to shut the guy up. I don't know about you, but there's no way I want to try to make a case on someone else when we got the killer in jail already."

Claire said, "What if you have the wrong man?"

The detective looked at her as if she were an annoying child. Finally, he said, "That's a question the jury will have to answer. We don't make cases twice."

Claire could see why Hallett preferred K-9 over the detective bureau.

■   ■   ■

It was still early, and Tim Hallett lay in his bed, hoping to fall asleep. He knew this feeling too well. This anxiety that things weren't going right. Now he found himself in the odd position of having Arnold Ludner as a bookend to his anxiety. First because Hallett wanted to put him in jail so badly, and now because he was convinced Ludner had nothing to do with the attacks on the girls.

He had gone over the situation and his feelings about it with Rocky. It helped to talk to someone and express his innermost thoughts out loud. Rocky never told anyone secrets, never interrupted, and never judged him. That's why he was currently breaking one of his rules and allowing the dog to sprawl on his bed as he played with the thick hair around Rocky's neck.

Hallett felt like a jerk. He had allowed his personal feelings to push the investigation, and now he was convinced he had pushed it in the wrong direction. He had the air conditioner on high, mainly to give him some white noise and drown the rest of the world out. He had turned off his phone not long after chatting with Josh and catching up on his son's day.

But now, lying with Rocky in bed and staring at the water stains on the ceiling, all Hallett could do was consider the Ludner case from every possible angle. His time in the detective bureau had not gone to waste, and he had always possessed good common sense. One of the first things he learned as a new deputy out of the academy was that you can't teach common sense. No matter how big and strong recruits might be, if they had no common sense, they would fail. It frustrated Hallett when he heard his older friends say their kids were adrift and maybe should become cops. Police work was not for everyone, and sometimes people didn't learn until after they had invested a lot of sweat and tears.

Hallett's common sense told him the variables in the case just didn't line up. It was like matching the right username and password on a computer. Almost like a logic puzzle. Ludner could still be the right suspect *if* the guy who attacked Michelle Swirsky was someone else. Michelle's attacker *had* to be someone else *if* Ludner was still at the compound. If all the facts Michelle had told Claire were true and Ludner was at home at the time, he couldn't be a suspect and there was still a killer running loose.

It hurt his brain to think about the case.

Then there was sediment from the canal. All three Ludners claimed they hadn't even been to a canal. And it was difficult to get a forensic scientist to make the definitive statement that the sediment had come from around Tina Tictin's body. They were all so used to getting beat down in court that they phrased everything in hypothetical terms. There was even a chance the sediment on the welcome mat could be a coincidence of some kind.

All of this examination didn't take into account his gut feeling that the Ludners were telling the truth. The sons had been watching their father. It was against his normal police instincts, but he couldn't ignore it. He could read people well and had the sense that these guys were telling the truth.

Hallett turned toward Rocky and said aloud, "Screw it. I'm glad I'm a dog handler and not a detective anymore." He knew there was some time before it all mattered. Ludner was being held without bond for the narcotics violations based on his criminal history, and the judge, who had kids of her own, didn't want to see a guy like that walking around free. Hallett was sure the homicide guys would put together a complete and detailed affidavit. That would take a little time.

Rocky sat up and started to turn his head like radar searching for a target. His ears stood straight off his head like horns. A moment later Hallett saw the headlights sweeping across the yard. He stumbled out of bed, dismissing the idea of grabbing his gun. The way he felt right now he wouldn't care if a gang member shot him in his own doorway. He was wearing shorts and pulled a dirty T-shirt over his head as he cracked the door and noticed a silver Mazda pulling to a stop next to his county-issued Tahoe.

Who the hell drives a Mazda? This question was answered almost immediately when the smiling face of Lori Tate popped out of the small car. The first thing she said was, "You're not answering your phone."

"Sorry."

"I was out here dropping off reports at the Belle Glade substation and wanted to see where you lived. I hope you don't mind me just dropping by."

Hallett said, "How'd you find it?"

She turned her head to look over her shoulder at the giant Christian school with a forty-foot steeple, looked back at Hallett, and said, "It wasn't hard."

Hallett gave her a tired smile and motioned her into the trailer. Rocky had been wagging his tail since he heard Lori's voice.

As she stepped inside, Lori said, "This is nice."

"Really? A trailer?"

"Out here, it's a mansion. And I bet your son likes playing with all the animals." She placed a hand on his bare arm and looked into his eyes. "You look exhausted."

"Been a tough couple of days. Anything new with you?"

"Actually it's kind of slow right now. Everyone in homicide is pushing Danny Weil to finish the affidavit and get Arnold Ludner charged."

"Already? What about the new attack?"

"What about it?

"Ludner has an alibi. We were watching him at his house when the attack occurred."

Lori said, "They don't tell me all that much, unless they need something."

Hallett looked away, wondering if they had new evidence. He glanced at the clock on his DVR and considered whether it was too late to call the office and find out what was going on. He needed a distraction to get away from this.

Lori said, "This is hard."

"What is?"

"Throwing myself at you without effect." She stood on her tiptoes and planted a long, wet kiss on his lips.

Hallett instantly felt his body respond and was shocked to realize how long it had been since he kissed a woman like that, not counting the slip with Crystal.

He could always call the office first thing in the morning.

■   ■   ■

Junior peered through the dirty window of his car, watching Michelle Swirsky's house pass by slowly. It was dark and quiet. Michelle's house had no lights on at all. Had his attack spooked her mother? He could park in front of the older, one-story house and no one would even notice. Michelle had already been interviewed by a local TV station, and he felt certain the telegenic young woman would make it onto the tube a few more times before her fifteen minutes of fame ran out. Right now he had no idea where she was.

It was only a matter of time before he found her. She had to go to school. She probably wasn't going to quit her job at Publix, and she certainly wasn't going to quit the martial arts class that had saved her life. He just had to be in the right place at the right time to see her.

He knew he had to plan his next encounter with the feisty young girl, even if it just meant a bullet in her face.

He owed her.

Usually Rocky liked the people that Tim liked. It was simple. The person Tim liked the most in the world was Josh. The same as Rocky. Sometimes Rocky's heart beat so fast when the little boy came into view that he thought he might tumble over. If he did, he would be happy tumbling over.

One of the things that confused Rocky the most was Tim and his interactions with female people. Not all female people, but some of them.

The person that Josh lived with was one of them. Sometimes Tim seemed to like her and sometimes he did not. But Josh clearly liked that person, and Rocky remembered living in the same building with her when he first came home with Tim. Her name was Crystal, and she had always been nice to him.

Some of the female people that came to their house with the animals smelled artificial. He couldn't pick up a scent because of all the other odors coming off of them. Usually they only came by the house one time. The female that was here now was different.

She paid a lot of attention to Rocky. She didn't smell artificial and wasn't skittish around any of the animals. She even ran with the two little yapping dogs all over the field and threw a ball for them.

Sometimes Rocky had to compete for Tim's attention with females. But he didn't feel that way with this female. It was like he shared Tim with her and got something more from it.

Rocky really wanted to see how Josh felt about her. That would help him understand how to deal with her. But the female surprised him by getting up and leaving the house during the night. Rocky had liked her light snores. It made her feel real.

As she left the house, she made a good sound that showed she was happy. Rocky understood that this was a person's way of wagging the tail they didn't have. He liked it because it made Tim happy.

If Tim was happy, he was happy.

■   ■   ■

Tim Hallett padded across the floor of his trailer to let Rocky run loose and do his business at exactly 7 A.M. It didn't matter how late they worked or what he ate, Rocky had to go for a trot around the property at seven in the morning every single day. He was the canine equivalent of an obsessive-compulsive. On the other hand, if Hallett had to wait until someone told him he could go to the bathroom, he'd be on a pretty regular schedule, too.

He left the door open so Rocky could slip back in after he'd made his rounds and visited each of the animals in their little zoo. Hallett sucked down a Gatorade and realized how much energy he had expended the night before. Lori had slipped out before midnight, and he felt like less of a gentleman because he didn't drive her home. He'd been raised to respect women, and he had a strong protective streak. Crystal had called it smothering, but his mom had called it good manners. His parents had enforced good manners sometimes with the threat of violence. It seemed to him that manners were going out of style. But Lori appreciated his offer for her to stay and his concern about her driving home at that hour of the night.

Hallett appreciated the attention from a pretty girl. He was a bit of a romantic at heart and viewed every date as the possible start to a long-term, special relationship. His friends had told him the concept was as corny as his "serve and protect" bullshit. Maybe that was just his personality. Life could be as simple as the right slogan. He'd found if you do your best, things tend to work out.

He picked up his iPad and navigated to the *Palm Beach Post* home page. His father had read the paper every morning of his life at breakfast. Hallett did the same thing but from a twenty-first-century perspective. He went directly to the sports page, as he did every day, then the local section, and finally the front page. Although a lot happened in Belle Glade and the other western Palm Beach County communities, it seemed like the people who lived in the eastern, urban areas had no interest in anything west of the Twenty Mile Bend.

Just as he was about to set down the device, an article on the second page caught his attention. It was pseudo-gossip column that covered politics as well as celebrities. The photograph next to the article made him freeze. It was a three-year-old photo of him as a detective.

"What the hell?" he mumbled aloud.

The article said, *The hero detective who saved a young girl was instrumental in arresting the man who skated on the charge. How could the sheriff's office allow someone with such strong personal feelings to be involved in another investigation of the child molester? My sources tell me that Tim Hallett, now a member of the Canine Assist Team, was the driving force of the investigation. Is he the only competent investigator at the giant sheriff's office?*

Considering some of the stories that had run in the column, this was not unflattering, but he knew there was going to be some serious fall-out. Everyone read this column. Especially at the sheriff's office, which was a favorite target of the writer. He wondered how long it would take for someone to say something to him.

Then his phone rang. It was the captain of the detective bureau.

■　　■　　■

Two hours later, as Hallett left the captain's office and shuffled through the detective bureau, Sergeant Greene, who had been in the meeting with them, said, "Tim, I'm not happy about the story either, but it didn't really paint you in a bad light. There was nothing negative about you in the entire article."

"But our whole team is being shifted back out to our regular duties."

"The captain had to do it for appearance's sake. The public only understands police work through the prism of *Law and Order* or *CSI*. That prick at the newspaper knows it and uses it to his benefit. You did nothing wrong. In fact, you all did a superb job."

"But . . ."

"But you know there's a lot more to police work than what we see on

TV. More things affect investigations than evidence and witnesses. And this stupid, useless little paragraph in the newspaper has cost me a great asset. But I don't want it to get you down, too."

"Any bets on who leaked the story?"

Sergeant Greene just shook her head.

Hallett nodded, turned, and walked toward the exit. As he passed John Fusco's desk, the detective looked up from a report and said, "Good luck, Farmer Tim."

It was difficult to resist the urge to punch the detective square in the face.

■　　■　　■

At lunchtime, sitting at his mother's kitchen table, Hallett couldn't believe how little things had changed since he was a child. If he was upset then, he found himself sitting at the same table, eating some incredible delight his mother had whipped up just to make him smile. Now, at thirty, as a veteran police officer, he had felt the need to come back to the same table and talk to his mother. The only difference was now he had the dog he always wanted.

Rocky sat on the floor next to him eyeing his brother. Every time Hallett showed up now, Bobby automatically left the room, took a quick shower, changed clothes, and returned. It seemed like a lot of work for a stupid habit.

His mom said, "Does this mean you're going to be out on patrol again?"

"I like patrolling with Rocky."

"It's just that I worry about you out there on the street. I've seen too many videos on the news of you at the front of the pack of sheriff's deputies chasing some robber."

"That's what a canine unit is supposed to do. The dog tracks, and the deputies follow."

His mother stepped across the kitchen and sat down at the table. "I don't know how that cute little Claire Perkins does it. She looks like a cheerleader or a prom queen."

Hallett let out a laugh. "Only if the cheerleader could kick your ass or the prom queen could shoot a perfect score on the hardest tactical course we have at the range. Claire does okay."

Bobby said, "I thought you were going to introduce me to her some-time."

"You've met her before."

"I mean like *really* introduce us."

"I'll tell you what, Bobby. She's a great girl and deserves a great guy, a guy who can pull his own weight in the relationship and has some po-tential. If you quit smoking pot, I'll arrange a perfect meeting between you and Claire." Hallett knew it wasn't right to pimp out his partner and use her as a reward, but if his brother managed to quit smoking pot, he was quite sure Claire would help him out by having dinner with Bobby.

His brother perked up and rubbed his bloodshot eyes. "You really think she'd have a problem with something as simple as smoking pot?"

"I *know* she would have a problem with it. She doesn't even like to be around cigarette smoke."

"You're a good brother, Tim. I'm sorry that jerk in the paper wrote the article that got you kicked out of the detective bureau again. But I promise I'll do my best today to cheer you up."

Hallett appreciated his brother's sentiment but wondered how far he had fallen when Bobby needed to cheer him up.

■   ■   ■

Darren Mori was pissed. And relieved. He was pissed that his friend Tim Hallett was taking shit. But he was relieved to be going back out on patrol, or at least available for assignment; he and Brutus got called on for special assignments, not usually regular patrol. There was a lot that went on in the detective bureau. Not just piecing together the evi-dence and facts of the case, but the subtle politics and the competition to see who would make the case first. The whole idea made him a little uncomfortable. He didn't have the experience Tim Hallett did of work-ing in the detective bureau, and he didn't have the confidence of Claire Perkins. All he wanted to do was focus on police work. That, and figure a way to sneak by and see Kim Cooper as soon as possible.

Darren understood that not everyone did everything perfectly. He knew he was stretched far too thin. Between studying for school, stay-ing in shape, practicing karate, keeping his parents happy, and now get-ting involved in a relationship with Kim, he barely had time to concentrate on anything but keeping his head above water. It wasn't an excuse; his father had taught him early in life that excuses never helped anything. He was a pragmatist. He knew there was only so much a human could do, and there was nothing he wanted to cut loose from his life right now.

Darren was certain there was no assignment in the sheriff's office that would intimidate Claire. Throw Smarty into the mix and they were like a superhero and her sidekick. Her looks could get her into anywhere, her smarts could figure out what needed to be done, and she was tougher than any SWAT team member. Sometimes Darren looked at her as the sheriff's secret weapon.

But Darren liked sticking to things he knew best. As he got more comfortable with Brutus and his ability to sniff out trouble, whether it was a bomb or a cadaver, Darren enjoyed working the assignments given to the Canine Assist Team. Very few canine units could afford to have their dogs cross-trained and equipped as well as this unit.

Because Brutus didn't track or bite, they weren't really used on regular patrol. But as long as they were members of the CAT, Darren was just happy they were all together. Sometimes he couldn't believe he got paid to hang out with a girl like Claire and a buddy liked Tim.

Now, walking out of the headquarters building, wondering where his partners were, he saw one of the homicide detectives, Danny Weil, stepping out of his car in the parking lot. He stood by the Taurus with the driver's door still open. Then he gave them his trademark smile and friendly wave and said, "Your boy Hallett is making us look bad."

Darren glared and wished Brutus would growl. "Someone screwed him on the news article because he was telling the truth. He just wants the right person arrested."

"We all do. That's why Arnold Ludner is in jail."

"What if he's not the right man?"

"How else do you explain the sediment in his welcome mat?"

As Darren tried to come up with a smart reply, Brutus tugged on his lead and started sniffing Danny's leg. Then he stuck his head into Danny's car. Immediately he started to react oddly and looked like he was going to alert. It took Darren a moment to realize what was going on.

Darren said, "You were at the crime scene out at the canal, right?"

"Of course."

He pointed at Brutus poking his head into the vehicle's open door. "He's alerting on the sediment you tracked into your car. That's exactly how the sediment was tracked into the Ludner house."

"I wasn't even at the Ludner house, doofus."

"But somebody from the crime scene was. There were a lot of us out there that day. Brutus and I were at both scenes. I was wearing different boots, so it probably wasn't me. Apparently, it doesn't take much of the sediment to make Brutus take notice. That's why he wants to alert on your floor mat."

The detective turned back to the dog sniffing inside his car.

It clearly frustrated the detective to have such a plausible explanation proven by a dog.

Then Brutus eased the situation by doing an abnormal alert Darren had never seen. Brutus peed on the front seat of Danny Weil's car.

36

In the two days since Tim Hallett had been tossed from the detective bureau and returned to patrol for the second time, he had barely eaten or slept, and now he was starting to feel the effects. He had done virtually nothing but consider the Ludner case from a hundred different angles. Now, nibbling at the edges of a sub and talking with Claire and Darren, he was at a loss for what to do next.

He said, "I wish cases were more black and white."

Claire said, "At least there haven't been any more news stories. It was just that one quick blurb that really didn't say anything negative about you at all. If you hadn't been reassigned, it was a very positive article."

"But everyone thinks I sabotaged the case to make myself look good. Some people even think *I* had the story planted. I can feel it around the headquarters building. Everyone thinks I want back in the detective bureau."

Darren asked, "Do you?"

Hallett looked down at Rocky, sitting comfortably on the ground, and said, "Not at all. The only thing I wanted was to stop the kidnapper. To stop Ludner. My problem is I couldn't conceive that the kidnapper was not Arnold Ludner. I was trying to make up for my error three years ago. I feel like a turd whenever I'm reminded of my exit from the detective bureau. Now I'll never get redemption."

Hallett thought about what he had said. Was he turning into that guy? The guy who only cared about what affected him? He said out loud, "Fusco and Weil will fight about glory and the real kidnapper might skate."

Darren said, "Brutus showed that pompous ass Danny Weil how sediment from the crime scene could've been tracked into the house by one of us. He alerted on Danny's car mat."

"The sediment never would've held up in court. It could've come from anywhere on the canal. Anyone of us could have tracked it into the house. It could've come from . . ."

Claire looked at Hallett and said, "What's wrong, Tim? Where else could it have come from?"

"We were watching the house the whole night from both sides, right?"

Both of his partners nodded.

"And only one person left during the entire surveillance, Ludner's son, Arnold Junior."

Darren said, "Yeah, so?"

"Could Arnold Junior be the attacker?"

Claire said, "The description from the girls was consistent. The attacker was a chubby, middle-aged man."

"We look at Arnold Ludner Jr. and think of him as being relatively young at thirty-five. But the guy looks like shit. And teenagers are notoriously bad at judging ages over thirty. Do you think they could've just gotten confused? He may not be chubby as much as he's *beefy,* having more muscle than fat, but that takes an experienced eye to detect. He could theoretically match the description, especially for as little as the girls saw him."

Darren said, "Fusco wouldn't want to hear that theory."

Claire said, "Neither would homicide."

Hallett smiled and said, "So I guess it's up to us to check it out quietly. If we have enough time before they indict Ludner. Any ideas?"

Claire said, "One of the detectives' theories is that the kidnapper uses stolen cars and possibly rentals."

"I still don't follow."

"The Ludner brothers had a rental car at their compound, a black Chevy."

Hallett considered it for a moment and said, "I see where you're going with this, but we're not in any position to issue subpoenas to rental car companies for their records."

Darren had a big smile as he said, "I might be in a position to get that information."

Hallett felt better just considering doing something proactive.

■   ■   ■

Junior needed to get out and drive around before he got back to work. Sometimes just doing minor chores cleared his head. But today nothing was easy because all he could think about was Michelle Swirsky. She had imbedded herself in his brain. He hated the thought of risking the police spotlight, but he could see no other path. It had something to do with what he had experienced with Tina Tictin. That ultimate display of power. When Katie Ziegler escaped, it didn't affect him like this. He moved on. Or maybe it had to do with the way Michelle had hurt him physically. He just couldn't let it go.

The idea of wasting all that effort to stay off the radar and make it tough for the cops annoyed him. Then he thought about Michelle, that athletic grace and fresh, beautiful smile. And the attitude that she thought she was better than him.

These girls didn't make a decision about what was going to happen and when, he did. He was the creator of this universe where he got to study girls and learn everything there was about their backgrounds before he opened a whole new world to them. The physical part, feeling them squirm or shake underneath his touch, was such a small part of the sensation. Knowing he had dominated them and had imposed his will, that was what made him feel so special.

He'd convinced himself that if he had finished things with Michelle, he could've lived off his memories and fantasies for at least a few years. But now he didn't see how that could happen. Not while she walked around so arrogant and carefree.

He tried to focus on something else. Anything. Then he gave in to the feeling and let his mind flood with images of what he imagined she would look like on the front seat of his car.

■   ■   ■

Darren had learned a lot about investigations in his time in the D-bureau. Fusco had helped him understand how to deal with people, and now he was gathering information without the use of subpoenas or any of the stuff he learned in the police academy. Police work really was about contacts. Knowing the right people and how they maintained information was the key to making things work. Even if he felt a little creepy asking Kim for the information.

He was honest as he stood in front of the Hertz counter and explained to her what he needed.

Kim looked at him and said, "I'm not supposed to give you any information like that. They're very specific in training. We need a subpoena, and I have to call our legal department." The whole time she was talking, she typed on a terminal but kept her eyes pretty much on Darren.

Brutus had put his paws up on the counter and laid his head so Kim could reach across and rub it. He had definitely figured this girl out even if Darren hadn't.

Then Kim said, "Hypothetically, no one by the name of Ludner has rented any cars from us."

Darren smiled as he realized how far out on a limb this girl was going for him. He appreciated it. But that didn't change the fact that he hadn't found out anything useful.

Then Kim said, "I can ask down the row. We all help each other, and they want to help me impress you." She gave him a wink as she hustled off to the left and talked to the girl at National Rental first.

About five minutes later she came back with notes written on the stationery from Sunshine Rental Vehicles, a small, independent company. Kim said, "Sunshine has horrible records, but they know a guy named Arnold Ludner Jr." She slid a sheet of paper across the counter to him. "He usually rents a car for three or four days about every two weeks. Always pays in cash. They thought he just traveled for work."

Darren looked down at the sheet of paper and smiled. It had all the dates going back for the past year. There were almost twenty different rental periods. He looked up and said, "You rock."

Kim flashed that perfect smile and said, "Yes, I do."

■　　■　　■

Claire Perkins had spent her four years at the Palm Beach County Sheriff's Office on patrol or in the K-9 unit. She had only done surveillance since working on the temporary duty assignment in the detective bureau. Even though the three Chevy Tahoes that she, Tim Hallett, and Darren Mori drove were unmarked, they were still large white SUVs. The fact that they were following a convicted drug dealer, who was probably looking for surveillance, made their job that much tougher.

She used to think that she'd been raised in a household with a drug culture. Her mom and dad had no problem with marijuana being smoked openly in front of her, and she knew that her dad, especially, used all kinds of other drugs. That was one of the reasons he was constantly changing jobs and also why her mother left him when Claire was a little girl. But seeing these two brothers brought a whole new meaning to the phrase "drug culture." These guys had combined capitalism and consumerism to make a small fortune. Even if their house didn't show it. With their brother as their lawyer, they weren't losing a lot in attorney fees every time they were arrested.

In a way, she was just going along with this idea to satisfy Tim Hallett and calm him down. Like most everyone else in the sheriff's office, she was not convinced of Arnold Ludner's innocence. There were just too many factors that could explain the attack on Michelle Swirsky while they had Arnold Ludner under surveillance.

Today, they had been following his son for about an hour and half on what looked like regular errands. She had monitored the radio in case they got a call, because this was just something they were doing on the side without any supervisory approval or guidance. They hadn't even told Ruben Vasquez what they were doing. Although she suspected the dog trainer would approve of them working as a team.

Arnold Ludner Jr. drove his gold Toyota Highlander to the jail first. That was to visit his father, she was certain. It also gave them a chance to gas up their vehicles and let the dogs out to run for a few minutes. No visitor in history had ever slipped in and out of the Palm Beach County jail in less than an hour.

Then Ludner made a stop at the grocery store and visited his mother in the neighborhood not far from where Tina Tictin had disappeared. So far, Claire was impressed that the guy would visit both his father and his mother. She knew a lot of men that barely paid attention to their parents.

Then, trying to stay well back of the drug dealer, all three Tahoes followed him into one of the rougher sections of the county, just west of the sheriff's office.

Hallett came over the radio. "I had to drive past him. I'll pick him up if he heads north on Military Trail."

Darren said, "I'll hang back this way in case he comes back south."

That left Claire with the "eye." She loved the slang the detectives assigned to some of their duties. The "eye" was simply the person who had the best view of the subject. It was really the narcotics unit that did most of the surveillance, but she enjoyed getting experience in anything that had to do with police work.

She pulled the Tahoe into a spot across the street. Smarty automatically sat straight and was ready to move. Every time she stopped the car, the dog hoped it was a chance for him to chase after someone. She could tell Arnold Ludner Jr. had no idea he was being watched as he approached the side entrance to a cheesy strip mall. He met someone coming out the door of an unmarked office and immediately grabbed the man by the collar of his shirt and whipped him against the wall. This wasn't something she expected.

Claire got on the radio quickly and said, "He's assaulting a white male, about forty years old. It looks like he might be trying to collect some money."

Hallett said, "If he goes too far, we have to make a move. This is much faster than I wanted to confront him, but it's your call, Claire."

Claire watched, hoping the confrontation would resolve itself. Then she saw Ludner reach in his pocket and pull something metallic out. There was no more time to wait. She jumped on the radio and called out, "I think he's got a knife. We have to move right now."

■ ■ ■

As soon as Claire had advised them what was happening on the radio, Tim Hallett roared up to the shopping center to back her up. She had already crossed the street into the parking lot. Arnold Ludner Jr. jerked his head up, released the man he was holding against the wall, and started to sprint across the lot toward the street.

Hallett brought the Tahoe to a screeching halt, stepped out of the door, and shouted, "Really? You're gonna run again?" It had no effect on the beefy man.

Hallett shouted, "I'm going to release my dog."

Now the man froze at the edge of the parking lot.

Hallett stepped around the Tahoe, drawing his pistol. In a stressful situation, all a cop remembers is training. He had gone through arrest scenarios a thousand times on the training field so that now it was automatic. He looked over the front sight of his pistol and scanned the area immediately around the suspect. He noticed one hand closed and shouted, "Drop it."

The metallic clink of the knife on the asphalt made Hallett hesitate. He took a quick glance to his right and saw Claire had the suspect covered with her pistol. Now he could go by the book.

Hallett said, "Raise your hands to the side."

Arnold Ludner Jr. complied.

"Now walk slowly backward toward me." When the suspect was ten feet away, Hallett told him to stop and drop to his knees, then out to a prone position. Hallett holstered his pistol, checking again to make sure Claire was in a position to shoot if she had to. He stepped forward, pulling the stainless steel handcuffs from their pouch and holding them in his left hand with the blades free to move.

He said, "Put your hands behind your back."

The drug dealer had been through the drill before. Still lying on the ground, he struggled to touch the backs of his hands behind his back.

Hallett slid in with one knee on top of the suspect as he smoothly slapped the cuffs on him.

Arnold Ludner Jr. said, "Why are you following me?"

"Why did you threaten that man?"

"I was just showing him my knife."

Hallett looked over his shoulder to see the man scurry into the office.

37

Darren Mori was upset he'd missed the confrontation with Arnold Ludner Jr. Those types of incidents, the kind where you pulled your gun and shouted at someone, were what he lived for. To him, that was the kind of shit that defined police work; the adrenaline rush after drawing a weapon, the thrill of doing something no one else in a civil society can do, made him regret his choice of surveillance posts. If he hadn't been sitting down the street waiting to watch the suspect drive south, he might've been in position to help with the arrest.

Now, Tim Hallett had asked Darren to go into the office and interview the victim while he talked to the suspect out in the parking lot. The porcine, sweaty little man had a scuff on his chin and kept insisting nothing happened.

Darren said, "He pulled a knife on you."

"Did he? If he did it was just to show it to me." The man had an odd foreign accent that Darren couldn't immediately identify. He was good with the different Caribbean and South American accents, but this definitely had a Middle Eastern flair to it.

Darren said, "How'd you get that mark on your chin?"

The man instinctively raised his finger to the welt, then pulled it away, saying, "Who knows how these things happen. I think this is just a huge mistake."

"What kind of office is this?"

"My office."

"What you do here?" Darren looked around the barren office that had a few empty desks and unused phones.

"I sell time-shares, but it's slow right now."

Now Darren's interest was piqued. "Can I take a look around?"

"Why?"

"Can I?"

The man looked down at the floor and shook his head. "No."

Darren leaned in close to him and said, "That shithead out in the parking lot is your supplier, isn't he?" He loved playing the bad cop even if there wasn't a good cop around. It was rare he got to be involved in this sort of discussion. But it did feel odd interviewing someone without Brutus at his side—even if the dog wouldn't be any help in a fight and wasn't particularly intimidating.

The man shook his head at Darren's assertion, saying, "No, we're just friends."

Darren gave him his best tough-guy glare and said, "Stay right here. We'll see what's going on."

■   ■   ■

Tim Hallett stood alone in the parking lot with Arnold Ludner Jr. Ludner's hands were cuffed behind his back, and he was leaning against the SUV. Rocky was inside his compartment right behind the shithead. Hallett liked the idea of letting the suspect worry about startling the agitated dog. He also liked the idea that if the situation went wrong, Rocky was just a quick push of a button away from helping him.

Hallett needed something to scare this guy. He was going to check his ankle and ribs for injuries similar to the ones Michelle Swirsky described, but he was hoping the guy would talk first.

Darren Mori came out the office and marched over to them saying, "The victim says he threatened him with a knife."

Hallett caught his partner's wink and knew it was just a ploy to make the suspect confess. The problem was the suspect's experience. He also knew his distributors well.

Arnold Ludner Jr. looked Hallett square in the face and said, "Bullshit. He didn't say that."

"He didn't say it or you didn't do it?"

The suspect just smiled. He really had the victim figured out. Finally, Hallett said, "Let's forget this whole ugly incident and talk about your dad."

"I already did. You didn't want to listen."

"Now I have a new perspective."

■   ■   ■

After ten minutes of talking and negotiating, Tim Hallett felt like he had developed a real rapport with Arnold Ludner Jr. That's why, at the suspect's request, Hallett had led him over to the side of the building and moved his handcuffs to a more comfortable position with his hands in front. Claire and Darren were tending to their dogs by their vehicles, which were now parked in the shopping center. No one had called this in yet, and Hallett thought he might be able to parlay it into a much bigger payoff than a simple assault with a knife. So far, he had violated several major policies for handling prisoners. The two men stood in a miniature breezeway underneath an overhang to the shopping plaza. Hallett had allowed the silence between them to last two minutes, hoping it might eat at Ludner's guilt. He wasn't sure how he wanted to phrase the questions, but he knew he wanted Arnold Ludner Jr. to say he had attacked Michelle Swirsky and that's why he was so certain his father was innocent. But that was a lot to ask.

Ludner leaned in and said, "Okay, I'm ready to talk." He lifted his handcuffed wrists and motioned Hallett closer.

Hallett felt the excitement run through his body, believing he was about to solve the biggest case in the sheriff's office right now. He stepped in closer and said, "I'm listening."

The suspect mumbled something and Hallett leaned closer.

Arnold Ludner Jr. bent down, then sprang up, driving the crown of his head into Hallett's face. At the last moment, Hallett turned and took the head butt on his forehead, but it still knocked him against the wall and onto the ground. As his vision cleared, he looked up to see Ludner running hard across the rear parking lot toward a residential neighborhood. Hallett didn't hesitate to spring to his feet and give chase.

He closed so much of the distance so quickly that he didn't bother to call for help or send Rocky after the pudgy doper. He wanted to deliver the payback himself. Hallett kicked it into high gear and hit the hefty drug dealer just as he reached the street. He delivered a high body block like a linebacker. Both men hit the ground, but Hallett had the luxury of using Arnold Ludner Jr. as a cushion. His handcuffed hands couldn't splay out and break his fall, so he skidded along the asphalt like a raccoon hit by a Lincoln Continental.

Hallett landed directly on top of him, facing the sweaty drug dealer. He glanced around quickly to see if anyone had noticed they weren't standing at the plaza. They were alone.

Hallett said, "Why'd you run, asshole?"

"Did you forget who I was? It's my job to run. It's *your* job to catch me."

Hallett thought about that for a moment. This guy was some kind of philosopher. Hallett pushed off him and helped the tubby man to his feet. He brushed off a couple of the pebbles stuck to his cheek and shoulders.

"I thought you wanted to help your dad."

The drug dealer said, "Why replace one innocent man with another? I know what you're trying to get at. I've never harmed a woman in my whole life and don't know why you think I had anything to do with the crime."

Hallett said, "I saw you leave the house the night Michelle Swirsky was attacked."

"I leave the house every night. I'm a fucking drug dealer. My brother's the one on probation. He's the one that has to be at home most times. That leaves me to go out and make collections and check on our distributors. What made you think I was connected with the attack?"

"You rent a lot of cars. That fits with the kidnapper."

The surly drug dealer said, "You never worked narcotics, did you? If you did, then you know anyone in my business transports the bigger loads of dope in rental cars. That way if we're caught and the cops seize the car, we don't lose nothing." He shook his head in disgust.

Hallett understood the reasoning but didn't want to give away any information that Fusco or homicide was holding back. Instead, he jerked up Arnold Ludner Jr.'s pants legs and said, "Let me see your ankles."

The drug dealer lifted each leg, one at a time, so Hallett could examine his bare ankles. There were no marks at all.

Then he yanked on Arnold Ludner Jr.'s shirt to examine his ribs. Nothing.

Hallett pulled the drug dealer to his feet and slowly started walking back toward the plaza. "You know what we suspect your dad of doing."

"I already told you I did. My brother and I aren't happy about it. We'd like to keep it from ever happening again." His tone was steady and serious.

"If I give you some dates, you think you could provide me with some alibis just so I could eliminate you as a suspect? It might mean we can focus on someone else and clear this up faster."

"If you're talking about the two girls that were kidnapped a couple of years ago, I can tell you right now I'll have the perfect alibi."

"What's that?"

"I was in jail." Then, after a few seconds he added, "Sherlock Holmes."

Hallett had moved so fast he hadn't checked simple things like that. It was still just a theory, but if the alibi was true, and right now he believed the drug dealer, he was back to square one.

38

Tim Hallett had already explained the bruise on his forehead as "just a minor mishap" to Lori Tate. They enjoyed the rest of their casual dinner at a Mexican restaurant on Forest Hill Boulevard with light banter about everything except the Palm Beach County Sheriff's Office and work.

Hallett had left Rocky at his mother's house, where he enjoyed running around her fenced backyard and chasing imaginary rabbits. The more time he spent with Lori, the more he was beginning to believe she was really something special. She didn't say much about her family except that she'd been born in Alabama and raised in North Florida, which explained her light southern accent.

When they had first come into the place, waiting for a table at the bar, they'd watched a local news show that featured a story on Michelle Swirsky, newly famous for her escape from an attacker.

Hallett noticed the reporter tried to sound like a teenager during the interview. She spoke like someone who watched too much MTV. It had to be awkward dealing with people like that.

Michelle said she hadn't realized how lucky she was at first when she escaped from the man. She hadn't even told her mother until she saw a news story about the murder of a teenager and the description of the man who killed her sounded a lot like Michelle's attacker. She had to do what was right.

Hallett smiled, knowing what the girl had escaped. She was lucky.

After dinner, when he ran out of conversation about movies he liked and answered her questions about his own childhood, Hallett hinted that he was still interested in what was going to happen with Arnold Ludner. He didn't mention any of his earlier conversation with Arnold Ludner Jr. As far as anyone was concerned—since there wasn't a complaint and the victim wasn't willing to talk, and Hallett was embarrassed that the guy had managed to get away from him, even if it was only for a few seconds—the incident had never occurred. He had released a slightly pissed-off Arnold Ludner Jr. from custody and gone about his regular patrol work.

Lori said, "I think homicide is going to charge Ludner very soon. I don't know for sure, because the detective, Danny Weil, doesn't mix with anyone in the office. No one trusts him."

"How'd he get the case?"

"He politicked hard to get something other than the drug shootings cases he usually gets. The sergeant gave it to him before it was linked to the others and became so high profile."

Hallett shook his head and thought how much of a role chance played in police work. Chance had screwed this case up in a big way.

■　　■　　■

Junior wrote out his plan like an engineer, calculating the odds of grabbing Michelle at the community college, at home, or at work. He realized he needed to take a breath, step back, and plan this thing out carefully, but he couldn't ignore the pounding drive that was forcing him to take action when his common sense said it that was ridiculous. What options were left?

The school had cameras and its own security force, as well as the occasional patrolling Palm Beach County sheriff's deputy. Everyone kept their eyes open where young people congregated.

Michelle's mother was so crazy right now that it was conceivable her house was an armed camp. He could find himself outgunned and outmatched by the high-kicking girl and her suspicious mother. Besides, there were too many neighbors who could see something and report it to the police.

That left the Publix supermarket where she worked. He hadn't seen any cameras in the parking lot. Michelle had to walk outside into the parking lot frequently to deliver the groceries purchased by the elderly people in the neighborhood. That could work.

It might take a couple of nights of surveillance and planning to get it right. Maybe he'd do it one night after he visited his father. He could use the idea of grabbing Michelle as a way to get through the ordeal of visiting his father in that nasty place. It smelled and gave him the creeps.

Junior wondered if he could wait. This urge to complete his mission with Michelle and teach her she wasn't better than him threatened to drive him crazy.

■   ■   ■

Tim Hallett noticed John Fusco cringe when he and Rocky walked into the detective bureau. He could hear the detective saying quietly to himself, "Don't come over here. Don't come over here." Then, when Hallett turned and marched directly toward him, Fusco muttered a quiet "Shit."

Hallett stopped right in front of the desk, and his dog sat immediately, staring at Fusco like a hound out of an old horror movie. Hallett said, "Can we talk rationally?"

"I don't know, can we?"

"I recognize that this is your case and I might've been overstepping the boundaries, but I'm concerned that we've arrested the wrong man."

"As concerned as you were that we hadn't done anything to arrest him in the first place? Concerned enough to hound me to take action? I can remember you pounding the drum pretty hard for us to focus on Arnold Ludner. Now tell me who else we can focus on."

"I know, I know. But haven't you ever made a mistake?"

Fusco took a moment, sighed, and said, "Look, Tim, most of this is out of my hands anyway. That jerk-off Danny Weil in homicide is the one driving the ship now. But if you came up with something, I might be able to show it to the sergeant in homicide."

Hallett didn't want to imply that Fusco didn't know what he was doing. He did. The obnoxious New Yorker was one of the most successful detectives in the whole county. But Hallett was desperate to stay involved in the case and was grasping at straws.

Hallett said, "I've been looking at photos of the girls, and they all have a similar look. Not necessarily hair and eye color but sort of an athletic, innocent look."

Fusco just nodded silently.

"And the fact that he has hot-wired vehicles so effectively means he might have a criminal background related to auto theft. Or he closely associates with someone who knows their shit."

Fusco said, "Or he's an auto mechanic."

"There is that, too." He reached down to rub Rocky on the neck, a nervous habit he had whenever he was at a loss for words. Then he blurted out, "The other thing I've puzzled over is the locations where he grabbed the girls. It seemed like he knew the best places to avoid detection and confuse investigations."

"Look, Tim, do you have a point?"

"I just want you to know I'm available if anything comes up you need help with."

"I understand what you're going through. It's tough to be kicked out of the detective bureau. Twice. But you still got your job, and you seem to like hanging out with your dog."

That earned a growl from Rocky as if he could follow the conversation clearly.

Fusco continued, "Let the detectives work this case. That's what we've been trained for."

"Will you at least keep an open mind? I know I pushed you toward Ludner, but I think you're making a terrible mistake."

Fusco was no longer angry at the dog handler; he just felt sorry for him. He said, "Sure, pal, I'll keep an open mind."

■　　■　　■

In the three days since he had talked to John Fusco in the detective bureau, Hallett had been on a roller coaster of emotions, from hope that the detective might listen to him to despair when he realized his career at the sheriff's office could be over. But, as usual, a combination of Josh and Rocky had lifted him out of his funk.

It was exactly the kind of Sunday morning Tim Hallett lived for. He had Josh with him for the weekend; they had spent the morning feeding the animals in the pens and watching Rocky chase wild rabbits on the edge of the school property. Usually he'd feel like a million bucks. Josh was dressed in a tiny button-down shirt with a short clip-on tie, ready for church. Rocky paced, knowing the church was one of the few places he couldn't go.

As usual, the TV was on in the background, and Hallett only paid passing attention to certain stories running across the local NBC station's newscast. This weekend show focused on human-interest stories more than breaking news, but it caught him up on life in the rest of Palm Beach County. No one ever did human-interest stories in Belle Glade.

Hallett glanced at the TV and froze. The entire screen was covered by a young woman's smiling face. It was Michelle Swirsky. He eased himself onto the bed, unable to take his eyes off the TV screen, and listened as Michelle recounted her attack in that cute, halting, teenage cadence. Then a voice-over asked the question, "Was this girl attacked as revenge for a Bernie Madoff–type scheme?" The story went on to say that Michelle's father was currently serving a five-year sentence in the Florida Department of Corrections for fraud and other crimes related to his Ponzi scheme.

Hallett recalled Katie Ziegler saying her father was in jail and that's why he wasn't available in case of an emergency. Could it be? He reached across the bed and snatched his phone, dialing the sheriff's office dispatcher. As soon as someone answered, Hallett identified himself and said, "Can you run a name for me, please?" After a moment he said, "All I have is a last name and location." He spelled out Tictin and the location in Lake Worth.

After a few moments the dispatcher came back on and said she had one name that came up through the Florida Crime and Information Center, better known as FCIC. She said, "I have a Robert Tictin, white, male, forty-eight years old."

Hallett said, "That's him."

The dispatcher said, "He's currently in the custody of Department of Corrections. Looks like the charge was possession with intent to distribute cocaine."

Hallett felt anxiety rise in him as he realized he'd found the connection between the victims.

39

Tim Hallett was on his own now. He didn't want John Fusco's pity, or to risk getting Claire or Darren in any more trouble. He had to run down this one lead. He even knew where to go. The girls who'd been kidnapped all had fathers in prison. It had killed him to sit on the information all day Sunday, but he knew there was nothing he could do. Now, he and Rocky were walking into the main probation office in West Palm Beach. Bill Slaton had to feel some sort of involvement in the case. He had supervised Arnold Ludner during his brief probation. The guy was an asshole, there was no doubt of that, but Hallett was sure he would jump at the chance to break a case like this. Who wouldn't?

If Slaton didn't want to help, Hallett could always limp into Fusco's office, explain what he had discovered, and see what happened. It was an odd feeling to be so isolated. The detective bureau wanted nothing to do with him. It used to be his home.

Hallett stepped into the seedy Probation and Parole building, and one look at his uniform and Rocky standing next to him sent two of the probationers scurrying to other exits. Even the secretary looked nervous. She reminded him of Crystal with less disposable income to spend on hair care products, fake nails, and wardrobe.

He stood in front of the secretary and asked for Bill Slaton. She just pointed down the hallway and showed obvious relief when Rocky stopped staring at her and focused on his walk down the narrow, thinly carpeted hall.

Hallett found the pudgy probation officer crammed into a minuscule office at the end of the building. Slaton almost looked embarrassed at being caught in such shabby accommodations.

True to form, all the probation officer said was, "What do you want?"

"To talk."

"About what?"

"The new Arnold Ludner case."

Slaton stood from behind his desk and leaned forward slightly, say-ing, "I deal with Detective Fusco. Does he know you're here? I'm way too busy to be distracted by some hot-shot patrolman."

Annoyed, Hallett stepped into the cramped office, allowing Rocky to slip in with him. Rocky tugged at his lead to lean in and sniff Slaton's leg. Before Hallett could let the probation officer know who was in charge, Rocky distracted him. He leaned down his head and put his paw close to his nose and made the same odd sound, like a lawn mower, that he'd made after finding the rag near Katie Ziegler.

Hallett was still processing what it all meant when the heavyset pro-bation officer said, "Get lost."

■   ■   ■

Rocky didn't strain on the short lead Tim had him on. They were going inside a building, and he knew he wouldn't be allowed to stray very far. Almost as soon as they entered the front door, two men ran out the back. The quick whiff that Rocky got told him the men smelled like a game he played with Tim. The smell came from a green plant that people kept in little bags.

All the people in the room smelled like they were scared. The fe-male person Tim was talking to behind the desk was clearly scared. Rocky could see it and really smell it. She was no threat. Not to Tim or to him or anyone else. Rocky just stared at her. A predator's stare. He stared at her because sometimes it was just fun to make people nervous. They made new smells and acted in odd ways. Rocky had to resist wagging his tail, it made him so happy.

Tim led Rocky down a narrow hallway and stopped in front of a very small room. Rocky couldn't even see inside all the way, but he could tell it was cramped and musty. There were mice that lived in the room. Rocky could smell them and heard one scratching next to him in the wall. Rocky didn't like the room or the voice of the person speaking to Tim.

As Tim communicated with the other person, Rocky stepped up to the door and peeked inside. A large man he had seen before stepped from behind a desk and moved toward him. Rocky leaned in and took a quick sniff of the man's leg.

The scent hit Rocky hard, making his whole body stiffen. That was it! The same scent that had confused him in the field with the tall grass. The predator's scent.

Without meaning to, Rocky had the same reaction and placed his head on the ground and his paw up to his nose. He also hoped Tim would see it was the same scent.

Rocky wished he could communicate more information to Tim. This was important. He just knew it.

■　　■　　■

Hallett felt an emotion close to panic as sweat broke out across his forehead. His legs were shaky as he led Rocky back to the Tahoe in the quiet parking lot, and both he and the dog were on edge. Did that alert mean as much as Hallett thought? Did Slaton pick up on it? There were a thousand explanations for the odd alert by Rocky. But the only one that bounced into Hallett's head was that Slaton gave off the scent on the rag found near Katie Ziegler weeks earlier. It sounded crazy. It was beyond the limits of what some dogs could do. But Hallett knew Rocky was special.

There were other factors that fit this crazy-assed theory. Slaton had access to the computers that would link the incarcerated men and their families. He would know the family situation for some of the girls.

There was a code among law enforcement to protect one another, but that didn't extend to serious crimes the way some silly TV storylines depicted. No cop wanted a criminal to get away with anything, especially if it was another cop. The code was more of a brotherhood that included playing by the rules and not hurting people. Sure, a cop could avoid getting a speeding ticket, but just about anything else got you booted out of the brotherhood pretty fast. There had been a time when cops might overlook drinking and driving, but now, with the focus from MADD and other groups, no one cut slack on a DUI. At no time would murder be ignored for a cop. Anyway, at no time was a probation officer considered a cop. Slaton was not even a well-liked probation officer.

Hallett needed to find someone to talk to and quick.

■   ■   ■

He caught Fusco in the parking lot of the sheriff's office. He didn't even waste time with a greeting. "I need to talk to you."

Fusco held up his hands and said, "I've been told to avoid you. You are a patrol unit not involved in investigations."

"Who told you to avoid me?"

"My bosses."

"Sergeant Greene?"

"No, above her. So you better move on. We have nothing to discuss."

"But I saw Bill Slaton this morning. The probation officer."

"So?"

"I'm not sure. But I have an odd feeling, and Rocky made an abnormal alert just like he did the day he found that rag near Katie Ziegler."

Fusco sighed and rubbed his hand across his face. "Now you want me to go after a probation officer because your goddamn dog has a theory about the case? Come on, Hallett, you're starting to lose it. I'll do you a favor and forget you ever mentioned this bullshit to me."

Hallett stared at the arrogant detective, resisting the urge to choke him because he realized it would only make him look crazier than he already sounded. He allowed the detective to walk away as he considered his next move.

■   ■   ■

Hallett immediately started to put his manic energy to use and looked for Ruben Vasquez at the training center. He found the dog trainer in close consultation with Claire Perkins.

Everyone expected cops to have all the answers when it came to crime. In fact, a modern police force had so many units and contained so much information that one person could never be an expert on everything. One of Hallett's strengths as a police officer was asking advice from the right people. The most knowledgeable person about dogs that Hallett knew was Ruben Vasquez.

Ruben looked up and said, "What can I do for you, Tim?"

He calmly explained what had just happened when he visited the probation officer.

Ruben said, "It was the same reaction to the rag?"

"Exactly."

Ruben nodded and muttered, "This could be big. Belgian Malinois aren't known for that kind of scent discrimination skills, but Rocky is an exceptional dog." Then he looked at Hallett and said, "And you're certain no one in the D-bureau is interested?"

"They won't even talk to me. The only issue is how much time we have before homicide submits an affidavit to the state attorney's office on Arnold Ludner. I'm not sure I can work this alone."

Claire spoke up. "You, Darren, and I will work it as a team."

Hallett liked that attitude.

40

Claire insisted on coming with Tim Hallett to the hospital that had treated Bill Slaton after he'd gotten injured during the arrest at the Ludner house. It was a simple but unofficial assignment. They wanted to look at his medical records from the day he was checked out for the injury. It was an absolute violation of patient privacy, and they weren't telling anyone at the sheriff's office what they were doing.

Claire felt a pang of guilt not telling John Fusco what they were doing. They were trying to start a relationship now that she was out of the detective bureau, and she had never been a good liar. That was one of the things she admired about John. He wasn't a good liar either. That's why she believed him when she asked if he had planted the story about Tim in *The Palm Beach Post*. Incredibly, Tim seemed to be the only one who had moved on from the incident. She and Darren were outraged that someone would provide information to a reporter like that. No matter what the reason, it just didn't feel right.

Claire believed it was important for her to come along to show Tim she believed in him and was willing to do whatever was necessary to solve this case. She knew Tim must be going through hell thinking about how he distracted the detectives from the real kidnapper by focusing on Arnold Ludner.

She didn't mind walking through hospital corridors in uniform. Unlike in most other places, no one seemed to notice a uniformed cop in a hospital. It was natural. When she walked just about anywhere else, people stared at her. She realized part of it was they weren't used to seeing a petite woman wearing a tactical vest and a gun, but part of it was just the public's curiosity with police work.

She'd been impressed how smooth Hallett had been as he went about discovering which emergency room doctor had treated Bill Slaton. There was no way they were going to get a look directly at the file, but a doctor might be able to tell them everything they needed to know.

In the emergency room she immediately noticed the young Indian doctor leaning against the counter at the nurses' station, filling out some paperwork.

Hallett called out, "Dr. Naza?"

The good-looking young doctor nodded as he focused on the papers.

"I need to speak with you."

The doctor still ignored them.

Hallett threw in an emphatic "Now."

That got the doctor to look up and assess them before he said, "What can I do for you?"

"We're just doing the follow-up on an arrest from last week where a probation officer got hurt. Do you remember treating Bill Slaton?"

The doctor thought about it for a moment, then nodded his head and said, "Portly gentleman, about forty-five?"

"That's him. Can you tell me how serious his injuries were for the report I'm writing?"

The doctor hesitated, then said, "I can't talk about a patient without his permission, even in a situation like this."

Claire liked how Tim Hallett stayed cool and professional even if he was lying his ass off.

"We're trying to file charges on the drug dealers that injured him, and I just wanted your quick opinion. We know he hurt his back. All I need to know is if you think it was serious or not."

After a moment of internal conflict he said, "It was obvious the man had physical stress, but I don't think it was a very serious injury. I told him a day's rest would relieve any of the discomfort in his back."

Claire pretended to make a few notes to add to their facade.

Hallett asked, "Did you notice any other injuries? Mr. Slaton said his ankle was sore and his ribs hurt."

Now that he was more comfortable with the conversation, the young doctor relaxed and spoke freely. He nodded his head and said, "I never looked at his ankle, but he had a previous injury that had already started to turn black and blue on the left side of his torso. It didn't happen from the same incident as his back. But that wasn't serious either. Just a little discoloration and, at most, a cracked rib. He seemed to be breathing all right, but I gave him a prescription for hydrocodone until the pain eased up."

Claire smiled as Tim nodded his head like they were in a professional consultation. Then Hallett asked, "Could you tell us how he might've come by the injuries on his torso? Did he offer an explanation?"

The doctor shook his head. "Isn't he one of you guys? Shouldn't you just ask him? I was busy that day and don't think I inquired."

Claire sensed the doctor getting suspicious and realized Tim did, too, when he said, "Thank you for your time. We'll be back in touch if we need something else."

She liked this kind of sneaky investigation as long as they didn't get fired for it later.

■   ■   ■

Even though it was only six in the evening, Junior wished he were a drinker so he could take something to steady his nerves. It wasn't just visiting his father, it was the building itself. Just the thought of the smell inside made his stomach flip.

But Junior intended to make use of his urge to grab Michelle Swirsky to get through this dreadful task. When he was finished visiting with his father, he could look for Michelle in earnest. Just the thought of her could get him through it.

He nodded to the attendants as he strolled through the hallways he knew so well and ended up at the semiprivate room where Mr. Goldman occupied the first bed. The retired builder had married a younger woman who took the first opportunity to dump him in this cesspool of a nursing home and run off with the yard guy. He loved telling Junior the story every time he came to visit his father.

Thankfully, tonight, Mr. Goldman was absorbed in the local news.

As soon as Junior stepped to the far side of the room, his father's yellowed eyes shifted to him.

He croaked, "Hello, Junior. What brings you around today? Has it been a week already?"

Junior said, "I'm a day early, Pop." Before he could say anything else, the newscaster on TV mentioned the name Michelle Swirsky, and his head automatically swiveled around to see the bright, youthful face smiling and talking with a young female reporter. He heard Michelle say something like, "I won't let the incident change my life. I'm just a little more alert."

Junior muttered, "Arrogant bitch."

From his bed, Junior's father said, "That little firecracker will go far in life. You could probably take some lessons from her."

"Take lessons, give lessons, it would just be nice to chat with her. You always told me to reach for my dreams. Who knows, she might be part of my dreams."

The old man said, "Does your dream have something to do with your dick?"

"Why?"

"You were a little creepy shit as a kid. Always peeking in windows and lingering too long when you shouldn't. Your mother just thought you were curious, but what did she care, living two hours away. At first I thought you were nosy, always trying to hear things the adults were saying. God damn if you didn't cling onto your mother like you were a tumor until she fled to Chicago." The old man suffered a coughing fit that startled Junior, and Mr. Goldman mumbled, "Keep it down, will you?"

When Bill Slaton Sr. had recovered, he wiped his eyes and looked at his son. "Then there was the time you showed your little pecker to the neighbor girl, remember? She laughed and you cried. I had to tell her parents it would never happen again."

Junior wondered if his father had lost it completely. He didn't know what the old geezer was babbling about. Then looking at the old man's face and recalling what it was like thirty years ago did something. It flipped a switch in his brain. It hit him all at once. He did remember.

He took a step back and felt the chair behind him. His legs seemed to give out as he plopped into it, still staring at his father. The next thing he knew he was back in his father's cluttered, two-car garage in Fort Wayne. This had been in autumn, near Halloween, because he had shown the girl from next door his ghost costume. Her name was Karen Olson and she was a classic midwestern Viking beauty, a year younger than him. He had been curious about the differences between men and women. He had seen his mom naked a number of times, but by now she was gone. He wondered what a younger female looked like. He also wondered if she wanted to see his penis. So, without asking or warning, he unzipped his pants. At first Karen seemed amazed. Even though she hadn't asked to see it, she wasn't afraid either. Then she started to giggle. Just the thought of it, even after all these years, made his blood turn cold. He wondered if his father could notice it past his cataracts.

Things had just gotten worse. Her giggles turned into an all-out mocking laugh as she said, "I've only seen pictures, but yours is a miniature. It's even kind of cute."

Junior hadn't known what to do. He was desperate to shut her up, but she kept laughing. Even after he had zipped up his pants and was trying to shove her out of the garage, her laughter cut into his brain. He had seen a hammer sitting on his father's workbench and wondered if bashing her blond hair would get her to stop. But he hesitated to pick it up and it was too late. She strolled home, her giggles echoing back into the garage and torturing him.

Karen Olson left on a fall vacation a few days later, and her family moved to Minneapolis because her father found a new job. Somehow, Junior had managed to block the whole incident, as well as the girl, out of his brain completely. It wasn't until Miss Trooluck showed him how to please a woman that he realized how he was interested in the opposite sex. Miss Trooluck had been kind and patient and didn't laugh when he pulled down his underwear.

More astonishing than recalling the memory of his brief encounter with the beautiful Karen Olson was his father's cold and calculating treatment to "cure" his problem. By this time in Junior's life, his mother had pretty much checked out of the family and moved to a suburb of Chicago. She only visited three times after she had moved.

His father's punishment was simple. If Junior wanted to parade around nude and show off his private parts—as his father called them in those days—his father would give him a lesson in modesty. He made young Junior strip down naked and then put a ribbon of Scotch tape across his penis, holding it up out of sight. That's where it had started. That's when he became the goddamn "dickless wonder." A chill went through him as the memories came flooding back to him.

He was a little kid, and the man he depended on most had taped his dick up, then chained him to a tree in front of the house like a dog. It wasn't cold out. It was a mild autumn. And it wasn't long, maybe an hour. But other kids had seen him. Other parents, too.

First the cops came by. The uniformed patrolmn had laughed at the innovative punishment. Then a lady from child protective services. If something like that occurred today, the media would've eaten his father alive. In those days the woman told him it was unacceptable and left. For good. That was it.

That's why Junior had handled the situation the best way he could. He forgot it. Completely.

Maybe that's why he didn't like cops. Maybe that's why he had a job that required him to go to people's homes and make a judgment on their behavior. Maybe that's why he was so fucked up.

His stomach tightened and all he could think about was Michelle Swirsky humiliating him.

Now he snapped back to reality as his father raised his hoarse voice, knocking him out of his memories.

Bill Slaton Sr. said, "What's wrong, Junior? You gone batty on me?"

Junior looked down and shook his head, trying to make sense of everything he'd just recalled.

His father said, "So you've moved on from your dick. I was afraid it would push you to do stupid things. Is your dick part of your dreams?" The old man's cackle reminded him of Karen Olson.

"No, my dick plays no role in this particular dream." It wasn't a lie. In fact, it was probably thanks to this old bastard's treatment that he hadn't had a meaningful relationship with a woman in nearly thirty years.

His father cackled, "So you're still a dickless wonder, huh?"

"I should be after what you put me through."

The old man nodded and said, "Finally starting to get some backbone."

Junior realized he had to finish things with Michelle to prove he had some backbone. Then maybe he'd deal with his father like a man.

41

Tim Hallett had scrambled to see Bill Slaton leaving work in his personal vehicle. It wasn't hard to follow the older Ford Taurus. He had studied the car's hood, matching it with the mental image of the partial photograph of the car where Michelle Swirsky was attacked. The whole theory was still far-fetched, and he had a lot to prove before anyone would listen to him. He thought about Fusco's comment that it was really Rocky's theory.

If the investigation had been sanctioned, he could match DNA, but for now that option was out. So was a photo lineup with the victims. They would blab to the detectives working the case and end Hallett's private investigation. This was one of the few viable options: surveillance.

Once again, the CAT was using three unmarked white Tahoes to follow a suspect. Technically, they weren't authorized to do the surveillance, so they weren't on duty, so they would only be fired for that, and not for the earlier breaking of the HIPAA and gaining unlawful access to medical information. What had he gotten himself and his friends into?

The whole thing could be a wild goose chase, but Hallett knew he had to play it out. Rocky seemed to be game as he paced in his compartment. He sure would like to get the dog close to Slaton again and see if he had the same reaction. But Fusco had already explained to him that he needed more to get anyone's attention.

As they drove through suburban West Palm Beach, Hallett called out the location of the Ford Taurus to his partners. The more he considered Slaton, the more sense it made. He had access to computers relating to Department of Corrections inmates. It would give him enough information to search online for family members as well. He really could pick his victims based on their background and was probably smart enough to do it based on jurisdictions so no one would link the different kidnappings together. He could have even learned to hot-wire a car from one of his probationers.

Hallett had already tried to call John Fusco, but he wasn't even answering his phone anymore.

Darren said he would call Sergeant Greene, but Hallett didn't know why his friend thought it would do any good.

Hallett backed off the Ford Taurus. Slaton wasn't driving crazily and signaled clearly before he turned. It wasn't like a dope surveillance. Slaton wasn't looking for anyone following him. After fifteen minutes he pulled into a nursing home in a run-down part of the county near a town known as Palm Springs.

Hallett knew the facility. This was where Crystal's grandmother, Ella, lived. He had been here dozens of times with Rocky and Josh, trying to visit more patients than just the elderly woman who helped raise Crystal. Why on earth would Slaton be coming here?

Hallett never actually saw Slaton walk inside the concrete building, but saw him march out about twenty minutes later. Hallett got on the radio and said, "Can someone else take the eye on Slaton? I'm gonna run inside and see what I can find out." He heard Darren say he'd be the lead car in the surveillance.

Rocky let out a short howl as Hallett slipped out of the Tahoe, then opened the rear compartment and put Rocky on a special decorative leash they used for nonpolice work. It let Rocky now he wasn't on duty, and it didn't look as threatening to people on the street. He was wearing casual clothes now, jeans and a button-down shirt left untucked to cover his pistol. Hallett was counting on the staff to recognize him and Rocky and allow him access to the building. He hustled to the front door of the nursing home and directly to the receptionist at the desk.

The cute, young Latin woman gave him a dazzling smile and said, "Hey, Deputy, what're you doing here so late?"

Whew, he had gotten lucky. Hallett said, "I'm supposed to meet a friend. His name is Bill Slaton." He was going to give more of his fake story when the receptionist volunteered, "Oh he's probably visiting his dad." She pointed behind her and said, "Down this hallway, then turn right, room 117."

Hallett thanked her as he and Rocky headed down the hallway, wondering if Slaton's father might let some information slip. They were delayed twice by elderly people who recognized their favorite dog and took a moment to pat his head. As always, Rocky held perfectly still and gave a quick wag of his tail to show his appreciation.

■   ■   ■

Darren Mori found he enjoyed the complexity of conducting surveillance. He was even multitasking. The Ford Taurus driven by Bill Slaton was two cars ahead of him, driving south on Military Trail. He called out the position to Claire while Tim Hallett slipped into the nursing home to see what Slaton had been doing there. The whole time, he was on the phone trying to reach Helen Greene. Someone had to know what they had found out. If John Fusco wasn't listening, maybe the sergeant would. She had impressed Darren with her patience and intelligence, and something told him she was more open-minded than most sergeants. He didn't know what else to do.

She finally picked up, and he smiled at her voice barking, "Greene."

Darren immediately said, "Sarge, it's Darren Mori. I'm calling you on official business, sort of."

"I hope this doesn't have anything to do with Tim Hallett's wild theories. For the past hour I've been studying crime scene photos from the Ludner house and the cane field where we recovered Katie Ziegler just because Hallett's gotten into my head. I like him, but there's nothing else I can do for him. The captain is talking about putting him on leave pending a psychiatric exam."

"That's going to make this request a little on the awkward side."

"Darren, what are you talking about?"

Darren considered his position but trusted Helen Greene. "We're on surveillance right now and could use some help."

"Surveillance of who?"

"Bill Slaton."

There was a sickening silence from the other end of the phone. Then the sergeant's voice cracked when she said, "The probation officer?"

"All two hundred and thirty pounds of him."

"Are you saying Tim thinks he's a suspect in the kidnappings?"

"Now that you say it out loud it does sound kinda crazy, but when you see all the little pieces, it makes more sense. We're on Military Trail north of Melaleuca heading south."

"You better give me a damn good reason not to shut this down right now." Her tone left no doubt that she didn't find this amusing.

Darren didn't hesitate to spend what little capital he had. "You told me when we found Tina Tictin's body that you owed me. I'm taking you at your word and calling in your marker." He saw Slaton turn right, then said into the phone quickly, "I gotta go." He gave her the radio channel they were working on and tossed the phone onto the passenger seat. Darren just hoped she was as honorable as he thought she was.

42

The man in the first bed quickly waived Tim Hallett off to the man in the second bed. The elderly man had jaundiced eyes and said in a harsh voice, "You're the guy who visits Ella, aren't you?"

"Yes, sir."

"You had a baby with a black woman that comes, too. I've seen him. He's a cute little boy."

Hallett still wasn't sure how to deal with old-school racism.

Then the old man looked down at Rocky and said, "I don't like dogs. You guys need to get lost. Ella's down the hallway."

"I'm not here to see Ella tonight."

"Why are you here?"

"I'm a friend of Bill's."

"You mean Junior? You just missed him."

"That's too bad. You know where he was headed?"

"That dickless wonder? No."

"I'm sorry, what?"

The old man coughed violently, then wiped his mouth with a dirty napkin. "I know he blames me for his crap life, but people need to take responsibility for themselves." His gauzy eyes focused on Hallett as best they could, and he said, "What about you? Do you like girls?"

The old man wasn't saying anything important to the case, but he was giving Hallett a vibe that made him believe even more that Slaton was their man. "Where was Bill going?"

"To chase his dreams. That's what he told me."

Hallett had a bad feeling. He nodded to the old man, then darted out of the room. By the time he hit the front door of the nursing home he was in a full sprint to his Tahoe. He grabbed the radio and shouted for someone to answer him and tell him where they were.

Darren Mori came on and said, "We're headed south on Military Trail."

Tim Hallett knew it was too risky to let Bill Slaton out of sight. It was too dangerous to risk him grabbing another girl while they tried to make a case. They needed to pull him over at their first opportunity. He'd make up the rest as they went along.

■　■　■

Rocky knew this place well. All of the smells and scents reminded him of the kind attention he had received here in the past. It also reminded him of the sorrow he sensed in the humans after some of the visits. These humans weren't always the same ones when he returned. Usually Josh would be with them and they would visit one female. But tonight, it seemed like Tim wanted to go somewhere else in the big building.

Rocky wished he could explore all the building, but he knew they were here for other reasons. He could sense an urgency in Tim. Most people here were lying down and were no threat, but Tim was still tense and hurried Rocky along.

Finally, they came to a room and Tim started talking to a man lying down near the window. Rocky could easily tell that Tim didn't like this man. But he was no threat. Rocky didn't think he could even stand up.

Tim took a moment to calm Rocky when he saw he was agitated. Rocky liked the feeling of Tim's hand as it ran from the top of his head all the way down his body to his tail, and Tim spoke quietly to him. Rocky wasn't even sure what the words meant, but he knew Tim wanted him quiet and still.

Something inside Rocky told him that a game was on the way and he would be able to run. He needed to run right now. A good run, chasing bad guys.

That's what Rocky hoped would happen soon.

■　■　■

It was after eight thirty and completely dark outside as Junior stood patiently in the parking lot of the Publix. He had seen Michelle Swirsky come out to the parking lot twice, but never farther than a few rows of cars. He figured that since she had been on TV, this job felt boring to her. She thought she was better than this kind of labor and better than him. The whole idea that she could get on TV and brag about what she did to him stiffened his resolve.

Bill Slaton had a hard time getting past the conversation with his father at the nursing home. Now, when he looked at Michelle, he saw Karen Olson's face. How different would his life have been if he had acted quickly in the garage? Would it have been just one dead girl or would he still need to do the things he did? His father's punishment didn't help, of that he was certain.

Michelle smiled at her customers; it looked fake, like she was practicing. He wondered if she wanted a career in broadcasting. The way she had talked about how she had escaped the kidnapper had captured everyone's attention. She explained that her tae kwon do instructor, who had been on one of the newscasts with her, had shown her everything she had done. He was a big, goofy-looking guy who worked for the Palm Beach County School Board Police. He seemed to have a way with kids. All Junior had heard was how great Sensei Rick was.

Now Bill Slaton Jr. noticed Michelle out in the parking lot retrieving empty carts instead of taking out an old person's groceries. He had seen some of the bag boys come out and do it, pushing twenty or thirty carts at a time back to the store from the outer parking lot. It looked like Michelle preferred to do just a few at a time.

He instantly realized this was his chance. If he was ever going to set things straight, he had to do it in the next few minutes. Each time she recovered carts, Michelle walked a few more rows out into the parking lot. For a girl who had been attacked recently she didn't seem to be paying much attention to the area around her.

Finally, she grabbed the cart just a few feet away from his vehicle. He called her by name. She looked up calmly, then froze; he knew she recognized him from their earlier encounter.

He stood next to his car with his pistol held low at his waist and pointed right at her. He worked hard to keep his voice calm and steady when he said, "I'll shoot you this time."

The girl shook her head nervously. She believed it.

He motioned the girl to enter the Taurus on the driver's side, then shoved her so she slipped into the passenger seat. He could tell she was so terrified she was confused, and that's what made the moment electric. The way he felt now, he could conquer the world.

He kept the gun pointed at her as he slid into the driver's seat and picked up his blindfold with his left hand. "Slip this over your head."

Michelle let out a gasp and cried out, "Why are you doing this?"

Junior loved it. Everything about this girl was exciting: the tears running down her cheeks, the way she was shaking like a cold Chihuahua, the quiver in her voice. She was shaking so badly she could hardly pull the homemade cloth blindfold onto her head.

Junior enjoyed keeping his voice so steady. "Hold up your hands and put them together." As soon as she lifted her hands, he wasted no time wrapping duct tape around them.

Junior intended to make sure her precious Sensei Rick wasn't going to be proud of what she did it tonight.

■   ■   ■

Hallett had listened to the surveillance and finally caught up with them headed south. Darren and Claire had stayed well back of Slaton driving his ratty old Ford Taurus and had lost him along the way. Right now Darren thought the Taurus turned into one of the shopping centers along the west side of the road.

Hallett let his eyes search the traffic in front of him and in the parking lots along Military Trail, dangerously ignoring the cars close to him. Rocky sensed the tension and sat up in his compartment, panting directly against the metal door that faced forward.

He slowed when he saw the brighter lights of a large shopping center and noticed the Publix grocery store that anchored it. Somewhere in a report he had read that Michelle Swirsky worked part-time at Publix. On a hunch he got on the radio as he turned into the shopping center.

Hallett said, "I'm searching the parking lot of the Publix. Is anyone available to go inside and check with the manager real quick? I think this is the Publix where Michelle Swirsky works."

Claire acknowledged him as she parked her Tahoe directly in front of the building. They were starting to veer off the original mission of finding Bill Slaton, but just the idea that Slaton was in the same area as his last victim worried him.

As he made a quick pass through the lot he still didn't see the Taurus.

■   ■   ■

Bill Slaton Jr. already felt some relief. That nagging feeling of unfinished business had vanished like a Budweiser at a Toby Keith concert. He felt powerful. Michelle was securely restrained and crouched down in the passenger seat of his car. She put up a brave fight to hold back the tears, but it only made her seem that much more vulnerable.

Junior enjoyed glancing over at Michelle as she sat perfectly still, sitting low in the seat the way he had told her to. Maybe she was a replacement for Karen Olson or some other woman who had screwed up his life. Women never knew how much influence they had with their little comments or silly laughter. This was one way to show them.

He hadn't realized how much the visit with his father had affected him. He needed to prove he was a man. Just hearing his father call him a dickless wonder made him want to go out and find five girls like Michelle. He'd always thought the insult was related to his lack of athletic ability until he recalled his father's "treatment."

The traffic was light, and he could just see a hint of the rising moon. He knew he had to act quickly. The managers at Publix would notice one of their employees missing, and after Michelle's notoriety on TV, no one would take any chances. He knew an abandoned gas station that had an office behind it. One of his probationers had found a way in and was living in the empty office. It was easier for Slaton to ignore the minor trespassing than to find housing for the homeless probationer.

He stole another glance at his prey as she sat silently. The blindfold left her nose and mouth exposed, and he pictured her beautiful smile.

He wished he could bottle this feeling.

■   ■   ■

Claire hustled through the automatic doors of the Publix, still dressed in her uniform with a, long-sleeve black T-shirt that said PBSO K-9 on the right sleeve and a black tactical vest. The combat boots she wore boosted her height to a total of five foot six. She had to look up almost a foot to the lanky manager behind the customer service counter.

The man, about her age, said, "May I help you?"

"Do you know if Michelle Swirsky is working here tonight?"

Then the man gave her an odd smile and said, "River, is that you?"

It took Claire by surprise, and she tried to figure out who this man was. She had to admit he looked familiar.

He gave her a broad smile and said, "It's Bill Shepherd. I used to live next to you in Lake Worth. Remember, my dad gave us rides everywhere."

Claire nodded and said, "It's nice to see you, Bill. We have a little bit of a situation. I need to speak with Michelle Swirsky, right now."

He just continued to stare and smile. "I had no idea you would grow up to look like this. I would've been nicer to you as a kid." He still had a goofy laugh.

"Look, Bill, I'd love to catch up with you later, but right now I want to make sure Michelle is okay. Is she working tonight?"

It finally sank in with the gangly manager that this might be important. He said, "Miss Hollywood? She was here tonight. I haven't seen her in a few minutes. Don't tell me she's followed in her father's footsteps and ripped someone off?"

Now Claire was starting to lose it. "Bill, we need to cut the small talk. Let's find Michelle."

The manager stepped through the door in the back of the small room and then appeared in the store, walking directly to a heavyset, older cashier. He spoke to her and then the cashier next to her. He walked back toward Claire shaking his head. "She went out to grab carts about five minutes ago, but no one's seen her since."

They did a quick check around the store and called for her over the intercom, but after two minutes Claire couldn't wait anymore and got on the radio to tell Hallett she wasn't here.

This complicated things.

43

Hallett tried to hide his panic after Claire reported that no one at Publix could find Michelle.

He all but screamed into the radio, "Do you see him?"

Darren thought he had spotted the Ford Taurus on Military Trail, but he hadn't seen it in the last minute. Hallett would never forgive himself if something happened to this girl because he didn't act quickly enough.

He mashed the button on his handheld radio and called out again. "You guys see him anywhere?"

Then a female voice that wasn't Claire came on the radio and said, "He made a U-turn and went north on Military Trail."

Hallett was about to ask who was giving the information when he realized it was Sergeant Greene. *Where the hell had she come from?* It didn't matter; they needed the help now.

He punched the gas as Rocky became more agitated in the rear compartment.

Sergeant Greene said, "I'll keep on Military, you take Lake Worth Road west. We'll do a grid search if we have to. I'm calling in more help now."

Hallett got on the radio and said, "Thanks, Sarge. I think I can explain this all in a few minutes. But we need to stop this guy and do it now."

A few seconds later his phone rang. "Hallett."

It was Sergeant Greene. She didn't sound angry, but she said, "You kind of need to explain it to me right now. Just the *Reader's Digest* version."

Hallett continued to search traffic but understood the importance of keeping the sergeant informed. He gathered his thoughts. "All the victims' fathers were in state custody. Slaton has access to the DOC computers. He tracked the sand into the Ludners' house and tried to lead us to Arnold Ludner. Plus, Rocky alerted to him when I spoke to him earlier."

The sergeant said, "I can add something."

"What's that?"

"While I was reviewing crime scene photos of the Ludner house, I saw a footprint on the walkway of a boot missing a square exactly like the cast Claire took out at the scene of Katie Ziegler's kidnapping."

"Unbelievable."

"I have crime scene matching them up now. We'll have an answer tonight."

Hallett said, "That should help seal it."

"That's not nearly enough for an arrest right now."

"We're not trying to arrest him, just stopping him for safety reasons. We can't risk him cruising the streets looking for a victim, and he may have Michelle Swirsky with him right now."

There was a pause on the line. Then the Sergeant said, "Keep looking. I'll get marked units over here."

That didn't make Hallett's gurgling stomach feel any better.

■　■　■

Darren Mori appreciated sitting so high in the Chevy Tahoe. It allowed him to look down rows of traffic and into parking lots easily. He'd just heard a call on the main radio asking for marked units to come into the area and help look for the Ford Taurus. The bulletin included a full description and a note to detain for Sergeant Greene if seen. He knew she was the right person to call. She had been tough but fair from the start, and Darren knew she liked Hallett.

Brutus sat up and let out the occasional bark. The connection between partners told the dog something was wrong. He might not have been trained to intervene in critical situations, but he still knew when his partner was tense. The way Brutus's head moved back and forth made it look like he was searching traffic with Darren.

He hoped Brutus's cadaver-searching abilities weren't going to be needed today. If this asshole really did have Michelle Swirsky, they had to act fast. Unlike in the movies, cops rarely faced situations like this, and Darren was happy he had the entire team out with him. It gave him confidence to know how well they had been trained.

Even though the situation was exciting, it forced him to look on the flip side and consider what that poor girl might suffer. The idea of her trauma, both physical and emotional, pushed Darren harder to get through traffic and cover more distance. He just hoped he was going to make a difference today.

■   ■   ■

Bill Slaton Jr. tapped the brakes on the Taurus before he turned. It was a habit his father had taught him when he was a teenager. Unless it was an emergency there was no reason not to warn the drivers behind. He had drummed the use of turn signals into the young man's head the way he had a thousand little things that had carried into Junior's adulthood. His father had screwed him up in more ways than Slaton could keep track of. Maybe Karen Olson had done worse, but he doubted it.

He turned into the parking lot, then took almost a full minute to survey the area. The lot had a tendency to be packed with homeless people and day laborers, but this time of night the laborers had gone home and the homeless were working the street corners. Slaton didn't know the story on the real estate but imagined one owner controlled the gas station, tiny strip mall, and other outparcels because he couldn't imagine why they would all close down at the same time. He hadn't seen active business in the plaza for at least eighteen months.

The lot looked clear.

Michelle had hardly let out a whimper, but Slaton wasn't fooled. He already knew what she was capable of doing and wasn't going to take any chances this time. He pulled through the lot with the intention of parking behind the office at the rear, but someone had piled trash in that exact spot. He could see broken wooden pallets and a half-burned, thin mattress and hoped that meant no one was living inside the abandoned office at the moment.

He could see no light coming out from the slits in the plywood covering the windows and saw no activity in the vicinity. He didn't mind taking the extra time to check the area because he knew it would also serve to disorient Michelle in the blindfold. However Slaton dealt with Michelle tonight, he couldn't leave the blindfold behind. There could be a load of forensic evidence stuck somewhere in the mass of dish towels, duct tape, and cotton. He'd incinerate it later, but right now, he didn't want to rush, so he could enjoy the feeling of power that was surging through his body. Slaton wanted to burn every moment of it into his memory for later use in his fantasy life. He intended to lie low for a long time after this. His visit from former detective Tim Hallett today had actually spurred him on to take action. If the cops really did doubt Arnold Ludner was the right suspect, it didn't matter if he struck tonight or not.

Slaton finally selected a spot away from the road between the office closer to the strip mall and another outparcel that looked like it was used to store equipment. He thought the car might be more difficult to see from the road.

The biggest risk, the one that scared him the most, was the walk from the car to the office. It wasn't far, and the lot was poorly lit, but he couldn't risk anyone noticing a girl with a hood over her head. He took a moment to pull on blue rubber gloves, then take one more quick look around the lot. Without a word, he opened his door and pulled Michelle out the driver's side.

As soon as she stood, he said, "Walk with me or I'll put three bullets in your belly and let you die painfully. Then I'll go to your house and get your mother, too." The little talk had its desired effect. She straightened up and matched him step for step. Once he was behind the office he breathed easier. He pushed on the loose board his probationer had showed him and shoved Michelle through into the dark, musty interior.

He popped on a tiny LED flashlight and could tell no one had spent the night in here in some time. He shoved Michelle onto some old blankets spread out on one side of the room.

He couldn't ask for anything more perfect.

■ ■ ■

Hallett had done a lot of surveillance over the years, especially the month he'd spent in narcotics. He'd lost suspects before and learned how to look for them when it happened. Every parking lot and side street was a potential hiding place. The difference was when he lost someone they were following because of dope, no one sweated too much about it. The suspect would turn up again, and even if he didn't, it wasn't like a young girl's life depended on it right at that moment. That added stress affected every aspect of the search.

One key difference right now was that he did not believe Bill Slaton realized anyone was looking for him yet.

Claire had stayed at Publix to gather more information and try to contact Mrs. Swirsky.

Sergeant Greene had called for more units, but a knife fight at a local bar had tied several up. Right now it was just Darren, the sergeant, and Claire helping Hallett look for the rogue probation officer.

The sergeant had an analyst back at the D-bureau trying to find Slaton's home address. That was the next place they intended to send someone.

Hallett felt ill at the prospect of what could happen. Rocky sensed his partner's discomfort and paced in his compartment, letting out an occasional whine.

Then Darren came on the radio and said, "I might see his car. We're west on Lake Worth road by the closed Shell station."

Hallett said, "I'll be there in less than a minute." He punched the gas and felt the SUV tilt as he weaved between two insanely close cars. An old man in a Cadillac honked at him and shot him a bird.

Rocky let out a short howl.

"It's gonna be all right, boy. We're gonna find her."

■ ■ ■

Bill Slaton tried to decide if he should strip her or not. His original plan was to just shoot her to relieve the feeling that she had conquered him. Then he considered strangulation. He had gotten such a charge out of choking the life out of Tina Tictin that it appealed to him. The only problem was that here he didn't have the luxury of water washing away any possible DNA evidence. Even though he had been careful, he knew how forensic scientists could lift samples from almost anything.

But at this moment, staring at the terrified girl who was completely disoriented by the blindfold, he considered his usual treatment before he decided how to end it for the conceited young woman. When he was finished, she wouldn't be on TV bragging about how she humiliated him.

As he weighed his options, Michelle mumbled, "Why are you doing this?"

"Why not? I can do whatever I want to you." Then he thought about what he had just said. He really could do whatever he wanted. It didn't matter what his father thought of him. He had the power and ability to change this girl's life any way he wanted. For the first time with one of these girls, he felt as if he might actually prove he wasn't a dickless wonder. He might make use of his penis. His father had a stronger effect on him than he gave the old man credit for. Calling him a dickless wonder had awakened something inside him. Now the questions fell to a more practical point. Did he have the time? Was it safe? Slaton chuckled. Hell no, nothing was safe. No one was safe. His own mother couldn't protect him. Just like Michelle's mother could do nothing to protect her.

In a way, he liked to think this was just more justice for her father, just like the other girls. They had all scoffed at the laws society had laid down and gotten whatever minor punishment some high and mighty judge passed down. He didn't want it to be easy for those men who sold drugs or stole money.

He reached in the dim light toward Michelle and started to yank off her pants.

44

Hallett pulled next to Darren Mori on the edge of the parking lot. He hadn't called for help yet. They wanted to make sure before they pulled everyone off the search. He knew the sergeant had heard Darren call out and would come looking for them in a few minutes if she didn't hear anything more. They could see the Taurus but had no idea where Slaton was. The car was empty, and there were several small buildings as well as the strip mall close by. To complicate matters, there was a man-sized hole in the wooden fence at the back of the lot that Slaton could've used to cut through to a safe house.

Hallett didn't want to alert the probation officer that they were in the area. He and Darren had only whispered and turned their radios all the way down. Rocky and Brutus were both on six-foot leads, straining to get moving. They knew something big was happening.

Rocky sniffed the air. Belgian Malinois were not known for their scent discrimination or air-scent tracking skills, but Rocky seemed to be changing everyone's perception of the breed's ability. Even Brutus was testing the air. He had no business being on a lead in a situation like this.

They moved quickly to the Taurus, and Rocky immediately picked up something, turning to the right and straining at the lead. There was no wind and no wildlife to distract him. He had definitely latched on to a fresh scent.

Hallett and Darren exchanged glances as Brutus pulled Darren another direction. Brutus wasn't specifically trained as a tracking dog, but he had certain instincts innate in all canines.

Hallett whispered, "Stay in sight."

Darren nodded as they both eased off at slight angles from the car.

Hallett was careful to step lightly and listen. He could almost tune out the normal traffic sounds as he paused after each step, listening for anything unusual. It seemed odd no homeless people were in the area and there were no crack dealers to scare.

Brutus startled him when he let out a bark from Hallett's left side.

■   ■   ■

Bill Slaton had Michelle's pants off when he sensed something outside. Still in a daze, Michelle let out a quiet moan of fear, prompting Slaton to pounce on her and clamp his hand across her face. He savored the panicked sound of her trying to suck air through her nose, but he realized this was not the moment to sit back and enjoy things. He listened.

A dog barked somewhere close by. He had to wonder if it was a police service dog. Probably just a neighborhood mutt. Either way he couldn't ignore it. He couldn't sit here and enjoy the few quiet moments with this girl who had plagued him. He was annoyed when he struggled to his feet and pulled the Beretta from his pants.

He had to snatch a peek into the parking lot.

■   ■   ■

Rocky tugged Hallett toward the small abandoned building. Hallett struggled not to have tunnel vision and focus only on the run-down cement structure. He scanned the parking lot in front of him and swiveled behind him before looking over to catch Darren's attention and silently guide him toward an outparcel as well.

Hallett's palms were sweaty as he rested his right hand on his Glock. He rotated the holster safety forward for instant access to the pistol.

A noise to the left attracted the attention of both deputies. Hallett drew his pistol as a thin black man stumbled through the hole in the fence. As soon as the man looked up, he froze, staring at the dogs, then disappeared back through the fence.

Hallett now concentrated on the one building. He considered how they should approach it tactically. There were no doors on the side facing him, and if he went around one end and Darren the other, they could be in the crossfire. He wanted to let Rocky get closer. He also didn't want to risk Michelle getting hurt.

Then, out of the corner of his left eye, he saw Darren react and reach for his pistol as he released Brutus's lead and the dog charged forward.

■   ■   ■

Rocky looked around this place with hard, unnatural ground that was rough on his paws and the buildings that popped up out of the ground. There was almost no grass and only a few trees that looked like they were dying. But Rocky had a scent. A scent just like the day in the tall grass. It was two people, a predator and someone who was scared. Really scared. Rocky knew the predator was the bad man from the building. *The bad man.* Rocky knew what to do. He tried to communicate it to Tim, pulling him toward a small building to the side.

Not only did he have a scent, Rocky could hear quiet human sounds that meant fear and sadness. They were coming from inside the building, and he was cocking his head to hear the sound as best he could. That's when the loud noise startled him. It only took him a moment to realize it was one of the loud things that Tim carried on his belt and made a noise like thunder.

Rocky turned and saw Brutus charging.

This didn't look like a game to him.

■   ■   ■

For a moment, Bill Slaton thought he might have startled a homeless guy, but as soon as he stepped through the small opening, he saw the deputy with the dog on a leash. Fleetingly, he recognized the deputy from the search at the Ludner house.

The deputy reached for his pistol, but Slaton already had the Beretta in his hand. He swung it toward the surprised deputy, ignoring the Golden Retriever, even as it approached.

At the same time, Michelle let out a scream. Everything weighed down on him at once when all he wanted to do was aim the pistol and fire.

■   ■   ■

Darren instinctively released the lead as he reached for his Glock and Brutus tugged hard. Slaton already had a pistol in his hand, but he was in an awkward position coming through the boards.

Darren stepped to one side as Slaton's pistol came on target. Then he saw Brutus, who had never shown any aggressive tendencies and had not been trained, charge Slaton, even distracting him with a snarl as he sprang into the air. He hit the fat man just as the pistol fired, and the muzzle flash filled Darren's vision. He heard a second shot.

The first bullet struck him in the upper chest and immediately knocked the wind out of him, as well as sending what felt like a strong electrical charge through every nerve ending in his upper body. The force of the bullet was unlike anything he'd ever experienced, and he dropped backward with the pistol still in his hand. Then he felt a jolting pain in his neck and didn't know if it was a side effect of the first round or if the second round struck him.

The last thing he noted before his vision faltered was Brutus latched on to Slaton's left arm.

■   ■   ■

Slaton fired twice at the deputy as the goddamn dog knocked him backward. Then he felt the searing pain as the yellow dog dug his teeth into his left forearm. He had held up the arm to fend off the dog, but had no idea how much it would hurt.

He panicked and squeezed the trigger of the Beretta. The first shot had no effect on the snarling hound. The second time the dog yelped and released its grip, but Slaton still felt a pain in his hand, and blood was pouring from his arm. It only took him a second to realize that not only had the dog ripped up his arm, but the bullet had passed right through the dog and struck Slaton's hand.

The dog was now on the ground whimpering, and the deputy was flat on his back. This was not the time for Slaton to feel sorry for himself. He had to get the hell out of Dodge. Now.

A shooting happens completely out of context to most people's lives, even cops. It is a rare and devastating occurrence. Those were the words from training that popped into Tim Hallett's head when he heard the shots and saw Darren go down.

Instantly he aimed his Glock and started to scoot in a sideways crab walk toward Darren, keeping his pistol up and pointed at the building where the shots had come from. He didn't dare release Rocky for fear he would charge the shooter. This could be considered contrary to his training, which taught that dogs are tools to protect people. But Hallett wasn't about to let his partner go.

As he cleared the side of the small boarded-up building, he caught a glimpse of Bill Slaton squeezing through another hole in the fence. He could also see Brutus was on the ground, whimpering. With every fiber in his body, he wanted to stop Slaton, but his duty and his loyalty were clear.

Rocky barked, then wailed at the sight of Brutus.

Hallett kneeled down to check his friend's pulse and see if he was breathing. Darren wasn't quite conscious, and his eyes couldn't focus. Hallett had seen these signs of shock in accident and shooting victims over the years. Before he started to unclip Darren's vest and search for the wound, he grabbed Darren's radio mic and made the call no cop wants to.

Hallett recognized how close to panic he was. He had to get it together to broadcast a call for help that was clear and concise. He depressed the microphone button and spoke in a voice louder than he intended. "10-24, shots fired." He gave their exact location. "We need immediate EMS." The numbers alone—10-24, officer down—would keep unnecessary traffic off the radio and attract cops from every district. He dropped the radio mic and yanked on Darren's vest before giving a suspect description. It would be a few minutes before anyone needed it anyway, and he had plenty to keep him busy at the moment.

Darren didn't make a sound.

■   ■   ■

Bill Slaton stumbled through the fence into a backyard covered with rotting, cracked plastic kids' toys. He still had his Beretta, and he was trying to stay calm. He surveyed the area but didn't see anyone and started to run, going through several backyards before turning toward the street in the quiet neighborhood. There he slowed down and started to walk along the cracked and uneven sidewalk. He knew a running fat man in this neighborhood would only draw attention.

He sucked in a couple of big breaths and wiped the sweat from his eyes with his bare hand. He couldn't believe what he had just done to get away from the scene. This was going to come back to bite him in the ass. The only question was what he would accomplish before some cop put a bullet in him.

His left arm was covered with blood, and the bullet hole in his hand trailed blood along the sidewalk. Then he got hold of himself and realized there were plenty of cars along the street and he had a skill most people did not. He saw a Honda in front of the next house and stepped out onto the street to get to the driver's side. He felt for his Buck knife inside his left pocket, wincing in pain as he jostled his injured hand.

Slaton had to stick the gun back in his belt to use his right hand to hold the knife and use it to crack the window. The first strike had almost no effect. As he brought his hand back for the next one he heard someone call out, "What the hell are you doing?"

Slaton's head snapped up to see a tall, muscular Latin man with no shirt and a gun in his hand rushing out of the house.

46

Hallett could feel the pulse stabilize in Darren's carotid artery. Now that he had the ballistic vest off and saw little blood, he realized the one bullet had struck the upper part of the vest. The second had splintered into his unprotected shoulder and neck. Claire had arrived and knew exactly what to do. She cut away the T-shirt, and they saw the discoloration of Darren's upper chest where the bullet struck.

Claire looked at Hallett and said, "I got this. Go find that asshole."

Hallett nodded, stood, and said, "Not just yet." It was hard to step past Brutus, but he had to find Michelle Swirsky. He wanted to cry out when he saw the blood splashed along the yellow fur of the Golden Retriever. Brutus's stomach was moving as he tried to breathe, but he didn't have the strength to lift his head. His front left leg was injured, and his chest was bleeding.

Now Hallett released Rocky, who immediately went to the injured dog and gently nudged Brutus's head with his nose, then licked the wound on Brutus's chest.

Hallett cursed when he realized he wasn't wearing a uniform and a ballistic vest and had no flashlight to pull off the tactical holder. He stuck his head in the building with the board ripped off of it and followed the beam of the small flashlight on the ground. Michelle Swirsky, wearing a blindfold, was tucked in the corner with her legs pulled in next to her.

Hallett said clearly, "I'm a police officer, Michelle. Are you injured?"

She sniffled but made no clear answer.

He stepped all the way into the building, saying softly, "It's okay, sweetheart. You're safe now." Squatting next to her, Hallett fumbled with the blindfold until it pulled free of her long brown hair. She looked startled, and he remembered he wasn't wearing a uniform. He also realized she wasn't wearing any pants. This was one more sensory overload he didn't need. He heard more cars pull up outside.

Then Claire Perkins called his name and leaned into the building. "The paramedics have Darren."

He sighed with a slight relief.

Now it was time to find Bill Slaton.

■　■　■

Rocky quickly scanned for any other threats, then took a moment to check his friend Brutus, who was hurt. Rocky tried to lick the yellow dog's wounds. Brutus whimpered quietly. That wasn't like him. Brutus never whimpered and was always the first to play rough when Rocky, Smarty, and Brutus played together.

Rocky looked up, trying to find the scent of the bad man on the wind. He was going to bite him. No matter what, Rocky had to bite the bad man hard.

This was a feeling Rocky had never experienced before. This was no game and it was not fun. He thought he understood Tim a little better now.

■　■　■

Bill Slaton didn't think he was technically panicked. He was functioning but recognized his heart rate and shallow breathing would catch up to him soon. This asshole with the gun didn't make things easier.

The man from the house didn't raise the pistol but shouted, "Get away from that car."

Slaton didn't look up from the window he was working on as he said, "Can't do that. It's an emergency."

That caught the man by surprise as he twisted up his face, then said, "Whatchu talking about, man? That's my girlfriend's car." He still didn't aim the pistol.

Slaton might not have been an actual cop, but he could read people, and this guy was all show. If he meant business he would've come out of the house shooting. Slaton pulled the Beretta and casually fired three quick shots without aiming. The idea was to frighten the man away, but he was surprised to see the guy go down. Slaton didn't have time to inspect his handiwork; he went back to focusing on getting into the car. He knew he didn't have much time.

The guy on the ground didn't mean shit. Slaton had just shot a cop, how much worse could he make things? It was liberating in an odd way.

■　　■　　■

As soon as he was convinced there was enough help on scene, Tim Hallett moved toward the fence with Rocky, ready to give chase to Bill Slaton. Hallett had a badge on a chain around his neck, hoping that would slow any antsy deputy who saw him. But as he pushed through the ragged hole in the fence, he wished he was in uniform with his god-awful, heavy ballistic vest. There was no time to get it.

Claire tended to the girl as Sergeant Greene and an extra paramedic did what they could for Brutus. When the young paramedic protested that he wasn't paid to work on animals, the sergeant snapped, "You better stop the bleeding and stabilize him or you might not make it off the scene in one piece."

Hallett burst through the hole in the fence instead of making a careful tactical entry. He risked that Slaton had moved on. It was a safe bet. Hallett also wished he'd been smart enough to grab a portable radio, but as far as he knew there was no one here to help him yet.

Rocky had a fresh scent and started to move into the backyard of the one-story house but stopped to nudge a plastic football like the one he played with at home. Without any encouragement from Hallett, the dog refocused on his job and was moving quickly through the backyard.

Hallett had his Glock out, scanning the bushes and the corners of the houses as Rocky led him through several yards. This was a rare case where he didn't give a warning that he was going to release his dog. Either he or Rocky was going to tear Slaton a new asshole.

He thought about Darren and Brutus on the ground and said a silent prayer. A veteran once told him there was no room in police work for vengeance, but right now that was a difficult concept to grasp.

Hallett heard three quick shots close by, and he picked up the pace. This was going to be over one way or the other in the next few minutes.

47

Claire used her sharp Gerber knife to cut the tape off Michelle's hands, then quickly helped her get dressed in the privacy of the abandoned office. She left the stubby flashlight lying on the ground, as well as the blindfold and shredded tape. That was something the crime scene people could deal with. Claire knew it was more important to get Michelle to a safe, comfortable place like her Tahoe, rather than worry about keeping all the evidence in perfect order.

Right in front of the building, Sergeant Greene and a paramedic comforted Brutus, who gave a faint pant. Her heart broke at the sight of the dog. She felt like his aunt. This sort of thing had never been covered in training.

Not far away, more paramedics arrived and helped with Darren. There were so many grouped around him she couldn't see her partner.

No matter how much she wanted to be next to him, comforting Darren or helping Brutus, her duty was to this traumatized girl. She guided Michelle so she didn't have to see too much of the carnage around her. Claire swallowed hard, trying not to let Michelle see how upset she was. This girl had been through enough already.

■　　■　　■

Hallett let Rocky pull him into the front yard and onto the sidewalk. He immediately saw a man on the ground in the next yard holding his hip. Slaton was standing next to a Honda, forcing the door open. He looked back at the man on the ground, and immediately Hallett worried that Slaton might shoot again. He couldn't risk it. Hallett let Rocky go and moved into a position to take a shot himself.

Neither Rocky nor Hallett made a sound, and Slaton didn't look up until Rocky was next to the car. The fat probation officer raised his pistol just as Rocky launched himself. The dog flew into the air, parallel with the Honda's roof. It was a true shock-and-awe maneuver.

Rocky struck Slaton high and latched on to his left shoulder near his neck. He knocked the probation officer off balance, but somehow the man managed to stay on his feet.

Hallett closed the distance in an instant and saw that Slaton still held the pistol in his right hand. Hallett had to shoot. He had no choice. He raised his Glock, realizing that Rocky was in the way. *He's just a tool.* That's all Hallett could think. He had no choice. He had to shoot.

■　■　■

Slaton sensed the dog before he heard the damn thing. It moved so fast and hit him so hard he had no chance to react. Jesus Christ, it was in his face. Then he felt the teeth dig in along his clavicle and literally saw stars. Now his left shoulder matched his mutilated left arm and hand. He was starting to really hate police service dogs.

Slaton tried to raise the pistol, intending to either kill the dog or shoot Hallett, who was rushing toward him. All the dog could do was bite, but Hallett could shoot him.

Blood squirted into his face, distracting him as the dog clamped down with a power he could barely comprehend.

Somehow he was able to force his arm up and look down the barrel of his pistol.

■　■　■

Rocky saw the bad man near a vehicle, heard the loud noises, and knew the man was dangerous. But that didn't matter right now. If he didn't act, Tim would be in danger. Besides, this bad man had hurt his friend Brutus. He didn't care how many loud things made noise, this bad man was about to get bitten. He had to keep Tim safe.

Rocky charged along the ground without making a sound. Just before he leaped into the air, the man turned and saw him. That made the bad man move just enough for Rocky to miss his throat where he had aimed. Rocky's teeth sank deep and solidly into the man.

Rocky was surprised the bad man was still standing on his two legs. Rocky clamped down harder and let his body hang limp, hoping to pull the man off his feet.

Rocky knew the man might be able to hurt him, but he didn't care. He just wanted to hang on. Then he heard Tim close by. The next noise startled him.

It was a loud thing.

■   ■   ■

Hallett ignored Slaton's cry of pain and the spray of blood coming from his shoulder. Instead, he concentrated on the front sight of his Glock. Rocky swayed in front of Slaton like the balance of a grandfather clock ticking back and forth.

He had no choice. Hallett squeezed the trigger. Once. Twice.

Slaton's gun fell to the ground.

So did Rocky.

48

Claire had Michelle fully clothed again and sitting comfortably in her front seat. Michelle trembled and grasped for Claire every time she shifted in the seat, as if she might leave the area. When Claire looked out the window, she saw Sergeant Greene on her feet and barking orders over the radio. Claire could hear sirens coming from every direction. Some were close and some were far off, but there was no doubt that all of them were headed to this spot.

Claire leaned out the window of the Tahoe but made sure Michelle knew she wasn't leaving. As much as she wanted to back up Tim, again she had to realize her duty was this girl's safety. She could see Darren move his head, and then he looked at the sergeant and croaked, "Brutus?"

One of the paramedics tried to quiet Darren down. The paramedic looked up at the sergeant and said, "He's in shock. It looks like his vest took one bullet, but it might've cracked his sternum. The other bullet fragmented into his shoulder and neck. We've gotta get him over to JFK right now."

Claire could appreciate how calm the sergeant stayed. As the only sergeant on the scene, she had a great deal to do. She glanced over at Claire and without saying a word, using only a facial expression, inquired about Michelle Swirsky sitting in the passenger seat. Claire gave her the okay sign with her fingers.

The sergeant said, "I'm going after Tim and Slaton." She wasted no time pulling her Glock from the holster on her hip and hustling toward the ragged hole in the fence.

■   ■   ■

Hallett stepped toward the open door of the Honda, his pistol on target. Bill Slaton was sprawled on the ground as blood pooled around him. His mouth opened and closed and he tried to say something, reminding Hallett of a snapper he once caught spearfishing. Hallett was in no mood to listen. He reached for the Beretta discarded on the street, picked it up, worked the de-cocking lever, and stuck it in the small of his back, secured by his belt.

Rocky eased away from the fallen man, snarling the whole time. The dog's face was covered in blood, but he didn't appear to be injured himself.

Hallett said, "Good boy. *Kalmeren.*" Telling the dog to calm down in Dutch seemed like the right thing to say. This was too much to happen in just one night. His head started to spin. Policy said he should give first aid to the injured man, but he had to check the victim lying on the lawn.

Hallett backed away from Slaton's twisted body and turned toward the man in the front yard. All he said as he approached him was, "How bad?"

The man moaned, "Bad."

Hallett kneeled down next to him and gingerly moved the man's hand from the wound. He'd seen much worse, but he wasn't going to tell the man. Then he saw the handgun that looked like a Ruger semiauto on the ground next to him. "Jesus, is everyone armed?" He reached across and took the pistol. He ejected the magazine and pull the slide back, causing a 9 mm round to pop out into the grass. He stuck the gun next to the one he'd taken from Slaton.

Sirens filled the air from almost every direction. Hallett turned to see Sergeant Greene jogging up behind him. He said, "Slaton's down and needs help." He was lucky it was the sergeant that found him and not some deputy who wouldn't recognize him. He called for Rocky, and the dog trotted up next to him.

Hallett turned back to the man and said, "We gotta get direct pressure on your hip. This is gonna hurt a little bit." He almost collapsed himself as he leaned down to hold the man's hand over the open wound just below his waist on his right hip.

Hallett knew he had to keep it together for a while longer.

49

Tim Hallett was adjusting to his forced administrative leave. It was much better than the last time he had to take some days off. This time the media was using words like "hero" and calling Rocky a "courageous dog," instead of mentioning how Hallett had used violence to coerce a confession from Arnold Ludner.

Bill Slaton was under guard at a local hospital, recovering from his left shoulder, arm and hand being shredded by two different dogs and a bullet. But his major injury was the two bullets Hallett put into the right side of his upper chest. Hallett had relived that moment of pulling the trigger while Rocky's body swayed in and out of his sight picture. At night he had nightmares about it, and during the day it popped into his head without warning. Bill Slaton had already been charged with kidnapping, and a new homicide detective had the rest of the case.

Even though he wasn't supposed to be acting in any official capacity during his so-called recovery leave, Hallett had stopped at headquarters to pick up a few personal effects. Of course, the only person he ran into in the D-bureau was John Fusco, who gave him a big smile, shook his hand, and said, "You can be a snotty prick, but you're not a bad cop."

Hallett just stared at him and said, "Thanks, I think." Then, as the detective started to walk away, Hallett reached out and stopped him, saying, "Fusco, be straight with me, did you plant the story in *The Palm Beach Post*?"

Fusco looked him in the eye, shook his head, and said, "You should know me better than that. If I have something to say, I'll say it right your face. And no one in homicide fessed up to it either. The story was actually positive about you. It just asked the same question I did: Why were you involved with this case?" He paused for a minute, patted Hallett on the shoulder, and said, "Let it go."

As he was about to leave, Sergeant Helen Greene came through the main doors, saw Hallett, and gave him a crushing hug.

Hallett said, "Thanks for coming out the other night. You saved the whole operation. But most of all I needed someone to believe me."

The sergeant looked a little uncomfortable as she said, "I believed you, Tim. Or at least I wanted to. History counts for something. I know you're a good investigator and could see connections in cases other people missed. But you'd been acting a little crazy, and I was told to keep you focused on things only K-9s could do. That's why I wouldn't let you get too involved in the actual investigation. But I still trust your judgment, and the loyalty of a friend like Darren is very convincing. When he called me, and I saw the photograph of the shoe print, I figured it was a sign from God. I had to help that night. And I'm glad I did."

"We're all glad you did." Hallett chuckled with her for a moment, then said, "Any other fallout around here about the case?"

She shrugged and said, "You know how it is. Once you were proven to be right about everything, everyone jumped on the bandwagon. But I heard Danny Weil is being transferred back to the road. We could probably work out a spot for you to come back if you want." She gave him an expectant look to show that it wasn't an empty offer.

Hallett thought about it for a few seconds, then shook his head, saying, "No thanks. I need Rocky to be a good cop."

■   ■   ■

Claire Perkins's heart skipped a beat as she saw John Fusco in front of the restaurant where they were meeting for their first official date. Now that CAT had been reassigned, she and Fusco could have any kind of relationship they wanted and no one would get in trouble.

As always, Fusco took a moment to straighten his tie and check his hair in the rearview mirror of his car. Then he zeroed in on her like a heat-seeking missile. They met between the cars, and she couldn't resist jumping into his open arms. It felt good to be embraced with passion. Sure, she gave Tim Hallett or Darren Mori a hug now and then, but it was like hugging a brother. She had missed the attention of a boyfriend. The sad thing was she hadn't realized how much until just this moment.

She took her time kissing him and making sure he couldn't confuse her intentions. She was dressed in a short black cocktail dress and heels that made her feel six feet tall. He had obviously just come from work, but he always dressed well, and his blue suit and red tie were a perfect match. He even held her hand as they walked into the restaurant and were immediately led out to a table that overlooked the Intracoastal Waterway. This was starting out to be the best date she had ever been on.

After the first glass of pinot noir, John reached across the table and grasped both of Claire's hands. He gave her a smile and said, "I have a crazy idea."

"I'm all ears."

"Even though we haven't actually dated, we've known each other for a little while. I thought we might try something bold."

She didn't want to rush him, but she couldn't wait to hear his idea.

"What if we skip all the normal dating bullshit and go away this weekend together? I can get us a room in Key West, and we could leave Friday morning. We wouldn't have a care in the world until Sunday night." He wiggled his eyebrows and gave her a goofy smile. "What do you think?"

"I love the idea, John. But I have to make arrangements for Smarty, and sometimes it can take a few days."

"You don't have a reliable kennel?"

"I would never leave him in the kennel for three days. I try to work something out with Tim or Darren for them to look after him. Plus, they couldn't be working, because I wouldn't want them to leave him alone for a whole shift."

Fusco released her hands and leaned back in the seat. "Now wait a minute. We are talking about your dog, right?"

The comment couldn't have hurt worse if he'd called her a nasty name. "If you think he's just a pet I love when it's convenient, I don't think you've been paying much attention to any of the dog handlers you've been working around the last month."

"No, I get it. You guys love your dogs, but there's more to life than caring for a dog."

"To someone like me that's like saying 'there's more to life than caring for a kid.'" She took a breath to control her tone. "It just means that you have no idea about things outside your tiny little world."

"Now hold on, are you really going to war with me over a dog?"

Claire realized this was a chasm she would never be able to fill. Not only did he just not get it, he wasn't smart enough and tolerant enough to even open his eyes. It was the age-old gap between dog lovers and people who didn't love dogs. To some people an innocent dog's life was more precious than a human's. It was an argument that could be made. She looked at John's handsome face. What a waste.

Finally, she said, "I'm not going to war with you, John. I'm surrendering and clearing the battlefield. I'd rather spend the weekend with Smarty at my little townhouse than a whole week with you down in Key West. I had higher hopes for you."

As she stood up and walked away from the table, part of her hoped that he would call out and apologize. But it just reinforced her opinion as he sat in silence and let her walk out the door. That was the dumbest move any guy could ever make.

■   ■   ■

Hallett stopped by the hospital to visit Darren and was surprised to find Ruben and Claire sitting by his bed and Darren's new girlfriend, Kim Cooper, lounging in a chair in the corner of the room.

He heard Claire say, "I can't believe they don't let dogs in here."

Hallett felt awkward around his friend, who was obviously depressed. When he sat next to him, all Darren could talk about was when he could see Brutus. It had fallen on Hallett and Claire to visit the injured dog at the veterinary hospital in suburban Lantana. The Golden Retriever's lower left front leg had been badly damaged, but a great vet was working to restore it. The jury was out on whether Brutus would resume his career. Overall, Brutus was recovering, but it was a sin that neither partner could visit the other while they convalesced.

Hallett pulled a wadded-up shirt from a cargo pocket. "We had this made up for you." He held up the T-shirt so Darren could see the front clearly. It had a sketch of three dogs straining at their leads and the words HONOR, DUTY, DOGS.

Darren's face lit up as he took the shirt. "Thanks, guys. It looks great."

They all seemed to take turns trying to cheer Darren up. He made another effort to smile, then said, "If they won't let me leave in the next day or two, you have to sneak me in to see Brutus."

Hallett said, "You mean kidnap you from the hospital?"

"I mean *rescue* me."

Now Kim stood from the chair and said, "You're not going to risk your health. Brutus will be fine."

Just hearing her say Brutus's name seemed to get Darren down. He said, "I wanted him to be a patrol dog, and when he finally acted like one, I wish he hadn't." He started to sob. "I'll never have another partner like him."

Hallett reached over and patted his friend's shoulder. "Brutus acted like that to save your life. Partnership is a two-way street. He'll still be around, even if he's not your partner at work."

Darren said, "I don't want to think about him not coming back."

Ruben shook his head, saying, "Let me worry about that."

■　■　■

After Hallett said his good-byes, Ruben followed him into the hallway.

The dog trainer said, "I owe you an apology. I was wrong."

"About what?"

He hesitated, obviously trying to gather his words. "I had the story run in *The Palm Beach Post*. I know the writer and made sure he didn't say anything negative about you personally."

"You? Why?" Hallett felt like he had been hit in the stomach with a shovel.

"It looked like our unit's mission was finished in the D-bureau, but no one showed any signs of wanting to move on. I thought you guys needed to be reassigned, but no one in administration listens to me, and Sergeant Greene would never move you. I had to do it to help our overall mission. We have to keep producing results or the Canine Assist Team is done. I'm sorry, I did what I had to do for the team. The mission is more important than any of us."

"I expected more of you, Ruben."

The dog trainer looked at him and said, "Then you probably need to know me a little bit better. I have a job to do."

"And we're just tools, like the dogs?"

"Sometimes, I'm afraid so."

"Right now I think you're the only tool in the unit." He spun on his heel and walked away from the dog trainer. He didn't think the week could get much worse.

■   ■   ■

A few hours after his emotionally draining visit with Darren at the hospital, Hallett was tired from playing tag with Rocky and Josh in front of his trailer. The activity never failed to cheer him up. He was trying to come to terms with Ruben. At least he understood why he did it. He might even be able to trust the dog trainer again someday.

Josh was inside getting ready to meet their visitor.

Rocky crouched low with his hindquarters in the air in his classic position to play tag. He let out a warning bark, and every time Hallett moved toward him, the dog used his lightning reflexes to hop from one side to the other.

The poodles, Sponge and Bob, each yapped once every time Rocky barked. Hallett was getting used to the little dogs and realized he wouldn't be getting rid of them. Just two small additions to the already sprawling family.

Then Hallett stood and stretched his back as he saw Lori's Mazda pull through the gate at the rear of the church.

A grin spread across his face in anticipation. This was the bright spot he needed in his week.

As she stepped out of the car, in a simple sundress, she gave him a dazzling smile. He greeted her with a hug and a lingering kiss. Lori leaned down and patted Rocky on the top of his head as his tail wagged furiously.

Hallett turned as he heard the door to the trailer open and felt the excitement build in him as his girlfriend was about to meet his son. He already had ideas of the activities all of them could do. All of them included Rocky.

Josh bounded out of the trailer and raced toward his father, skidding to a halt right next to him.

Hallett said, "Lori, this is my son, Josh."

She leaned down and shook his tiny hand.

Hallett couldn't argue with the manners Crystal was teaching the young man. He caught something else in Lori's expression. She looked up at him as if there might be a problem. Hallett said, "Josh, do me a favor and go check the animals real quick." The boy turned and darted toward the pens, with Rocky right on his heels.

He'd given bad news to too many people in his career as a road patrol deputy to want to wait for it himself. He took Lori in a quick embrace, then asked point-blank, "What's wrong?"

She looked down at the ground and said, "Nothing we can't talk about later."

"After this past week of surprises, I can't wait for another."

Lori appeared distraught as she looked down at the ground. Biting her lower lip, she finally said, "I got a job offer."

"From who?"

"The FBI crime lab."

"Where?"

She looked down at the ground and mumbled, "Virginia."

"You're thinking about it?"

Then she dropped the bomb. "I took it already."

His head was spinning. All he could do was stammer, "What, when?"

"I know it's a lot to process. And I did take us, our relationship, into consideration. But at the end of the day, you've got Josh and Rocky. You'll be fine."

Hallett just stared at her, not sure of what to say.

Lori said, "I'm sorry, but it was hard finding the right time to say something."

She was right in everything she said. He was disappointed she was leaving, but when he looked over at his son playing with his partner, he knew she was right. He'd be fine.

Lori said, "I need to go. It's too hard to stay here with you. You're weakening my resolve." She stretched on her tiptoes and kissed him.

Then she was gone.

Josh came running back to Hallett and said, "Where did the lady go?"

"She didn't want to play today. Now it's just us boys."

Josh gave him a smile and said, "Cool," as he ran off with Rocky in close pursuit and Sponge and Bob trying to keep up. Hallett let a smile blossom, then chased after his son and his dogs.

50

He had placated Darren for an extra day; then on Monday they made their break. It was exhilarating in a way, but it was also pretty easy. Hospital security was geared to keep people out, not in. The hardest part was helping Darren get dressed. His upper body was black and blue, with four ribs broken, and his neck and shoulder were carefully bandaged. It was the fear of infection and internal bleeding that had kept him hospitalized for three days.

Now, after stuffing pillows under the sheets like in an old-school prison break, Hallett and Darren walked slowly to a rear elevator, then left the hospital through the back door, where Claire was waiting in her Tahoe with Rocky and Smarty sharing the rear compartment. Hallett had to slide in next to them for the ten-minute ride to the veterinary hospital west of Lantana.

No matter what the hassle, it was all worth it once Hallett saw the effect Darren had on Brutus. Instantly, the dog went from lying quietly in a large kennel to jumping up like a puppy, his head banging against the grate as he got used to standing on just three legs. The left front paw was heavily bandaged, with a splint stabilizing it as well.

Once out of the kennel, he licked Darren's face and whimpered like he was crying. Brutus wasn't the only one. As Hallett wiped a tear away, he turned and caught Claire openly sobbing.

She managed to croak, "Not a single word to anyone about this."

He cleared his throat and said quietly, "I'm going to get Rocky."

■   ■   ■

Once outside, Hallett took Rocky off his lead and let the dog run free for a few minutes, chasing the occasional pigeon or squirrel. Hallett walked along the shaded trail near the parking lot and leaned down to pick up a discarded plastic Gatorade bottle. As he was fully extended, he heard Rocky approach and then felt the dog nip him on the backside. He stood and turned around to see Rocky crouched low, ready for a game of tag. It instantly lifted his spirits.

Then Rocky winked. There was no stress, the light was good, and Hallett knew what he saw. Rocky winked, and he had done it with purpose. Somehow Hallett knew his life could never be boring while he had so much to learn about what made Rocky tick

He had a partner and a family who loved him. Everything would be okay.

■　■　■

Rocky wanted Tim to be happy. Tim needed to be happy. Since Josh was not here, it was up to Rocky to ease Tim's sadness. The little boy made both of them happy and should have been around them more. But now it was just up to Rocky.

He waited for the perfect chance. Then Tim bent slightly, and Rocky ran behind him to jump up and give him a nip on his hindquarters.

Tim spun around and looked at Rocky. Slowly his teeth became visible, and Rocky knew he was making Tim happy.

All Rocky wanted to do was make Tim and Josh happy. And to play a game every once in a while.

Maybe a game where he got to catch a bad man.